TOM CLANCY

CHAIN
OF
COMMAND

Also by Marc Cameron
Available from Random House Large Print

Tom Clancy Shadow of the Dragon
Tom Clancy Code of Honor
Tom Clancy Power and Empire

TOM CLANCY

CHAIN OF COMMAND

★

MARC CAMERON

RANDOM HOUSE
LARGE PRINT

Copyright © 2021 by The Estate of Thomas L. Clancy, Jr.; Rubicon, Inc.; Jack Ryan Enterprises, Ltd.; and Jack Ryan Limited Partnership

Cover art and design by Eric Fuentecilla
Maps by Jeffrey L. Ward

The Library of Congress has established a Cataloging-in-Publication record for this title.

ISBN: 978-0-593-45982-9

www.penguinrandomhouse.com/large-print-format-books

FIRST LARGE PRINT EDITION

Printed in the United States of America

1st Printing

This Large Print edition published in accord with the standards of the N.A.V.H.

"Special Forces is a mistress . . . She will love you, but only a little, seducing you to want more, give more, die for her . . . And in the end, she will leave you for a younger man."

James R. Ward, OSS

PRINCIPAL CHARACTERS

UNITED STATES GOVERNMENT

Jack Ryan: President of the United States

Anthony Hargrave: Vice president of the United States

Dr. Caroline "Cathy" Ryan: First Lady of the United States

Arnold "Arnie" van Damm: White House chief of staff

Mary Pat Foley: Director of national intelligence

Mark Dehart: Secretary of Homeland Security

Dan Murray: United States attorney general

Jay Canfield: Director of the Central Intelligence Agency

Brian Wilson: Director of the Federal Bureau of Investigation

Tom Vogel: Chairman of the Joint Chiefs of Staff

Scott Adler: Secretary of state

Robert Burgess: Secretary of defense

Jason Bailey: Admiral of the United States Navy, chief White House medical officer

Robbie Forestall: Commander of the United States Navy, adviser to President Ryan

Carter Boone: Commander of the United States Navy, vice president's physician, White House medical office

Marci Troxell: Commander of the United States Navy, First Lady's physician, White House medical office

UNITED STATES SECRET SERVICE

Lawrence Howe: Director

Gary Montgomery: Special agent in charge, presidential detail

Maureen "Mo" Richardson: Special agent in charge, FLOTUS detail

Karen Sato: Assistant special agent in charge, FLOTUS detail

Keenan Mulvaney: Special agent in charge, vice presidential detail

THE CAMPUS

John Clark: Director of operations

Domingo "Ding" Chavez: Assistant director of operations

Dominic "Dom" Caruso: Operations officer

Jack Ryan, Jr.: Operations officer/senior analyst

Adara Sherman: Operations officer

Bartosz "Midas" Jankowski: Operations officer

SPECIAL FORCES OPERATIONAL DETACHMENT ALPHA 0312, AFGHANISTAN

Brock: 18A, Captain
Guzman: 180A, Warrant officer
Ward: 18B, Ops sergeant
Thelan: 18F, Intelligence sergeant
Megnas: 18E, Communications sergeant

1

WASHINGTON AIR ROUTE TRAFFIC CONTROL CENTER
LEESBURG, VIRGINIA
TIME TO DECIDE: SIXTEEN MINUTES

Tim Goode grabbed the edge of the desk and pushed his padded chair away from the radar console, rolling it forward and back, bleeding off nervous energy while he took a scant moment to study the electronic blip moving northeast. At least once a day some clueless pilot flew their little Cessna or Piper or Beechcraft across the imaginary line that fenced the United States capital.

"Bewitched, ballsy, or bewildered?" Goode muttered under his breath, rolling his chair all the way forward again. A low growl rumbled in his chest.

Seriously, dude? All you gotta do is look at the chart . . .

Dozens of blips and corresponding transponder codes moved across his scope. It wasn't like this moron was the only aircraft he had to worry about at the moment.

Goode adjusted the mic on his headset—as if that would do any good—and tried the radio for the third time.

"Aircraft on a sixty-degree south of Nokesville, identify yourself on this frequency."

Nada. Nothing. NORDO.

Aircraft were not permitted within thirty nautical miles of the Washington Reagan Airport VOR—the SFRA, or Special Flight Rules Area—unless they met three specific criteria. They needed a flight plan. They had to be in communications with air traffic control. And their transponder had to squawk on the assigned frequency.

This inbound numbnuts was batting zero for three—and making a beeline for the capital at a hundred and twenty knots, covering two miles every minute.

Goode waved over his shoulder for a supervisor with his left hand. His right moved for the computer mouse on his desk, activating the red and green signaling lasers located around the SFRA. Aided by radar tracking, the intense beams were aimed directly at the offending aircraft, warning the pilot to make an immediate one-hundred-eighty-degree turn.

See it—flee it.

This guy continued inbound with no response, undeterred by the warning lights.

At this point, Goode reported this Track of Interest to the Air National Guard duty officer at the Eastern Air Defense Sector, or EADS, 390 miles to the north in Rome, New York. Her name was Lieutenant Mary Wong. Both were frequent fliers when it came to SFRA incursions, and the two had spoken many times before.

"Got another TOI for you," Goode said, getting down to business with the particulars. "Bullseye two-four-zero degrees for thirty-one nautical miles. Airspeed 120 knots."

Bullseye was the VOR at Reagan National Airport, the center of the restricted airspace circle.

Lieutenant Wong kept Goode on and notified her commander, who had a direct line to the United States Coast Guard Blackjack helicopter crews at Reagan and the F-16s with the 121st Fighter Squadron at Andrews. Both of these units were immediately placed on a heightened state of alert.

It cost the American taxpayer over fifty thousand dollars to scramble a single F-16, so no one took the action lightly—nor would they hesitate once certain trip wires were crossed.

"Who is this guy?" Lieutenant Wong said. "He's bullseye two-four-zero degrees for . . ." She paused, then spoke again. "Still NORDO?"

Goode tried the offending aircraft on the radio once more before answering Wong. "Correct," he said. "Either he's having radio problems or he's ignoring me altogether."

Wong was in deep conversation with her supervisor, ticking down the checklist of responses for an incursion into restricted airspace. Goode watched the green dot, expecting to see a Coastie MH-65 launch on his screen at any moment.

TIME TO DECIDE: TWELVE MINUTES.

The inbound Track of Interest met the criteria for an immediate Operation Noble Eagle (ONE) conference call. Lieutenant Wong began by contacting 601st Air Operations Center at Tyndall Air Force Base—Continental U.S. NORAD Region (CONR) headquarters near Panama City, Florida, where Lieutenant General Rhett Farrer served as the CFACC, or Combined Forces Air Component Commander.

The commander of NORAD/NORTHCOM, four-star general Mike Hopkin, was enduring a root canal at a specialist off base in Colorado Springs at that moment, so his J-5, Major General Steven Armstrong (the joint director of policy and planning), stood in for him on the phone in the N2C2—NORAD/NORTHCOM Command Center. In this capacity, General

Armstrong was armed with Civilian Aircraft Engagement Authority—a benign way of saying he'd been delegated the responsibility from the secretary of defense through General Hopkin to give the shootdown order so an F-16 Falcon could blow this little four-seater civilian airplane out of the sky.

Neither Goode nor Lieutenant Wong spoke the words aloud, but both knew that if this pilot continued on the same course, he would have his choice of the Pentagon, the Capitol, or the White House as targets.

Nine hundred miles north of Tyndall and sixteen hundred miles east of Colorado Springs, the scramble sirens sounded at Andrews Air Force Base. Captain Scott Hill and Lieutenant Rich Waggoner sprinted across the flight line to their waiting F-16s.

TIME TO DECIDE: ELEVEN MINUTES.

TWENTY MINUTES EARLIER:

Early mornings were George Cantu's favorite time for flight lessons. His wife would drop their three-year-old daughter at daycare about now, and then head to Culpeper Middle School, where she taught seventh grade—a far more dangerous endeavor than instructor pilot, to George's way of thinking. The air was crisp and dense enough that the little Cessna would leap off the runway when the time came. Cooler mornings meant new students didn't have to deal with much turbulence during the period in their training when they were still trying to get past the notion that the wings might spontaneously fall off the airplane during flight.

Stainless-steel tumbler of coffee in one hand, flight bag in the other, Cantu went straight from his old Toyota Tundra to the apron behind the hangar where his red-and-white Cessna 172 squatted on the tarmac, dazzling anyone lucky enough to look at it in the bright morning sun. He wanted to perform a quick preflight inspection before Mrs. Szymanski arrived.

The cell phone in his hip pocket began to buzz, shattering the reverent solitude of the flight line. It wasn't his wife or Mrs. Szymanski, or any other number he recognized, so he ignored it and shoved the device back in his pocket to continue the preflight.

Good news could wait and bad news found you one way or another.

Mrs. Szymanski would, of course, do another complete check of the airplane as part of her training, but in the end, he was pilot in command. The aircraft was his responsibility, no matter who happened to be sitting in the left seat. Besides, it gave him a few minutes alone with the 2006 180-horsepower high-wing baby he loved only slightly less than his wife and daughter.

A whisper of wind from the north brought the earthy root beer smell of sassafras from the nearby woods. The day was bluebird clear with not a cloud to be seen. Pilots called it CAVU— ceiling and visibility unlimited. To the west, the Blue Ridge Mountains were clear and bright, without a hint of their usual haze. Once in the air, Cantu would have an unimpeded view toward Chesapeake Bay, some ninety miles to the east. This was the kind of superbly flyable day that made him yearn to get airborne as quickly as possible.

For him, the preflight of his little airplane was a labor of love, a way to connect, to let his bird speak to him, tell him about any complaints or issues.

He gave each wingtip a little tug to make sure they were still secure. The fact that only two bolts held each wing in place was always an interesting topic of discussion between instructor and any new student.

Working his way around the plane, Cantu checked the control surfaces, the tires, ran his hand along the propeller to feel for any nicks or cracks that might be invisible to the naked eye.

His cell phone rang again when he was under the wing draining a small amount of fuel into a clear vial to check for water. Annoyed, he fished the phone out of his pocket with his free hand. Same number as before. Important enough to keep bugging him, so he answered.

The glass vial of fuel slipped from his hand and smashed into the tarmac before the caller had spoken two sentences.

Cantu swayed in place. Sweat ran down his back and beaded on his forehead despite the cool air. This was all wrong. He couldn't have heard correctly.

"What did you say?"

The electronically distorted voice repeated the horrific instructions, oozing cruelty. **"Georgie, if you want your wife and child to live, get in your airplane and taxi to the south end of the runway. Do it now."**

Cantu leaned against the Cessna, attempting to steady himself. His voice was breathy, impotent. "Wait . . . What?"

The phone fell silent but then rang again a half-second later. This time, it was a video call. His wife knelt in their driveway, examining a flat tire on her Subaru. The footage was probably being shot from across the street. His little daughter stood beside her mommy, holding the fuzzy blue bath towel she dragged with her everywhere she went.

"Theresa!" he shouted. "What is happening?"

"**She can't hear you, Georgie,**" the distorted voice said. "**We took the liberty of putting a little bullet in her tire, you know, to slow her down. But hey, it's just as easy for us to put a bullet in her or the snotty kid.**" The voice darkened. "**Now get your ass in the plane. I'm not gonna tell you again.**"

Cantu moved on autopilot, quickly but woodenly, scanning the surrounding buildings and trees for any sign of watchers as he climbed into the Cessna.

"**Yes, Georgie,**" the voice said. "**We have eyes on you, just like we can see your pretty little family.**"

"Please—"

"**Do you have an earpiece?**"

"I . . . an earpiece? . . . Yes. Earbuds."

"**Put them in and keep me on the line. The wind is from the north, so I assume you'll take off on 32?**"

"Um . . . yes. Runway 32. That's right," Cantu said. "I'll do what you want. Just . . . please . . . don't hurt them."

"**It's not up to me, Georgie,**" the voice said. "**You hold their salvation. Follow my instructions to the letter or you may as well be the one pulling the trigger. That's not what I want. But I won't lose sleep over it.**"

"No, no, no!" Cantu said. "I'll do whatever."

"Put in the earpiece. You speak only to me on the phone. No matter what happens, do not use the radio. Understand?"

"Yes. I understand."

"Then move your ass," the voice said. "Once airborne, assume a heading of northeast by east until I tell you otherwise."

"Roger, northeast by east," Cantu said mechanically, angry with himself for speaking so calmly to the man who had threatened to murder his wife and child.

Dispensing with any run-up, he increased throttle and let off the brakes, steering with shaky legs to the south end of the runway. The voice had instructed him not to talk over the radio, so he made do with a visual check out the windows. He could see no other traffic, so his takeoff roll was short. Instructor pilots were not easy to rattle, but Cantu felt certain he was about to throw up. He was airborne in an instant. The cockpit of his little airplane, the place he'd always felt at home, was now an uncertain hell.

He gained altitude quickly, glancing down to see his student, Mrs. Szymanski, shielding her eyes from the sun, no doubt wondering why her crazy instructor had taken off without her.

The monstrous voice spoke again, jarring Cantu out of his trance. "You're tempted to press the mic button on your yoke. That would be a fatal mistake. We would know. And then . . . Well, Georgie, I don't have to tell you what would happen to your kid."

Cantu banked quickly, leaving the undulating green of the Shenandoah behind him, heading northeast by east as instructed—directly toward Washington, D.C. His heart beat wildly, rattling the prison of his ribs.

The bright orange United States Coast Guard MH-65 Dolphin helicopter appeared out of nowhere. The surprise appearance surely on purpose to elicit fear and compliance from the pilot of the offending aircraft. The chopper cut a path in front of the Cessna, banking hard and coming around as if on a strafing run.

Sweat stung Cantu's eyes and glued his back to his seat. He'd known it was only a matter of time before they sent aircraft to intercept.

Heavily armed aircraft.

Air traffic control had been bending his ear on the radio without letting up for the past ten minutes. He ignored them, too terrified to answer but nauseated at the thought of what was going to happen when he did not. He pushed thoughts of exploding fireballs out of his mind and stared straight ahead, watching the ribbon of the Potomac River grow increasingly large off his nose. The warning lasers had hit him as he approached the SFRA—red and green flashes he knew were meant specifically for him.

Teaching would-be pilots in the skies around Washington, D.C., he spent a good deal of time discussing the Special Flight Rules Area that surrounded the capital with an invisible ring. He warned students of the nightmare of response aircraft and the real-world possibility of getting blown out of the sky.

Now he found himself living the scenario he'd warned so many others about.

Cantu knew exactly what the caller wanted as soon as he'd been given an azimuth. But he flew on without thinking, willing his hands to stop shaking on the yoke. Would he kill others to save his family? What wouldn't he do? He'd considered purposely crashing into the forest south of Manassas, but these monsters would probably kill his wife and daughter out of spite.

The Coast Guard Dolphin called him by tail number on the radio, direct, but much friendlier than the voice on his phone.

"**. . . United States Coast Guard helicopter off your left door. You have entered restricted airspace. Turn south immediately and follow me. Acknowledge by radio or rock your wings if you hear me.**"

An electronic marquee similar to a bank clock

in the helicopter's side window displayed the same instructions in scrolling red LEDs.

Cantu clenched his teeth, resisting the overwhelming urge to answer. He chanced a peek at the Dolphin's pilot, who stared back at him buglike behind the dark visor of his helmet. The helicopter seemed close enough to reach out and touch—sleek, official, and fast. Cantu didn't see any weapons, but fully expected the chopper's door to slide open at any moment and reveal a machine-gunner.

The Dolphin pilot repeated his command, but the cruel voice in Cantu's ear drowned him out.

"We can hear the Coastie, too," it said. **"Ignore him and continue to fly. You are an American citizen. They will not shoot you down. They are bluffing."**

"These guys . . . they're not bluffing," Cantu whispered, mostly to himself. His mouth was a desert, barely able to form words.

The Coast Guard chopper drifted closer, repeated instructions to follow a third time before drifting away—making room for something with bigger teeth.

TIME TO DECIDE: SEVEN MINUTES.

"Copy that," General Armstrong said. He stood in front of one of the many computer screens in the NORAD/NORTHCOM Command Center, eyes locked on the radar signature of the offending aircraft. He was fully prepared to give the shootdown order if it came to that, though he would have gladly stepped aside and yielded to his boss if he'd come into the N2C2. But that wasn't happening.

Firing on a civilian aircraft wasn't the kind of decision you made peace with each and every time you faced it. Events like this unfolded at lightning speed. You had to get your head wrapped around it from the very beginning, before you stepped up and took the job. You followed procedures, listened to the boots on the ground and eyes in the sky—and then, if everything fell within a certain clearly defined box, you gave a nod of your head to blast some poor son of a bitch out of the sky. Procedures were supposed to save you, allow you to sleep at night.

Maybe.

So far, no one had pulled the trigger.

On September 11, 2001, District of Columbia Air National Guard fighter pilots Lieutenant Heather "Lucky" Penney and her CO, Colonel Marc "Sass" Sasseville, scrambled to intercept and stop United Flight 93 after the World Trade Center and the Pentagon had been hit. The pilots had no missiles, nor ammo of any kind, and resolved to ram the airliner in a suicide mission to save countless others on the ground.

Unbeknownst to them at the time, passengers had already taken control of United Flight 93 and crashed into a Pennsylvania field.

With brave men and women like that, no one was getting into D.C., not on Armstrong's watch.

The Coast Guard MH-65 pilot reported a single person on board the TOI, looking bewildered and lost, crying.

Crying.

Well, hell, Armstrong thought. Tears were a bad sign, particularly when combined with a thousand-yard stare.

Armstrong leaned forward, both hands flat on the counter. This situation was turning to shit right before his very eyes. Dangerous for people on the ground, and, General Armstrong thought, deadly for the little Cessna if it did not deviate. He checked the red clock above the radar screen.

TIME TO DECIDE: SIX MINUTES.

2

Anna Kapoor, commissioner of the Food and Drug Administration, perched at the edge of the couch across from President Jack Ryan, clutching the leather folio in her lap until her knuckles turned white. He couldn't blame her. It was nerve-racking enough just being summoned to the Oval Office at any time of the day, but an early-morning meeting to discuss the President's pet Pharmaceutical Independence Bill prior to his daily intelligence briefing put her on the spot with two of Ryan's closest advisers—his chief of staff, Arnie van Damm, and the director of national intelligence, Mary Pat Foley. Both were astute pros, tough customers—though, as usual, Arnie looked like he'd taken a nap in his clothes.

Ryan had appointed Kapoor FDA commissioner six months earlier, and by all accounts she was doing a terrific job. Some in government felt the Food and Drug Administration, under the Department of Health and Human Services, was one of the more mundane cogs in the massive wheels of bureaucracy—until there was an **E. coli** outbreak on their favorite green salad.

Armies needed three basics to fight: bullets, beans, and bandages. No matter on which side of the fence Americans fell regarding the Second Amendment, in everyday life most spent far more time thinking about the latter two components of that equation. Beans and bandages fell under the purview of the FDA.

Short and round, Commissioner Kapoor appeared much younger than her fifty-six years, and privately joked that the few extra pounds filled in all her wrinkles. She wore a royal-blue suit and large glasses with gaudy red frames that might have looked unprofessional on some, but suited her olive complexion and gave her the look of a friendly university professor. Her stage fright notwithstanding, Kapoor was direct in her initial presentation, as well as in her answers to questions. When it came to all matters FDA, she was a subject matter expert, having come up through the ranks straight out of Harvard, a welcome relief from the many professional bureaucrats that kept the wheels of Washington turning.

"There are some realities we must address as we move forward, Mr. President," Kapoor said. "The pharma bill you're proposing will definitely impact Indian and Chinese markets. There is no question we have a problem with supply. From the past issues with heparin to bad antibiotics, the list of generic drugs that have been either tainted or nearly inert is a lengthy one, and, frankly, that list grows weekly. The sheer amount of raw pharmaceutical ingredients the United States imports from China is staggering, and growing exponentially every year since 1992. Manufacturing plants in India produce the vast majority of the generic drugs we consume in the United States."

Mary Pat Foley met Ryan's eye and gave him a little nod of approval. "I think you picked the right person to push this bill."

Kapoor nodded softly in thanks and then continued. "Frankly, Indian manufacturing companies depend on the higher prices the United States pays to subsidize the cheaper prices at which they sell product to the rest of the world."

Ryan rubbed his chin. "I'm not trying to be protectionist here, at least, not to the detriment of other countries, but the fact remains that it is nigh unto impossible for your people to properly inspect plants in China or the subcontinent. There is without a doubt corruption and shoddy manufacturing everywhere in the world, including facilities in the U.S. But we can clean up our own house easier than someone else's eight thousand miles away."

Van Damm chewed his bottom lip. "It wasn't that many years ago that a whistleblower won something like ninety million bucks for exposing a pharma plant in Puerto Rico, the very place we're trying to resurrect manufacturing."

"Ninety-six million," Kapoor said. "But you are right on point, Mr. van Damm. I would assure you, the FDA has changed since that time. We are more aware."

"If companies want to move offshore," Ryan said, "let's make it palatable for them to move off of our shore. There was a time when Puerto Rico was the medicine cabinet of the United States. We'd certainly have an easier time inspecting plants there."

"Much easier," Kapoor said. "The simple fact that diplomacy requires my team to give lengthy notice before inspections to Indian manufacturing plants makes such inspections not only burdensome, but, for the most part, near worthless as compliance tools. You see, Indian culture runs on workarounds or 'jugaad' for very nearly everything—similar to what we call 'hacks,' but much more pervasive. Actions we would certainly view as cheating in American culture are simply shrewd business practices there. But I have to say, this phenomenon is not unique to India. Most of the rest of the world operates by cheating and cutting corners as a matter of course. In India, we just have a word to describe it." Kapoor shook her head. "Now, I am in no way saying that everyone in India is dishonest. For heaven's sake, much of my extended family remains there and they are quite successful and happy. But do you know what? When they are ill, they pay the extra money to purchase name brand medication from the United States."

Van Damm bounced a fist on his knee, eyeing the commissioner. "Are you ready to testify to all this in front of congress, knowing that parts of that testimony might upset members of your family?"

Kapoor was quiet for a long moment, then took a deep breath. "Mr. van Damm, I was raised by Indian parents to do what is right. I do not blame some worker or even a manager who is trying to feed his family for coming up with the most lucrative way for his company to do business. I do, on the other hand, blame the business owners, the fabulously wealthy men and women who care nothing about the efficacy of their product and focus only on the bottom line. I would speak the hard truth about food and drug safety if that truth cast a shadow on India or Indiana."

Foley smiled at that. "She's good, Mr.—"

Ryan had just lifted his favorite Marine Corps coffee mug to his lips when four United States Secret Service agents burst into the Oval Office. Freshly on shift, they wore pressed suits, had perfectly cut hair, and not a single smile among them.

Ryan stood immediately, as did the other three in the room.

There was no need for a code word or a

lengthy explanation. When Secret Service agents barged in mid-meeting, something serious was going down.

Gary Montgomery, special agent in charge of Presidential Protection Detail, or PPD, appeared in the door half a second later and gave Ryan a curt nod. He was a big man, a collegiate boxer for the University of Michigan, imposing but light on his feet. Just the sort of person Ryan wanted running point with his protection. He was back-lit by the hall lights, and his sudden presence added to the urgency of the situation.

"Mr. President," Montgomery said. "I need you to come with me to the PEOC." The PEOC (pee-yok) was the Presidential Emergency Operations Center, often referred to as "the bunker."

Foley held her notepad to her chest and beckoned the startled FDA commissioner closer.

Kapoor looked around the room. "What should I do?"

"Come with us," Ryan said. "We can talk down there."

Van Damm gave a slow shake of his head and loosened his tie, even more than it already was. "What manner of bullshit are we dealing with today?" he whispered to no one in particular.

There were certain events that the Secret Service believed demonstrated the mood of the moment around D.C. And if that mood approached anything at all close to violent, even if the threat or action was not aimed directly at the White House, it precipitated a trip underground. If a demonstration got out of hand in front of the Pentagon, the Secret Service hustled POTUS to the PEOC. If the Supreme Court Police mixed it up with rowdies on the SCOTUS steps, it meant a trip to the PEOC.

Montgomery took up a position directly behind Ryan's left shoulder, within easy reach. Two more agents led the way, with two others behind. Van Damm, Foley, and Kapoor followed, with two agents bringing up the rear.

"The First Lady?" Ryan said before they'd even made it out the door of the Oval.

"She's fine, sir," Montgomery said. "I just spoke to Special Agent Richardson. They're almost to the Institute."

Ryan nodded as he walked. Thankfully, Dr. Cathy Ryan, one of the world's leading ophthalmic surgeons, had two procedures to perform that morning and was already out of the White House. She wasn't fond of these little trips to the PEOC. Perpetually on the move, doing surgery, jogging, cooking, Ryan's wife of more than four decades turned into something of a caged cat if she was kept bunkered up for very long. She loved to read, but wanted the option of getting up and going outside if the mood struck her.

Trips to the PEOC were an annoyance for

Cathy, but they were soul-crushing for Arnie van Damm.

Located below the East Wing, the PEOC was first constructed during the Truman administration. It had received constant upgrades since that time, but the long hallways and subterranean odor made sure it retained a musty Cold War ambience. Van Damm made it clear virtually every time they took the trip that it felt like the KGB was taking them down a dead-end hallway to put a Makarov bullet in the back of their skulls.

Van Damm pointed out on countless occasions that if a coup ever happened, this was where it would go down.

"**Et tu**, Arnie," Ryan would say, every time.

A series of conference rooms and spartan living quarters, the PEOC was staffed twenty-four hours a day by the White House Military Office. Essentially a smaller version of the Situation Room with flat-screen televisions and sophisticated communications equipment, the PEOC allowed the President a safe haven from which he could continue to see to the business of the country during a threat to the White House.

"Inbound civilian aircraft has violated the SFRA . . . just a precaution," Montgomery said as he ushered the little group quickly down the hallway.

"And he's flying directly for us?" van Damm asked.

"Yes, sir," Montgomery said over his shoulder.

"Fighters?" Ryan asked.

"F-16s on station now," Montgomery said. "He's still refusing to yield."

"There's an airplane coming toward us?" Kapoor whispered to Foley.

Ryan answered for her. "Looks that way."

"He's refusing to yield with tactical fighters crawling up his ass?" van Damm said, shaking his head, incredulous. Everyone in the hallway had been around long enough that they knew there was no easy explanation for human stupidity—or violence.

3

Two F-16 fighters blew past off the left side with a full-throated roar, heading north, tossing the little Cessna and making George Cantu feel like his chest would surely explode. He was a bug on the fighter's windscreen, puny and insignificant. Capable of speeds over 1,500 miles per hour, the Falcons had to significantly rein in their speed to stick with Cantu's single-engine Cessna for even a short time. They rolled slightly away, a display of the AIM-9 Sidewinder missiles on their wingtips.

Short-range air-to-air missiles.

"Cessna pilot, Cessna pilot, this is United States Air Force armed F-16. You are in violation of restricted airspace. Acknowledge by radio or rock your wings if you understand."

Cantu stared at the mic button on his yoke, but left it alone.

The Falcon pilot's voice crackled over the radio again. **"Cessna pilot, I say again, this is United States Air Force armed F-16. You have been intercepted. Rock your wings to acknowledge."**

Fifteen seconds ticked by. Cantu licked sweat

off his upper lip. Then came the demand, direct, but icy calm.

"Cessna pilot, follow me or you will be shot down."

Pulling ahead, the jets split, the one to the right dropping a brilliant array of orange flares directly in front of the Cessna. Cantu gasped. For a split second, he'd feared a missile launch.

"Please . . ." Cantu said to the lonely cabin of his little airplane. His shoulders shook so dramatically he feared the yoke might snap off in his hands. "Theresa . . ."

The voice in his earpiece prodded him on, reminding him of the deadly consequences to his family if he deviated from his instructions.

The fighters came around again, executing a sudden snap roll in unison. They banked left, accelerating in a great arc, one trailing the other to disappear behind him.

Cantu's little red-and-white airplane poked along, alone in the clear blue sky, flying directly for the bone-white LEGO sets of government buildings on the far side of the Potomac.

He thought of his wife. His little girl. And prayed it would be over quickly.

The resolve in the fighter pilot's voice had been unmistakable. He was coming around to shoot.

Cantu saw the plane a millisecond before he heard it. It flew straight up from below like a rocket, a scant five hundred feet off the nose of the Cessna. Afterburner scorching a path, the jet shot upward, GE turbofan engines providing over thirty thousand pounds of thrust, and creating enough wake turbulence to shake the smaller airplane as if it had been seized by a giant hand. Cantu was an experienced enough pilot to know the powerful fighters could have worked together to create turbulence much worse. No. This was a warning. A head butt to let George know they were serious. The last thing they would do before they blew him and his airplane into tiny pieces.

TIME TO DECIDE: TWO MINUTES.

"What is with this guy . . ." Armstrong muttered.

There was zero doubt that the Falcon would splash its target when the order was given, but winning this kind of one-sided battle still contained an aspect of great loss. The fighter's AIM-9 Sidewinder would do a number on the puny Cessna, blasting it out of the sky with little effort, but there would be fallout; burning metal pieces the size of a microwave could do a lot of damage to people and property on the ground.

Vehement curses died on General Armstrong's tongue, never seeing the light of day. Every word spoken on the radio and in the room was being recorded for future dissection by Monday-morning quarterbacks for months and years to come. The transcript of the shootdown would become part of some congressional record, Air Force Academy textbooks, and dumbass memes on the Internet.

Without commentary, General Armstrong issued a simple order to the lead F-16 pilot and gave code-word clearance.

"Roger that," Captain Hill said in his soft, unflappable Kentucky drawl. **"Comin' around now. Weapons hot. He should splash over Rock Creek Park. Missiles in twenty seconds . . ."** He paused. **"Stand by, NORAD . . . TOI is complying with my order. Turning south, away from the capital."**

Moments away from shooting down a civilian aircraft or rolling away for an escort, it didn't matter. Captain Hill's tone of voice never changed.

A smile of relief crept over General Armstrong's face, relaxing for the first time since this shitshow started.

The Cessna pilot finally broke radio silence, his words gushing out as if a dam had burst. He blubbered his name through sniffs and gulps, breaking down in hopeless sobs. He stammered out an address in Culpeper, Virginia, and begged someone to help his family, screaming that that they were in danger from some madman.

Captain Hill answered in the ever-steady

voice. **"I'll pass that along,"** he said, and then directed the pilot to proceed southwest and follow the U.S. Coast Guard Dolphin to Davison Army Airfield.

The pilot acknowledged amid more pleas to save his family.

Hill's voice crackled over the radio again. **"We're checking on them, George, but I need you to understand. You must maintain your present heading and land without delay at Davison. ATC has been notified. Every airplane in the area is holding just for you. Do you understand?"**

"Okay . . . Roger . . . Davison . . . Airfield . . ."

"You're going to see us pull away," Hill continued. **"But we are still here. You need to start communicating directly with air traffic control again and do not deviate from this course unless specifically instructed by them . . ."**

In the N2C2, General Steven Armstrong gave a stoic nod and said a quiet prayer of thanks. He'd dodged the history books—this time.

4

The vice president had stumbled getting on the plane.

Karleen Lynch, a fifty-eight-year-old retired investment banker and the United States ambassador to Japan, had raised four children. She knew sick when she saw it.

The ambassador walked briskly, pondering Anthony Hargrave's health as she made her way up the broad sidewalk along Sakurada Dori in concert with her small protective detail of Diplomatic Security agents, one in front, one alongside, and one in a black Toyota sedan trailing slowly. The agents often referred to her among themselves as the "ambo," as if **Lynch** was too long a word.

All of them walkers, Lynch and her team outpaced small knots of uniformed high school students, dark-suited Japanese salarymen, and local Tokyo residents who were on their way to walk the grounds at the Imperial Palace. Long-legged and fit, Ambassador Lynch preferred to be moving when she chewed on a problem.

The President—through the SecState—had

tasked her with a very specific mission for this trip. To that end, she needed the vice president to be on his A game the moment he arrived in Japan. That shouldn't have been a problem. Tony Hargrave was normally the picture of vitality, strong jaw, perfect hair, and an honest, toothy smile. On any other day he could have graced the cover of an outdoor adventure magazine, but when she'd watched the news footage of him trudging up the stairs to board Air Force Two, he'd looked pale and lethargic, like he needed a healthy dose of homemade chicken and dumplings—Lynch's remedy for almost any malady.

That was hours ago. She hoped he'd gotten some rest on the plane ride over, because they had much to do and almost all of it would be under the scrutinizing eyes of people who didn't exactly have the best interests of the United States at heart.

The reception that evening was going to be hell. Pranjal Varma, the Indian foreign minister, was already in Tokyo. He'd been gunning for her for two days—and she'd been deftly avoiding him. His chief of staff had called her office no less than six times, insisting on a meeting to discuss India's grievances toward the Ryan administration's Pharmaceutical Independence Bill.

Lynch skirted a small queue of government workers, young, lower ranks, all in dark suits or dark skirts and white shirts. They were lining up at a food cart to pick up stacks of bento, lunch boxes of rice and fish or plum or scant bits of meat, to carry back to their senior staff inside the offices along white avenues. She caught the odor of curry, and found herself wishing she had time to stop.

Not today.

She was under instructions from State to keep off the radar until the vice president and secretary of state arrived. That evening, they would all sit down for a friendly dinner with the Japanese prime minister, who had agreed to host a meeting. Indian Foreign Minister Varma could vent his spleen there. Cordially. With a referee. Over sushi. And many cups of warm sake.

It wasn't as if Varma was going to breach the walls of the embassy, but it felt wrong to Lynch for her to hide behind a couple of strapping young Marines and an iron fence. Diplomacy was an art, and sometimes that art required one to take a long walk.

The Sōri Kōtei, as the Japanese prime minister's residence was known, was a scant two thousand feet away from the United States embassy in Tokyo. It was close enough that if the CIA wanted to aim one of their fancy listening devices in that direction, they could sit at their desks and easily pick up conversations among the uniformed guards patrolling lush gardens of sago palm and Himalayan cedar. Considering the guests in attendance tonight, the Agency, along with Diplomatic Security and advance agents of the United States Secret Service, had been doing just that for the better part of a week.

The reception was scheduled to begin at six p.m. It was now half past noon. Ambassador Lynch could have waited five hours, put on her walking shoes, and hoofed the short distance up Sotobori Avenue and arrived at the prime minister's residence early enough to change into more fashionable heels. Instead, she wore those walking shoes and made her way northeast, skirting the great stone walls and mossy moats of the Imperial Palace, and crossing busy Daimyo-Koji Avenue to reach the palatial red-brick façade on the Marunouchi side of Tokyo Station.

Inside the cacophonous, teeming maze of levels that went down and down and down, Ambassador Lynch and her Diplomatic Security agents boarded the surprisingly uncrowded Ōme rapid service train directly to Fussa, the front door to United States Yokota Air Base. A DS agent in the black Toyota sedan paralleled her route on surface streets just in case the ambo needed him.

The agent driving the Toyota met Ambassador Lynch at the Yokota south gate with a change of clothes more suitable to meeting the vice president of the United States. The base security commander let her use his office to change.

She arrived on the flight line as Air Force Two touched down. Foreign Minister Varma had known she would be there and sauntered over to stand beside her, extending his hand.

He was young for such a crucial government office—equivalent to the U.S. secretary of state—early forties, wearing a red silk tie and an expensive midnight-blue wool suit that would have fit right in on the top floor of a Wall Street investment firm. Lynch had often thought that neckties were a construct of powerful fat men who wanted to distract attention from their ponderous bellies. Not so with Foreign Minister Varma. Everything about him looked perfectly chiseled—broad shoulders, coiffed hair, piercing hazel eyes. He could have been a Fortune 500 executive or the captain of a baseball team. They were on opposite sides of this pharmaceutical issue, but Lynch couldn't help but like the guy—which was, she supposed, the reason he was in this particular job.

The two of them exchanged greetings while their respective protection details eyed each other coldly like warring factions parlaying under a flag of truce—swords sheathed, but within easy reach.

"Your President is making life difficult for all

of us," Varma said after pleasantries were exchanged. "I do not have to tell you—"

Fortunately, a Boeing 757—white with a powder-blue belly—turned off the taxiway, twin Pratt & Whitney engines preempting all conversation. Since Vice President Hargrave was on board, it was designated Air Force Two.

Varma clasped his hands in front and gave Lynch an amused smile, conceding that she'd eluded him again for the moment. She suspected he'd only wanted to practice his objections anyway, before he moved on to the big leagues—the vice president and the secretary of state.

Unlike Lynch, Secretary of State Scott Adler was a career Foreign Service officer. As such, he had a reputation for looking down his nose at political appointees. They were, he felt, hacks who'd been gifted positions for which he'd worked his entire life. Somehow, Lynch had won him over, likely because she was a better than average poker player, a game at which Scott Adler excelled.

Diplomacy, indeed.

A DS agent who was part of SecState's advance team spoke into the tiny flesh-tone mic clipped to his lapel, alerting his cohort around the perimeter that "EAGLE is on the ground." A nearby Secret Service agent on the VPOTUS detail followed suit.

PAINTER, he said, was planning to work the ropes immediately after he got off the plane.

Casual onlookers might think the area around the flight line was a circus, but in truth it was a well-choreographed dance.

Ambassador Lynch's protective agents melded with the dozens of other men and women in suits—the Diplomatic Security secretary of state detail (EAGLE), the U.S. Secret Service Vice Presidential Protection (PAINTER), and a healthy contingent of Air Force law-enforcement personnel.

For now, Japanese Security Police stood at the outer perimeter. Lynch counted a half-dozen—but their presence would grow exponentially as soon as Hargrave and Adler departed Yokota Air Base.

SPs from Mobile Security Squad 3 were tasked with the protection of foreign dignitaries and were there to meet their counterparts. Tokyo Metropolitan Police officers with at least five years of uniformed experience and a third **dan** in at least one approved martial art, these were steely-eyed men with dour expressions and suits that matched down to their neckties.

And they saw everything.

The Japanese government gave permission for a very limited number of firearms to be carried into their country. Their own protection officers often carried a diminutive SIG P230 in .32 caliber, which, according to Lynch's detail agents, was akin to not being armed at all. At best, her agents said, it was a passable gun for fighting one's way to a larger gun. The Japanese government adopted a don't ask, don't tell policy when it came to U.S. agents bringing in weapons, clearly stating their rules but knowing full well that virtually every agent had a SIG or a Glock under their jacket. Lynch suspected the higher-ranking SPs were present not only to liaise with arriving protective details, but to make certain no one caused embarrassment with a pistol that was easily spotted by the public—or by one of their bosses.

As it turned out, the Americans and the Japanese were all cops at heart and found common ground immediately, despite the language barrier.

The vice president appeared at the door of Air Force Two first, wearing a charcoal-gray jacket that accented his perfectly styled gunmetal hair. Flashing his trademark smile, Hargrave was greeted by the Air Force band, the Yokota Base commander, local city leaders, and the governor of Tokyo—who had his own protection detail, SP Mobile Security Squad 4.

Smile notwithstanding, Hargrave's shoulders sagged as if carrying some unseen burden. It was worrisome, but Lynch was placated some when he trotted down the steps.

Secretary of State Adler followed, balding, older than Hargrave and considerably frumpier.

Both men wore tailored suits, though Hargrave's was clearly newer, where Adler's was road-weary, as befitting the wardrobe of a globe-trotting secretary of state. The men walked the receiving line together, shaking hands, bowing. As the Secret Service agent had warned, Hargrave took a couple minutes to work the ropes, pressing the flesh with a few onlookers, who were for the most part Air Force families stationed at Yokota.

Secret Service personnel in an armored limousine eventually whisked Hargrave away to a waiting UH-1N Iroquois a hundred meters down the flight line. This particular bird comprised parts from several helicopters that had seen service during the Vietnam War. The sleek new MH 139-A Grey Wolfs that would replace the aging "Twin Hueys" were still months away from delivery. The governor of Tokyo was well aware of the chopper's history and opted to return to the city via the longer route with his motorcade.

Old and leaky as they were, if the Hueys were sound enough to assign to personnel of the 459th Airlift Squadron, then Vice President Hargrave, a former U.S. Army Apache pilot himself, insisted that they were good enough for him. He invited Foreign Minister Varma and one of his security agents to ride with him. Secretary Adler had asked Ambassador Lynch to accompany him, and since he was riding with the vice president, so was she.

The helicopter was extremely loud. Unfortunately, because the crew chief provided each passenger with a headset and mic, Varma was able to talk their ear off during the entire fifteen-minute journey to the helipad on the roof of the Sōri Kōtei, the Japanese prime minister's office.

Lynch closed her eyes while the Indian foreign minister gave full-throated voice to his country's numerous grievances regarding President Jack Ryan's "disastrous, protectionist, and ill-conceived plan."

The vice president listened patiently, offering no excuse or rebuttal for his boss's agenda. Perhaps he knew that the best form of diplomacy was keeping his mouth shut.

Or maybe, Lynch thought, he was just too sick to argue.

S cott Adler's late mother (**of blessed memory**) would have said poor Tony Hargrave looked like he was about to plotz (collapse) and, as Jewish mothers were prone to do, she would have recommended a healthy meal of chopped liver.

Adler and the VP were old friends from the days when Hargrave came aboard State after leaving the military. He'd always been one to have an easily upset stomach—odd for someone who flew attack helicopters.

Adler was a detail man—and an expert poker

player, much to the chagrin of his cohort at the Fletcher School of Law and Diplomacy, where he'd graduated first in his class. He'd worked his way up the ranks of career civil servants at State. Fluent in the language, culture, and politics of Russia, he was naturally drawn to the Soviet side of the department—a busy place during those halcyon days of the Cold War. He spoke enough Japanese to converse and had done some negotiations a few years earlier when the two countries teetered on the brink of war. At the moment, he was making a miserable go of trying to give up cigarettes for the . . . eighth time in his adult life, which made him at once jittery and hyperaware of his surroundings. The subtext in the vice president's conversation—or lack of it—told Adler something was wrong.

Hargrave spoke Russian as well, and had worked for Adler in the beginning. Even then, it was easy to see that this smooth-talking former Army chopper jock was one of "those guys" who was destined to rise above his peers. The limelight followed him, and nobody seemed to mind it, because he was a genuinely good soul. Hargrave had moved on to politics, winning a House congressional seat in his home state of South Dakota—and eventually catching the eye of Arnold van Damm and other Party elders to replace an ailing Richard Pollan as vice president.

Hargrave bummed a Rolaids from Keenan

Mulvaney as soon as the Huey touched down. The Secret Service special agent in charge of his detail could always be counted on for an antacid. Mulvaney gave him the Rolaids, along with a wary side-eye, but said nothing.

Foreign Minister Varma stood a few feet away with a pinched expression, looking as though he might need something for his stomach as well.

"You okay?" Adler asked Hargrave when they were standing side by side on the plush red rug in the grand foyer of Prime Minister Mori's residence. The vice president was the boss here, but Adler was the senior man and in many ways thought of Hargrave as a favorite nephew. "Maybe you should get with Carter, let him check you out."

Hargrave mustered a wink. "I'm good to go, buddy."

Dr. Carter Boone, commander, United States Navy, was one of the White House physicians who routinely traveled with the vice president. As with physicians who traveled with POTUS, Commander Boone remained within quick access in case of emergency, but just far enough away that he wasn't as likely to be injured in the event of attack or catastrophic accident. If all went well, Dr. Boone would spend the entire evening dressed in a tuxedo, doing paperwork in a nearby office.

Hargrave beamed as Prime Minister Mori and

his wife came down the stairs to meet and greet the visitors.

"Seriously," he said out of the corner of his mouth, eyes focused on the prime minister as he gave Adler a playful nudge with his elbow. "Don't worry about me. I'm just as tired as you look, that's all."

But it turned out to be more than that.

Much more.

Prime Minister Mori was a gracious host, regaling his guests with the bloody history of the official two-story residence, which was built in 1929. His wife, a quiet, birdlike woman who said little with her lips but much with her eyes, squirmed uncomfortably as Mori recounted with vivid descriptions the two bloody coups that had occurred within these very walls, the murders being the apparent birth of the ghosts who walked the carpets at night and had kept many prime ministers from occupying the residence at all over the years.

For the most part, Foreign Minister Varma ate quietly, handing out periodic verbal jibes to demonstrate his mood. One of them—Adler didn't hear it—must have been aimed at the ambassador.

Hargrave cleared his throat, his smile vanishing.

"I understand your government is upset about President Ryan's proposal, but—"

Varma shot a playful wink at Lynch. He dabbed at his lips with a linen napkin and got down to business now that he had the vice president's full attention. "Forgive me, but the United States speaks of such matters much the same as I am told ancient samurai did in this beautiful country. When one warrior killed another in battle he might say **'kiri sute gomen.' I cut you, I throw you away, I am sorry.**" Varma glanced at Prime Minister Mori, making his case. "Please excuse my pronunciation. It is extremely glib for the vice president to say that India is merely **upset**. Much of the world outside the United States of America depends heavily upon affordable generic pharmaceuticals manufactured by companies in my country. President Ryan's plan to subsidize plants in Puerto Rico is nothing less than protectionist. These businesses will undercut Indian companies, killing a vital market and cutting off access to the poor around the world."

Scott Adler struggled to hold his tongue.

"Mr. Foreign Minister," Hargrave said. "I can assure you, the United States has no wish to keep vital medication from the poor. We do, however, assert our need for pharmaceutical independence, preferring to get our medications from plants that are available for monitoring and inspection."

Varma chewed on that for a long moment, then said, more darkly than before, "We deeply resent any implication that our plants do not cooperate in the fullest."

"I'm not implying, Mr. Foreign Minister," Hargrave shot back. "I am speaking frankly. It is almost impossible to get inspectors into your facilities without giving them so much notice that those inspections are virtually worthless—"

Prime Minister Mori raised an open hand, smiling softly like a wise grandfather. "Gentlemen," he said in perfect English. "My wife has prepared a delicious custard for our dessert. These matters are quite weighty. I fear talk of them now will sour the experience. I urge you, let us postpone this discussion until afterward, for the sake of—" He stopped mid-sentence, the sparkle vanishing from his eyes. "Hargrave **Dono**," he said, speaking as much to his own aides as to the vice president. "**Otsukaresama desu. Daijobu desu ka?** Are you unwell?"

Adler turned to see his friend had gone chalky white. Sweat beaded along the vice president's forehead and dotted his upper lip. His eyes fluttered. He swayed in his chair, listing sideways. He would have toppled over had Adler not caught him.

Hargrave's special agent in charge who'd been seated along the wall sprang to his feet, speaking into his lapel mic. "Medic, medic, medic," he said. "From Mulvaney. Dr. Boone to the dining room for PAINTER. Immediately."

Special Agent Mulvaney helped ease the vice president to the floor and put him on his back, elevating his feet with a cushion Mrs. Mori gave him.

Ambassador Lynch pushed away from the table and moved in to assist. "Is he choking?"

Foreign Minister Varma crowded closer and asked if he could be of any help, shrugging off his own security until they all but hauled him away.

"I'm fine," Hargrave said, breathless, moving his jaw from side to side like he might be sick at any moment. He was far from fine.

Secret Service agents seemed to materialize out of the curtains, forming a human shield around the vice president, who now blinked up at Adler and Special Agent Mulvaney. As secretary of state, Adler was one of the few people on the planet who wasn't summarily dragged away by agents during such an event.

Hargrave grabbed his hand. His grip was weak and unsettlingly cold, but he held on. He turned his head slightly, looking at Mulvaney. "Let him . . . stay . . . He is . . . my friend."

There was something so incredibly moving about the way he said the words. Tears welled in Adler's eyes. Tony Hargrave, one of the strongest, most vibrant men he had ever met, one heartbeat away from the presidency of the United States, had turned into a frightened little boy.

Mulvaney gave Adler a wary nod while he notified the motorcade outside to get ready to move. Agents were already en route to Toranomon Hospital, just across the parking lot from the U.S. embassy less than a kilometer away. Advance agents had spoken with the surgical staff weeks before, as they did at hospitals in every venue POTUS or VPOTUS visited in preparation for a medical emergency. Trauma staff would be ready—whatever this turned out to be.

Prime Minister Mori's close-protection agents escorted him from the dining room out of an abundance of caution. Japanese Security Police assigned to the VPOTUS detail remained nearby, vigilant but out of the way. The lead SP relayed a play-by-play of events to his command post over radio, alerting marked police cars to prepare for an escort to Toranomon.

Adler's own Diplomatic Security agents rushed in and attempted to cajole him out the door, but he shrugged them off, still holding Hargrave's hand.

Dr. Boone pushed his way through the knot of agents and dropped to his knees beside the stricken vice president.

"Stand by for PAINTER to be on the move to the ambulance," Special Agent Mulvaney said into his lapel mic. Then to Dr. Boone, "Paramedics are on their way in now."

"Copy that." The doctor gave a curt nod, then focused on his patient. He kept his voice calm and low.

"What's up, Mr. Vice President?" He gave a reassuring smile as he searched his patient for signs of trauma. "Tell me what we have going on here."

Hargrave pointed to his belly, wincing at a new and sudden pain. He swallowed hard. "I feel like shit, Doc."

Boone pressed his fingers alongside Hargrave's neck. "Your pulse is rapid, Mr. Vice President. We're going to get you to a hospital and check things out. Could be appendicitis. When did this start?"

"The flight . . ." Hargrave whispered, wincing again. "I don't know . . . Maybe before." A tear creased his temple "My gut feels all . . . I don't know, shaky, like it has a mind of its . . ." His face twisted into a mask of pain, mouth opening and closing like a gasping fish. His eyes fluttered and then closed.

Dr. Boone lay a hand against Hargrave's abdomen, high at first, under the rib cage. He paused for a moment, then moved it lower. All pretense of calm drained away. He cursed under his breath, then turned quickly to Mulvaney.

"Inform Toranomon Hospital the vice president

has a triple A rupture," he snapped. "Abdominal aortic aneurysm. Let's go!"

Adler loosened his grip and Hargrave's hand fell away, thudding against the carpet.

The muscles in Boone's jaw tensed like cables.

It was standard Secret Service procedure to have an ambulance staged on standby outside. Three Japanese paramedics hustled in moments later with a rolling gurney. Boone gave them a rundown while they lifted Hargrave together.

"Triple A?" Adler whispered, half to himself.

"A major artery has burst in his abdomen," Boone said. "**The** major artery. He has massive internal bleeding."

"But you can fix him?" Adler felt himself go cold. "Right?"

"We have to take him to the hospital, per protocol," Boone said, looking as if he'd been kicked in the gut. He leaned in closer so only Adler could hear. "Someone needs to inform the President. I'm sorry, Mr. Secretary, I have to go."

5

The Secret Service gave the all-clear allowing Jack Ryan and the others to emerge from the PEOC thirty-seven minutes after they'd been hustled down. An exercise in hustling, the trip back and forth along subterranean hallways and dim stairwells proved to be an unsettling way to digest one's breakfast, especially for his chief of staff.

Ryan asked Commissioner Kapoor a few more questions while they were in the PEOC and then excused her as soon as the Secret Service allowed everyone to go topside. Arnie reminded Ryan none too subtly that as much as he wanted to focus on the Pharma Independence Bill, there was a hell of a lot going on at the moment.

Ryan was accustomed to a full threat board, but this was ridiculous. The usual saber-rattling by Russia, China, North Korea, and Iran had seen a noticeable uptick in the past hundred hours. Each of these countries had serious internal problems—famine, civil unrest, natural disasters—but those who underestimated the intelligence apparatus of any one of them did so at their own peril.

Ryan had no doubt that operatives and analysts were even now delighting their overlords with news of turmoil in their "Main Enemy"— the United States.

A spate of deepfake videos, all featuring Jack Ryan in some compromising position, now flooded multiple platforms on the Internet. Attempting to get the videos taken down only gave them more publicity and caused them to trend. At the same time, ransomware cyberattacks on the city of Baltimore, Red Hook Terminal, and the D.C. Metro system had left tens of thousands in the dark and on foot. Two Metro trains on the Green Line had collided, killing three and wounding dozens.

So far, U.S. intelligence hadn't been able to pinpoint an origin of these attacks. At first there'd been some belief that the perpetrators belonged to People's Liberation Army Unit 61398, one of China's military hacking units based in Shanghai; other analysts felt the digital tracks were wrong and that the hackers were from GRU's 26165, a Russian military intelligence unit that was particularly active with disruptive cyberattacks. Still others in the community pinned the attacks on Iran. There were, in fact, so many opinions as to provide no clear opinion at all. In some ways, the identity of the perpetrator did not matter. An attack against the United States by one aligned with the best interests of the others.

If the President of the United States was busy seeing to his own problems, he was much less likely to fret over a few new islands dredged up from the ocean floor by the People's Liberation Army-Navy in disputed waters, or to make much of a stink over Russian troops taking their war games perilously close to the border with Ukraine.

And now someone had apparently tried to fly a plane into the White House.

"The pilot's name is George Cantu," Brian Wilson, the FBI director, said from his seat at the end of the sofa. Wilson was one of the few men Ryan knew who could really pull off a bow tie. "He's thirty-five years old, no criminal record, no history of mental illness that we've been able to ascertain. We have him in custody now. He knows very little, if his story is to be believed."

Ryan surveyed the room from his chair by the fireplace. "Someone mentioned the threat to the man's family. Have we checked on their safety?"

Gary Montgomery sat on the same couch as Wilson, nearer to the door. He always seemed to stick just a little bit closer in the moments after a heightened threat to Ryan.

"We have agents with Mrs. Cantu and her daughter as we speak, Mr. President."

"Good to hear," Ryan said.

Foley and Homeland Security Secretary Mark Dehart sat on the opposite sofa.

Van Damm was on his feet, pacing, hands together, up, clicking a thumbnail against his top teeth. He'd never been a fan of the PEOC. The tomb, he called it, and swore he'd rather die in a fiery blaze than suffocate several stories below the East Wing of the White House. It would take him a few minutes to regain the swagger of the shrewd political operative that he was.

Ryan took a sip of coffee and gave a contemplative nod.

"Are we still certain that this pilot was coming for us?"

Secretary Dehart tapped the screen of his tablet computer and turned it to face Ryan. "This is the Culpeper airport. According to Mr. Cantu, the mysterious caller threatened to kill his family if he didn't follow instruction exactly. The voice ordered Cantu to fly northeast by east immediately after takeoff. He was then to continue until he was given more detailed coordinates." Dehart tapped the screen again to start an animation of an aircraft superimposed over a map of the restricted zone around the Washington, D.C., area. A dotted line extended from the nose of the plane.

Mary Pat leaned forward, getting a closer look. She shook her head. "That course would have put him directly over the White House."

"Or directly into it," van Damm said.

"What about the wife," Ryan asked. "Was her car damaged, as Cantu claimed?"

"It was, sir," Montgomery said. "What appears to be bullet holes going through the sidewalls of the front and rear driver's-side tires. The bullet that took out the rear tire may be lodged inside the muffler."

"I have techs on the way over there now," Director Wilson said. "To take custody of the muffler and preserve the bullet if it's in there."

"Nobody heard a shot?" Mary Pat asked.

"Apparently not," Montgomery said. "I'm sure the Bureau will do a more thorough canvass. But according to my agents, the neighbors report seeing a dark blue sedan that was possibly a Ford Taurus. Neighbor lady wasn't sure of the make but knew there were two men in it that didn't lift a finger to help Mrs. Cantu change the tire." He shrugged. "She wasn't going anywhere anyway, with two flats."

Director Wilson rested both hands on his thighs. "As Gary noted, we're doing a thorough canvass of the neighborhood, preserving any bullet or fragments from the muffler, and, of course, a full background on Mr. Cantu. Techs are digging into his phone now, but so far we're not getting much useful to help us identify the caller."

"Run it by me again," Ryan said. "What the caller said when he gave Cantu his first directions."

"That they had eyes on his family—"

"No," Ryan clarified. "What did they say regarding the direction they wanted him to travel? His exact words."

"Ah." Wilson nodded. "The caller ordered Cantu to fly 'northeast by east.'"

Ryan took a sip of coffee and thought about that for a moment. "Anyone here familiar with that term?" he asked at length. "I mean, how it's used specifically."

"I presume it's what it says," Foley said. "Kind of northeast."

"Could be just that," Ryan said. "But all the airplane pilots I know use actual numbers to indicate heading. Northeast by east is a direction on a mariner's compass rose." He nodded at Montgomery, whom he knew kept a small sloop-rigged sailboat on the Potomac.

"That's correct, Mr. President," the agent said. "Northeast by east is . . ." He did the math in his head. "Fifty degrees and fifteen minutes. Halfway between northeast and east northeast."

Van Damm stopped his pacing and raised a doubtful brow.

Ryan read his look. "I know it's in the weeds, Arnie," he said. "But we should at least consider the fact that our caller may have spent time in somebody's Navy."

Van Damm gave a shake of his head. "We dodged a bullet on this one, Mr. President. The press would have had a field day if you'd shot down little Lucy Cantu's daddy."

"I doubt Lucy Cantu's daddy would have been too happy about it, either." Ryan stood, prompting everyone else in the room to stand as well. He didn't think he'd ever get used to that—but it did have the benefit of keeping things moving.

"Whoever is behind this knew our fighters would shoot down a light aircraft," he said. "Their aim wasn't to kill me, it was to preoccupy us. To take our mind off the pressing business of running the country—and I choose not to let that happen. So I'll leave it to you experts to get to the bottom of things." He glanced at Arnie. "Let's have what's next. I'm ready to talk about something besides some poor schmuck being forced to fly his airplane into my living room."

Ryan knew from experience that it was almost impossible to steer a meeting back to raw intelligence once anyone broached the topic of immediate threat—like somebody crashing a small aircraft into the White House. Every person in the Oval was action-oriented. There was a hell of a lot of analysis going on at the moment, with intelligence so raw it was still a steaming pile on the ground. If Ryan let every attack or threat of attack derail his day, he'd never get anything done.

In a nation made up of well over three hundred million, people were going to disagree with him, some enough to try and kill him. Some saw him as the enemy—the face of all that was wrong in the country—and Ryan was not one to plead or alter his behavior to change anyone's mind on that notion. The buck truly did stop with him. He publicly fell on his sword far more than he touted his victories. His approval rating was generally high, but there were always a few who were in the middle of the national equivalent of road rage, whipped into a murderous frenzy by any one of the many imperfections in a democratic republic. These "special ones" saw nothing but a red mist with Ryan's face in the center. As Gary Montgomery periodically reminded him while they ran on treadmills in the White House gym, the bullet that kills you has no dogma—political, religious, or otherwise. It's not fanatical or insane; it's just lead.

Arnie looked out the ballistic glass windows toward the Rose Garden and the South Lawn as the others filed out of the room.

"Kapoor and her team are briefing Senator Chadwick this afternoon regarding your Pharma Independence Bill—"

Ryan frowned. "**My** Pharma Independence Bill? Damn it, Arnie, we've talked about this."

Van Damm raised both hands. "I know, I know. Outside this office it's **the** Pharma Independence Bill." He heaved an exhausted sigh. "There are more than a few folks on our side of the aisle who see this move as a betrayal to U.S. pharmaceutical companies. We're talking billions of dollars here, even trillions."

"We are." Ryan nodded. "And billions of lives. You heard Kapoor's statistics. I'm not trying to run anyone out of business, least of all American interests. Giving tax incentives to companies who build in Puerto Rico won't force anyone to move there, but it will Incentivize them."

"I'm only suggesting we tread lightly," van Damm said. "Mr. President, you are the face of this . . . **our** . . . Pharma Independence Bill, and that's making you a lot of very powerful enemies."

Ryan sat down and rested his hands flat on the desk, giving a slow nod. "You want me to tread lightly because someone has decided to hate me . . ." He scoffed. "Yeah, Arnie. That sounds just like me. Let's have—"

There was a knock at the door and Mary Pat Foley returned, her mouth agape. Half a second later Gary Montgomery stepped in from the main hall, looking just as stricken as Foley.

Ryan stood, his mind immediately turning to Cathy . . . or one of the kids. The look on Mary Pat's face told him to brace himself for the worst.

He whispered. "What is it?"

Montgomery nodded at Foley, who swallowed once, struggling to regain her composure.

"Mr. President," she said. It was not like Mary

Pat to be at a loss for words, but her mouth opened and nothing came out for some time. Finally, "Sir, I have Scott Adler on the phone. The vice president is . . ." She swallowed again. "Jack, Tony Hargrave is dead."

6

Stunned, Ryan gathered Foley, van Damm, and Montgomery around his desk and put the secretary of state on speaker. He offered Foley a tissue, but could tell she'd compartmentalized her grief for the time being.

"Dr. Boone was present when he passed," Adler said, sounding hollow, shell-shocked. "The prime minister waived any investigation on Japan's part. It'll still take some time, but I should be able to fly him home in the next few hours."

"No foul play?" van Damm asked.

Foley shot a glance at Montgomery, who'd received a quick briefing over the phone from Special Agent Keenan Mulvaney. He shook his head.

"No, sir," Adler said. "According to Dr. Boone, Tony's aorta ruptured where it ran through his abdomen. The internal bleeding was massive and immediate. He passed away before we could even get him outside to the ambulance."

"It just . . . ruptured?" Ryan said, half to himself. "Nothing leading up to it?"

"I don't know," Adler said, exhausted. "Maybe. He looked so tired during the flight. I told him he should let Dr. Boone check him over, but you know Tony. He wouldn't have it . . . I should have been more persistent."

"This isn't your fault, Scott," Ryan said.

"I know that, Mr. President," he said. "Logically, anyway. But . . ."

"This . . . is out of nowhere . . ." Ryan stammered, something he rarely did. "Thank you, Scott, for taking care of the details."

"Tony Hargrave was my friend, Mr. President. I'm glad I was here for him."

Foley sniffed back tears again. "What about his wife?"

"It just happened," Adler said. "She has no idea. Prime Minister Mori has issued a media embargo on this until we've had time to notify her. Fortunately for us, the Japanese people are generally rule-keepers so they should stay quiet."

Van Damm drew a deep breath. "What about Varma? Would he leak it?"

"He appears to be genuinely concerned," Adler said. "Despite our disagreements. He's promised a one-hour delay before he notifies his government."

Ryan glanced at Gary Montgomery, who understood what he wanted without a word.

"Your motorcade is ready to depart when you are, Mr. President."

"Very well," Ryan said. "I'm going straight to the Observatory to tell her myself, Scott."

Foley opened her mouth to speak, but again, couldn't get the words out. She took Ryan up on his tissue and sniffed back more tears. "I'm sorry to break down like this . . ."

"It's understandable," Adler said on the other end of the line. "Tony Hargrave made everyone laugh. It's only natural that his loss will make people cry." He cleared his throat. "If there's nothing else, Mr. President."

"Keep us posted, Scott," Ryan said. "I'll meet you at Andrews when you arrive."

Adler ended the call.

On his feet, Ryan checked his watch and then glanced at Foley. "How would you feel about riding with me to see Phoebe? I'd take Cathy, but she's in surgery this morning."

"I'd be honored, Mr. President," Foley said.

Ryan turned to van Damm. "Get with Jason and have him make sure Dr. Boone takes a good look at Scott. He's not a young man anymore and this is going to be exceptionally stressful for him."

Navy Admiral Jason Bailey was the chief physician over the White House medical office—and Carter Boone's boss.

"Of course," van Damm said. "And I'll make an appointment for you at the same time. Tony was your friend, too."

Ryan scoffed, shrugging on his suit jacket. "I'm fine."

"I'll bet that's just what Tony told Scott."

Ryan waved him off and turned to Montgomery. "Let's get going."

The agent spoke into his lapel. "Limo from Montgomery. SWORDSMAN coming your way."

"Jack," Foley said, more familiar under the weight of Hargrave's death. "Are you feeling what I'm feeling?"

"What's that?" Ryan's mind reeled with a thousand different tasks he needed to complete. "That we're under some kind of coordinated attack?"

"Exactly." Foley steeled herself again. "Leave it to me, Mr. President. We'll smoke out who's behind this."

"I know you will," Ryan said, walking.

Arnie followed Ryan into the hall. "I hate to broach the subject now, but it's my job. We need to be thinking about what's next. The markets, the country, the rest of the world . . . They're all watching. They must see that we can handle this. Considering everything else going on, you need to name a new vice president sooner rather than later."

"Got it." Ryan gritted his teeth, trying very

hard not to snap. Arnie was correct, but that didn't make his message any easier to hear. "But right now, if you don't mind, I want to inform Phoebe Hargrave that her husband is dead before she learns about it on CNN."

7

Concrete docks and jetties at the Puerto de Frutos jutted into the river like uneven teeth on a broken comb. East of Tigre city the waters braided through countless islands and canals, eventually joining the Uruguay River at Punta Gorda before flowing into the Río de la Plata. This "River of Silver" was more estuary or bay of the Atlantic, more than a hundred miles across. In the late seventies and early eighties, the Argentine military junta disposed of dissidents in these silty waters, naked, and often still very much alive when they were pushed from military helicopters.

The **Guerra Sucia**—this Dirty War when military rulers disappeared tens of thousands of young people suspected of being communists or socialists, who were imprisoned, tortured, raped, and then eventually burned or dumped into the sea—was not so very long ago. The man selling empanadas on the corner might well have been a guard at a secret prison. The gray-haired woman with a flower in her hair could have had a daughter among the disappeared.

The memories were still very much alive, but buried deep like the dark waters far below the surface. You had to know where to look for them. Now, tourists, both Argentine and foreigner alike, flocked to the Río de la Plata and the lush Tigre Delta.

Dominic Caruso, a special agent with the Federal Bureau of Investigation, at least on paper, surveyed the scene while his partner (and girlfriend) Adara Sherman focused their target. Tall, clean-shaven, with dark hair, he walked like an American and he knew it. Self-assured, alert, taking up a considerable amount of emotional space with his presence alone. Hell, the FBI had poured a whole can of whip-ass on him during new agent training at Quantico. He was a member of an elite force of cops, a top cop, FBI—except he wasn't, not in truth. He was something different now. Something even more elite, or, at the very least, nimbler.

Fit to the extreme, Adara was Nordic blond to Caruso's dark and swarthy. She kept her hair short, absent any murder handle, as she called braids or ponytails. A lifelong learner, she had a working knowledge of six languages beyond English, two of which she spoke with fluency. Perhaps her best asset as an intelligence operative was her ability not to look like an American. Sherman had the ability to morph from college sorority sister to frumpy librarian by simply putting on a different hat.

Today she was a tourist, in a dark polo and khaki shorts—which showed off gorgeous legs born from hours of CrossFit.

Caruso and Sherman, both members of an off-the-books quasigovernmental intelligence organization known as The Campus, made their way down the divided boulevard of paving stones, keenly but surreptitiously focused on the raven-haired woman named Guillermina Rossi. Argentines spoke Spanish like Castilians, so they pronounced the name **Gizhermina**.

Walking thirty meters ahead, their target, or "rabbit," wore a loose cotton shirt that hung past her hips over faded jeans. Her thick hair was pulled back in a wide band made of the same unbleached cotton material as her shirt. Though Rossi was their target, she was not their objective. Sherman and Caruso were after the man she was going to see. Darko Begić, a Serbian national wanted for the systematic rape of twenty-seven Bosnian women and the murder of their fathers, brothers, and husbands. The horrific war crimes had been committed decades before. Begić had been a youthful twenty-year-old thug then, roaming the streets of Srebrenica with his paramilitary gang of other young thugs.

The fruit market was at once a tourist destination and a jumping-off point. Covered mahogany tour boats sat rafted together on the chocolate-brown water like floating buses, two or three deep. Passengers queued up under shadowed awnings clutching tickets for sightseeing tours into the jungled maze of rivers flanked with mansions and stilt houses. A floating store, stocked with kerosene, snacks, and gaseosos—what Argentines called soft drinks—churned the water as it chugged southeast, ready to serve the people who had the good fortune to live on the delta full-time.

"Something's off," Sherman said, speaking into the mic dangling from her ear. She chased a drip of dulce de leche ice cream down the side of a sugar cone with the tip of her tongue, keeping her voice low and reserved because of the many passersby. "I'm just not getting that killer-gun-moll vibe from this one. She's too . . . I don't know . . . pretty . . ."

Caruso took a bite of ham-and-cheese empanada and gave a contemplative nod at the raven-haired woman before locking eyes with his blond girlfriend. He flipped the switch in his pocket so he could speak only to Adara and not broadcast across the net.

"Attractive and badass can go hand in hand," he said. "You are exhibit A in that regard."

"Aww," Sherman said. "You know all the right things to say."

Ahead, Rossi disappeared around the corner of a stall along the river selling grilled beef. A muscular young man in a white shirt and sunglasses followed—likely a bodyguard.

Sherman took another lick of ice cream as she picked up her pace. Today, she and Caruso posed as the couple they actually were, making it easy to banter naturally back and forth. It was a weekend, and the heavy crowds gave them plenty of cover.

Guillermina Rossi wasn't alone—but neither were Caruso and Sherman.

John Clark, director of operations for The Campus, spoke over the net. The team had dispensed with their usual Sonitus Molar Mics for this operation and gone with simple white earbuds connected to their cell phones via hardwire. It seemed every third person shopping along the boulevard had a similar earpiece, so they fit in perfectly.

"Our rabbit still have her friend in tow?" Clark asked.

"Yep," Caruso said, popping the **p**. It helped keep passersby at ease if they dispensed with military jargon. "Dude's got no neck. I'm thinking it's probably mirror muscle, maybe even juicing. But he'd be a handful." Caruso chuckled. "He's kinda fond of those muscles, too, judging from how tight he wears his shirt. Not too bright, because I'm seeing printing from a pistol in his belt every time he rolls his shoulders—which is a lot."

Rossi had been alone when she boarded the Mitre train at Retiro Station in downtown Buenos Aires. The musclebound young man had joined her when she reached the docks.

Most of the team had followed her to Tigre on the train, but Clark and his son-in-law, Domingo "Ding" Chavez, traveled in a rented Toyota van, braving Buenos Aires's notorious traffic while they were kept apprised of the rabbit's moves by those on the train. Clark now patrolled the streets along the riverfront. It was his job to scoop up the entire team if things hit the proverbial fan.

Chavez was already on the water in an open sixteen-foot fiberglass boat. He'd negotiated with a mom-and-pop rental company for two vessels as soon as they arrived. Jack Ryan, Jr., was at the helm of a second small runabout.

If Guillermina was going to meet Begić somewhere on the delta as they believed, she'd have to do so in a boat. Chavez and Ryan planned to pick up the others as soon as she boarded anything that floated.

Former Delta Force operator Bartosz "Midas" Jankowski lagged behind Caruso and Sherman, rounding out the team. He stood ready to take over as the eye if Guillermina or her new friend smelled a tail.

"Maybe this new meathead is security for Begić," Midas offered. "Come to take her to him."

"Could be," Adara said. "She's made a couple of turns around the shops. She's either killing time or running countersurveillance, probably a bit of both. The thing is . . ."

Her voice trailed off. Caruso could tell by the way she chewed on her bottom lip that she was thinking hard about something.

Clark, two blocks away and eager for intel from his team, prodded over the net.

"Let's have it," he said. "I don't care if it's just a gut feeling."

Adara gave a slow nod. "What's that saying about Argentines? 'They're a bunch of Italians who speak Spanish but think they're Brits living in France.'"

"Pretty damned on point if you ask me," Midas said.

"I don't think I've been around a more well-coiffed group of people," Adara said. "Nearly everybody we've run across looks like they're dressed for a fancy date, even if they're just hitting the corner market to stock up on dulce de leche. This girl looks like she's going camping, not to meet her filthy-rich war-criminal boyfriend."

Ahead, Rossi stopped in front of a shop selling

long knives, the kind gauchos customarily carried in their belts. Meathead looked at the blades while Guillermina talked on her cell phone, gesticulating wildly with her free hand as she spoke.

Caruso brought the others up to speed over comms.

". . . She's becoming more animated," he said. "Excited about something. Look sharp. Maybe Begić is coming to her. We could be looking at an imminent arrival."

"Well, shit," Chavez said.

The plan had been to follow her to Darko Begić's location and then let the FBI legal attaché in Buenos Aires take it from there with the local gendarmerie. It was one thing to follow the bad guy's girlfriend who, at best, was running shoddy surveillance-detection measures. Begić was bound to be traveling with competent muscle. The Campus team would still attempt to see where he went, but surveilling people who did not want be followed required a much larger group than The Campus had at their disposal.

"Prefectura," Jack said. "Four of them in an open patrol boat, heading southeast."

Prefectura were the border patrol of Argentina.

"Not surprised," Chavez said. "Their local HQ is just around the corner."

"Okay, boys," Adara piped up. "Something's going down."

Guillermina ended her call and stuffed the

phone into the pocket of her jeans. Flicking her hand at Meathead, she motioned him toward a set of steps that led from the market to the water.

Caruso relayed what they'd seen.

". . . Ding, Jack, you have eyes from your positions?"

"Affirmative," Ryan said. "I see a lone boat diver—looks like maybe a teenage kid—just pulled alongside the pier. Rossi and Meathead are getting on board."

"Perfecto," Caruso said. "On our way. Can you pick us up and still keep her in sight?"

"Can do," Ryan said.

Chavez, slightly farther upriver, called out for Midas to come to him.

"Rossi and her muscle are pulling away from the pier now," Ryan said. "Heading downstream. Falling in behind that mahogany tour boat that's abeam the second jetty."

Dom and Adara cut left between the curio store and the ice-cream shop, hustling down the concrete steps to hop over the gunnels of Ryan's skiff at the same moment he motored up alongside the pier.

Ryan sat on an overturned plastic bucket, the makeshift helm of skiff drivers the world over. Ball cap pulled low over his eyes, he steered the little boat with the tiller arm of a thirty-horse outboard motor.

With Dom and Adara seated and settled, he

waited for two kayakers to squirt by, then pulled the tiller toward him and arced the little boat smoothly away from the concrete wall.

"Heat check!" Adara suddenly said, her voice grim. "Rabbit's doing a one-eighty."

Guillermina Rossi was heading back to land, and the Campus operators were out in the open, sitting in their boats.

Everyone but John Clark.

8

NIGHTINGALE.

Something as audacious as kidnapping the First Lady of the United States deserved a good code name.

"The operation is well under way." The Spaniard's voice poured out of the speaker, sounding puffed up with his own importance—as usual.

It was late evening, far later than a man of Harjit Malhotra's means should have been in the office, but, Malhotra thought, working late was one of the reasons he was a billionaire. That and the stars. The snarling din of traffic hardly reached the fifteenth-floor windows of his Banjara Hills office. His secretary was still there, too, beyond the polished teak door. Kashvi was an exquisite girl, with the most delicious mole at the small of her back. He'd get to her soon, after his call, no matter how long that took.

As he spoke, Malhotra gestured at the air with the katar that he kept on his desk. One of his many expensive playthings, the jewel-encrusted push-dagger had a fat triangular blade that resembled a long shark tooth. Historically, it was used to protect oneself against tiger attack. Malhotra imagined sliding it into the Spaniard's neck. Speaking with this man was always tedious, but this time, he bore welcome news. At long last.

Spinning his chair slightly, Malhotra tapped the touchpad on his laptop to wake it up, savoring a news story regarding Vice President Anthony Hargrave's death. He glanced across the top of his computer at the stuffed Bengal tiger that stood, fangs bared, to the right of his office door, and thought of the perfect timing. A smile crawled across his broad face as if he'd just tasted something deliciously sweet—or Kashvi's mole.

"Did you have anything to do with this?" he asked the Spaniard.

"Hargrave's death was coincidental," the voice on the other end of the encrypted VOIP line said. The man spoke English, precise, like he was highly educated, but with a decidedly Spanish accent. "A gift of fate, señor. Neither I nor any of my men can claim responsibility. Still, we will capitalize on the consequences of the death. Make no mistake."

Malhotra stabbed the katar into the front of his lap draw, then pulled it out and pitched it on the desk to keep from marring his beautiful desk any more than he already had. This Spaniard could make him so angry. The smile vanished as quickly as it appeared when he thought of the latest debacle.

"And what of the civilian aircraft? I was under the impression it would be blown out of the sky by the American Air Force. We have missed a valuable opportunity. The press would have roasted Jack Ryan alive had he shot down one of his own citizens! Now you have wasted time and resources. Have you not given the Americans the opportunity to demonstrate they are more than capable of protecting their White House? This is exactly the opposite of the outcome I want. Ryan is stubborn, bullheaded. He will keep pushing this bullshit legislation of his until we—and by **we** I mean **you**—turn his world on its head!"

The Spaniard yawned on the other end of the line. Someone with lesser ears might have written the sound off to a glitch in the VOIP connection, but Malhotra was sure this mercenary prick had just yawned at him. The son of a bitch actually yawned!

"Señor Malhotra," Gil said. "My men are working on exactly the scenario that we have spoken of all along. If what you want is—"

The billionaire cut him off.

"What I want you to do is rain hell on President Jack Ryan in many small doses," Malhotra snapped. "I am sure I made that clear in our initial discussions."

"Crystal clear."

"Operations fail for a reason," Malhotra said. "Who is to blame for this business with the airplane?"

"The pilot deviated from instructions given by my men," the Spaniard said, as if shrugging off the question. "A shootdown proved to be unsuccessful."

"Unsuccessful?" Malhotra smashed a fist against his desk, upending a silver tray containing a seventeenth-century Mughal tea set and narrowly missing the dagger. Cups and saucers went over the edge, crashing to the carpeted floor. "Deviated? I sincerely hope your people had the good sense to slaughter that pilot's family for his inability to follow instructions."

"They did not," the Spaniard said, sounding smug, as only a Spaniard could. "That would have turned what the authorities view as an untraceable crank call into a murder investigation—which would bring unnecessary scrutiny at the moment."

Malhotra's buxom secretary poked her pretty head in to check on the noise of the tea set hitting the floor. She gave a little start when she saw the tiger, as she always did, and then looked at Malhotra, raising her perfect eyebrows to see if he needed assistance.

Malhotra slammed a hand on the table again. Conversations with the Spaniard always made him want to choke someone—maybe not to death, but at least until they squirmed and admitted that Malhotra was the boss. He glared at the secretary for a long moment, seething, thinking how her tremulous throat and wide chestnut eyes would admit he was the boss . . . under a wide variety of circumstances. He waved her away. She offered a subservient dip of her head before pulling the door shut, softly, as Malhotra required. She would pick up the mess when she came in later.

He'd paid sixty thousand dollars for the tea set. Extremely rare, but he'd find another one somewhere. One could buy anything with enough money.

The Spaniard demanded a great deal of that, but he was a hireling. It galled Malhotra that this man exuded the air of an equal, as if it were he and not Malhotra who called the shots. Señor Gil liked to point out that in order for his plans to be successful, he had to retain tactical control while Malhotra kept command authority. Soldier double-talk horseshit, that's what that was, and Malhotra knew it. Authority was nothing without control.

Still, he had to admit that this Spaniard was a force to be reckoned with. If the stories were true, he had served with distinction in the Spanish Special Operations Unit, or UOE. Known colloquially in Spain as "the Unit," it was absorbed into Special Naval Warfare, where Gil, it seemed, felt his skills and acumen were overlooked by younger, newer officers. Sidelined, he discovered other soldiers from all around the world who'd found themselves in similar situations—marginalized for whatever reason—and the Camarilla was born.

One did not find men like this from searching websites—or even the Dark Web. Everything was by word of mouth. Referrals.

He'd met the Spaniard three times face-to-face, early on during the initial negotiations. The meetings had taken place in Malhotra's office—an arrangement he had hoped would give him, as the Americans called it, a home-field advantage. It did not. Each time, Señor Gil had brought with him dour men, four in all over the course of their meetings, as if to show off his muscle. Of varying ethnicity, these men shared a common gravitas that drew tremulous smiles from Kashvi. All of them were apparently hired for their ability to shoot beams of contempt from their eyeballs, obviously present to intimidate. Malhotra had considered calling some of his security people into the meetings but decided against it. These Camarilla men would have viewed even the best of his people as food, bothersome flies to swat.

But Malhotra wanted the toughest, which was why he had engaged the Spaniard in the first place. The fact that the men who worked for him were certainly murderers at once unsettled him and put him at ease. Still, he was paying a lot of money, and felt he was owed a certain modicum of respect.

Money was a funny thing. Malhotra had risen from a comfortable portfolio just south of eight hundred million dollars to billionaire land overnight, all because of a fluctuation in the market. Heady stuff for a forty-year-old who inherited the company from uncles who had no children of their own.

As a lowly millionaire, Malhotra had dutifully worn a suit to the office every day. Now, like many men of his status, he dressed however he wished. He needed to impress no one, excepting perhaps his present girlfriend, who was pretty and smart but not quite smart enough to suspect anything untoward about Kashvi. She would suss it all out eventually. Women had a knack for that sort of thing. When she did, he'd find a new one. The flavor of the month was a twenty-eight-year-old fashion designer from Mumbai who dressed him like he was one of her runway models. That morning she'd laid out a pair of chinos and a white linen shirt, like he was going for a photo shoot on the beach instead of working at his office. He didn't care about clothes any more than a shark cared about the look of its own skin. The world was his ocean. The board of directors was weak, a show. He owned the company—and answered to no one.

Except for Reinhardt Roth. That was the one man on earth he wanted to please, for the moment at least. If Herr Roth stayed happy and Roth Pharmaceutical purchased MalhotraMed Pharma Corp, in two weeks' time Harjit Malhotra would increase his net worth over tenfold, making him safe from market fluctuations. In order for that to happen, Jack Ryan needed to put an end to this incessant harping about American independence from generic drugs manufactured in India. Señor Gil began to tick off the successes of his organization's multipronged attack on the American President.

Malhotra listened, leaning back in his Brandywine leather chair, scanning his vast art collection. Among his prized possessions were two Renoirs, a sculpture of Kankalamurti carved from human bone, and a three-hundred-year-old French translation of the **Kama Sutra** that he kept on a lighted wooden stand to the left of the door, open to the most delicious illustrations that caused Kashvi to avert her eyes each time she walked into the office.

The stuffed Bengal tiger crouched to the right of the door opposite the **Kama Sutra**. Glass eyes blazing with wild fury, the beast's lips pulled back in a fierce snarl, exposing daggerlike fangs.

On a small lectern beside the tiger, resting against crushed black velvet, was the howdah pistol that had killed it. Malhotra purchased the Harris Holland double-barrel along with ten rounds of .577 Snider ammunition—projectiles as large as his thumb—for eighteen thousand dollars. It was a pittance to pay for the joy of using a nineteenth-century weapon to bring down such a savage adversary. Some billionaires let others fly them into space for a few seconds. Malhotra preferred his adrenaline to spring from something more visceral.

Malhotra bounced a fist on the arm of his chair, suddenly tired of listening to the Spaniard drone. His uncles had taught him that if someone was allowed to speak too long uninterrupted, they began to believe that they were in charge of the meeting.

"I assume your men are ready."

"They are," the Spaniard said.

"They had better be," Malhotra said. He knew a thing or two about hunting dangerous things. "Taking the First Lady from under the noses of her Secret Service protectors is not something to take lightly."

"Of course," Gil said, yawning again.

Malhotra frowned. **Saala kutta!** Literally, **brother-in-law dog.**

"I would not be so concerned if I merely wanted you to kill her. But your mercenaries must not only take her, but keep her alive. If Ryan finds that his wife is dead, he will grieve but move on. Given even the slightest possibility that he might save her, that man will be consumed. I trust your mercenaries are up to that task."

"They are," Gil said, dead calm. "But I would remind you that my men are not mercenaries, señor. Mercenaries fight for money. Men of the Camarilla fight for the joy of the conflict itself." He gave a little condescending grunt, as if his words were too lofty to be understood by a non-soldier. "And, more important, they fight for each other."

Malhotra nodded to the stuffed tiger and mouthed the word **mercenaries**.

The tiger said nothing, but Malhotra felt certain it agreed.

9

Ding Chavez watched the scene unfold from his vantage point fifty meters upriver. "You're already committed, Jack," he said over his radio. "She's gonna get hinked up unless you continue heading into the water the way you've already started."

Midas grabbed the skiff's rail, ready to haul himself up and get off the boat.

"I'll take up the eye," he said, groaning. "Pretty smart brush-off technique."

"Hold what you've got," Chavez said.

One hand on the rail, Midas turned to look at him. "You don't want me to follow?"

"I need you to drive the boat."

Midas gave a curt nod. "You're the boss."

"Come and take my seat," Ding said, handing off the tiller and trading places. "You've been behind her awhile. Good chance she's already spotted you. For all we know, Begić has a countersurveillance team watching the whole fruit market. I'll be a new face."

"She's back on the pier," Adara said. "We'll lose

sight of her in ten seconds, as soon as we go past this tour boat."

"Got her," Chavez said. "For the moment, anyway."

He watched Guillermina Rossi and Meathead climb to the top of the stairs as if they intended to keep shopping. Lower in the water, Chavez's view was obstructed by the concrete wall of the pier after they had gone only a few feet.

Chavez piped, "Has anyone got an eye?"

Clark's voice came over the net, rough as ten miles of gravel road, but steady and comforting nonetheless. "I have the eye," he said. "Both are pretending to browse at the knife shop at the end of the road, but it's pretty obvious from the way they're looking over the top of their sunglasses that they're checking their six—scratch that. The girl's staying put but Meathead is walking south, toward the city, his head on a swivel."

"I'm on my way up," Chavez said. "We're right below you."

"Standby where you are," Clark said, falling silent.

Chavez glanced from Midas to the stairs. Both looked like dogs eager to be let off the chain.

"Meathead has stopped," Clark said. "Rossi is—okay . . . they're heading back to the boat. On your toes, boys and girls. These two aren't exactly pros, but they are looking hard to find a tail."

Chavez cast off the bowline and nodded at Midas to take them away from the dock.

Clark came across the air again. "Oh, and by the way. Guillermina keeps touching the hem of her shirt. I'm thinking Meathead's not the only one who's armed."

Two kilometers downstream, Guillermina Rossi's boat arced north, leaving the wider main river to enter a shadowy canal. River laurel, palms, and towering evergreens lined the banks. It looked to lead toward a lesser fork of the Paraná, one of the larger rivers that flowed from Argentina's interior.

Midas kept to the main channel, motoring past the canal's entrance. Ryan's boat had let them pass shortly after pulling away from Tigre. He now brought up the rear, allowing him to make the turn as a fresh set of eyes.

With Midas at the tiller, Chavez's skiff continued downstream for a full minute before doing a one-eighty in front of an oncoming tour boat to motor back to the canal.

"How about a sitrep, Jackie Boy?" Chavez asked. A white egret looked on from the marshy shallows as they passed, a tiny fish held crosswise in its daggerlike bill.

"Taking it slow," Ryan said.

"This place is idyllic," Adara said. "Quaint

TIGRE, ARGENTINA

N

Arroyo Abra Vieja

Luján River

Puerto de Frutos

Begić's House

Municipalidad de Tigre

Prefectura
San Fernando

Canal San Fernando

© 2021 Jeffrey L. Ward

houses. Kids fishing off the docks. Like the Deep South with a South American feel . . . Huckleberry Bolívar. If Darko Begić is here, he picked a beautiful place to hole up."

"How about Rossi and Meathead?" Chavez prodded. He couldn't help but agree with Adara. Patty would like this. He'd bring her here someday—when he wasn't hunting a war criminal.

A scant thirty feet wide, this new waterway was beyond quiet, absent the heavy traffic of the larger throughfare—the riverine equivalent of a Tigre suburb. The eastern bank boasted immaculate stilted homes nestled among manicured gardens of swaying palms and thick-hipped cypress trees while the west side of the canal looked slightly wilder, with bushes and reeds choking stretches of undeveloped shoreline between equally pristine houses with impossibly green lawns running down gentle slopes to the water's edge.

"Hard to fade into the background when there are no other boats but us," Ryan said. "It's like following someone down a deserted side street. They know we're here, we just have to hope they don't—"

He fell silent.

Chavez waited a beat. There were three radios in Ryan's boat. One of them would sing out eventually and bring everyone up to speed.

Then Ryan's voice piped over the net, measured

but direct. "Another boat coming our way. Could be Begić. Just pulled away from a dock on the west bank a hundred meters ahead."

"Outstanding," Chavez said. "Mark the coordinates of the house where he's staying and continue upstream—"

The staccato pop of gunfire carried over the water. A flock of small green parrots rose out of the trees at the bend ahead. A father fishing off a wooden dock with his son grabbed the boy by the arm and hustled him up the slope, away from the rattling sound of danger.

Midas rolled on the throttle without a word from Chavez, cutting a white V in the brown water and bringing the little boat up on step.

"This is a hit," Ryan said. "Rossi's not coming to meet Begić. She's coming to kill him."

Chavez and Midas rounded the bend an instant before Begić's driver rammed Guillermina Rossi's boat broadside. The Serb's skiff was larger, maybe twenty feet, with a center console and an upswept bow that rose higher in the water. Begić ducked low, using the console and his driver to shield himself from Rossi and Meathead's pistol fire.

In the scant moments before the boats collided, Chavez saw Begić had two bodyguards, one of whom lay wounded on the transom behind his boss. The other sprayed Rossi's boat with automatic fire with an Uzi. Meathead jumped to cover Rossi but caught a gutful of bullets as the heavier boat plowed straight into them.

The upswept bow on Begić's boat crushed the smaller vessel. Driven upward by the impact, the larger boat came completely out of the water, its propeller cavitating and screaming as it sailed and sliced over and through Rossi's fiberglass skiff.

Begić's driver was killed in the melee, either by gunfire from Rossi or by the impact of the collision. The boat began to slow, settling into the water. Rossi had gone overboard, along with her driver. Begić scanned the surface, gun in hand, waiting for her to pop up.

Caruso, the only one in the other skiff who was armed, sent a round into Begić's stern as Ryan raced to put their skiff between Rossi and the Serbian.

Begić shouted something unintelligible. His bodyguard let the Uzi fall against a sling around his shoulders and took up the helm, rolling on power to roar downstream toward Tigre.

Still on step and going full throttle to reach their friends, Midas arced their boat quickly to the right, avoiding the oncoming vessel as it shot past. Begić fired twice, assuming Chavez and Midas were part of the ambush. The shots went wide. Fortunately, the guy with the Uzi was too busy driving the boat.

"You good, Jack?" Chavez shouted. Midas had yet to slow down.

"All good!" Ryan shouted back. They were close enough now they could have heard each other without the radio had it not been for the screaming engines. "We'll fish out Rossi!"

Chavez glanced over his shoulder at Midas. "Got 'em?" He clutched the gunnel as Midas stood the little boat on its side, arcing into a tight turn that took up the entire width of the canal.

"Oh, yeah," Midas said. "They've got a bigger engine." He shot Chavez a tight grin and settled in at the tiller. "Good thing I'm a better boat driver than Señor Uzi."

10

Begić's larger and faster boat continued to pull ahead as they sped upriver toward Tigre. Both vessels slalomed in and out of the steady parade of tour boats and pleasure craft.

A hand on each gunnel, Chavez leaned well over the bow, willing more speed out of the motor.

Begić's boat slowed, then turned up one of the finger canals cut between the concrete piers. Cutting left, it disappeared in front of a line of squat mahogany tour boats rafted together at the docks. Midas and Chavez rounded the flotilla in time to watch the Serbian leap over the side of his skiff and sprint up the steps. His driver sped away without looking back.

Midas nosed toward the pier. "Come take the tiller!" he shouted. "I'll go after him!"

Chavez ignored him, hopping over the rail when they were still two feet out. Midas was no spring chicken, but Chavez had more than a few years on him. Fortunately, Begić was older than either. Catching him shouldn't be a problem.

Hopefully. Still, Chavez dispensed with any witty comeback, saving his breath for the chase.

Arms pumping, Chavez hit the top step at a full sprint. The crowd of fruit market shoppers, already alerted to a wild man rushing up from the river with a pistol, began to murmur and shout when they saw Chavez in hot pursuit.

Begić spun, realizing someone was following him. He shot from the hip, missing Chavez but scattering startled market-goers. Chavez ducked behind a T-shirt shop, then did a quick peek around the corner, squatting low so his brain-pan wouldn't present such a predictable target if Begić happened to be lying in wait. No worries there. The guy was hauling ass, pistol in hand, but not looking back.

Chavez followed at a sprint, chuffing like his cousin's '66 Shovelhead Harley.

"He's cutting right," Chavez said between breaths. "First side street . . . Left again . . . parallel to the piers . . ." He scanned for a street sign. "Sarmiento . . . South toward the main road out front."

The Serbian continued to shove his way through crowds. Small shops gave way to traditional brick buildings, furniture stores, art galleries, restaurants—and far fewer people. Begić sped up, now with a straight, unimpeded path as he ran toward a waiting white sedan idling in the street at the next corner. He touched his ear, adjusting an earpiece, speaking to someone as he ran.

Sirens wailed from every direction, growing louder. Policía. They were close.

The driver of the white sedan had clearly had enough. Spooked by the oncoming police, he sped off, leaving Begić high and dry, still half a block away.

The Serbian stutter-stepped, threw up his arms in protest. Chavez couldn't hear what he said, but imagined a string of colorful curses. Begić didn't slow down for long.

Fifty feet behind him, Chavez brought everyone up to speed over the radio. "He's turned northeast again . . . cutting between some buildings to the same street where he jumped out." Chavez matched his pace, not wanting to risk getting a bullet to the face if he got too close. "He's on his phone with someone."

John Clark chimed in. "Returning to his boat, maybe?"

"Could be," Chavez said.

"That's affirmative," Midas said. "I have eyes on his boat driver. No Uzi in sight, but he's sitting in the skiff in front of the northernmost tour boat in the canal, almost to the main river. The tour boats are rafted three out from the dock. Four or five have just come in from delta tours.

The whole place is a mess, crawling with vessels and people."

"Copy that." Chavez slowed to a trot so as not to prompt Begić to take any more wild shots and risk hitting the crowd. "He's winded," Chavez said, panting himself. "I'm fifty feet behind him."

"Jack," Midas called out. "What's your pos?"

"About a hundred meters downriver," Ryan said. "Coming up on the easternmost Tigre docks now. We have Rossi on board. According to her, Begić raped and murdered her sister about a month ago. She came to settle the score—"

"Haul ass this way," Midas said, "and we'll help her do that. Move toward the front where the driver is waiting. It's okay if he sees you."

"Roger that," Ryan said, trusting the former Delta operator to know what he was doing.

"Begić's boat can't get any closer to the pier than he already is at the moment," Midas said. "Too many other boats in his way . . . Press him, Ding. Keep him moving. I have an idea."

Chavez listened as he ran, grateful for a break from using his wind to keep everyone updated.

Begić slowed a step as he reached the raft of tour boats, his head snapping back and forth, considering his options. The three vessels in the back of the line were in the process of disgorging dozens and dozens of passengers, packing the pier and blocking the Serbian's way forward.

"Moving in," Ryan said.

Begić threw up his arms, waving wildly as he spoke to someone through the mic dangling from his ear. Unable to move forward, he dispensed with the stairs and leaped over the railing to the roof of the nearest boat, landing on the fiberglass roof. Some sixty feet long and eighteen feet wide, the boats made for a slick but unimpeded escape route. Begić crossed the vessel nearest the pier laterally, leaping to the next boat in the raft, and then the next until he reached the outer vessel, at which point he ran forward again.

Chavez followed him over the rail, grateful for his Lowa boots with grippy soles. He jumped from the inside boat to the middle, running parallel to his target. Both men had been pushing all out for over five minutes. Chavez was in better-than-average shape, running well over twenty miles each week, though appreciably slower than he'd once been. Not too many years ago he would have run this asshole into the ground, ripped the dude's arm off and beat him do death with it. But these full-on sprints had him fading. Fortunately, Begić was in worse shape, sucking the proverbial pond water, wheezing, staggering, fueled by little but adrenaline and hate.

Chavez gained on him now with every step.

Tour operators and boat crews began to shout from the pier and decks below, chastising these two crazy men for marring the tops of their beautiful vessels with heavy boots. Crowds of market-goers gathered at the rail. They shouted insults, well practiced in the Argentine art of escrache—public shaming—until Begić turned and fired two more shots. The bullets smacked the wood behind Chavez, missing him, but close enough to make him dance instinctively to the side.

Screams rose from the crowd at the pop of gunfire. Most stampeded away en masse, but a few hunkered down and tried to film with their phones.

Begić built up speed as he reached the bow of the rearmost tour boat. His boots pounding away on top of the roof, he gathered himself up to leap across the gap. He made it, landing at the aft deck of the next in line, but only just. A knee slammed against the unforgiving fiberglass in the process before he was able to haul himself up the ladder to continue his forward run.

Less than twenty feet behind him, but one boat closer to the dock, Chavez ducked his head and pumped his arms, willing himself to go faster. This would all be over soon—one way or another.

Begić jumped down to the next and final boat in line, floundering again, scrambling to his feet and up the last ladder, limping badly now. Chavez was able to gain another couple yards.

Almost neck and neck, running on parallel boats, Begić must have heard Chavez moving up on him. He raised the pistol as if to shoot, but Ryan, or someone off the bow, blew an air horn, grabbing the Serb's attention.

Confused at seeing Guillermina Rossi so soon after their last encounter, and surely taking her for a threat, he stutter-stepped again, trying to work out which way he should go.

Ryan hit the air horn again.

Chavez angled to the right at the sound of the blast, launching himself across the gap to the adjacent boat and plowing directly into the exhausted Begić. Chavez bent his knees and dug in like he was hitting a tackle sled in football practice. Unable to control himself laterally, the Serb toppled over the side, dropping fifteen feet into Midas's skiff. Chavez pulled up short, letting himself down in a more controlled fashion to keep from breaking anything.

Begić writhed on the plywood deck, not quite so lucky.

Cowering behind open hands, he moaned something in Spanish that Chavez couldn't quite make out over the sound of his own breathing.

Midas pointed the little skiff into the river, blocked from view of the pier by the larger vessels. He turned south as a fiberglass launch full of Prefectura officers arrived from the San Fernando station upstream. A coast guard patrolling the country's waterways, the Prefectura Naval Argentina was even larger than the Navy, so there was little doubt the entire market would be swarming with them in no time.

For now, the arriving officials were armed with stale information, still scanning the roofs of the large tour boats for the reported troublemakers.

Chavez pulled an oily canvas tarpaulin over the stunned and groaning Darko Begić. Midas motored downstream a kilometer, turning gently off the main river onto an industrial waterway at the edge of Tigre proper called the Canal San Fernando.

Begić's moans grew louder, higher in pitch. "I have money," he said, wincing as he spoke from what were surely fractured ribs.

Chavez put a boot to the man's shoulder, not a kick, but a stern reminder that he should keep quiet. It didn't help.

The Serbian squirmed until he was able to peek out from under the canvas. "Camarilla? Who hired you? One of the girls? Not Guijita, surely . . . I hear you guys are unbribable—but everyone has a price. Correct?"

Chavez ignored him.

"How does double sound, my friend?" Begić whined like a mosquito now. "I swear it. Don't take it for yourself if your honor is at stake. Surely even the fabled Camarilla needs operating capital?"

Normally, Chavez would have been happy to let a prisoner spill his guts with all the intelligence information he wanted to vomit up, but frankly he was having a hard time getting past the fact that this guy was a piece-of-shit child rapist. No, Begić needed to go have his day in court in the Hague or wherever they sent him—Bosnia, with a bunch of female prison guards, if there was any justice in the world.

Chavez used the toe of his boot to turn Begić's face toward the deck, grinding it against the filthy plywood so there would be no misunderstanding. He wasn't interested in talking.

Midas took the little skiff past the Prefectura station on the left where a half-dozen uniformed officers prepared small runabouts to join the search for the man who had shot up the fruit market. Normal boat traffic on the river had not stopped during the recent melee and the enforcement officers had no idea the men responsible had run toward them instead of away.

Ryan followed in his boat with Dom, Adara, and Guillermina Rossi.

Still winded, Chavez breathed an uneven sigh of relief when he saw his father-in-law with arms folded standing in front of the van alongside the scrubby dirt bank of the canal. The scattered buildings were run-down and far apart, with several overgrown vacant lots in between what few there were. Bits of trash and nests of tangled fishing line blew over the moist dirt on a breeze that gusted up off the main river.

Clark peered north, past his arriving team-mates. "His boat driver?" he asked. "The one with the Uzi?"

Adara Sherman shook her head as she hopped over the side to help Chavez wrangle the wobbly Serb from the boat. "Señor Uzi was going upriver at warp speed last time we saw him."

Begić hunched forward, hands bound with zip-ties, and stifled a cough. **Yep,** Chavez thought, **broken ribs.**

The Serb switched to English. "What now?" he sneered. "Why bring me on land just to kill me? It is common knowledge that Camarilla takes no prisoners."

John Clark looked from the Serb to Chavez, thought for a moment, and then waved away some notion. "We need to move. Now."

Chavez prodded Begić forward, up the bank toward the waiting van.

The Serb stopped in his tracks. "You are not them?" Begić gasped. He looked heavenward, muttering a whispered prayer. Tears filled his eyes—and then he began to laugh.

Guillermina Rossi stepped out of Ryan's boat a scant ten feet downriver. She stumbled over a gnarled little bush, but caught herself and smoothed her wet clothing with unsteady hands. Begić chuckled at her mishap, his smallish nose crinkling in bitter disdain. "I know **you**, Guijita." He leered at her translucent blouse, still soaked from her plunge in the river. "So these people are merely your thugs. All this? For what, my darling? Revenge?"

Rossi bowed her head, water dripping from wet hair. Broken twigs and bits of leaf clung to a flushed face.

Chavez glanced over his shoulder toward the mouth of the canal, checking for followers—Prefectura officers or otherwise. A rush of adrenaline shot down his arms when he turned back and caught the momentary flash in Rossi's eyes.

He'd seen that look before.

Rossi's hand came up quickly, holding a small semiautomatic pistol. Her first round would have hit Begić square in the head, but Chavez bumped her elbow, deflecting her point of aim enough that the bullet ripped through the man's jaw, destroying several teeth before exiting below his right ear. Rossi fired again, the second round striking the Serb in the wing of his pelvis, dropping him like a sack of sand.

Chavez wrested the pistol away, cleared it, and threw it into the river.

11

Clark had everyone moving before the Serbian hit the ground.

"Let's go!" he said.

He didn't have to tell everyone that gunshots were ass-magnets for the boys and girls in blue.

Adara ripped open a packet of QuikClot from the pocket kit she was never without and stuffed treated gauze into the pulsing wound in Begić's hip. Hands restrained, he writhed in the mud like the injured snake that he was, spittle and bits of tooth clinging to the tattered flesh that had once been his cheek.

"Missed any arteries," Sherman said when she stood, covered to the elbows in blood. She gave the Serb another tight-lipped visual assessment and then nodded. "Can't do anything about the face wound, but he should live until they get him to a hospital."

"So we're good?" Ding asked.

"He'll live," Adara said. "But he's not going to look pretty for his trial."

"Works for me." Ding waved his hand in

a circle over his head and rallied his team into the van.

They left Darko Begić on the riverbank with the other bits of soggy trash, a copy of his Interpol Red Notice taped to his back. The notice was not actually a warrant, but an Interpol document that stated there were outstanding warrants in other countries and that those countries were eager to extradite if the subject was located. Argentina, still sensitive about their reputation for harboring Nazis after World War II, would see that he was given medical treatment and then promptly extradited to stand trial for his crimes.

At the wheel of the minivan, Clark sped down Avenue Santa Fe, melding with heavy traffic that flowed toward downtown Buenos Aires.

Guillermina Rossi slumped deeper into her seat, apparently resigned to going to prison for the rest of her life for avenging her sister's murder. She stood on the side of the road trembling when they dropped her at Victoria Station with no explanation. Completely spent physically and emotionally, she fell to her knees on the concrete and wept.

"No one thought to search her?" Clark said the moment they were moving again. His voice was tight, brimming with disappointment.

Adara sat in the back row beside Dom, beating her head softly on the headrest in front of her.

"I missed it completely," she said. "Rossi had a pistol in her hand when she went into the water, but I saw her drop it. What with everything else, I didn't think to look for a second."

Dom put a hand on her shoulder. "She wasn't a threat."

"The hell she wasn't," Clark said. He glanced in the rearview mirror like a father scolding rowdy children on a road trip. "She just wasn't a threat to us." He paused, letting the notion sink in that they'd **all** missed a hidden gun. Such things happened, but that shouldn't make anyone feel better about it.

Clark let the team brood on that as he drove south on surface streets, muscling his way through Buenos Aires traffic, where aggression and momentum gave one the right of way.

He broke the silence as he took the on-ramp to the Highway Panamericana. "Anybody want to tell me what else went wrong?"

Chavez, riding shotgun, glanced sideways, already aware of where this was going. "We were outnumbered by the situation," he said. "Small-group tactics might work in a highly kinetic action like we just experienced, but there are still too many points of failure, too much that is completely out of our control. A foot surveillance turned into an ambush on the water. If Rossi had been running anything other than half-ass surveillance detection she would have burned us before we ever got to the water. This was only a win because we were lucky."

Ryan spoke next. "We had our entire team on the ground and Begić very nearly got away. Soon or later we—" He paused, took his phone from his pocket, and then raised a finger. "It's Gavin. I need to take this."

Gavin Biery was the Campus director of information technology. When he called, it was usually something important. Clark gave Ryan a nod and then looked at the rest of his team in the rearview mirror. "Junior's right," he said. "We need more people." In truth, he and Chavez had been discussing this for some time.

"A half-dozen would cover more bases," Midas offered, forehead against the side window, hypnotized by the traffic. "But even two would help exponentially."

"We'll go with two for now." Clark didn't say it, but he knew just where to start. He took his eyes off the traffic long enough to glance in the mirror again to see Ryan becoming more animated on the phone with Gavin. The kid had something. Clark could see it in his face.

"There is something else we should talk about," Ding said. "What do we know about Camarilla?"

"**Little room?**" Midas said, shaking his head. They'd all heard of the Camarilla, but no one had been able to come up with any hard intel.

Caruso spoke next. "The Bureau believes the group is tied to at least two recent political assassinations. One in the Caribbean, another in Germany. Both the victims had less-than-stellar reputations so no one got too wrapped around the axle about their deaths. Still, a shadow group working for the highest bidder is worrisome."

"More than one of those," Adara said.

"Yeah," Caruso said. "But this seems to be something different. Almost like they have state funding—and, if the hype is true, a sort of patriotism."

"That's too weird," Midas said.

"Camarilla," Clark mused, changing lanes to get out of the way of a speeding bus.

"An inner circle," Adara said. "Political cronies surrounding a leader—like Andrew Jackson's unofficial Kitchen Cabinet. They had the ear of the President, and did his bidding, but without holding actual government office."

Clark looked at Chavez with a raised brow. "Given a certain point of view . . . in the cold dispassionate light of day—that would be a description of The Campus."

Ding gave a contemplative nod, looking out the window again. They passed yet another parrilla and the smell of fire-grilled meat filled the van. "Begić seemed sure we were going to kill him when he thought we were Camarilla. Probably a good idea to dig a little deeper into who they are."

"Fair enough," Clark said. "But Adara's right. There are all manner of Camarilla out there. It's a dangerous world with lots of work for those who are action-oriented—some of it honorable, some of it more nefarious. But there's not exactly a shortage of muscular guys with tats and tight T-shirts who've spent a considerable amount of time downrange. Most of them are salt of the earth. The others . . ."

Ryan ended the call and pumped his fist in the air.

Chavez twisted in his seat to look over his shoulder. "Whatcha got?"

"It's not nothing," Ryan said. "But not a lot, either. Get this. Seventeen deepfake videos that we know of popping up all over the Web. They're extremely realistic, purporting to show my dad doing everything from cheating at golf to getting a lap dance at a strip club on K Street."

"Okay," Clark said, to show he was listening.

"Gavin and I took a hard look at three of the most recent ransomware attacks—the Baltimore power grid, Red Hook Terminal in New York, and the D.C. Metro. Money from two of the ransomware attacks went to the same virtual currency wallet. Metadata from four of the deepfake videos has common characteristics with one of those ransomware programs."

"So they are linked," Clark said.

"Sort of," Ryan said. "Gavin calls them commonalities, mostly the style in which pieces of code are written. But get this. Everyone from NSA to Defense Intelligence was sure we'd find out Russia or China or Iran behind this. Hell, even I thought as much."

"So which is it?" Adara asked.

"None of the above," Ryan said. "These guys appear to be operating out of Japan."

"Japan?" Adara said. "You think there could be some link to the VP's death?"

"SecState was on-site with Hargrave when he died," Clark said. "It sounds like the VP was sick long before he left for Japan. It's just that no one realizes it. We'll keep an open mind, but his death looks coincidental." He eyed Ryan in the mirror. "And Gavin's intel sounds a little on the thin side, as far as evidence goes."

"Probably not enough to get the Bureau to move quickly," Ryan admitted.

Clark changed lanes again, rumbling past a truck full of cattle. The odor of manure hit him as they drove by. The smell of money—on many levels.

"Very well," Clark said. "Write it up and we'll blue-file what you've got to Foley."

A blue file was what The Campus called any report submitted from them for use by an official government intelligence or law-enforcement agency—always through Mary Pat Foley. Thoroughly scrubbed of metadata and identifiers, the information apparently came "out of the blue" but was deemed credible on its face by the director of national intelligence. Components within the seventeen intelligence agencies under her purview would dissect the information and compare it with raw data they already possessed.

There was a good chance this one would end up in an intel stack, waiting for more information until it became "actionable."

Hard experience had taught Clark to be a realist, but if he had a fantasy, it was to backtrack one of the wormy little ransomware assholes who fired off these malware bombs from the safe space of their computer lair, and meet them face-to-face.

Someday.

"I'll double-check with Foley," he said at length. "But in the meantime, does Gavin have an actual address?"

"Narrowing it down," Ryan said. "So far just somewhere around Tokyo Station."

"Very well," Clark said. "Jack, Midas, you leave directly from here for Japan. Snoop around and see what you can find." He squinted into the mirror, giving Ryan the warning glare that the kid always seemed to need. "Intel only, Jack.

No action until Foley and her shop have a chance to have a look at what we give them."

"Always," Ryan said.

"That's rich," Clark said and chuckled. "Sherman," he added, drawing sudden interest from Adara. "You speak a little Japanese, don't you?"

"Hai, chotto dake," she said. **Yes, only a little.** "I'm conversant. Not fluent by any stretch."

"You go with them, then," Clark said. "If today taught us anything, it's that there's strength in numbers."

Dom Caruso banged his head softly against the side window, clearly peeved that his girlfriend was heading off for an adventure without him.

"What's the plan for the rest of us?" he asked, deadpan.

"Recruitment." Clark met his eye in the rearview. "The three of us are the last legacy Campus operators. We're going to find us some new meat."

12

The former legionnaires on this Camarilla team droned constantly about death in a faraway place. Lately, Leo Debs, formerly of the London Metropolitan Police, had come to believe that faraway place might very well be Texas.

Far from the senior man, Debs's background as a close-protection officer by way of British SAS put him in tactical command of this operation.

The early dawn air hung cool and crisp over the Buffalo Gap mountains, like the first bite of a good apple. Spent brass was strewn across the ground. Freshly ignited smokeless powder and the comforting smell of gun oil mingled with the flinty odor of the surrounding mesquite trees.

But for the crowded field of fresh cardboard silhouette targets, the area in front of the fifteen-foot dirt berm could have been mistaken for a junkyard. Used targets, riddled with bullet holes, littered the hard-packed clay. Rusted fifty-five-gallon drums stood here and there between the target stands and the backstop, charred black at their rims like burn barrels. Carpet remnants and old mattresses were laid out to the right of the targets, end to end in a long meandering line. Four ceramic garden gnomes sulked beside an earthen berm, peering over shriveled ears of prickly pear cactus fifty meters from where six Camarilla operators gathered at a chalk line in the pink limestone ground. They were more gargoyles than gnomes, small to simulate greater distance, and decidedly unfriendly, just as Leo Debs wanted them to be. These represented Secret Service Uniformed Division snipers.

The former close-protection officer had set up ten standing cardboard targets, painted gray, in a loose diamond formation. He'd painted dark sunglasses on each, identifying them as the inner bubble of the First Lady's Secret Service detail. In the center of these grays stood an eleventh silhouette with two pink balloons taped to the chest, Dr. Cathy Ryan. Her Secret Service code name was SURGEON. Someone, likely Taylor, had drawn nipples on the balloons and a pair of sultry lips on a third balloon fixed to the head. Debs had set up ten more gray targets among a dozen others that were unpainted brown cardboard.

The grays in the crowd wore various painted badges—San Antonio PD, Bexar County Sheriff's Office, Texas Rangers. Others were simply gray, representing plainclothes officers. There would be countersurveillance in the crowd, of course, undercover Secret Service looking for just the sort of threat the Camarilla posed. Debs and his men would sort out those threats as they presented themselves. They were all damned good at sorting.

Fortunately for Debs, the venue of the First Lady's event worked to his advantage. Any area navigable on foot on the walk between the buildings to the west and the San Antonio River to the east was relatively narrow, forcing the outer ring of protective personnel to bunch closer than they normally would have. The Secret Service would set up barricades, staffed by local law enforcement, generally one every six feet. In some locations this would have meant an army. Today, these LEOs were the six blue targets, directly in front of the firing line.

In reality, the barricades would be set up a dozen yards or more from the venue where the First Lady would help with the dedication, creating a no-man's-land that Debs and his team would have to cross to get to her. That risk was unacceptable.

Debs's six-man team stood at the firing line, looking between the shoulders of the blue targets. Each carried an FN P90 submachine gun on a single-point sling under a light cotton jacket along with one extra magazine. Described as a personal defense weapon, or PDW, the stubby little FN P90 looked decidedly futuristic, though it had been around since the nineties. A hair over two feet long with a Gemtech suppressor, carrying fifty rounds of high-velocity 5.7x28 steel-core cartridges, the PDW was an effective weapon for offensive action, especially at closer range against adversaries wearing body armor.

As small as the firearms were, there was no way Debs and the others could have gotten them past the inner rings of local law enforcement and Secret Service personnel.

For a variety of reasons, he needed the target—and her phalanx of guards—to come to him.

The operators stood relaxed, arms at their sides, masking the threatening demeanor that came so easy to each of them.

A loud **whoomph** rolled from a barrel nearest the berm, followed by a small curl of gray smoke—not enough to be visible from the road. Another barrel blew, then another, and another. The team advanced at the fifth puff of smoke, taking out the blue targets directly in front of them with point-blank shots to the back of each neck.

At the same moment, the garden gnomes at each end of the berm evaporated into clouds of ceramic dust, courtesy of four quick 7.62 NATO rifle rounds sent from Pea and Rook.

The team advanced quickly, steadily, habitually careful not to cross up their own feet. Short burps from their P90s impacted each blue and gray target—and others, too. It didn't matter, so long as no one hit the First Lady.

All Secret Service targets down, Debs safed his P90 and parked it on the sling at his side. Then, wrapping his arms around the pink target, balloons pressed tight to his chest, he fell sideways onto the nearest mattress. The six other team members had fanned out in a line as they fired, along the mattress, falling now like toppled trees moments after Debs. Half a breath after the last one hit the mattress, there was a suppressed **whoomph** from a barrel to the left and a wisp of smoke curled skyward.

Nowak, a brash former operator with Poland's GROM, called out elapsed time from his position beside the pickup.

Six-point-three-five seconds from the first shot to the last.

I t would be so much simpler just to cap her ass," Fermin Pea observed ten minutes later.

Debs and his six-man team were on their feet again and gathered with the others around a sheet of plywood balanced on two waist-high sawhorses, studying a model of the San Antonio River Walk.

Debs glanced up, a die-cast Hot Wheels ambulance in his hand, but said nothing. Pea didn't need to be convinced of the plan. The Salvadoran was only thinking out loud. He had, after all, been part of its design. They all had. Still, Pea wasn't wrong. Killing Cathy Ryan would have been infinitely easier than extracting her alive. Blasting her off the face of the planet along with her entire team of Secret Service agents would have been a straightforward endeavor. Taking out those same Secret Service agents but leaving FLOTUS alive—now, that would require choreography and finesse. Hence the drills they'd walked through seven times up to this point. The most recent being the only time the pink target came through unscathed. Executive protection training, including that of the U.S. Secret Service and the London Metropolitan Police RaSP, planned for attacks on the principal. Debs and his team were going to attack the agents themselves.

For Debs and the others to be successful, they had to grab Cathy Ryan **and** get away. The fewer extra holes she had in her body, the better.

Debs had heard it said many times during his training with the Metropolitan Police that it was nigh unto impossible to protect someone from an assassin who was willing to give their life to complete their mission. He'd found this to be true, mostly. But it was also true for a highly trained assassin with money to burn when they didn't care how many innocents they killed in the process. Debs had folded the panic caused by dead and wounded bystanders into his plan—as long as no bullets struck the First Lady.

Command structure in the Camarilla was

loosely based on seniority. Half the men present had more time in the group than Debs, but he was the expert at dignitary protection, so it naturally followed that he would be the expert at dignitary kidnapping. Everyone, even Taylor and Rook, deferred to him. Burt, the third Legion bloke, had taken an IED blast to the face in recent years, and did whatever they told him, which was mostly picking up spent brass and doing the dishes.

"Good walk-through," Debs said. "I'd like to shave a full second off under these controlled conditions. That gives us a buffer against the unknowns we'll face in the real world."

He set the toy ambulance a block away from the red circle that signified the snatch site.

"Given those same unknowns," Debs continued, "the details of this op must be burned into our minds and muscles—from the macro ten-thousand-foot view to the micro of that glimpse of your reflection in some poor Secret Service sod's Ray-Bans when you pop him in the face."

A murmur of agreement ran through the group. They were all pros and understood the need for study and repetition. For NIGHTINGALE to be successful, the details needed to occupy their every waking hour and invade their dreams.

A line of blue house paint, light enough that he could make notations on it with his mechanical pencil, meandered the length of the plywood.

The San Antonio River. Cardboard from Kraft Macaroni & Cheese boxes cut to size formed the façades of important buildings like the Alamo, and the many hotels, restaurants, and shops along the River Walk. Popsicle sticks signified bridges and other important landmarks. The die-cast Hot Wheels cars that represented ambulances and the Secret Service motorcade were much larger than scale, but that couldn't be helped.

The white queen from a cheap plastic chess set represented Cathy Ryan—Secret Service code name: SURGEON.

They called her NIGHTINGALE.

As soon as the client identified the President's wife as the target, Debs began to scour public records for upcoming travel. There was no doubt that they should take her on the road. The White House was too well fortified. The hospital where she worked was a possibility, but the sheer magnitude of law enforcement and military in the D.C. area made escape more wishful thinking than well-designed plan.

The Association for Research in Vision and Ophthalmology conference committee had announced FLOTUS as their keynote two months earlier. Along with her speech to ARVO, Dr. Ryan was to help dedicate a Texas council on youth literacy memorial alongside the river. Politicians and their spouses could always be counted on to dedicate some monument or memorial. Such preplanned events caused no end to the headaches for their protectors, and with reason. Broadcasting the exact when and where of the protectee's appearance was a boon to those who wanted to do them harm.

Armed with the knowledge of where Ryan was going to be at a given moment in time, Leo Debs had planned what he would do were he the one tasked with protecting her, working backward from there. He'd gone to San Antonio and strolled the River Walk like a tourist, identifying weaknesses and vulnerabilities and then figuring out how to exploit them.

The Secret Service had done a cursory advance by the time Debs made his first on-the-ground study. Unlike a visit from POTUS, they had yet to weld shut manhole covers and the like. They would come through again before the event, patrolling with explosive-detection K9s, tightening routes, buttoning up danger areas, increasing river and walking patrols—but by then Debs was already ahead of them.

And the simple fact remained. Dr. Ryan was not the President, so she would get a fraction of his level of protection.

Effective personal security consisted of concentric rings like the layers of an onion, with fluid air and river support. The innermost ring being a detail of close-protection agents, placed to afford them a 360-degree view around the First Lady.

The detail supervisor would be within arm's reach of the First Lady at all times. News footage of previous events allowed Debs to identify the special agent in charge of SURGEON's detail as Maureen Richardson. He'd met her during his former life, and knew her to be a capable, by-the-book operative.

By-the-book was exactly what he needed for this to work.

Leo Debs could look at the map and predict with a reasonably high degree of certainty exactly where the First Lady's Secret Service detail would post themselves during her event. He knew the foot formations they would use to surround her as she made her way down the River Walk from the ARVO conference venue where she was scheduled for a short meet-and-greet before the dedication. He knew where the snipers would set up to give them the best field of view. The optimum number of state and local officers forming the edge of the interior ring between the crowd and the First Lady was common knowledge.

More important—crucial to the success of NIGHTINGALE, Debs knew exactly how the First Lady's detail would react to specific stimuli. The so-called special relationship between the U.S. and the UK saw the Secret Service frequently offering advice and training to Her Majesty's protective officers. Constable Leo Debs had been the recipient of many such trainings, both in London and at the USSS training facility in Beltsville, Maryland.

Debs knew what they would do because they had trained him to do the same thing.

He placed one red poker chip on a box representing the roof of a building two blocks to the north and another on a building adjacent to the convention center.

"NIGHTINGALE is, for the most part, a series of hammer blows—big, loud, messy, and relatively indiscriminate as to who they kill."

Taylor, the Aussie, balanced the point of his KA-BAR fighting knife on the corner of the plywood and gave a low chuckle. "So long as it's not us or Her Highness."

Debs smiled. "Relatively indiscriminate. Think of NIGHTINGALE as a series of sledgehammer strikes with a couple of precise surgical operations in the middle."

Fermin Pea used his index finger to trace a line in the air over the River Walk and rubbed the stubble on his formerly tattooed chin with his free hand. "Timing is gonna be everything."

Rook studied the board, thinking. "Always is."

"By the numbers," Debs said.

"One: Nowak is already through the Bexar County Emergency Operations Center firewall." He lifted the white queen and set her down again in the same spot on the River Walk. "When

SURGEON reaches this mark, Nowak will blast out an emergency text alerting everyone with a cell phone of a possible gas leak. The agents directly around the First Lady will be focused on the crowd so they won't look at their phones, but perimeter agents and the command post will. It'll take them a couple seconds to register the text, at which point the CP will notify the SAIC via radio.

"Two: Seconds after the agents are made aware of this possible gas leak, Nowak will send up—"

Soulis, once upon a time a member of the Greek 1st Paratroopers Lokatzides, or Mountain Raiders, piped up, interrupting the briefing. Among the shorter members of the team, he had intensely green eyes that held many stories, most all of them secret. The brigade had roots back to the Sacred Squadron, a free Greek unit attached to the Allied 1st SAS. That was enough for Debs to like the guy, but he was a steady man, too, when that sort of thing counted. Soulis was tasked with force protection—countering anything from the outside that could bite Camarilla operators while they were otherwise engaged in their assigned duties or unwinding by the fire drinking a beer. This included perimeter security, a series of camera feeds he'd meshed together so he could monitor them from a Panasonic Toughbook that he was never without. Sitting inside a new-model Dodge van less than ten feet from the plywood diorama, he looked up to catch Debs's eye.

"Sound contact cameras four and five," he said, adjusting a set of headphones. "Northwest perimeter."

"Mics?" Taylor asked.

"Can't tell," the Greek said. "The mics on these cameras are programmed to pick up sharp sounds as well as discernable movement." He used a small joystick to operate the pan-tilt-zoom features on one of his cameras. "Don't have the right angle to get the plate number," he said. "Outer perimeter must be tits-up. I'll get some redundancies set up as soon as we get this issue sorted out."

"You're saying sharp sounds," the big Aussie said, raising a woolybooger eyebrow. "As in my ex-wife's bitchin'?"

"As in gunfire," Soulis said. "I'm thinking someone is having target practice on the ranch next door."

"Well, shit!" Taylor said. "That is all we need."

A husky boom drifted through the bony mesquite branches.

"That sounded like a little more than target practice," Pea said.

"Could be off-the-shelf Tannerite," Soulis said. "But I'm guessing that boom came from something a little more substantial. I'd say it was a claymore."

"A claymore?" Rook pounded a fist on the plywood table. "I thought the ranches around us were supposed to be vacant. These dickheads start blowing things up and we'll get a load of unwanted attention." He waved his hand around the firing range, littered with targets and brass. "We got a little too much here to hide if some ATF asshole comes nosing around."

"Shooting ain't illegal," Pea said.

"No," Rook said. "But it's damned sure a clue. We fly under the radar or we don't fly at all."

"Any visual?" Taylor asked the Greek.

Soulis checked the cameras again and then looked up, shaking his head.

"No joy. They're still shooting. Cameras four and five face at an angle, basically parallel to our boundary for more coverage. They would pick up anyone who passes, but not approaching from ninety degrees. I am getting some interference with the wireless—and a humming sound. There's a good possibility they're operating some kind of drone."

13

The Camarilla men fanned out, staying in contact with encrypted radios and hard-wired mics and earpieces. All of them, even Fermin Pea, who hadn't seen actual military experience, knew what it was like to be downrange when the shooting started and commo went tits-up. Without communication they were simply ten individuals, highly skilled and lethal, yes, but still individuals. When they worked in concert, they were terrifyingly effective destroying angels.

A few idiots plinking at soda cans and blowing shit up should pose no problem at all—as long as they disappeared.

It was just an hour after sunrise, with fingers of fog still crawling across the ground through thick mesquite, prickly pear cactus, and yucca plants. There were hogs here, and whitetail deer, but it wasn't deer season and few people went to the trouble of hunting hogs early in the morning.

Rook and Taylor—joined at the hip as usual—took point. Debs and Pea pulled rear flank, watching the team's six o'clock. The rest of the team spread out shoulder to shoulder, belly-crawling through the scrub cedar and prickly pear cactus, blackened by harsh temperatures of the past winter. Rook reminded everyone of the high likelihood of scorpions and rattlesnakes as they made their way toward the periodic pop of gunfire.

Bringing up the rear, Debs lost sight of everyone but the boots of the men directly in front of him in the thick scrub.

Taylor's Aussie drawl buzzed in his ear.

"Two assholes . . . strike that . . . three, I say again, three assholes. Judging from their targets and barricades, I'd say they're practicing to hit an armored truck."

"I don't give a shit what they're doing," Rook said. "We haven't exactly been quiet. They'll know we're here, which means we need to shut them up permanently before they can tell anyone else. I'd like to take them out right now, but two of them are around the corner in that pickup. I can't get a good read on how well they're armed. That old barn is blocking my shot. Too much of a chance one would get away if I pop the other . . ." More silence while Rook continued to observe. Then, "The guy out front moves like he's not your average Airsoft warriors. He's kitted up like the real deal, chest rig, rifle plates, CZ Scorpion on a single-point sling. And the Greek was right about the drone."

Taylor cut in. "I'll be damned. They got a claymore strapped to the front of the drone. That's bigger than the ones we're using."

The hornet whir of a large drone filled the air, carrying through the trees. It grew increasingly louder, then suddenly fell quiet.

"Okay," Rook said. "This shitbag is gathering up his toys and heading toward the truck. Debs, you're closer to the gate. Head that way on the double and see if you can cut them off, or at least slow them down enough that Pea and I can get a good shot. That guy has looked our way a half-dozen times. They know they have neighbors. Get them stopped whatever it takes, because we gotta dump 'em in a very dark hole or this whole job is over before it starts."

14

Royce Vetter expected to be shot at any moment.

He'd not put eyes on the men on the adjoining property this morning, but he knew they were up to something big. At first he thought they were law enforcement. Those assholes practiced in the mountains once in a while, but the longer Vetter listened to the suppressed weapons and precise volleys of fire, the more he came to realize that the group on the old Spivey ranch was something else.

It made sense, really. The end times weren't just somewhere in the distant future. They were now. Those with eyes could see it plain. Stood to reason that other groups would be getting their shit together. Still, Vetter didn't want anything getting in the way of his plan, so they did the test he needed to do, then hauled ass.

Thirty-eight years old, with a well-earned beer belly and a salt-and-pepper flattop, Royce was the self-appointed leader of the three men in the pickup. Along with their individual rifles, each carried a Glock 19, a chest rig with four spare magazines, a fighting knife, and, in the case of Corbin Lilly, a pouch with his Leatherman and a few surprises to make an IED out of pretty much anything he had on hand—if it came to that. Zip, the third member of the team, carried a short shotgun he'd sawed off himself. All of them needed new long guns. Good ones, full auto, short barrels, maneuverable, quiet when set up correctly.

Preparing for the end times took a shitload of money, and Vetter had figured out a surefire way to grab a ton of it. Sure, a couple guards would die. Hell, they'd better, or Vetter's plan wasn't worth the paper towel it was written on.

Corbin Lilly, a year older than Vetter, a tow-headed blond with a sparse beard the color and consistency of corn silk no matter how hard he tried to grow it out, whom Vetter considered his second-in-command, braced himself against the dashboard, his window rolled down.

"Brush is too thick to see anything over there." Corbin half turned, keeping his voice low, though the shots had come from at least a hundred yards away and the bouncing pickup was making all kinds of racket.

Zip wore a black flannel shirt buttoned all the way to the top like he was going to church. He'd caught a mesquite thorn under his eye early that day and a curtain of blood had dried on his cheek.

"Sorry," Zip said. His real name was Merlin. He was trustworthy as a good dog but seemed to make a hobby out of doing stupid shit and then apologizing for it. "I didn't know anyone was living over there when I found this place."

Corbin started to say something, but Royce raised a hand, hushing him. He glanced sideways at his passengers as he negotiated the rutted red clay. "What'd y'all hear over there?"

"Weapons fire."

"Right," Vetter said, skirting a dead prickly pear that had slumped into the road. "But what kind of fire was it?"

"Automatic fire," Zip said.

"Ah," Vetter said, "Taking advantage of this teaching moment. But not just any automatic fire. There must be a half-dozen guys shooting over there and every one of 'em is completely in control. Three-round bursts, engaging multiple targets—" A smile spread across his face. "Did you hear that little beep before the last volley of fire? Pretty sure that was a shot timer."

"Somebody's got tactical training going on," Corbin mused.

Royce thought that over. There were several shooting schools located around, but the trouble with growing up in Abilene was that by the time you got as old as Royce, everyone pretty much had you dialed in for who you really were. Both of the good schools had instructors who would have been all too happy to send Royce down-range and use him as a target.

Royce's wife had a decent job at the auto parts store off Highway 277, good enough anyway that she'd bought them a nice flat-screen TV. It was great for games, but the guys would come over and watch YouTube tutorials about shooting drills and tactical movement. You could learn a shit-ton on the Internet about homemade suppressors, improvised explosive devices, cell-phone triggers, tremble switches, the works—but eventually you had to go out to a range and practice. Corbin had apprenticed with an electrician in high school and knew his stuff when it came to circuits and soldering irons. He'd built two extremely potent mini claymore mines out of plastic travel soap containers following an online tutorial. They'd tested one at an old gravel pit, but they were saving the second for something more useful.

Zip piped up. "Maybe we should go talk to these guys. We'd need some more guys on the crew if we want to do some bigger jobs in Fort Worth or Dallas. Maybe we should go check them out. See what makes them tick. We might have a lot in common."

"Too risky," Vetter said. "We stick to the plan as is."

Zip shook his head, unconvinced. "You said it yourself. These guys have control of their weapons. We could use some trained dudes on our squad."

Vetter hit a rut a little harder than he needed to, just to get Zip's attention. "We're gonna leave before they see any of us. Pretty sure those trained dudes would shoot us in the face if we try and approach them."

"Why?"

Vetter scoffed. "Because that's what I would do."

15

Debs ran as fast as he could, P90 SMG held tight against his chest, crashing through brush, leaping cactuses. Mesquite thorns slashed his arms and face, narrowly missing his eyes. The gate was a quarter-mile away, over the crest of a long hill that the team used to conceal their actions from the road by sight and sound. Fortunately, the shooters from the land next door hadn't rushed cleaning up their drone, and Debs slid down the front side of the hill and stashed his rifle behind a prickly pear about the same time the black pickup reached their own gate. A blond man wearing a camouflage T-shirt got out, revealing at least one long gun in the cab with his two companions. Debs had a Browning Hi-Power in a waistband holster at the small of his back under his shirt, but resolved to jump for his rifle if these guys decided they wanted to be unfriendly. Blondie looked up periodically at Debs as he worked the combination, like a hyena might glance up from a kill to check for lions, and then dragged the gate open and waved the truck through.

He counted to four on each breath in an effort to calm himself after the sprint. Loose stones still skittered down the hill beside the darker earth of his fresh tracks. Hopefully these guys weren't accomplished trackers, and if they were, Pea and Rook would put an end to their tracking days with a couple hunks of lead.

Debs slipped a pair of Mechanix gloves from his pocket, and pulled them on. He pretended to inspect the fence, jiggling T-posts and checking tension on the barbed wire. He had no tools, but didn't think the guys in the truck would be alive long enough to notice.

His back to the road, busy with his chores, Debs gave the occupants of the pickup a neighborly wave as they approached. As he expected, the men wanted intel about what he was up to as much as he wanted to know about them. Tires popped on the limestone gravel as the truck slowed, then rolled to a stop.

Debs turned and peeled off his gloves and found himself looking directly at the open passenger window ten feet away. Blondie kept his hands inside the cab where Debs couldn't see them, as did the dude in the middle, his ball cap low over his eyes like he might be sleeping—or stoned. The driver had a broad jaw with a bit of an undercut that made him look like a pit bull—an insult to pit bulls, really.

"Lose somethin'?" Blondie grunted.

"Checking the fence," Debs said. He didn't bother to hide his accent, expecting Rook and Pea to turn the men's heads into red mist at any moment. When that didn't happen, he leaned against the nearest T-post and flashed what he hoped was a nonthreatening smile.

The pit bull behind the wheel spoke. "Been doing some shooting."

It wasn't a question.

"A fair bit," Debs said, still smiling, wondering why none of these guys was missing a brain stem about now. The pickup had stopped cold, at a slight angle on the road. Perfect targets from the perches Pea and Rook would be in now, looking at them through the reticles of their scopes.

"Sounded like more than a fair bit," Blondie said.

Debs shrugged like he didn't care. "I figure everybody around here has a good range on their land—keep the deer rifles sighted in." He didn't mention that he'd heard them shooting as well.

"Deer rifles," Pit Bull mused.

A white Chevy Impala topped the hill to the east, throwing up a rooster tail of dust. Blondie and the middle guy in the ball cap turned to look over his shoulder, but Pit Bull stayed focused on Debs.

Debs took a deep breath as the vehicle got closer. It had a light bar on top. That's why Rook and Pea were AWOL. Taylor County Sheriff's patrol. For a fleeting moment, Debs thought the

assholes in the pickup were undercover law enforcement. No, they were too nervous for that.
The approaching squad car explained why these
guys were still breathing, though. Pea and Rook
would have been able to see the car well before
Debs, and held fire until it went past. Even then,
a county deputy seeing the men together was a
problem. This would need to be taken care of
somewhere away from here.

The patrol car roared past, on his way somewhere, but tipping his hat as he went by. The
poor cop had no idea of the deadly bubble he'd
just driven through.

The transmission under the black pickup gave
an audible clunk as Pit Bull threw it into gear
and took the opportunity to leave.

"Take care," Debs said, waving.

Blondie rolled up his window without another word.

Debs memorized the license-plate number as
they went past. Pit Bull was the leader. They'd
find out where he lived, have a little chat to locate
the other two, and then dump the lot of them
before one of these hillbilly arseholes started
shooting his mouth off about the military types
practicing with automatic weapons. This was
one bloody stump that needed to be cauterized,
and fast.

16

White House Chief of Staff Arnie van Damm stood at the bookcase across the Oval Office from Ryan clicking a black Skilcraft ballpoint pen almost enough to be annoying. The four others in attendance at the meeting occupied their customary seats near the fireplace and on twin couches. The CoS often kept himself slightly apart when he was working through some particularly difficult problem. He said it helped him retain his own voice while remaining part of the larger conversation. Ryan couldn't help but marvel at the man. Decades of government service, chief of staff to four presidents, face-to-face meetings with the most influential people to walk the planet, and through it all he remained unchanged. His off-the-rack suits were clean—normally—but by the time he had his assistant take one to Goodwill, he'd pretty much worn the life out of it. In a world of Montblanc pens and embossed leather folios—Arnie van Damm relied on a government issue Skilcraft and a stodgy Forest Service green memo pad. The sleeves on his beloved Eddie

Bauer wash-and-wear dress shirts were perpetually rolled up to his elbows—uneven when he was deeply engrossed in some issue, which was more often than not.

"Governor Davis called this morning," van Damm said. "She wanted to offer her condolences and drop a none-too-subtle reminder of how instrumental she was to the Party in the midterms."

Mary Pat Foley folded her arms across her chest, shaking her head slowly like she was disappointed in one of her children. "That woman's about as subtle as a yeast infection."

The men in the room stared at their own shoes.

Talking politics fell just short of drinking hemlock to Mary Pat Foley, but Ryan trusted her opinion and asked her to be present for this strategy session.

In truth, he had all the members of his cabinet advising him on possible names for a new vice president—but there were a handful of people in whom he placed a greater amount of trust. Some of those had accompanied him to Andrews Air Force Base four hours earlier to stand beside Phoebe Hargrave. Everyone in the hangar, including the media, had waited in stunned silence as the Air Force band played "Hail Columbia" as the late vice president disembarked the plane, this time in a flag-draped metal coffin.

Secretary Mark Dehart and Lawrence Howe,

the director of the Secret Service, greeted Keenan Mulvaney, the special agent in charge of the vice president's detail. As head of Homeland Security, Dehart's own protective element fell under the logistical umbrella of VPPD, the Vice Presidential Protection Division, and thus Mulvaney's overall supervision. The Secret Service agent all but moped down the air stairs, his face deadpan, normally square shoulders sagging in defeat. He had a boyish face to begin with, but coming off the plane he'd looked like a high school senior who'd singlehandedly lost the championship game. The person whom he was charged to protect was dead. No matter that it wasn't his fault. Mulvaney's entire body bent with the burden of Hargrave's death. His boss and his boss's boss had come not only to pay respects to the vice president, but to take care of their man.

Secretary of State Scott Adler, red-eyed from emotion and groggy from lack of sleep, had shaken the President's hand and then, as a family friend, offered to ride with Phoebe Hargrave. The vice president was her husband, but he also belonged to the people of the United States. She'd need assistance dealing with the White House machine regarding funeral arrangements, and Adler aimed to be there for her.

Ryan had ordered his secretary of state to go home and catch a few hours' rest as soon as he

got Phoebe Hargrave settled. He'd gotten nothing more than a cursory nod in return.

Director Howe had gone with Special Agent
Mulvaney to Secret Service headquarters, but
Ryan had asked the others in attendance to return
to the Oval with him—Foley, Dehart, Secretary
of Defense Robert Burgess, and Attorney General
Dan Murray—hoping, he'd said, to pick their
brains.

They'd spent the past hour discussing the value
of executives over legislators. Though a governor
brought the executive chops of leading a state,
foreign policy experience was often sorely lack-
ing. Congressional representatives and senators
might have a little more experience with issues
overseas, but their "secret sauce," according to
van Damm, came from the fact that they spent
an inordinate amount of time trying to get themselves reelected—almost from the moment the
polls closed for the election that got them seated
in the first place. It was greasy, distasteful stuff,
working the phones for donations—in leased
space across the street or down the block from
official offices to avoid campaigning on government property. But with that distasteful work
came large Rolodexes of donors—names of people who knew other people with the power—
influential people who could swing large blocks
of the nation. In short, what made legislators so

appealing as candidates for higher office was not their foreign policy experience or their lengthy CV dealing with complicated matters of running the country—their worth lay in the fact that "they knew a guy."

Ryan didn't give a rat's ass. The Party, on the other hand, cared a great deal, and it was van Damm's job to trumpet that message.

The secretary of defense spoke next. A gruff civilian warhorse, Bob Burgess was as disgusted by politics as Foley was, but he knew how to play the game. "Micky Dunn reached out to me last night," he said.

"The gentleman from Pennsylvania," Dehart said through a sardonic half-smile. Dehart had represented Pennsylvania as a U.S. senator before Ryan ambushed him to serve in the cabinet. "Congressman Dunn has somehow managed to get himself elected nine times . . . He's a horrible human being, but he does sit on House Ways and Means and chairs Homeland Security."

Burgess chuckled. "He brought that up more than once during our conversation. He implied . . . hell, he told me straight-out that it was his turn to get a seat at the table what with all the help he's given your administration."

Ryan used the flat of his hand to smooth the fabric of his slacks over his thigh—something his old man used to do to take a breath and keep control of his temper. "His turn? He said those exact words?"

"He did, sir," Burgess said.

"Originally," Ryan said, putting on his professorial voice, "some of the framers wanted House terms to be three years like the British House. Others demanded terms no more than a single year. Anything longer, they felt, was tyranny."

Burgess smiled. "They probably had guys like Micky Dunn in mind."

"To be blunt," van Damm said, "there is a long list of people who believe it's 'their turn.' Many of them know they wouldn't pass the scrutiny of an FBI background colonoscopy. What they're really after is the chance to say you considered them. Bragging rights. They just have to let it leak they were on some short list. That way they can say the decision was theirs not to take the job . . ."

Ryan shifted slightly in his chair, catching Mary Pat Foley's attention while Arnie continued with his lesson in prudent political philosophy. The director of national intelligence raised her brow slightly, a twinkle of understanding in her eyes. They'd worked together for a very long time, Ryan and Foley—decades now. They'd felt the Cold War thaw under their feet as the world changed around them—and then noticed the recent chill as the pendulum began to swing the other way. Of all the people Jack Ryan knew, Mary Pat Foley understood him better than anyone except Cathy—and there were some things even Cathy would never know.

Arnie continued to pontificate on the minefield of all the people Ryan was likely to upset, no matter who he nominated for vice president.

Foley lowered her gaze and shook her head. The movement was ever so slight, but it was clear enough to Ryan. Without uttering a word, he'd checked to see if she was at all interested in the job of vice president. She gave her answer with that tiny gesture and a crooked smile.

Not only no, but hell, **no.**

The door from the secretaries' suite opened and Scott Adler walked in, stopping short when he saw the gathering. He wore a clean suit but the same depleted expression he'd had at the hangar. He'd likely wear that for some time. Ryan caught the odor of cigarette smoke immediately. Adler had started up again. You could hardly blame the guy. There were times that he . . . No, Cathy would kill him.

"I'm sorry, Mr. President," Adler said. "Betty told me to just come on in. She must have thought I was supposed to be a part of . . . whatever this is."

"Always, Scott." Ryan waved him in. "I depend on your counsel. But I feel certain you could serve the country better were you to get a few hours of sleep."

Adler ignored the suggestion. "You're meeting about Tony's job, aren't you?"

"The vice presidency," Ryan said. "We are."

"I knew the vultures would be circling," Adler said through clenched teeth. His eyes welled with tears. "But I'd hoped we could at least get arrangements for a service in the works. A day of mourning, flags at half-mast. Small things, but I think they're important."

Ryan sighed. "I gave the order to lower flags across the country and at every base and embassy ten minutes after we first spoke. As you know, I addressed the nation shortly after we got the news, and will address them again in . . ." He glanced at his watch. "Four hours. I need to have some things moving by that time. It's important for the American people to know we have a plan. For the world to know."

Adler stood still for a long moment, eyes shut, breathing through barely parted lips.

Ryan gave him a moment to continue, then rose and walked across the room to shake his hand. The others followed suit.

"I only hope to be as good a friend as you were to Tony," Ryan said. "Now go home and get some sleep."

"Of course, Mr. President," Adler said. "Please forgive me."

"Not at all." Ryan looked around the Oval, smiling at his friends, old and new. "We take care of one another. And speaking of that. I've got an appointment with Senator Chadwick coming up."

Adler chuckled. "I'll definitely want to be long gone for that."

The others filed out of the room after him, Arnie still perusing the names and notes in his little green memo book. Foley lagged behind a few steps so she had a modicum of privacy with the President.

"I'm not a statesman, Jack," she said when everyone was out of earshot. "I hate cameras. Always have, even as a little girl. If I had my way I'd appear before congress behind a black screen with my voice electronically altered like I was in the witness protection program or something. I just do not get all the look-at-me-please-validate-my-existence stuff on social media. Creeps me right out."

"This I know," Ryan said, grinning. "I only—"

She cut him off. "I am a spy, Jack. I was born a spy and I will die a spy. That's all there is to it. You understand what I'm telling you?"

"Loud and clear, my friend."

The fact that he'd never had to actually offer her the job and she'd never had to refuse him meant that whomever he chose could be his "first" choice.

"Now," the DNI said, heaving an I'm-glad-we-got-that-over-with sigh. "If I may offer some unsolicited advice."

Ryan waved his hand across the desk. "By all means."

"Don't offer the job to that woman—"

The statement took Ryan so off guard that he snorted. "Michelle Chadwick as vice president?"

"Good lord, Jack, don't even whisper those words. That's how you summon the devil. She's playing all nice for this pharmaceutical bill, but I promise you, she would be more than happy to see ninety-nine percent of your agenda crash and burn." Ryan started to interject, but Foley, going full steam, didn't appear to notice. "I know she came through by outing that Chinese spy when he tried to recruit her . . . but I've gotta tell you, simply refusing to commit treason doesn't exactly warrant a medal. That woman would have your guts for—"

Ryan raised a hand. "Mary Pat. Don't you worry about that." He gave a grim smile. "Senator Chadwick is beyond the pale even for a team of rivals."

17

Debs parked the Dodge down 14th Street in the shade of some scrub oaks, away from any other houses. Fermin Pea got out of the passenger side. The remnants of the face tattoos he'd had removed cast odd shadows below his eyes—like he'd smudged his skin with telltale bits of ash.

Like Debs, Pea press-checked his pistol out of habit—not that stupid racking-a-round-in-the-chamber shit like they did in the movies, just a simple movement of the slide a couple millimeters to be certain there would be a round in the chamber when he needed it.

If things went as planned, they'd be needing some momentarily.

County records showed the license plate on the black pickup came back to someone named Royce Vetter. A staggeringly easy Internet search revealed Vetter's cell-phone number, his address in the northern edge of Abilene, and how long he'd lived there. It took Debs all of two minutes to find him on social media. No doubt about it. This was the guy with a jaw like a pit bull. Another two minutes of scrolling through Vetter's friends revealed that Blondie's name was Corbin Lilly and the sleepy guy in the ball cap was Merlin Swain, but he went by Zip. Neither Swain nor Lilly were married, and judging from their social media pages, neither looked to have a girlfriend.

Debs and Pea would sort out Vetter and his family while Rook and Taylor took care of Lilly and Swain, respectively.

Vetter's status was "married," and a teenage boy named Chris with the beginnings of the same pit-bull jaw showed up in a few of the pics. There was a daughter, too, Rene, on the gaunt side of athletic-looking, twentysomething, broody, with a floppy mop of flaxen hair over a high side-shave. Photos made it look like she was someplace with palm trees, California, maybe, or Arizona. It was just as well, though she did have an interesting look that made Debs kind of want to meet her, if only for a few minutes before he sorted her out.

He and Pea kept their ball caps pulled low in the event they passed any porch cameras. They saw no one, and the two driveways they passed were empty.

A pixie of a woman with dyed auburn hair, plumped lips, and fake lashes big enough to confuse an amorous tarantula met Debs and Pea at the door. The house was small, with peeling paint and sagging gutters. A tarped Trans Am occupied center stage on a patchy, sunburned lawn.

Inside the house, Mrs. Vetter's domain looked to be neat and tidy as far as Debs could make out through the small crack held open by her. Her name was Margaret, but Debs thought she looked a hell of a lot more like a Trixie or a Bunny. He'd known a stripper in Grimsby named Star who could have been this little firecracker's sister. She kept one hand behind the frame and out of sight like she had a shotgun back there.

A runty brown dog, a Pomeranian, maybe, stuck its head around the woman's leg, growling through the screen.

"What's he done this time?" she asked, brushing a tired lock of hair out of her eyes.

Pea, who stood to the left of the door, gave a little shrug. "What do you think he's done, Mrs. Vetter?"

"Nice try," she said. "Anyway, you missed him by, like, an hour."

"No worries." Debs pulled a card out of his shirt pocket. "We'll leave our number and—"

"You're not cops," Margaret said. "Not with that accent. Not unless the bobbies at Abilene PD started recruiting from across the pond." She said the last in a mongrelized mix of posh and Cockney—the way Americans seemed to think everyone from England spoke.

"Oh, hell, no," Pea said. "We're not cops. But we need to get in touch with Royce. It's important."

Margaret never took her eyes off Debs. "You're that guy from the old Spivey place out at Buffalo Gap who Royce was yakking on and on about. Some kind of militia shit going on out there, to hear him tell it."

Debs forced a smile, but his heart skipped a beat. This woman had just sealed her fate. "Nothing as exciting as all that, I promise." He pushed the business card toward the door. "Here's my cell number. If you would ask him to give me a ring."

"Give you a ring?" she sneered, again with the derisive Cockney accent.

"It's about a job," Debs said, pushing the card forward. "An extremely lucrative job at that."

The woman brightened at the idea of a paycheck, and opened the door a crack to accept the contact information. "I'll have him call you when he gets—"

Debs let go of the card before she could grab it. She glanced down instinctively as it fluttered to the carpet, allowing Debs to plant his fist square in her nose.

She staggered backward, tripping over her own feet. Debs followed his punch through the door, hitting her again before she could bring up the shotgun, this time in the side of the head, quickly gaining control of the weapon. She fell, landing hard on her butt, the wind leaving her in a painful **whoompf**.

The little rat dog had a spinning shit-fit right then and there, whirling and barking and generally trying to eat its own tail.

Debs shooed the thing away with the side of his boot, sending it sliding across the floor into the dining room.

Pea came in behind him, pistol up, scanning the living room and adjoining hallway. The house was surprisingly clean, with stacks of folded laundry on a neat but tattered couch across from a big-screen television.

"You alone?" Pea asked.

Rat Dog came to its senses and began to bark again, even louder now, focusing on Debs.

A feral growl started somewhere deep in Margaret Vetter's chest. "My husband is going to kick the shit outta both of you."

Pea put the toe of his boot to her hip, hard like he was kicking a field goal. The apparent boredom in his voice belied the ferocity of the kick. "I asked if you're alone."

She toppled sideways, writhing in pain, hurting too bad to scream. She nodded, catching her breath, still seething. "Yes, I'm alone."

Pea checked anyway, padding down the hall and returning in less than a minute with a quick nod. "We're good. Boy's room looks lived in. Girl must be staying elsewhere."

"You leave my kids be—"

Debs hunkered down to look at the woman face-to-face, but the dog rushed in and tried to latch on to his gun hand. It would have seemed brave under different circumstance. Debs stood and sent it flying with another sideswipe from his boot.

"Polly!" Margaret said. "Be still!"

Debs shot a glance at Pea. "Would you take Polly in the kitchen and convince her to be quiet? Margaret and me, we need to have a proper chat."

The Salvadoran scooped up the little dog by the scruff of the neck and carried it through the door. Seconds later, it fell silent.

"Don't you hurt my dog," Margaret said, "so help me—"

Debs gave her another smack to the side of her head—hard, because, as he'd learned from every single one of his mother's boyfriends, there wasn't much point in hitting someone if you were going to be soft about it.

" 'Leave my kids be. Don't you hurt my dog,' " Debs said, mimicking Margaret Vetter's Texas accent. "You're making a shit-ton of demands for a woman with a gun to her head."

The bravado suddenly fled, she began to cry. "Please . . . What is it you want?"

Debs patted her cheek, softer now. "Focus for me, Margaret. What gave Royce the idea that me and my mates are some kind of militia?"

She touched her ear, then pulled the fingers away to check for blood. "He . . . I don't know. He's into that kind of thing. Militias. End-of-days stuff."

Debs pulled back to hit her again.

She raised an open hand to ward off the blow, fading like a boxer. She'd been hit before.

"Stop, stop, stop." She shook her head. "He heard your suppressors or something. Really. I'm not sure. I'm telling you the guy is crazy. Loves to blow stuff up. Says he's on a mission from God or some shit."

"What are they up to?" Debs asked. "Royce and his friends."

She just looked at him, chin quivering. "What . . . What are you gonna do to me when I tell you?"

"We're not interested in you, love," Debs said. "We only want to talk to Royce. Tell me what he's planning."

"He talked about a money truck," she said. "Like, you know, an armored car."

Debs shot a glance at Pea, then returned his focus on Margaret. "When? Which armored car company?"

"That's all I know," she said. "I overheard him talking to Zip about it. You know, money for their cause." She reached up and pulled aside the collar of her shirt, exposing a dark purple bruise. "Royce let me know in no uncertain terms that I needed to haul ass and leave them be when they talked about their apocalyptic shit, and that's exactly what I did."

"So you have no idea which armored car company he was talking about?"

"I swear—"

The back door swung open with a loud smack. She flinched, but Debs put a finger to his lips to shush her. He nodded to Pea, who went to check it out.

"Mom!" a youthful voice yelled. "I am actually going to kill him this time. Do you hear me! That son of a bitch stole my three-thousand-dollar UAV. I saved all year for—"

Sixteen-year-old Chris Vetter froze when he walked into the living room to find the muzzle of Fermin Pea's Glock leveled at his face.

"Mom?" he whispered. "Who . . . What's going on?"

"It's okay, mate," Debs said. "I want you to have a seat by your mum and we'll get this all sorted out."

Margaret patted the carpet beside her and gave her son a shaky nod. "It's okay . . ."

Debs looked the terrified boy up and down and smiled. Damn if the boy didn't look just like his father. Poor kid.

"You know who I am?" Debs said, flaunting his British accent.

"Mister," Chris said. "I got no earthly idea, but I'm thinking you're the bastard who hit my mother." He started to rise, but Margaret grabbed his sleeve.

Debs raised a wary brow. "Your dad never mentioned me?"

"My dad's a nutjob," the boy said. "When he's not sitting around planning for the failure of society with his dickhead friends, he rips off things I've busted my ass for."

"You heard him," Margaret said, tears welling. "Royce steals from us. He beats the shit out of us." She hung her head. "I wish he'd been here so you could kill him. That's what you're going to do. Isn't it?"

Debs gave her a little nod. "Your husband hits you?"

"Hu-huh." She whimpered. "All the time. I'm not lying when I say I hate him. I'll tell you whatever you want to know, but I swear I don't know anything more."

"Sounds like he's not much of a man," Debs said. "Pack a bag. Both of you, until we sort this out."

Margaret heaved a deep sigh, rising to one knee. Her shoulders dropped and she relaxed a notch, thinking she was going to live through this.

Debs put a bullet in the back of her head the

moment she turned. Pea took care of the boy. Both used suppressed nine-millimeter Glocks, not silent, but quiet enough the neighbors wouldn't hear. The 5.7 projectiles from the FN pistols and SMGs they'd use for NIGHTINGALE were unique, too apt to link them to San Antonio.

If they made it to San Antonio.

First, they had to find Royce Vetter and sort him out.

Pea checked both bodies to make sure there were no screwups. The Salvadoran didn't like to talk about it, but on two of his previous hits the bullets had decided to skirt the skull of his targets, zipping under the skin, knocking them out but leaving them very much alive. He'd had to hunt them down and kill them again. Tedious, not to mention embarrassing. And it had pissed Taylor off to no end.

The blood and gore on the carpet said that was not the case here, but Pea checked anyway.

"Think we need to call the boss?" Pea asked, as they slipped around the corner to where they'd stashed their truck. The shadows on his neck of some of his older tats had grown darker, which always happened when he got flushed from excitement. "Maybe we should tell him we're a no-go until we get this guy?"

"It may come to that," Debs said. He thought of all his planning, the countless hours and effort he'd expended, all going up in flames because

some end-of-days arseholes decided to go shooting on the ranch next door. He ground his teeth
until his jaw hurt, going over his options. "We
know they're planning to hit an armored car.
Statistically, that doesn't usually go well for the
bad guys . . . We need to find them and make
sure." He glanced up at the Salvadoran, struck by
a sudden thought. "Hey. What did you do with
that little dog?"

"It's in the fridge," Pea said, wiping a drop of
blood off his cheek with the back of his hand.
"Don't worry. I left it some water."

18

Ding Chavez inserted a fresh magazine in his Glock 19, press-checked to make certain there was one in the chamber (an ingrained habit), and holstered the weapon. They ran a hot range beneath Hendley Associates. No point in carrying an unloaded gun, even on the range. Chavez removed his Peltor earmuffs and set them on the folding shelf in front of him alongside four nine-millimeter ammo boxes, two of them empty. Like many shooters his age, Chavez suffered from some measure of hearing loss, so he doubled up on ear pro with silicone earplugs underneath noise-canceling muffs. He removed the bright chartreuse earplugs and let them dangle on a string around his neck.

In the same motion, he pushed the button on the left wall of his shooting station. One stall to his right, John Clark did the same and both their targets raced toward the two shooters on hanging tracks. Overhead lights illuminated hits—and misses—as the targets trundled along.

Hendley Associates, the financial arbitrage firm that provided the "white-side" cover for The

Campus, sat in a semisecluded greenbelt within jogging distance of Old Town Alexandria. From the outside, it was one of many steel-and-tinted-glass structures that dotted the south side of the Potomac—DoD, the United States Marshals, and Amazon owned virtually everything that wasn't a hotel or condo in Crystal City. Old shops and historical buildings still graced the area between Arlington and Alexandria, but tucked into quiet streets lined with oak and sycamore trees lurked satellite offices for many alphabet agencies.

And Hendley Associates.

On the roof, powerful antennas picked up burst feeds from Fort Meade and Langley—made possible by a little insider help from the ODNI and Mary Pat Foley. Two stories below ground level, out of sight and sound, the multimillion-dollar fifty-yard weapons range kept Campus operators adept and their secrecy intact. Underground bunkers and ranges were not exactly uncommon in the D.C. area.

Chavez spent as much time here as he could. The range was his chapel, the narrow shooting station with folding barricade his confessional.

Spent brass littered the polished concrete floor. Powerful exhaust fans roared overhead, filtering lead and gases from the air. Negative pressure sucked the door shut each time anyone entered or left the range, making Chavez feel the constant need to clear his ears.

The targets rattled to a stop, within reach of each shooter. They were using Realistic Targets, the same colored drawings Chavez had used decades earlier when he'd first gotten into this business. Anyone who'd gone through firearms training with a federal or local agency in the past thirty years had very likely faced, among others, "Red Plaid Man" and "Brown Suit Woman." Paper overlays allowed the characters to carry a camera, or a knife, or binoculars, or a badge.

Today, they carried guns.

Red Plaid Man, a mustachioed dude with a wool cap and lumberjack shirt, looked suspiciously like a guy Chavez had once worked with. Today he'd chosen Brown Suit Woman as his adversary. Her beret and stern visage combined with the large handgun to make her look like she might be affiliated with the Baader–Meinhof Red Army Faction of the nineteen-seventies. Three-dimensional bad-guy targets, 360-degree video shoot-don't-shoot houses, and hyperrealistic Simunition scenarios had certainly improved training in the last twenty years, but Brown Suit Woman and Red Plaid Man were nostalgic, like the smell of Hoppes #9.

The A-zone of the Realistic Targets was just that, realistic, a bowling pin–shaped area encompassing heart, lungs, and head—the areas of the body that, when perforated, were most likely to let enough air in and enough blood out to stop an assailant from trying to kill you. Shot groups within that vital area demonstrated weapons proficiency—but Campus operators wanted much more than mere proficiency. Every one of them strived for perfection. Adept, Clark called it. A cut above. Top shot. That took more than practice.

It sounded odd or even affected to voice the words aloud, but being adept meant treating your weapon like a samurai treated his sword—as an extension of his body. The mechanics of proper grip, sight picture, and trigger control didn't happen by merely shooting over and over. Form had to be critiqued, tweaked, and then tweaked again, then it had to be drilled and drilled and drilled—until everything came as second nature. Many people could drive a manual transmission, but someone who made the effort to actually practice timing, clutch, and shift danced through the gears like butter without sacrificing speed. Becoming an adept shooter—a gunfighter—took perfect practice, under stress.

Like competing against your father-in-law.

Clark and Chavez had used Sharpies to draw eight-inch circles center mass on each of their targets, forcing them to be more precise with their aim.

Chavez ran a hand over the paper target and blanched at the four rounds out of a hundred that he'd pulled outside the black ring. Her eyes, one green, one blue, glared back at him, mocking his failure. The shots were still center mass, producing a ragged hole in his target that could have been covered by a fist. But at twenty-five yards, four shots had wandered low and slightly right of her handgun, just across the Sharpie circle. As far as Chavez was concerned, anything outside the ten-ring on a nice, comfy range with a controlled environment was a miss. Full stop.

Clark was more practical. His target was a bit ragged. A hand injury courtesy of a hammer-wielding Russian had left him with nerve damage and a bunged-up trigger finger. For a time, it had been touch and go whether he'd even be able to shoot again at all. A dyed-in-the-wool .45 ACP fan, he'd carried a SIG P220 for decades, but the long double-action trigger pull had left him shooting like a mere mortal after the Russian went to town on his hand with the hammer. Clark had gone back to the clean break of the single-action trigger on his Wilson Combat 1911—and returned to his normal prowess.

For Clark, semi-accurate speed trumped super-accurate precision all day long. No matter what Ding Chavez did, his father-in-law always seemed to edge him out in speed on the draw.

Chavez shook his head at the target and used the Sharpie to make a small tick mark next to his four outliers so he could tell them apart from any others after the next round of fire.

"How'd you do?" he said, knowing full well how Clark had shot. The man was a machine, getting off at least one round while Chavez was still bringing up his pistol—and Chavez wasn't exactly slow.

Clark poked his head around the divider and pointed to his ears. "What?"

Chavez nodded to his target, a grapefruit to Chavez's orange, but every shot inside the circle. Every. Single. Shot. The bastard.

Clark stepped behind Chavez to get a better look at the damage to Brown Suit Woman. He clucked a little, tipping his head at the four offending hits, but said nothing.

He didn't have to. Ding Chavez was a firearms instructor.

"A little too much finger on the trigger," Chavez said, assessing himself. "Pulled them low." He changed the subject. "I was thinking about what you said in Argentina . . . about this Camarilla and how The Campus could be viewed the same way."

"It's true," Clark said. He began to load magazines with .45 ammo from his vest pocket as he spoke. "That argument's pretty damned easy to make—a private, off-the-books group. The difference is that we work for the good guys instead of the highest bidder. A noble purpose, as it were."

"For sure," Chavez said. He'd been chewing on this little tidbit of philosophy since Buenos Aires.

It made sense. In strictest terms, much of what they did fell well outside the confines of what was legal. But that's what made them nimble, able to navigate the realities of a very dangerous world. It was also what made recruiting exactly the right individuals as operators critically important. Rules of engagement were, more often than not, left up to the boots on the ground, absent the picky little constraints of oversight or review boards. Campus operators reviewed one another, themselves, and demanded incredibly high standards. They needed new blood, deeper ranks, but the mere idea of that terrified Chavez.

"We'll dig into the list of possibles this afternoon," Clark said. He topped off the last of seven mags and tapped the spine against his open palm. "We need more people. Pronto. At any rate, you about ready to go again, Weedhopper?"

"Just say 'one, two, three, go,' Mr. Clark."

Brown Suit Woman and Red Plaid Man clattered out to the twenty-five, the speed of their short journey causing the bottom edge of the paper to bend slightly toward the shooters in the breeze.

"I'm going to work on speeding up a hair," Clark shouted from around the corner, ear pro already in place. "You see about tightening those shots—but keep your speed up."

Chavez's target would have won him Expert scores at any agency or department. It was near perfect. Another man might have taken offense at the suggestion for improvement, blown it off as advice from an overbearing father-in-law. But Clark wasn't picking on him. Neither of them would settle for a **near** perfect score. What they did wasn't a game, and somewhere out there, someone was practicing just as hard.

Chavez pushed the thoughts of recruitment out of his mind. How could they possibly screen someone for what they needed on the team? Someday they were going to make a mistake and pick the wrong person, either someone who didn't have enough scruples or someone who had too many.

19

Conventional wisdom said Steven "Chilly" Edwards should have been more than satisfied with his lot in life. The Abilene Police Department let him ride around all day on a Harley-Davidson Electra Glide. When he wasn't on the motor, he was runnin' and gunnin' as a sniper with APD SWAT. It was a good gig and his dad, a Taylor County Sheriff's deputy, reminded him of it every Sunday when they got together for dinner. Motor officer, SWAT sniper . . . Getting paid for it was just gravy. Still, Chilly was always on the hunt for something bigger. His older brother was FBI, Hostage Rescue Team no less—Delta Force with handcuffs. He was also a sniper. APD was a great place to work—good guys, fantastic gym, one of the coolest badges on the planet—but Chilly yearned to take his skills on the road.

Rolling on the throttle, he signaled, shoulder-checked, and then leaned the beefy Electra Glide onto the sweeping exit ramp that would take him off Interstate 20, where he'd spent the last two hours working traffic to southbound

Highway 277—where he would continue to work traffic. Chilly poured on more speed, merging with the river of cars and pickups. He looked where he wanted the bike to go—a truth in both riding and life in general.

Taillights flashed and vehicles began their abrupt, stoppy-starty inchworm dance as soon as he hit the highway. Drivers had a tendency to freak out when they saw a motorcycle cop, especially the college kids from any one of Abilene's three universities. A motor officer wasn't on his way to another call—an alarm or domestic or some kind of squabble—no, a cop on a bike was actively hunting for someone to pull over, and everyone knew it.

A soccer mom in a blue Ford Expedition dropped her cell phone when Chilly chuffed past. She just let the phone slip right out of her hand, eyes locked straight ahead, pretending she didn't see him. Maybe, just maybe, he wouldn't see her. He went with it, hoping the surge of adrenaline she'd gotten was enough to remind her not to text and drive. The guy in a white pickup ahead drifted into his lane, then back again. Chilly eased up on his speed, faded back, out of the danger zone. The guy was wearing an earpiece, lips moving like he was on the phone. Hands-free. Like that made a lick of difference.

Ride like everyone is on crack and out to kill you was doubly true when you wore a badge.

Of course, not **everyone** was out to kill Chilly. The PD and the citizens of Abilene had a pretty good relationship, as relationships between cops and citizens went. But riding the big Harley put him in the wind in more ways than one. He'd heard it said that people rode motorcycles for the same reason a dog stuck its head out the window of a moving car. The logic made perfect sense to Chilly. It was undeniable that being on a bike made one a target, either from someone who intentionally wanted to hurt him or from some damned driver with his head up his ass. The Brits called them SMIDSY accidents. Sorry Mate I Didn't See You . . . APD had lost a good man to one, years before Chilly had come aboard and the powers that be had decided to put all motor officers in blindingly bright yellow bicycle shirts along with blue uniform slacks and knee-high leather boots. Chilly didn't mind the high-viz uniform. He was thirty years old, five-ten, a muscular buck-ninety with dirty-blond hair he'd kept cut short since he got out of the Army. The GI Bill put him through school at Hardin–Simmons—a stone's toss away from his parents' house.

His dad wasn't too keen on the history major, calling it "a degree just for showing up"—but, hey, it was a diploma. That was enough to get him an interview with the FBI. With his experience on APD SWAT—and an elder brother speaking on his behalf—he received a tentative fast-track offer for HRT after he did two years in one of the Bureau's large offices. He'd already passed the physical and polygraph and was just waiting on the background investigation to be completed.

Until then, Abilene PD paid him to ride a Harley and shoot things.

The driver of the white pickup, still gabbing on his hands-free phone, drifted out of his lane again, halfway this time, nearly running a Ford Focus off the road. **Idiot.**

Chilly lit him up with the red-and-blues at the same moment the call went out for an officer assist. He was close, rolling up on the 10th Street exit in a quarter-mile, so he activated the mic on his helmet.

"Dispatch, Tom 26, go ahead and attach me to that call."

"10-4, Tom 26."

Chilly turned off his red-and-blues and rolled past a noticeably more attentive driver in the white pickup. He took the 10th Street exit to loop back around to the call—a double-wide trailer, west of the highway off 14th. Chilly had been there before. Most everyone on patrol had at one time or another. Dispatch always sent two officers, no matter the kind of call. Royce Vetter believed he was ushering in the last days or something. Apparently that job meant he had to fight every time he was arrested—which was a lot. It was only a matter of time before he went to guns instead of fists. Everyone who dealt with him noted in their reports that he was losing touch with reality.

Chilly slowed after he made the turn onto 14th Street, half a block from the double-wide. Derek Franjul stood in the street waving him forward. Face taut, his normally olive complexion had gone pale. A bulge the size of a cantaloupe in the front of his uniform shirt writhed like some kind of alien was about to burst out.

Chilly removed his helmet and hung it on the bike, looking from Franjul to the double-wide and then back to Franjul again. "What the heck have you got under your uniform?"

"It's a damned dog, if you can believe it," the officer said. "The door was open. I woulda waited, but Vetter's truck isn't here. His wife and kid were both dead when I got in there. Blood and . . ." He shook his head. "It's all over the walls."

Chilly glanced at the house again, hand tapping the butt of his pistol, making sure it was where he left it. He thought seriously about grabbing the folding M-4 from his bike pannier, but decided against it. "What about Vetter?"

"Gone." Franjul shook his head. "Just Margaret and the boy. I can't remember his name."

"Chris," Chilly said. "You sure they're dead?"

Franjul exhaled slowly, shaking his head, recalling the scene, judging from the faraway look in his eyes. "Oh, yeah. They're DRT, dude. Dead Right There."

Chilly had seen death before, in the Army and since coming aboard the PD. Sometimes the human body lived through getting both legs blown off by an IED. Other times, your heart blew up while you were sitting on the pot.

"You were telling me why you have a dog tucked inside your uniform shirt?"

Franjul gave a little start, coming out of his trance. "Oh, yeah. I heard crying coming from the kitchen so I went in before you got here. Vetter—or whoever did this—put the damned dog in the refrigerator, if you can believe it. I'm trying to warm the poor little guy up."

"Could be DNA on its fur," Chilly said.

Franjul groaned. "You're startin' to sound like an FBI guy already."

Chilly peeked inside the open door, careful not to touch anything. Franjul was right. There was no doubt Margaret and her son were dead. Both shot in the back of the head, both on their knees when it happened. Neatly folded laundry was stacked on the couch. More in the hamper, clean, waiting to be folded. Absent was the smell of old potato peels and rancid socks that graced so many homes they went inside. This one smelled like bacon and cedar. Family photos on the wall undisturbed but for a bit of blood spatter, most of which had been directed downward, suggesting the killer had been standing, aiming toward the floor. The human melon did crazy things when impacted by a high-velocity projectile. It was important to look for where the majority of the spatter was and not get too hung up on a few dots and dabs here and there. These two had been executed—and whoever did it stuffed their pup in the Frigidaire, the sick bastard.

"Detectives and a supervisor are on the way," Franjul said. He fished the squirming dog out of his shirt and held it in both hands, away from his body. "You think there could really be DNA?"

"They can get DNA from someone's breath now," Chilly said. "So I wouldn't be surprised one way or another."

Franjul pulled the shivering dog closer to him again. "Royce Vetter is a grade-A asshole, but I never figured him to blow his wife's brains out—or one of his kids'."

Chilly glanced at the other officer. "That's right. Vetter's got a kid in college."

"Margaret's kid, from when she was in high school, I think." He tipped his head toward a photograph of a young woman in her twenties, slim, pleasant, funky haircut. "Rene . . . Tatum, I think. She was barrel racing last time I heard, living over in Eastland near her daddy."

"You seem to know a lot about her."

"I bought her a drink after a rodeo last year," Franjul said. "She's . . ." He grimaced. "A handful. I'll just say that."

Chilly gave a low whistle. "Somebody will need to tell her about her mother."

"Yeah," Franjul said. "And keep her from killing her stepdad."

"That doesn't make sense," Chilly said. "Margaret and Chris were knelt on the floor and dispassionately executed, shot from behind. You ever known Royce Vetter to do anything without losing his shit? If he'd killed them, he'd have used a ball bat, face-to-face—and then burned the entire house to the ground. No, this is something else—"

The sergeant rolled up in his Tahoe, throwing a nod to the two officers. He stretched on a pair of blue nitrile gloves with a snap as he met them near the front porch. He'd already been briefed by phone.

"I'm assuming since you called off the ambulance that we have no pulses?"

"That's correct, sarge," Franjul said. "No pulses. Two DOAs." He gave a quick rundown on what he'd found, including the dog.

The sergeant gave a nod to the squirming Pomeranian. "What's with the dog?"

Franjul filled him in about the refrigerator.

"Could have DNA from the killer on it," the sergeant said.

Chilly gave the other officer a knowing side-eye.

"Edwards," the Sarge said. "You touch anything?"

"I haven't gone inside yet," Chilly said. "Just looked through the door."

"Go ahead and bounce, then," the sergeant said. "The sky's gonna open up and shit badges all over the place at any moment now. I need at least a couple officers on the street taking care of problems that are not double homicides."

"Copy that," Chilly said, at once disappointed he wouldn't be a part of the investigation, but perfectly happy not tiptoeing around gobs of brain matter in search of evidence. He turned to go, but suddenly froze, throwing his arm sideways to keep the sergeant from taking another step. He nodded to the chipped sidewalk leading from the porch.

"Totally missed this when we walked up." Chilly pointed to a partial boot print, stamped in blood on the dusty concrete. He moved away, then tapped Franjul's leg.

"Let me look at your sole."

"Well, that sounds creepy as hell," Franjul said, lifting his boot. "It's not mine. See."

It was a waffle-stomper boot, but the pattern was unique, angled with small V hashmarks, more like a tire than a boot. Chilly didn't recognize it from anything he'd seen before. Whoever had left the print was walking away from the house. There was a partial word visible where Chilly imagined the arch would be, but he couldn't make it out.

"He stepped in blood." Chilly snapped a photo with his phone. "Good chance there's a better print inside."

"I'm sure there is." The sergeant gave him a tight smile. "Good job finding this one. Now get back out on the street."

20

Ryan slowed the treadmill to a plodding jog so he'd be able to talk with Gary Montgomery without wheezing. He'd come to appreciate the Secret Service agent's solid, decidedly apolitical perspective. Montgomery, wearing a dark blue University of Michigan football T-shirt, jogged easily for someone who stood over six-two and tipped the scales somewhere around two-fifty.

"How's Mulvaney holding up?" Ryan asked.

"He's doing well," Montgomery said. "I appreciate you asking. The vice president's death came as a shock, as it did to everyone. Mulvaney's been running VPPD for a good while now. Mrs. Hargrave trusts him. He's able to help her navigate some of this . . . and doing that helps him deal with everything."

Montgomery's hands swung naturally at his sides as he ran, light on his feet like when a boxer skipped rope. He looked straight ahead, glancing periodically at the numbers on his treadmill. He'd explained early on that he would never go all-out when they were in the gym, ensuring that he always had enough in reserve to take care of his primary duty—protecting. He appeared happy to answer Ryan's questions, but never gave unsolicited advice except for when it came to matters of security.

"You've been a fly on the wall in quite a few of my meetings over the past few hours," Ryan said, jogging, feeling like he was in a race. They were going nowhere, but the big guy was winning. "I'd be interested to hear your opinion."

"My opinion, Mr. President?"

"On my nomination for the next vice president."

Montgomery glanced around the gym, though he knew they were alone with another agent posted outside the door.

"Remember how badly you wanted the job when President Durling asked you to accept it? I was a fairly new agent then, working another assignment, but your feelings on the matter were common knowledge among the agents throughout the Service."

"Is that right?"

Montgomery turned and looked at him as he ran. "You didn't want it, did you?"

"It was the last thing I wanted," Ryan said. "I was only moderately comfortable as national security adviser . . ."

"And there you go, sir," Montgomery said. "Respectfully, you should pick someone who feels the same way you did—driven to serve, but more than a little pissed that the responsibility falls to them."

21

Leo Debs spotted Royce Vetter's black pickup truck in the east parking lot of the Harmony Suites Hotel across the street from the EastGate Mall. A beige armored car idled some hundred feet away at the northeast corner of the building.

Two armored transport companies serviced Abilene and surrounding Taylor County, with a third making periodic trips to and from Fort Worth to the east. Routes and times, of course, were secret, so Debs, Pea, Rook, Taylor, and another team member named Ramos split into separate vehicles, dragging a net across the city as best they could, focusing on check-cashing and payday loan services since they were likely to deal with large amounts of cash over credit card transactions. Banks were a bad bet for robbery. Some geniuses got away with it once or twice. Debs had planned a couple, as exercises, but had never followed through. Too many safeguards—trackers, dye packs, cameras out the ass. Armored cars, on the other hand . . .

Debs thought about where he'd pull the job if

he had planned to hit an armored car. A semi-crowded spot to blend in or remote so there would be no witnesses—he could see value in both. He'd need easy access to a highway. Most important, the portion of the route when the maximum amount of cash would be on board. ATMs could hold as much as two hundred grand a pop when they were full, but that was likely closer to twenty or thirty thousand per machine a city the size of Abilene.

The new mall east of town was a good bet. A check-cashing store, heaps of motels—each with at least one ATM, and the mall itself. If the crew caught a truck loaded for deliveries, it could be a sweet score.

He'd just parked in the Sears parking lot and thrown his favorite pair of Zeiss binoculars to his eyes when his hunch paid off.

He punched Pea's speed dial into his mobile and gave him the location.

"Hang on," Debs said, scanning. His voice buzzed against his hands as he panned the binoculars. "I've only got eyes on Vetter and Blondie in the truck. Zip's going to be running counter-surveillance somewhere around here."

"I'll let the others know," Pea said. "Ten minutes out if I don't want to risk getting pulled over."

"Yeah, mate," Debs said. "That's the last thing we need . . . hang on . . ."

Debs fell silent as Vetter and Blondie got out of the truck, carrying the drone. Both men wore brown slacks and tan shirts. They weren't uniforms, but could easily have been mistaken for guard uniforms by a casual observer.

Vetter launched the drone. As suspected, they'd affixed a device that looked like the one they'd detonated earlier at their range. A split second later a ball of fire rose into the sky from a parking lot to the north, followed by a low, percussive boom as the sound waves reached Debs.

"Car bomb in the Home Depot parking lot," he said.

The drone rose straight up, well out of hearing range to the guards inside the heavy truck, then loitered directly overhead. Security protocols said the driver would remain locked inside the vehicle while the messenger exited and performed a delivery or pickup. If anyone was near the vehicle, they simply waited inside to open the door. The drone allowed Vetter to get his device close—very close—to the armored car without arousing suspicion from either guard.

Another bomb rocked the Home Depot parking lot, setting off car alarms and drawing the attention of anyone in the mall parking lot to the north. The guards inside the armored truck proceeded with their work, outside sounds muffled by the reinforced metal box. The moment the passenger door opened, Vetter brought the drone straight down. It hovered a scant two feet behind the messenger as his boots hit the pavement to exit the vehicle. Vetter detonated the device immediately. It might have been homemade, but it was deadly effective, spraying a conical pattern of ball bearings that shredded the messenger and dropped him in his tracks.

It would have been a good plan but for the heavy steel divider on the far side of the messenger that boxed the driver in. A few pellets got through the talking holes—just enough to terrify the driver and make him throw the truck into gear.

Morons . . . There was a ninety-nine percent chance these Airsoft warriors would get themselves killed in the next ten minutes. But even those odds weren't good enough. If by some remote chance they survived this and were arrested, they'd start looking for bargaining chips—like information on a bunch of dangerous-looking blokes holding target practice out Buffalo Gap way.

Debs checked the distance with a laser rangefinder—one hundred and forty-seven meters. No worries there. He could have driven closer, but he had a good spot, parked between an empty panel van and a pickup with a camper shell. The suppressed FN SCAR 17L CQC was short, only a ten-inch barrel, chambered in 5.56 NATO and meant for close-quarters combat. The color of flat, dark earth and fitted with a Gemtech suppressor, it wouldn't be noticeable unless someone happened to be looking straight at his truck—unlikely, with everything else going on outside.

In the SAS they would have called this a soft-kill rifle—relatively slight in caliber compared to his heavier 7.62 or the larger hard-kill rifle he normally employed as a sniper. The soft-kill would be less likely to overpenetrate and wound an innocent. Debs didn't so much care about that—he used the SCAR because it was small.

The armored car bounced over the curb and onto the street, leaving the messenger's lifeless body in a lonely-looking heap in the middle of the parking lot.

Vetter's plan wasn't bad, per se. The problem was it was just half a plan. He and Blondie had thought to murder the two guards remotely and then stroll up to the truck in clothes that made them look like they belonged there. They would use the dead guard's keys to unlock the back and make off with the money—soulless in its simplicity. In a way, Debs regretted having to kill them.

Remaining behind the wheel, Debs lowered the window and rested his rifle on the door frame, turning his body slightly to get a good sight picture through the Schmidt & Bender eight-power scope. He had a clear shot on Blondie, but Vetter was still blocked. Another step and he'd have them both. Neither would make it to the armored truck . . .

Then two cowboys walked out of the barbecue joint in the front of the hotel, into the parking lot. Debs pivoted the gun slightly, watching their faces through the reticle of his scope.

They'd seen the drone explode, the guard fall, and, more damningly, they saw Vetter drop the drone controller as he and Blondie hustled toward the armored truck as it pulled away with the passenger door swinging open.

The men from the restaurant were both armed. Filled, no doubt, with good intentions, they must have called out at the same time they drew sidearms from their waistbands. Devoid of proper training, they stood rooted in place as they brought their weapons up. Vetter and Blondie both turned at once, shooting as they moved, diving for cover behind their pickup.

Debs wanted to curse but took a deep breath instead, and squeezed off a round at Blondie's ear. Glass from the passenger window deflected what would have been a perfect hit, apparently wounding Blondie in the shoulder from the way he listed sideways.

One of the cowboys had fallen to one knee on the pavement, reloading while his partner continued to spray the black pickup with well-aimed fire from his sidearm. Perhaps they weren't so poorly trained after all, Debs thought.

Vetter had his pickup in gear now and sped out of the parking lot, fishtailing onto the frontage road. Undaunted, the cowboys jumped in their own truck and gave chase. Windshield shattered by multiple rounds, Vetter had to lean out the window to see. Panicked, he turned to the right to meet the cowboys' truck almost head-on. He spun the wheel hard left, jumping the curb and bouncing into the mall parking lot—heading straight for Debs.

Debs leaned in, lining up another shot, but the cowboys attempted a PIT maneuver, untracking but not spinning the black truck.

Vetter cranked left, sideswiping a live oak tree as he headed north in the parking lot, cutting between parked cars in an attempt to shake his pursuers. The cowboys stayed tight on his tail. Their pickup was newer, and more responsive, allowing them to roll up alongside and bump Vetter's left rear tire with their front quarter-panel. The truck spun, crashing into a parked minivan.

Vetter and Blondie came out shooting. Vetter carried a small backpack. Blondie wore his.

Sirens wailed in the distance. The cowboys continued to shoot, but slower now, likely running low on ammo.

Vetter and Blondie fled into the mall.

Debs caught a flash of movement from the corner of his eye, and turned to see Zip, the sleepy-eyed member of Vetter's crew, pull up in front of the Sears exit in a maroon Buick LeSabre. He was on the phone.

A mall security patrol in a white Toyota truck rolled around the corner from the southwest at the same moment Vetter and Blondie rushed out the double doors.

Seeing two armed men rushing toward the getaway driver, the security patrol rammed Zip's Buick, sending Vetter and Blondie scrambling the way they'd come, back into the mall.

Debs cursed. He was close now, just a few dozen yards away. If these assholes would just stay still for half a second he could end this thing.

The mall security guard remained in his truck, slumped over the wheel and apparently knocked unconscious by the impact. That made things easier. Debs located the only security camera he could find outside the mall and took it out with a double tap from the SCAR 17—if one worked, two would work better. Zip sprang from his wrecked Buick and rushed for a woman in a small Hyundai SUV backing out of her spot. Now Debs cursed. The crowded parking lot made it impossible to get a good shot. He pulled a bala-clava down over his face, then, giving the area a quick scan, got out of his pickup and trotted around the line of cars to find Zip brandishing his pistol at the woman in the SUV, pounding on her driver's-side window, promising not to hurt her if she would just open the door. That was rich.

Debs gave a shrill whistle and then shot Zip twice in the neck.

He let the short-barreled SCAR fall against his body on the single-point sling, parking it behind his back. Without pausing, he trotted forward as if to check the dead man's pulse. Judging from the condition of Zip's throat, there was little hope in finding one.

Debs stooped long enough to snatch the dead man's mobile phone from his pocket, made sure his eyes were opened, and used his lifeless face to unlock it, then trotted away without making eye contact with the terrified woman in the SUV.

Sirens wailed as police units drew closer.

People dashed from the mall's main entrance, heads down, running for their lives. At least one, a woman who could have been a grand-mother, clutched a screaming toddler to her chest and limped her way into the parking lot, the thigh of her blue jeans dark with blood from a bullet wound.

A throaty roar pulled Debs's attention to his right, and he turned to watch a police officer in a bright yellow uniform shirt chuff by, jumping the curb and gunning the throttle against the tide of fleeing patrons to ride his Harley Electra Glide through the double doors, straight into the mall.

22

Officer Scott Ritchey was first on the scene. He'd been at the Whataburger less than a mile away from the Home Depot when he heard the first explosion. A torrent of 911 calls flooded dispatch before he'd arrived on the scene, first reporting the car bombs, then, more frantically, at least one active shooter.

Dispatch held the channel for Officer Ritchey.

It had seemed like a good idea at the time, riding in on the motorcycle, allowing him to move much more quickly than he could have on foot. The Harley's 1700cc V2 engine wasn't exactly quiet under normal circumstances, but inside the confines of the department store it roared like a caged bear.

Crouching to make himself a smaller target, Chilly scanned for any sign of the shooters. The tile floors had been freshly waxed the night before and he could feel the front wheel shimmy like he was riding on oiled pavement. He loosened his grip on the handlebars, letting the big bike have

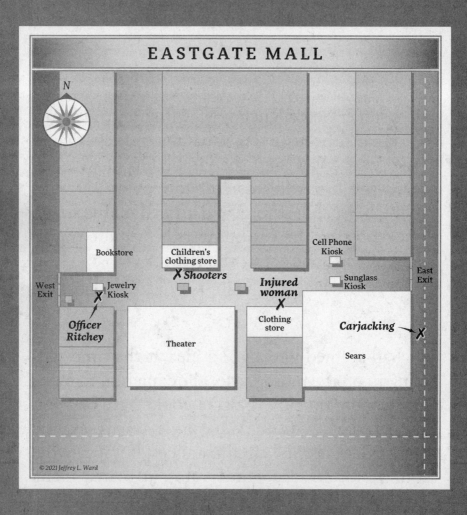

EASTGATE MALL

N

Bookstore

Children's
clothing store

Cell Phone
Kiosk

X *Shooters*

West
Exit

Jewelry
Kiosk

*Injured
woman*

X

Sunglass
Kiosk

East
Exit

X

*Officer
Ritchey*

Clothing
store

Carjacking

X

Theater

Sears

© 2021 Jeffrey L. Ward

its head. Like a trusted horse, the Harley stayed upright, rolling easily past perfume counters and racks of clothing before squirting out onto the industrial carpeting of the mall.

A woman who looked to be in her sixties hunkered behind the sunglasses kiosk, pointing down the hall in the direction of the cinemas. She jerked her head away as a bullet tore through a row of Ray-Bans directly in front of her face.

Rounds creased the carpet at Chilly's feet, forcing him to cut to the right. He pulled the bike behind a kiosk selling cell-phone cases, dismounting quickly to pop open the right pannier, keeping the bulk of the motorcycle between him and the shooters as best he could.

A woman in a bright yellow sundress lay on the floor beneath a rack of bargain clothing to his left. Blood soaked the carpet around her torso. She lifted one arm, then moaned something Chilly couldn't make out. The bump in her sundress told him she might be pregnant.

Rounds snapped off the carpet and thwacked the wooden kiosk, pinging against the metal bike, tearing Chilly's attention off the wounded woman. This was no good. He crouched lower. No good at all. The shooters couldn't see him, but the flimsy kiosk provided only concealment, not protective cover. Luck was the only reason he hadn't caught a bullet. Sooner or later, that luck would run out.

He ripped the folded Colt AR-15 from the pannier on the back of his bike, along with a small chest rig and four thirty-round mags from the opposite box. The Colt was an SBR, or short-barrel rifle, with an eleven-inch barrel and a LAW Tactical Adapter that retained the buffer spring allowing him to fold the stock and store the gun in the side case of his motorcycle. A small 1-8 Nightforce NX8 scope rounded out the weapon. As a sniper, he would have rather had his larger Accuracy International .308, but he was plenty comfortable with the Colt at the distances he would be shooting inside the confines of the mall. He removed his helmet and set it next to his motorcycle.

A pitiful, whimpering cry from the woman in the yellow dress tugged at the corners of his concentration. Every active-shooter drill he'd attended hammered home the need to pass wounded civilians in order to stop the threat. Leaving a few to die in order to stop the killing. Hard enough to think about in training. In real life it was heartrending. Pinned down by gunfire, Chilly's hands were tied—for the moment.

The woman struggled to lift her head, then collapsed against the carpet, beckoning him over with her left hand. She held something in her right, but the angle made it impossible to tell what it was. Rifle in hand, Chilly gave her a grim smile and raised a finger to let her know he needed a minute. She nodded, fully expecting him to come save her. That's what cops did. They didn't run off.

Another round zinged off the carpet. Someone down the hall screamed.

Another voice crackled in Chilly's earpiece. "Responding units, this is Ritchey. I'm pinned down beside that little jewelry kiosk across from the bookstore. Two shooters barricaded inside the kids' store across from the watch place. They must have been trying to get out the back and I went past them. Both shooters are white males, both wearing dark brown pants, tan shirts. Some kind of uniform, pretty sure one is Royce Vetter. Possible—"

A string of shots cracked both over the radio and down the broad hall.

Officer Ritchey paused for a moment, probably returning fire, Chilly thought, then spoke again. "Vetter's holding at least one hostage. White female. Short, dark hair, white T-shirt and jeans."

"Scott, this is Chilly. I'm southeast of you." He described his position and the stores immediately around him.

To his left, the woman in the sundress called out again. Louder this time, heartbreaking. ". . . can't hold on much longer . . ." Her chest shuddered as she spoke. She brought her left hand to her belly, cradling the unborn child.

Chilly checked his options. She was out of the line of fire but bleeding profusely from a wound in her biceps. He could attempt to save her, but that would give the shooters the chance to make a break for it if they decided to. Pockets of shoppers huddled inside almost every store. Everyone in the mall was in danger.

Splinters flew as more rounds punched through the plywood kiosk, making Chilly's decision for him. The shooters were calculating now, putting their rounds up, down, side to side. They knew Chilly was somewhere back there and searched for him with every round like a deadly game of Battleship.

He had to move. Fast.

Other units called out over the radio as they secured the mall's perimeter. Any moment, they'd begin to pour in from every entrance.

Bullets slapped the carpet between him and the woman in yellow.

"Hey, Scott, Chilly here. Cover fire on my mark if you can. I need to move."

"Copy that," Ritchey said.

A round pinged into the Harley's gas tank, spilling gasoline. Chilly watched gasoline fountain out onto the carpet. **Well, that sucks . . .**

He gathered himself up to move, keying the radio. "Three, two, one, mark!"

Down the hall, Scott Ritchey fired three pistol

shots, a second apart, pulling the shooters' attention his way.

Hopefully.

Chilly dove for cover inside the clothing store beside the wounded woman.

Her eyes fluttered when she saw him. She gave an exhausted nod toward her right hand.

Chilly froze when he saw it.

He keyed his mic again and spoke firmly into his radio.

"Bosco! Bosco! Bosco!"

Responding officers gave him the channel. Clutched tight in the wounded woman's right hand was a bomb.

"My fingers are really, really tired," she whispered. "He told me I can't let go . . ."

Her voice trailed off.

Staying low, Chilly moved closer, pressing a hand on the woman's wound, attempting to stanch the flow of blood.

He tried to keep his voice calm and, he hoped, soothing. "He told you something?"

She swallowed, gathering what strength she had left. "He said I had to hold on or it would . . . explode." She stifled a sob. "I . . . I'm so sleepy. I don't think I can do this much longer."

Hand pressing flat against her shoulder, Chilly studied the device, narrating on the radio. "Three-inch-diameter PVC, capped at both ends, about ten inches in length. No visible fuse, but the female gunshot victim holding it says the person who gave it to her said it would detonate if she lets go."

Mitch Kyle, the tactical bomb tech, spoke next. He was six minutes away.

"Ask her if she feels a bump or nub sticking out on the device."

Chilly relayed the question.

The woman shook her head. "No. It's . . . smooth." She grimaced through a hard swallow, panting to catch her breath. "He said . . . He . . . He told me it was a . . . I don't know, a photon cell or something."

"A photosensitive circuit?"

"That's it." An exhausted nod.

Chilly repeated what he'd learned, then said. "Okay, Mitch. Can I, like, cover it with a shirt or something?"

"You can," the TBT said. "But a ten-inch pipe bomb can do a lot of damage. Whatever you do, don't change the environment. Zero light can come in. Do you copy? Zero. No. Light. Whatsoever."

"Copy. Only a teensy bit of light . . ."

"I'm serious, Chilly," Mitch said. "Don't try to be fancy. Unless you can move at something like seven hundred million miles an hour, you're not fast enough to beat that circuit. I've got a bag I can put it in. Be there in four minutes."

Four minutes, Chilly thought. This might well be over in one.

"I wish . . ." The woman shook her head, her voice as pale and blue as her skin. "This is going to be so hard on my other kids . . ."

"We're gonna be just fine," Chilly said. "Then you can introduce me to those kids." He nodded to her stomach as he wrapped his left hand around the woman's fist, keeping her fingers pressed tight against the bomb. "Boy or a girl?"

"Baby girl," the woman whispered.

"Cool," he said. "You can introduce me to her, too." He gave her hand a squeeze. The woman's heart rate was off the charts, her face increasingly pale. "Let's you and me hang on to this together."

He keyed his mic. "Scott, I need to deal with a situation here. Give me a heads-up if those guys start my way."

"Copy," Scott Ritchey said. "But if they start your way, I'm gonna shoot 'em."

"What I like to hear," Chilly said. He called for the SWAT commander. "Sergeant Johnson, Chilly."

"Go for Johnson."

"Sarge," he said. "Looks like Royce Vetter and his buddy have decided to turn this into their Alamo and make a last stand. They've got homemade explosive devices of unknown material." Chilly gave the wounded woman a wan smile as he looked at the device wrapped in their joined hands. "If it's TATP or something similar, could be pretty unstable. I'd advise the team not to deploy any bangs when you come in. Could set something off unintentionally—and I'm right on top of one at the moment."

"Copy," Johnson said. "No flash-bangs."

"You have an ETA?"

Johnson responded. "I'm two minutes out on I-20. Others are arriving as we speak and forming up in the parking lot. Hang tight."

"Copy that," Chilly whispered, and then turned to the woman underneath him. "My name's Steven. What's yours?"

She blinked terrified eyes. "Lois," she said. "Lois Wright."

"Okay, Lois," Chilly said. "We need to stop the bleeding in your arm. Can you hold the pipe real tight again for a second while I grab a couple of those sweatshirts?"

She nodded, hand on her belly, cradling the baby.

"You making a tourniquet out of the clothes?"

"Nope," he said. "I have one of those in my pocket."

"I'm afraid losing all this blood is gonna hurt the baby."

"I'm not gonna lie," Chilly said. "Situation's not optimum. But babies are tough. And we're going to stop the bleeding and get you to a hospital—"

"As soon as you get this bomb out of my fist."

"Yep," he said. "Right after that."

He talked as he worked, hoping it would help keep her focused. "My name is Steven, but everyone calls me Chilly."

Her eyes narrowed. "Why?"

"Not sure," Chilly lied. "Maybe because I'm built for times just like this."

"Like this?"

He grinned. "Yeah, you know, defusing bombs and stuff."

Lois turned to look at her hand. "You know how to defuse this thing?"

"Not really," he said. "But I have an idea that should work until the real bomb tech gets here."

He dragged a half-dozen of the darkest color sweatshirts and hoodies off the nearby rack—maroon and navy blue. Then he wrapped his fingers around hers again, holding tight. He dug the RATs tourniquet from the pocket of his uniform slacks with his free hand, keeping an eye out for any approaching shooters. Essentially a flat bungie cord with a locking cam, the RATs was small enough to carry with him virtually anywhere. Still holding her hand and the bomb, Chilly rolled half across her body, snaring her wounded arm in the loop. It took some maneuvering to get the tourniquet past the bullet wound and all the way up under her armpit.

He held the free end of the elastic and gripped her hand tight around the bomb. "Hold on. This is gonna hurt when I pull it snug."

Lois gave a pinched grin. "This is my third kid. I can deal with it."

A fearsome boom shook the mall to the west—toward Scott Ritchey and the shooters.

Chilly looked up, eyeing his rifle on the ground beside him, both hands tied up at the moment.

Panicked screams came from around the corner—another explosion, and then the sickening pop of gunfire.

Ritchey's voice poured over the radio. "Chilly! Heads up! One shooter down, one shooter working your way. I can't . . ." Ritchey coughed. "Sons of bitches have smoke grenades."

More shooting. A riot of more screams.

"Hold what you've got," Chilly whispered to Lois. He piled four sweatshirts flat on top of the PVC pipe bomb, layering them for maximum effect before he slid his hand away from Lois's. Another hoarse boom shook the walls. This one closer, around the corner.

"He's coming your way," Ritchey said. "I can't see shit. I got no shot!"

"Keep your hand where it is," Chilly said. "Don't try to pull it out, no matter what happens." He piled the remaining sweatshirts over her hand and arm, hopefully blocking any and all light—as long as she didn't try to pull away. Snatching up the rifle, he turned to her a final time.

"Could you tell my husband I love him? My kids . . ."

"You're gonna tell them," Chilly said. "Hold on now for me, Lois. This'll all be over soon."

Her eyes fluttered closed. "One way or another . . ."

A shrill scream pulled Chilly's attention back to the shooter. On his belly now, rifle to his chest, he shimmied to the corner of the store. A quick snapshot around the corner with his phone showed Royce Vetter, wearing rifle plates and carrying a black SMG. He dragged a teenage female by the elbow, walking from store to store, shooting anyone who got in his way. Clouds of thick gray smoke hung on the still air behind him. Mall patrons darted back and forth through the shadows like characters in a video game. Ritchey must have really had his hands full.

Billy Johnson, the SWAT sergeant, filled the lull in the radio.

"Can you give me a sitrep, Chilly?"

"Stand by," Chilly said, still flat on his belly.

He'd turned the magnification on his scope down to 2, almost as low as it would go. Even so, his target was close, a couple dozen yards away, filling the reticle with his head. Chilly took a deliberate breath as he let the crosshairs settle over Royce Vetter's left ear.

Settled, he half exhaled and then squeezed the trigger.

Chilly kept watch through the Nightforce, ready to shoot again if he'd somehow missed or pulled his shot. He hadn't.

Gun and hostage both slipped from Vetter's grasp as his muscles quit functioning. His right leg buckled a fraction of a second before his left, causing him to crumple and twist at the same time, corkscrewing to the ground.

Chilly keyed his radio. "Ritchey, you clear?"

"Affirmative. One down on this end."

"Second shooter down, Sarge," Chilly said. "We should be clear, but there could be someone we don't know about."

"Copy that," Johnson said. "Sending in teams from the bookstore and the theater. Mitch is en route to your location."

"Copy," Chilly said. "Visibility is crap, Boss. Tell 'em not to shoot the guy in the bright yellow uniform shirt."

23

Adara Sherman stood from her business-class seat and tiptoed up and down, rolled her shoulders, moved her neck from side to side. She then made a pilgrimage to the lavatory, not because she needed to but because the flight from Ministro Pistarini International Airport, outside Buenos Aires, to Tokyo-Narita was interminably long, putting her driving to the airport, on an airplane, or waiting for a connection for some twenty-nine hours straight.

Business class was vastly superior to being crammed into the sardine tin in coach. But as good as they were, apart from some rare and extremely expensive exceptions, if you had to sit in the same type of seat for an hour in your own living room, you'd be looking for better furniture. Comfort was a relative thing, and right now, Adara Sherman was relatively exhausted. She couldn't remember ever being so tired. Not in college, not in Navy Boot Camp—during the winter in Great Lakes, Illinois, or Corpsman training, or pulling double watches aboard ship.

No, this was something different. This fatigue went all the way into her bones.

She sat back down, smiling politely at the male flight attendant who walked by with a glass of wine for the lady in the seat behind her. Hypnotized by the whir of the air-conditioning, jostled by the slight, almost imperceptible buffeting of the monstrous Japan Airlines 747 at forty thousand feet, Adara leaned over and rifled through her backpack. She came up with a stack of index cards, each bearing a Japanese phrase on one side and the English translation on the other.

If she couldn't put her exhausted brain to sleep, she might as well put it to use. In the movies, the spies could spiel off multiple languages whenever the need arose. In actual life, at least for Adara Sherman, it took constant practice and review. When she had any downtime at all, she was reviewing flashcards, reading history, or memorizing maps.

Across the aisle and one seat forward, Jack and Midas slept soundly, Jack with some book about investment banking hanging out of the seat pocket, Midas with a copy of **Wired** magazine on his chest. For as long as Adara had known these guys, they'd been able to put themselves into a sort of suspended animation during long flights. Damn them.

Adara asked the attendant for a ginger ale to

soothe her gut and then flipped the first index card and went back to work.

W hen it came to dealing with her husband, the First Lady of the United States nearly always got her way.

And she hardly even had to try.

She had back-to-back surgeries that morning. Jack had reading to do, and briefings, and meetings . . . and more reading. She found it extremely sexy, the way he always had his nose in a book or newspaper. The alarm had gone off at ten minutes to five. Jack was already up. She could hear him in the bathroom, brushing his teeth.

Stretching, Cathy Ryan rolled over and clawed for her glasses on the nightstand, slipping them on so she could check her phone and make sure there were no last-minute cancellation texts from her assistant. Satisfied that her morning was still a go, she yawned through another shivering stretch, and then swung her legs off the edge of the bed. She wore underwear and a T-shirt—loose enough not to completely embarrass Jack's chief of staff or the Secret Service if they had to burst into the White House Residence unannounced. Jack had never been the kind of guy who wanted her in skimpy silk gowns, preferring her in one of his shirts and little else. If she remembered correctly,

Jack Junior became a reality while she was wearing a robin's-egg-blue button-down from Brooks Brothers.

Good thing they hadn't been in the White House Residence for that one . . .

Jack came out of the bathroom, still brushing his teeth. Half dressed, he wore black socks, boxers, and a white shirt with the top button already buttoned and waiting for his tie—like an earnest little boy getting ready for school. The side of presidential life only Cathy got to see.

They'd gone to sleep talking about poor Phoebe Hargrave and the suddenness of her loss. Jack was still brooding over who to pick to fill the office of vice president. He had a funny way of holding his left eyebrow when he brooded. It was cute, but he always ended up with a headache.

Peering over the top of her glasses at her husband of four decades, Cathy Ryan decided to change the subject.

"Been working out?" She knew she had to be careful with the flirting or he'd suggest they run a little late for work.

Ryan patted his belly with his free hand. "I recently read that, statistically speaking, women prefer a man with a dad bod to that of someone who is über-fit and musclebound."

Cathy gave a contemplative nod, musing. "Let me see . . . Gerard Butler dad bod or Gerard Butler with a Spartan six-pack . . ." She shook her head. "You know, pretty sure I'm good either way."

Ryan went back to brushing his teeth. "Dad bod it is," he said around the brush, giving her a wink. He came back a half-minute later, a red-and-blue-striped tie draped around his neck. "Remind me. What's the opposite of a presidential pardon? I want to see that Gerard Butler is on that list."

Cathy grinned. "I know you can't make it, what with everything going on, but I'll miss you in San Antonio with me."

In truth, Jack had never been planning to attend her San Antonio speech. Before Tony Hargrave's death he'd been tied up with an event in Dallas with the president of Mexico. Now even that had been postponed.

"Me, too," he said, watching her while he tied his tie. "I'm sure you'll have all those eye surgeons eating out of your hand with that speech."

She let her head fall to one side, blond hair draping her shoulder. She was fully aware that her husband had focused with laser precision on her legs.

She swung her feet slowly back and forth.

Jack stopped tying mid-Windsor and let the ends of the tie fall. "I'm sure I'd be the dumbest person in the room anyway."

"An ARVO conference crawling with ophthalmologists," she mused, batting lashes. Sometimes, she couldn't help but tease him. ARVO was the Association for Research in Vision and Ophthalmology. "You'd be bored out of your skull. Besides, I'm sure making you sit through my speech one more time is against the Geneva Convention or something."

"One cannot learn too much about retinas and corneas and . . . all that other medical-y eye stuff. Anyway, you know, I'd be perfectly content listening to you read the directions on the back of a box of macaroni and cheese."

She stood to walk toward the bathroom—giving him no indication whether this meant **"Meet me back in bed in five minutes"** or **"I need to get ready for work."**

She stopped at the doorway and turned, standing hipshot, one hand on the frame. "Ya know, I'd love for you to come with me to San Antonio for a lot of reasons. Monte Harper's supposed to speak. It might behoove you to carve out ten minutes to have a talk with him."

"Dr. Harper?" Ryan said. "Your friend from Johns Hopkins?"

"His daughter called me last night," Cathy said. "I was going to talk to you about it then, but what with Tony's death and all you have on your plate . . . He's on his way home from doing cataract surgeries in Afghanistan. His wife, Naomi, is an ob-gyn. She's with him teaching women about pre- and postnatal health. You're going to want to hear what they have to say about their experiences with generic antibiotics. I think it'll help garner support for the pharma bill."

"We could use all the help we can get on that one," Ryan said.

Cathy gave a little nod. "You should get them up here as soon as they get stateside. They're eager to talk to you. Naomi's done an informal survey of many of her colleagues around the U.S. and they've come up with some pretty convincing anecdotal evidence. It probably would be good for you to talk in person."

"I'll get them on the calendar," he said. "Text me their contact info when you get a minute. Did you know we allow India and China several days' notice before we inspect their manufacturing plants?"

Cathy gave a sardonic smile. "I did know that."

"Of course you did."

"Look at it this way," she said. "A doctor prescribes a generic drug for a urinary tract infection. If it doesn't work, do we blame the drug for being too weak? No, we blame the bacteria for being resistant—and we resort to something else."

Jack leaned in and kissed her on the cheek before fumbling with his tie, forgetting where he was already in the process of tying it. He started for the bathroom, where he'd have a mirror.

Cathy stayed put.

"Truth be told," she said, blocking the door with her hip. "I don't really want to go to San Antonio, either, not for this. Conferences should be about going to breakout sessions that pique your interest or chatting at the bar with friends. The ARVO committee invited me so they could draw in attendees, but if I try to attend anything other than the opening ceremony, my protective detail will plug up all the corridors. I'll just frustrate everyone who can't get where they need to go. I love Mo Richardson to death, but dragging along a full complement of Secret Service personnel everywhere I go sucks the life out of me."

"I feel your pain," Jack said. He kissed her cheek again. "You'll be terrific. Mo's a seasoned professional. She'll tell her team to blend in."

"Mo's on vacation for two weeks. Her sister's wedding. Karen Sato is running the show while she's gone."

"You want me to send Gary?" Jack said.

Cathy scoffed. "It's not that. I trust Karen. She's just a little more tightly wound than Mo, more likely to hover, if that makes sense."

"They get paid to hover," Jack said. "Hovering is literally in their job description."

"I know that, Jack." Cathy checked her watch and did the math for her commute to the hospital before reaching for her husband's tie. "Here," she said. "Let me help you with that."

He tilted his head to give her space, but instead

of finishing the knot, she slid the tie off his neck and tossed it to the floor.

He looked down at her. "I thought you had to be at the hospital."

She squeezed past him, heading back into the bedroom, exaggerating her walk so as to leave no question about her intent.

"I have a couple minutes to spare," she said. "Patients benefit when their surgeon is an emotionally whole and happy person. And anyway, Mr. President, I thought we might discuss a few things you'll be missing while I'm in San Antonio."

24

The telltale squeal in Adara Sherman's ears told her the JAL 747 inbound to Tokyo-Narita had started its descent. She passed Jack on her way back from the lavatory, getting one more walk in before the seat belt light came on. He glanced up, gave her one of his patented Jack Junior winks, and then went back to working on his notebook. He'd trimmed his beard, closer, less mountain man. Midas slept. The guy could sleep anywhere, apparently having no guilt to burden or keep him awake. Working with these guys was the best job in the world, and Sherman knew it.

The flight from Buenos Aires to Tokyo, with a short layover in New York, was so long as to be sickening. About to bounce off the walls, she'd walked the length of the plane a dozen times to keep her circulation going. Somewhere over Hawaii, she'd resolved never to try and be an astronaut. She'd reviewed the intel from Gavin regarding the hackers. Made notes. Boned up on her Japanese language. Studied her notes and then made more notes. Between all that, she thought about Dom and sipped ginger ale.

She'd just dozed off again when the JAL pilot bounced the landing at Narita and shook her awake. Wooded hills surrounded the airport some thirty-five miles east of Tokyo. The fourteen-hour flight wasn't bad enough. Now they were looking at dragging their bags down umpteen levels below the terminal to reach the Narita Express train into the city.

It was early morning in Japan, twelve hours ahead of her body clock, which was still slogging along on Buenos Aires time. Sherman found herself running on fumes, a pit in her stomach. Grimy and pinched in all the wrong places from wearing the same clothes for thirty-plus hours, a hot shower was calling her name by the time she walked down the jetway. She forced a smile at the uniformed medical officer. A thermometer the size of a movie camera was mounted on a tripod alongside a squishy green antimicrobial carpet that every passenger had to walk down. Clearance through Immigration went quickly, with all three of them traveling under alias passports provided unofficially by Mary Pat Foley's shop. Adara cleared first and made her way to baggage, where her roller duffel was already doing the merry-go-round with a hundred others. She had to climb to get the thing and was ready to bite Ryan's head off when he bounced up with his own suitcase.

"What?" she said, wary of his sudden giddiness when she felt so shitty.

Ryan held up his phone, leaning in so as not to be overheard by the throng of other travelers in the crowded baggage claim area.

"Gavin narrowed down the address for the hacker space," Ryan said. "Someone appears to have hacked into the Japan Railways system—and they're siphoning off a shitload of power. Gavin suspects Bitcoin mining."

"Seems weird," Adara said. "Why would someone go to all that trouble setting up the hardware to mine Bitcoin when they're already making millions on ransomware attacks?"

"Greed," Midas said. "No skin off their nose if they get the power needed for their little mining operation for free." He rolled his shoulders, curling his ballistic nylon duffel bag for a few reps to get some exercise. "It's a fair bet these shitbirds are contracting for some state actor, so they probably have to voucher all the payouts and hand them over for the motherland or fatherland or whoever the hell is pulling the strings."

Adara frowned. "We knew our target was somewhere around there. Are you saying it's right in the station?"

"Not in it," Ryan checked his phone again, wiping the sleep from his eyes with a thumb and forefinger. "Nearby. On Eitai-dori. It's a street that runs under the tracks to the north. It connects the east and west sides so you don't have to walk through the station itself." He closed his eyes and groaned reverently at a memory. "Yuki and I went there a couple times for sushi. Little restaurants, boutique shops. All very Japanese, but it reminds me of some of those taverns under the L train in Chicago."

Yuki—Yukiko Monzaki—was an agent with kōanchōsa-chō. The Public Security Intelligence Agency was akin to the FBI counterintelligence, CIA, or MI6, responsible for gathering intelligence and conducting counterespionage activities against both internal and external threats to the people of Japan. She'd worked with The Campus in the past. She and Jack had had a short relationship, but work had always gotten in the way. Adara liked her, but knew the relationship was doomed from the beginning. It was difficult enough juggling work and home life with Dominic Caruso, and they worked for the same agency—not to mention the same government. The United States and Japan were peers and allies, but they each had goals that put their own citizens first. It was an open secret that even friendly countries spied on one another, which meant Jack and Yuki spent as much time guarding what they said to each other as they did trying to communicate. It had ended amicably, as far as Adara knew, but Jack was a sensitive guy, and though he threw around his good looks and playboy façade, broken relationships left a mark—particularly the good ones.

Ryan shuddered a little as if from another memory and then shook his head, coming out of a stupor. "Anyway, it's the perfect place to hide a hacker space. People come and go by the millions and the power usage is camouflaged by all the electricity consumed by all the trains. I'm not an engineer, but the bullet train has to suck up a ton of power."

Midas yawned, stepping back and forth from one foot to the other. "We're booked at the Marriott Courtyard a couple blocks away from the station—walking distance."

"It'll be good to stretch our legs," Adara said, feeling better to have a clear way forward.

"Agreed," Midas said. "I say we drop our stuff at the hotel and then go check out the little shops near our target. Maybe grab some breakfast."

Ryan nodded. "Even operators of international intrigue have to eat. I know a place a block from our target that specializes in chawanmushi. They have great mentaiko, too."

"Mentaiko?" Adara asked.

"Spicy cod roe," Ryan said. "From down south near Fukuoka."

"Cod roe," Midas said, rubbing his stomach. "The breakfast of champions. I'm game but I need a half-hour at the room. I can never bring myself to take a dump while I'm wedged into an airplane toilet."

"It's a plan, then," Ryan said. "Midas takes a tactical dump, we go grab some mentaiko, and then ruin the day for some asshat hackers."

Adara put a hand on his shoulder. "You know what?" she said, sleep-deprived and unable to stop grinning. "I am suddenly reminded that I have the best job in the world."

The Narita Express train ran every thirty minutes and took just over fifty minutes to reach Tokyo Station from the airport. The walk to the hotel, while less than a kilometer, took time because of the endless sea of humans coming in and going out of the station. Thirty-one hours after leaving Buenos Aires, Adara finally kicked off her shoes and sat at the end of her hotel bed at the Tokyo Courtyard. Jetting around the globe looked cool in the movies, but there was a price to be paid for world travel, and Adara could see it in the lines around her eyes every time she looked in the mirror. It took everything she had to resist the urge to fall into the bed and get horizontal for just a few minutes. Instead, she took the time to grab a quick shower before changing into a white three-button polo and a pair of khaki slacks that Dom said she looked good in. She rounded out the outfit with a pink terry-cloth ball cap that was more about style than function. She was plenty prepared to kick someone's ass if she had to, but she liked pink and wasn't afraid to admit it. Jack and Midas met her in the lobby by the little upscale hamburger joint, looking freshly scrubbed, also wearing hats as a guard against the many surveillance cameras around the city.

Midas stopped across the narrow Yanagi-dori at a bank of five vending machines selling everything from iced coffee to mixed nuts to tiny amber bottles of a vitamin drink called Oronamin C— one of which he bought and chugged like it was hair of the dog.

"Everyone zeroed in on a weapon of some sort?" he said as they hung a left off Yanagi west onto Aogiri-dori between aging tan brick apartments and a construction site for more modern structures of glass and steel.

"Of course," Adara said. "But don't forget, Clark said this is a fact-finding mission only."

"I know," Jack said. "But facts lead to other facts, and pretty soon you're . . . well, you know. Things happen."

25

The entrance to the address Gavin had found for the hacker space was easy to find but impossible to get into without being seen. This was going to take patience and a lengthy surveillance, much of it in the open, in the most populated city in the world, where all three of them stuck out drastically from everyone else in the crowd.

Adara considered herself a bit of a foodie and would have tried the mentaiko and rice that Jack recommended for breakfast, but the spicy fish eggs seemed a little adventurous. She opted for chawanmushi—literally "steamed in a teacup." The savory egg custard was much easier on her churning gut.

Japanese breakfasts were traditionally small, but none of the three ate even all of what they'd been served. Eating made for excellent cover during a surveillance. It allowed them to sit in one place for a lengthy period of time, sipping tea and nibbling on something while they feigned reading the **Asahi Shimbun** newspaper or scrolled through their phones.

The shop across the street from the target location, still in the shadow of the raised tracks, sold small bowls of soba—buckwheat noodles—in a salty broth. There were no tables outside, but a raised counter on the sidewalk where she and Midas could stand shoulder to shoulder, slurping out of their bowls while they watched. Jack loitered a half-block away, connected via hardwired earpiece and cell phone, eating a plastic container of gyūdon—thinly sliced beef and onion in a rich sauce over rice. The mentaiko had been his recommendation, but he apparently needed something a little more substantial than fish eggs and rice for breakfast.

Adara used a pair of disposable wooden chopsticks to toy with her buckwheat noodles while she studied the floor plan Gavin had sent to her phone. The place looked to be plumbed for a bathroom and break room/small kitchen. The main door to the address was inside a covered cave-like tunnel that looked to serve a small, two- or three-car parking lot for the office occupants. The back door was accessible from an extremely narrow alley—just wide enough for a bicycle or scooter. With no outside handle, this heavy steel door was for use in case of fire or earthquake and opened from the inside only—a no go. The floor plan showed a small suite of three rooms through the main door off the right side of the garage, possibly offices, but more likely a combination office/living quarters for a building attendant.

Periodically a bald meathead came out of the shadows to stretch his legs and look up and down the street before going back inside. There was no mistaking him for anything but security. He was white, early forties maybe, with a hatchet face and ropy neck muscles that rose out of his powder-blue dress shirt. His gray slacks were tailored and pressed. His shoes were sturdy Rockports, meant for activity, and the lengthy periods standing. Dom had several pairs just like them.

The guy was aware. Adara had to give him that. When three-quarters of the men and women in the developed world—and maybe even more than that—walked around cut off from the sounds of the world by their earbuds, or hunched over their phones reading news that was happening thousands of miles away, or playing games that were happening nowhere, Baldy's phone was in his pocket and his eyes and ears were open—constantly scanning, listening, looking for anything out of place. As far as Adara could tell, he didn't have a handgun on him. That didn't mean that he didn't have a weapon within his reach, but that he could deny if some police officer got too nosy. Shortly after the Campus operators had arrived, he was replaced by a second meathead. This one was Japanese, also with a soldier's bearing, buzz cut, and similar business-casual dress. The two men chatted for a few minutes before Baldy went inside. The Japanese man stayed on the street for a few more minutes, scanning as his partner had been doing, and then retreated into the shadows.

Midas attached a ladderlike device called a Yagi antenna to his cell phone and aimed it across the street. About a foot long, the setup was similar to equipment used for war-driving, the process of driving or cycling around and locating all the hackable Wi-Fi access points in a given area. Foot and vehicle traffic was sparse but steady, allowing him to focus on the target in between passersby without the clutter of other cell phones and vehicle Wi-Fi IDs. "Not getting much Tempest," he said. "Which makes perfect sense. If these guys are pro enough to scam bajillions of dollars online, they'd be the careful sort."

Tempest was the NSA code word for electronic data leaking into the air from devices. It could be something as basic as the melody of tonal blips on a keypad that could give away the number of an entry code, or the MAC address or Bluetooth ID on someone's smart dishwasher. Wireless routers, copiers, cell phones—they all showed up on the scanner.

"These guys are going to have their computers hardwired in," Midas said. "I'm guessing they've got a smart TV . . . I have each of the two security dudes' cell phones when they're outside, but I lose them when they go in."

"We're looking at this like they're security for the hackers," Ryan said. "What if they are the hackers?"

"Taking turns pulling security . . ." Adara mused.

"Maybe," Midas said. "I realize I'm stereotyping here, but these two don't fit the profile for someone who spends their day glued to a computer screen inventing malicious code."

"They do look like soldiers," Jack said. "I'm just surprised this place is so small. I'd expected a big Russian troll farm Chinese fiction factory with row after row of cell phones and laptops banging out fake news and incendiary posts. If Gavin's floor plan is right, this place is hardly large enough for five or six, and they'd be crammed in tight if they have enough computer hardware to be mining Bitcoin."

"True enough." Midas shrugged. He hefted a padded nylon computer case. "I brought the laser mic. I'd get a vibration off that window on the parking shack, but the angles are wrong. Too much traffic cutting in front of the laser here at street level. We'd be lucky to get every tenth word. If we go higher, the edge of the building cuts off my line of sight."

"What about a slap?" Adara asked.

"They'd get a look at our faces when we put it up," Midas said.

A "slap" was a small microphone that transmitted at GSM or 2G digital networks, so called because of its small size and the user's propensity to slap it against a wall or the back of some piece of furniture as they walked by. Its tiny size left room for only a small battery, giving it a finite shelf life. The ones Adara and Midas carried were disguised as a chunk of gray concrete that could be dropped on virtually any sidewalk next to a building without garnering a second look, and a woman's wallet, complete with ten thousand yen in small bills—about ninety dollars—a couple of credit cards, and a voter registration—nothing with a photograph.

Adara looked at her watch. "It's been nearly an hour since the last shift change. This guy always has a bottle of water in his hand when he strolls outside. He'll be looking for his bald buddy to give him a push any minute now. I'll stroll by and drop the purse. With any luck our guy's greedy enough to pick it up."

Midas stayed where he was, sipping bubble tea. The earbud in his right ear kept him in communication with Adara, who had made her way to the end of the block before crossing the street and hanging a left, putting her on a direct course for the target. In one hand, she carried a paper map she'd picked up in the lobby of the hotel, unfolded so it flapped in the breeze, touristy. In the other, she gripped the strap of a nylon backpack, rigged so she could pull a cord with her thumb and drop the wallet out of an unzipped pocket.

Right on time at the bottom of the hour, the bald guy ghosted into view in the shadows, ready to relieve his Japanese partner. Adara reached the edge of the garage opening, seemingly absorbed in her fluttering map. She stumbled a bit as she went by, then looked down at her shoes, one of which she'd untied before crossing the street. The bald man hooked a thumb over his shoulder toward the garage at about the same time Adara knelt to tie her shoe.

The slap wallet tumbled out of her backpack right on cue.

Just inside the opening to the garage, the two targets were still deeply engrossed in their own conversation. Neither appeared to notice Adara or the wallet.

She finished with her shoe and stood, walking away without glancing back.

The bald guard's head snapped up. He'd apparently heard Adara's footsteps on the pavement. Midas couldn't hear what was being said, but instead of sneaking out to retrieve the dropped wallet without alerting Adara, the guard walked directly to it, shouting for her to stop.

The man looked inside it, thumbed through the money while Adara made her way back to him, fawning, grateful. She kept one hand on top of her pink ball cap to keep it from blowing off in the wind. She reached for the wallet, but the man pulled it away as if taunting her, holding it just out of her reach. He appeared to lecture her for a moment, before handing it over. She ducked her head in thanks, and then pointed at her map. He shook his head. She ducked her head again and turned, consulting in the map as she walked away.

"He seemed like kind of a dick," Midas said. "Way to stay in character—"

"Hang on," Adara cut him off. "Give me a second." She waited a half-minute to speak again, when she was well out of earshot. "Jack, are you hearing us?"

"I am," Ryan said. "Whatcha got?"

"I overheard pieces of a convo when I was dropping the wallet," she said. "Good news, there are apparently only two hackers up there. Bad news is I'm fairly certain these guys are about to kill them."

"You sure we're talking two hackers?" Midas asked over comms when Adara joined Jack up the block. She ran the risk of being recognized if she returned to her original vantage point across the street.

"I couldn't make out all of the conversation, but I clearly heard the bald one say 'supposed to kill both of them and wipe everything.' **Both** makes me think two."

"It does," Midas said. "Any idea when they plan to go about this said killing and wiping?"

"Nope," Adara said. "Is Baldy still pulling guard duty out front?"

"His little gopher face poked out of the shadows a couple seconds ago," Midas said. "There's a chance he could be leaving the dirty work to his partner. For all we know, it's going down as we speak."

"Could be," Adara said. "But did you catch how that guy toyed with me when he was giving me back my wallet? There's a cruel streak there in his eyes. He'll want to be part of any hit. I can almost guarantee it. Besides, that asshat called me **sweetness**."

"Okay, then," Ryan said. "We'll need to get upstairs before they follow through. I can call Yuki, but she's by-the-book to the extreme. She never met a rule she didn't want to follow to the letter. Once we get her involved, she'll shove it up the chain and that's the end of it as far as we're concerned. It'll be out of our hands. Probably out of hers, too. If they treat this like a tactical callout, any data is going to be dumped before they get inside."

"And if they don't," Midas added, "these guys will murder the hackers and dump the data anyway. If we turn it over to Yukiko, at least we'll have a couple live prisoners to interrogate."

"**Yuki** will have live prisoners to interrogate," Jack reminded them. "I'm telling you, her bosses will shut us out and we'll get nothing."

"Can't you use any of that Jackie-boy charm on her?" Midas offered.

Ryan's sigh was audible over the line. "Afraid I used all that up on Yukiko Monzaki a long time ago. I recommend we do it ourselves."

"I can't believe I'm saying this," Adara said. "Especially after the look Clark gave me before we left. But I agree with Jack. Let's not forget six people died on the D.C. Metro because of these assholes. No, these guys have graduated to the big leagues. We're not only talking about evidence of millions of dollars in extortion money, we're talking about murder. Not to mention these bastards out front are about to commit more murder."

"Okay," Midas said. "What's the plan, Jack?"

"The plan?"

"Come on," Midas said. "We've been working with you long enough to know you've been planning to go in since the moment we laid eyes on the place. You gotta have a plan."

"Now that you mention it," Ryan said, "these

two look like former military. They're not going to be tricked or intimidated. For all we know they're holding the hackers prisoner—"

"Maybe . . ." Adara said, unconvinced.

"So . . . I say we slock them," Ryan said.

A slock was a primitive weapon, more common in prison than outside—a padlock dropped into the toe of a sock that was then swung as an impact weapon.

"And you have a sock with you, of course," Adara asked.

"In my pack," Ryan said. "No lock, but it's better to use rock or sand anyway. I'll use some pieces of concrete rubble from that construction site."

"Figures." Adara wasn't surprised that Jack had come prepared. All of them trained on field-expedient weapons—broom handles, their own belts, socks full of rocks. Clark was proficient with all of them. Firearms and knives were difficult to come by in Japan, so they'd use what they had at hand. "We should do it now," she said. "Get Baldy while he's alone. They don't appear to be talking to one another by radio, at least while they're out front, but they could have cameras."

Midas gave a low whistle. "I like the concept, but I think we should wait until just before the push, while the Japanese dude is on his way down to meet his partner. He's less likely to see anything if there is a camera."

Adara thought through the variables. "What's to stop the hackers from dumping all the data if they see us taking out their guards?"

"That's the tricky part," Jack said. "Midas knows the most about computer tech. He should be the one to rush in and stop them from deleting files. There's a two-foot length of pipe leaning against that construction fence over there. Adara, you up to slocking the guards? I'll follow up with the pipe."

"I am," Adara said. "But, as a medic, I've gotta tell you, I once saw a guy who was hit so hard in the head with a ball-peen hammer it broke the wooden handle and he still put up a hellacious fight."

"She's got a point," Midas said. "The human skull is a marvel. Hard to say how it's going to react." His voice fell low, more somber. "That's why you can't be intent on just knocking someone unconscious. If we're going to do this, you have to aim for the outfield. If they die, they die."

"Okay, then," Jack said. "There is another scenario."

"Yes, there is." Adara looked at her watch. "About fifty of them. The shift change is about to happen. Let's talk about it while we're moving into position."

Had anyone asked Adara Sherman if these men guarding the hacker space needed stopping, she would have answered with an unequivocal yes. Was she prepared to kill them? Still yes. But if someone asked if she was comfortable that it fell to her to kill them, the response would have been more complicated. She'd taken more than a few lives over the course of her career, but that had always been in the middle of a rescue or the heat of battle. This was going to be different. She wasn't planning to fight anyone. She and Ryan were essentially going to beat these two men to death, suddenly, without warning. This was an assassination. She'd seen enough violence to know it would be brutal and it would be messy. What it would not be was easy. She was no John Clark, nor did she want to be. This one was going to haunt her.

A lot.

Adara approached first, timing her gait so there was no one else walking with her. Fortunately, it was well before lunch and pedestrians were sparse on the sidewalks under the tracks. She wore the pink hat again and waved to Baldy with her flyaway map like they were old friends. The sock full of rocks was stuffed in the back of her waistband, the empty "handle" portion hanging out like a tail. Ryan followed a dozen steps behind with the length of heavy pipe hidden up the sleeve of his shirt. Midas came from the opposite direction.

Adara had just crossed the threshold toward Baldy, when not one, but two Japanese men came running out the glass door into the garage—and both of them moved like soldiers.

26

The proverb his old man had told him about knowingly putting a poisonous snake in his pocket slithered into President Jack Ryan's mind each time he thought he might be able to trust Senator Michelle Chadwick. The perpetual sneer of disdain across her angular face all but screamed that she hoped to put a dagger between his shoulder blades at the earliest possible convenience.

A little of Michelle Chadwick went a long way. It didn't help that Ryan had to meet her at nine p.m., a time when he'd much rather have been . . . well, doing just about anything else.

Tall and thin (Cathy described her as bony), with a hawkish nose that made her look put upon even when she smiled, Chadwick was the senior senator from Arizona. She was serving her third term, backed by family money courtesy of her grandfather's Scottsdale real estate fortune. One of the Senate "cardinals," she chaired the subcommittee for Homeland Security on Senate

Appropriations. As such, she wielded an inordinate amount of power, which she often used to lambast anything Ryan was trying to accomplish.

She had, however, proven herself a patriot and worked with the administration when she'd been approached and blackmailed by agents of Beijing. In that brief moment, her interests and Ryan's had been the same. She'd warned him that such a situation was a once-in-a-blue-moon event— and then the pharma bill came along.

"My people are basically for it," she said, settling herself in on the couch across from him like she planned to stay awhile. She kicked off a shoe and let it dangle on the tip of her toe. Cathy did that, Ryan thought, and she did it much better. "You're going to have a problem with Iowa and a couple other states with pharma manufacturing bases. The big guys aren't too keen on generics as it is, and having our generic medicine cabinet so close to home in the Caribbean sorta bugs them. On my side of the aisle, we're happy for more access to healthcare in the form of generic drugs, but opponents are calling this—"

Ryan raised a hand. "I know, I know, capitalism for the poor working stiff, socialism for the wealthy business owners."

"And they have a point," Chadwick said. "But we can get around it. It needs to happen, and if we both—avowed political enemies that we are—put our faces on the bill, then it's got at least a breath of hope to pass."

Ryan took a sip of coffee. "I need to ask you. Why?"

"Why am I cooperating?"

"To be blunt, yes."

Chadwick gave a little shrug. "The stats are all over the place on the subject of where this country gets our medication, but you know the Twain saw, 'There are three kinds of lies: lies, damned lies, and statistics.' A hell of a lot of people on your side of the aisle point to eighty percent of our drugs being from China and India. The PRC definitely produces a large percentage of the chemical precursors to various drugs, but some scholars who are much smarter than you or me point out the number of finished drugs from India or China, while still substantial, is a good deal lower than eighty percent."

She paused for effect.

"I'll bite," Ryan said. "Where are you putting the number?"

"That's the problem," Chadwick said. "No one seems to know. One side says eighty or ninety percent, the other side says that's not correct but can't counter with a real number. That's what bugs me." She took a long, slow breath and then exhaled slowly. "Truth is, my aunt almost died from a urinary tract infection. The generic antibiotics she got from her corner drugstore didn't even come close to touching it." She leaned forward as if confiding something extra-important. "Made in India, by the way. I paid for an independent test and the results came back with less than half of the active ingredient her medication should have contained."

"Is your aunt okay?"

Chadwick closed her eyes and shook her head. "It is really difficult to dislike you . . . She's better now, once we got her real antibiotics."

"Which plant?" Ryan asked. "The generics, I mean."

"MalhotraMed," Chadwick said. "Here's my point. The United States needs more pharmaceutical production plants, not fewer, and they must be nearer our shores, where we can get over and perform timely inspections."

"I'm with you," Ryan said. "Obviously. I'll mention MalhotraMed to Secretary Kapoor and see what data she has."

"It won't be much," Chadwick said. "I've already done a deep dive. FDA Inspections is a bureaucratic nightmare."

"So she says," Ryan said. "I'll check anyway. It's information we'll need to know to move this bill along."

Chadwick reached down and slipped the errant shoe back over her heel, scooting forward in her seat.

"I meant to lead with this," she said. "But I was

so sorry to hear about Tony Hargrave. He was a genuinely wonderful soul. One of the few in Washington."

"Thank you," Ryan said, knowing Chadwick had more on her mind.

"I assume you're working diligently to find someone to fill the office."

"There are many smart people working on that right now," Ryan said.

"Good," Chadwick said. "What with all the spot fires springing up of late, I think it's important to the American people to get some good news."

"Spot fires?"

"You know what I mean," Chadwick said. "Ransomware attacks by the dozen, all those bothersome videos."

Ryan scoffed. "Seems like deepfakes would be just the sort of thing that worked in your favor to discredit me not very long ago."

"Oh, it still works in my favor," Chadwick said. "At least as far as slowing down some of your politics, but that doesn't mean I condone it." She rested her arm along the back of the couch and toyed with the fabric absentmindedly. "Do you have a short list yet?"

"Getting shorter," Ryan said.

"Anyone I'd know?"

Ryan had to smile at that. He looked at his watch and stood.

"My cue to leave," Chadwick said, taking the time to smooth a frayed bit of thread on the upholstery before getting to her feet. "Just remember, whoever you nominate has to get through the Senate, which means getting through me. We're working on this Pharma Independence Bill, but we're not friendly enough for you to ramrod someone through."

"Wouldn't dream of it," Ryan said, half expecting her to slither out the door.

27

The bald one went down fast, much more quickly than Adara expected. His two Japanese partners were not so easy.

Foreign tourists were not uncommon around Tokyo Station, but Baldy was a professional and gave Ryan a once-over when he approached. Ryan feigned a limp, attempting to appear less threatening—a tough thing to do with his imposing height.

Adara pushed the map toward Baldy with her left hand, asking for help finding Shibuya. "... it's ... like ... supposed to be the busiest crosswalk in the world. Who'd come to Japan and not want to see that ..."

Baldy retreated a couple steps in the shadows, instinctively seeking the cover of the parking garage. He tugged Adara along with him, as if to get her away from Ryan.

She hit him with the slock when he turned away, hard, putting her hips into it. A baseball weighed about five ounces, and the sock-rocks were roughly two baseballs. They impacted Baldy at the base of his skull, a rabbit punch.

Swaying on his feet, he had enough wherewithal to turn, blinking stupidly at Adara and
then at Midas as he ran past, heading for the
door. Jack used the two feet of pipe to great effect, connecting with the same spot Adara had,
then, on the backswing, creasing the side of the
man's bald head as he fell—out cold, his brain
rapidly swelling if it hadn't already been detached
from its stem. Blood ran from his nose as if from
an open faucet.

A bark from Midas and the sound of the door
flying open jerked Adara's attention behind her.
The first Japanese soldier all but flew out the
door, intent on saving his partner. Midas cupped
the back of his head and shoved as he went
by, throwing the startled man off balance. He
caught the second man by both shoulders, pulling him into a knee to the groin before tossing
him over the side of the stoop to meet Jack.

"Leaving 'em to you!" Midas said, as he grabbed
the door before it shut and ducked inside, disappearing up the stairs.

The entry was on a raised concrete stoop, three
steps but well over two feet high. For whatever
reason, treads on stairs in Japan were often longer, the risers taller, forcing the walker to take a
step and a half before dropping to the next level.
It worked to Adara's advantage, forcing the first
Japanese man to take the quicker route straight

over the edge without having to stutter-step down. The added height made him feel superior, and he raised his fist on an outstretched arm in a sort of Superman punch, aimed directly at Adara's face.

Grounded, she stepped to the side like a matador and swung the sock with everything she had. The blow was a glancing one, staggering her opponent but not even coming close to taking him out of the fight.

Behind her, Jack was dealing with the new arrival. Adara could hear the pipe clanging when it hit bone. She was too busy with her own opponent to check his status. She swung again, an uppercut this time, intent on looping the slock and catching him on the jaw when momentum brought it around again. The man faded like a boxer, bobbing to allow the weapon to whoosh by mere inches over his canted head. He regained his footing quickly, drawing an expandable baton from behind his back and flicking it open with an ominous crack. He looked back and forth from Adara to Jack, yelling encouragement to his friend. His jaw tensed when he glanced over his shoulder to see that Midas had made it inside.

"What do you want?" he asked in perfect English, absent any trace of an accent. A trickle of blood ran from his ear where the slock had hit him.

"I want you to put that baton down," Adara said.

"I will put it down your throat," the man hissed.

Jack tagged his opponent in the neck. He fell to his knees, allowing Jack to rush in and jab the pipe into Adara's man, impacting him above the kidney. It didn't penetrate, but it hurt like hell, and gave Adara the opening she needed.

The Japanese man swung wildly with the baton.

Adara smashed her slock into his good ear. During training Clark hammered into them not to be married to any one weapon or attack, but to be ready to exploit any weakness an opponent offered them.

Rather than attempting another swing, Adara dropped the sock and leapt onto the Japanese man's back, snaking one arm around his throat and locking it in place with the other in a rear naked choke. In the same movement, she wrapped his torso with her legs, hooking him with her heels so he wore her like a backpack. He staggered backward with the added weight, twisting his head just enough to continue getting air. The man wasn't large, not much taller than Adara, but he was incredibly powerful, with a bull neck and strong fingers that dug into her arm, attempting to peel it away from his throat. He pedaled backward, aiming for the concrete stoop, planning, no doubt, to fall into the sharp concrete edge—and break Adara's spine.

She cranked hard, bending her wrist inward so the base of her thumb ground into the man's carotid. His grip against her arm loosened a fraction. He stumbled, swayed, pounding against her forearm with his fists in an attempt to free himself.

Then he humped up, going rigid like he'd tripped or—

Jack drove the length of metal pipe into the man's belly. This time it went in, penetrating like a spear. The man flailed wildly, hitting her in the forearm again and again. She held fast, squeezing, taking every inch of space as it was offered until she'd robbed him of blood and oxygen to his brain until he fell. Ryan withdrew the bloodied pipe and swatted at the man's hand, to Adara's surprise, knocking away an out-the-front blade he must have drawn while she was choking him.

She slid to the ground, feeling a sudden heat in her arm.

Jack grabbed the man by his forelock and slammed his head twice against the concrete deck for good measure before rushing to Adara's side.

"Where's your guy?" she asked, feeling queasy.

"He's down for good," Jack said, giving no further explanation. He frowned as he examined the gaping slashes on her forearm. "He got you good."

Somehow, he'd tagged her on the cheek as well, cutting her almost to the bone without her even knowing she'd been hit.

"Missed the major arteries," Adara said, grateful to see blood dripping and not arcing out of her butchered arm. But it was dripping **a lot**. "Our priority now is to get these guys hidden behind a car. For all we know some ramen delivery guy has already called the police."

"Shadows give us plenty of cover," Jack said as he helped drag the three men behind a Toyota van and deposit them in a pile. "Unless someone heard the scuffle, I think we dodged a bullet. This entire dance went down in about twenty seconds."

Adara's phone began to buzz in her pocket. She fished it out with her good hand. It was Midas calling from a hardline—and he was evidently watching them on camera.

"Are you guys coming up or not? There's some stuff you're definitely going to want to see."

28

Midas buzzed Adara and Jack through two inner doors, one at the bottom of the stairway and another that led into the main rooms at the top. He had the two hackers sitting on a low futon couch when they arrived. Both Japanese, one male, one female, they looked as though they'd been plucked from a university campus. The girl, whose name was Takako, wore a pair of lime-green cutoff overalls. Brightly green rubber bands kept her hair up in perky dog ears, one of which was dyed cotton-candy pink, the other deep red, giving her a startling, Harley Quinn sort of look. In contrast, her hacking partner, a boy of nineteen named Hatoru, wore a conservative blue three-button polo and khaki slacks. His dour expression and black glasses made him look like he would have been carrying a slide rule and wearing a pocket protector a few decades earlier.

The actual hacker space was small, maybe ten by ten, with a folding plastic table and four laptops attached to larger flat screens. The adjacent room was half again as large but stuffed with banks of computers that were, as Gavin Biery had expected, mining Bitcoin. A clear drape of plastic sheeting hung over the doorway so the air-conditioning had to cool the hardware in only one room. Empty food containers and cellophane wrappers formed a mountain in the back corner. In the opposite corner, with a good view of the door and a wall-mounted video monitor, were two soft leather chairs that had obviously been where the off-duty guard posted himself.

Takako was by far the more talkative of the two. **"Nan de, son'nani jikan ga kakatta no?"** she sniped, fuming. **Why did it take you so long?**

Adara glared back. She'd taped the wound on her face and was now wrapping gauze from her backpack around her wounded arm, in no mood to be schooled by some pink-haired hacker punk. **"Nan da, yo?"**

Takako rolled her eyes and threw her hand dramatically over her forehead. "We have been leaving tracks for you to find for over a week," she said in English, which was better than Adara's Japanese.

"Over a week?" Midas said. "The ransomware attacks have been going on almost three."

Hatoru nodded. "The men who had us, the men we saw you kill on camera, they watched us constantly. The bald one knew enough about code that he could check our work."

"Shoulder-surfing every minute," Takako said.

"It is impossible to work with someone staring over you like that. If they knew how to do it, then why did they bother to take us?"

"This is pretty skookum," Midas said, looking at the setup.

"I don't know what that means," Takako said. "Skookum?"

"It means really good," Midas said, still looking over the computers. "I'm going to have to get someone who knows a hell of a lot more than I do about this." Each laptop and phone got its own Faraday bag that Midas had brought along for that purpose. The metal mesh liners in the bags prevented their contents from sending or receiving any Wi-Fi or radio signal. The devices might still have a booby-trap command to wipe the data if certain keys were pressed or if the wrong passwords were entered, but if they were removed from the Faraday bags in a digitally secure room, outside actors wouldn't be able to control them remotely.

Takako raised her hand like a student in class. "Oh, oh, that would be me," she said, sneering. "I know what to do."

Adara finished tying off the bandage. "Oh, no, you don't. You're not going anywhere near that hardware."

Takako smacked her own forehead. "**Bakayaro!** If we wanted to shred everything it would have been shredded already."

"Be that as it may," Adara said. She took a seat in the leather chair, blinking to clear blurred vision. The massive adrenaline dump and blood loss made her feel woozy.

Jack found a stash of the little Oronamin C drinks like the ones Midas seemed to like and peeled back the top on one.

It was small so Adara slammed two in a row, feeling the sugars give her system the comforting jolt it needed. "I need clothes that don't have blood on them," she said to the girl. "You're about my size."

Takako shrugged. "They bought me these clothes," she said, pulling at the overalls. "So I didn't stink, they said. You can have them if you want. I prefer my own clothes."

Adara groaned. "Well, I can't go out like this." She motioned for the girl to step into the next room with her.

"So they took you against your will?" Midas asked.

"Yes," the boy said. "Our parents believe us to be at university."

Takako stuck her head around the corner, half dressed. "And our friends think we have snuck away together to our favorite love hotel in Shinjuku."

The boy smiled, his face flushing crimson.

"Who were they working for?" Jack asked. "These men who took you?"

"We saw only these three," he said. "No one else."

"Their names?" Midas asked.

Hatoru looked over his shoulder and leaned forward as if to answer, but Takako returned and met his eye. He fell back against the futon and shut his mouth. Takako flopped down beside him, now wearing a loose pullover sweater and cutoff jeans that were so short the pockets hung below the legs.

"We never heard their names," she said.

"At first I thought they were going to take the ransom money we made for them and just kill us," Hatoru whispered.

Takako finished his thought. "We have been watching, listening to the way they speak. They do not even care about the money. I think they just want to cause harm to your country. But they were still going to kill us. Soon."

Midas was on the phone with Gavin, his back turned, speaking in rapid, hushed tones.

Adara heard a zipping sound, like duct tape being peeled off a desk, just before Midas turned to face them.

Takako and Hatoru heard it, too. Both sat up straighter.

"Okay," Midas said. "We're taking the laptops with us."

Takako started to protest.

Midas lifted a Glock pistol from behind the

stack of Faraday bags and pointed it at Takako. "I'm surprised they left you with your very own handgun within such easy reach."

Takako raised both hands. "Okay, okay, okay . . . We weren't prisoners," she said. "Not to begin with. More like contractors. But they **were** going to kill us, I swear it. Hatoru heard them talking this morning about bringing in another hacker to take over when we were . . . you know, out of the pic—"

"Guys!" Adara said, nodding to the security monitors. "We have company."

They watched as a Japanese man got out of a dark Toyota sedan inside the garage and then paused as if sniffing the air. Looking back and forth, he stooped to examine a pool of blood, and then followed drag marks out of the frame toward where Adara and Jack had stashed the bodies. He appeared a moment later, his movements jerkier, agitated. He looked directly at the camera above the door for a moment—long enough for Midas to snap a photo of his face on the monitor—and then jumped back in his car and sped away.

"This is not good," Hatoru whispered.

"That guy is probably on the phone right now," Jack said. "Calling in some cleaners. We need to scrub the security archives, kill the cameras, and haul ass."

"First part's done," Midas said, clicking the keyboard below the monitor.

Adara nodded to the two hackers. "What about them?"

Midas stood, backpack full of Faraday bags over his shoulder, and held up a roll of duct tape—presumably the one used to tape the pistol under the computer desk.

Jack went into the bathroom and shut the door to make a call.

Hatoru began to nod frantically while Midas taped his hands behind his back. "Your partner is correct. That man will call someone to come and kill us. You must let us go. We are otaku, gamers." A tear ran down his cheek. "We did not wish to hurt anyone."

Midas gave him a hard pinch on the fleshy back of his arm, under his biceps, bringing a pitiful yowl.

"Losing millions of dollars hurts," Midas said. "Those people on the train you hacked died . . ." He pinched the kid again, bringing another yelp. "Dying hurts. Stealing shit is bad." **Pinch.** "Killing people is bad." **Pinch.**

Haruto's chest heaved, huffing and puffing between snotty sobs like he was going to hyperventilate.

"So." Midas looked him dead in the eye. "Unless you want to tell us who is behind all this, shut your mouth and take a seat. I think I speak for every person on the other end of the computers you're scamming when I say I don't give a shit if that guy sends his goons to saw you both into pieces and drop you into Tokyo Bay."

Midas raised his hand as if to administer another pinch, but the kid jerked away, falling backward into the futon, quivering.

Takako glared. "You are very cruel man."

Adara grabbed the tape from Midas and spun the girl around to restrain her. "Get used to it."

Ryan stepped out of the bathroom and gave a shrugging thumbs-up. "We leave them here."

Haruto began to thrash. "They will murder us!"

Takako looked up, blinking doe eyes, trying to coax up some tears. "**You** are killing us."

"You did this to yourselves," Midas said. "And it's probably gonna hurt . . ."

Sirens wailed in the distance, growing closer as the Campus operators rounded the block two minutes later toward the Marunouchi side of Tokyo Station. Midas walked twenty yards behind. In addition to checking in with Chavez, Ryan had called 110, Japan's emergency number. With over forty thousand police officers in the city, and the Japanese propensity to yield to authority, response time would be near instantaneous.

"You were kind of harsh," Adara said to Midas over her earbud. The bright green overalls brought her plenty of stares from passersby, but not nearly as much as her blood-soaked clothes would have.

"My nana lost over thirty grand to scammers," he said. "Those pukes just made me think of what happened to her."

"Surprising Chavez wanted them left for the cops," Adara said.

"Mary Pat is looping in the FBI legal attaché and the Agency station chief as we speak. They'll be all over this."

Hi-Lo sirens began to scream around the corner, responding in a swarm.

Adara picked up her pace, falling in with the crowd of commuters entering the packed train station. "They're going to give descriptions of us." The odor of perfume shops and bakeries drifted with the push–pull tide of tens of thousands of people.

Shoulder to shoulder with Jack, she looked directly at him while they walked. "Maybe Mary Pat's shop can do something with their phones. You took photos of their faces?"

Ryan groaned. "I did."

"So you know what you have to do, right?" Adara asked.

"I know." Jack groaned again. "I already texted her and told her we wanted to meet and show her some photos."

A pinched expression crossed Adara's face, like she'd eaten a snow cone too fast. "You didn't call her? Jack! You just sent her a text? After not talking to her for how many months?"

"I don't know," he said. "A few."

"No communication and then a text out of the blue?"

Jack's phone buzzed in his hand as Yukiko Monzaki of the Japanese Public Security Intelligence Agency replied.

Adara leaned closer, attempting to read the message. "What did she say?"

Jack jerked away, slowing his pace, letting the crowd of perturbed commuters part and flow around on either side of him. He groaned a third time, like an old man getting up from a soft chair, then read the message aloud.

" 'I am busy . . . You will have to come to me.' "

"When?" Midas asked.

"Five-thirty this evening," Jack said, reading the next text. "An address in Akihabara."

"Five-thirty." Adara sighed. "That's the best news I've heard all day."

She pushed the memories of the fight in the garage to the back of her mind and focused instead on the hot shower and soft bed that awaited her. But first they would all split up inside the train station, ducking into different bathrooms along the way, and change into different hats, windbreakers, and parachute pants they all had stashed in their daypacks. They'd run at least an hour of SDR—surveillance-detection routes—before meeting back at the hotel. With any luck, they'd be able to elude any facial-recognition software and have enough time at the hotel for Adara to stitch up her wounds and maybe even grab a nap.

29

The news ticker on the side of Harjit Malhotra's computer screen said that #POTUS, #President, and #JackRyan were trending.

Malhotra bounced in his seat between sips of strong cashew liquor and scrolled through every social media platform he could think of. Every other tweet was something about the American president.

He is failing.

How can he be trusted?

Is he the man everyone has long believed him to be?

He was absolutely worthless at protecting the country from these hackers!

America deserves better!

Piss pour leadership. (Malhotra wondered if that typo might have been on purpose.)

There were, of course, tweets and posts voicing full-throated support, but as in life, detractors outweighed vocal champions exponentially.

He watched streaming videos of Ryan flirting with women, disrespecting the flag, and quipping glibly to a cabal of wealthy businessmen about the millions he'd made by playing the markets. The videos were fake, but there were enough of them to sow seeds of doubt. Human beings would believe even the most outlandish lie as long as it fell close to what they wished to be true.

And still, the fool, Ryan, pressed his protectionist pharmaceutical bill. The man was a runaway polo pony that would not turn no matter how much you goaded it with the spurs.

Malhotra muted the sound on his computer and looked up at the Bengal tiger across his office.

"That idiot American President has made millions through shrewd investments," he said to the beast. "But I have made a few shrewd investments of my own." Malhotra shrugged, certain the tiger understood. "A few million dollars can buy you a billion-dollar war if those dollars are put in the hands of a military man with the balls to make things happen."

30

Dr. Monte Harper's local assistant stood beside him in the felt yurt. Hollow-cheeked, with a shy, inquisitive face, the young girl hunched over the supine patient, fly-swatter in one weather-chapped hand and an umbrella in the other. A red scarf draped her head, but her smile remained uncovered. In other parts of Afghanistan she might be in a burka and forbidden to go to school. She certainly would not have been assisting a male doctor, let along speaking freely with him.

There was never enough food in the remote Wakhan Corridor of eastern Afghanistan, but at least here she could go to school. Her name was Laleh and she was thirteen.

Harper adjusted the light on his microscope to illuminate the interior of the unblinking eye that stared up at him, held gruesomely wide by a wire speculum. He made a tiny frown-shaped incision through the white of the eye with an instrument called a crescent blade, small, keeping the fluid inside the chamber. The cataract-damaged lens would come out through this tiny opening and an artificial one would be introduced in its place. He'd just tunneled into the interior when Laleh suddenly spoke.

He'd have to talk to her about that.

Along with her native Khik zik, she spoke Tajik, Pashto, and better Russian than Harper, who was self-taught. In another part of the world, she might have her sights on medical school. Here, she would milk sheep, churn butter, and cook her family's food over a fire of burning yak dung.

"Soldiers are coming down the valley on horses," she said. "I heard the men talking. The trail from the north must be clear enough to pass."

Winter snows had receded early this year, allowing Wakhi shepherds to make the twenty-mile migration, or kuch, with their herds of yaks and fat-bottomed sheep from their wheat fields below to the high valleys of the Big Pamir over four thousand meters in altitude. The junction of three of the world's highest mountain ranges—the Pamirs, the Hindu Kush, and the Karakoram—was known as the Pamir Knot. The Bam-I-Dunya, or Roof of the World.

The Wakhi spent their winters in the valley of the Wakhan Corridor, a thin buffer strip of land bordered by Tajikistan, Pakistan, and China. Carved out in an agreement between Great Britain and Russia during the spy vs. spy era Rudyard Kipling dubbed "the Great Game," the Wakhan Corridor was meant to ensure that the British India and Russian holdings in Central Asia did not share a common border. It was an afterthought to most Afghans—remote, small—some two hundred miles long and forty miles wide at its widest point, and surrounded by toothy, cathedral-like peaks, many of which were perpetually covered with snow and ice. The people here had never had to deal with the Taliban or terrorism. Their fight was to stay alive, to deal with the wolves and bears that preyed on their flocks, to eke out a living in a place so barren that yak dung was the only source of fuel for cooking fires. Naan bread and shirchoy—salted milk tea—made the bulk of their diet. Intense glare, dazzling snowfields, and thin air were the perfect recipe for early blindness due to cataracts. One in five mothers died during childbirth. Infant mortality was so high that many families did not settle on a name for their children until they were three or four years old. The average life expectancy was thirty-five.

It was the perfect place for the Harpers to spend some time.

Dr. Harper glanced away from his patient long enough to catch a tremor of worry in the girl's eyes.

It was always something. Harper and his wife were here in the summer grazing camp known as Vagd Boi with the full knowledge and support of both the Afghan and the United States governments. They'd come on their own dime, donating medical care and expertise, and still some warlord was about to ask them for baksheesh—a payoff.

"Are you sure they are soldiers?" he asked.

"Yes," Laleh said. "They came down from Tajikistan last year, to help the Afghan Border Police. A patrol once bought a yak from my mother but they did not pay enough for it. What are you to tell a man who wants to buy a yak for a bargain price if all you have are stones?" She began to breathe heavily, causing the umbrella to wobble and drip.

Melting snow from an overnight dusting rained from the yurt's heavy felt roof, making Lelah's umbrella crucial. Wet yak hair and the dung fires smoldering in adjacent yurts gave the makeshift operating theater a barnyard feel, necessitating the flyswatter. Bright battery-powered lights, packed in by yak and horse along with the rest of the equipment, illuminated the hazy interior of the yurt, making the red throw rugs and pillows all the more vibrant.

"Maybe the soldiers come for eye surgery," the girl said. She'd made it clear she wanted to be a doctor herself. Nizari Ismaili Shia were relatively progressive when it came to educating their daughters, but the backbreaking work of field and dung fire made more than a few years of school a distant dream. Harper's wife hoped to change that, and he hoped to help her do it.

"Perhaps," Harper said, focusing now on his patient's cloudy lens.

The procedure was known as SICS, small-incision cataract surgery, and it gave sight back to tens of thousands of rural people, most of whom could barely afford to feed themselves, much less spare the costs of travel for a medical procedure of any kind. It was not uncommon for prospective patients to hear by word of mouth that the Harpers were in the area and hike many miles to visit their makeshift clinic. Often, they were the first doctors they had seen in their lives.

"All the way from China," the girl said. "A far, far journey."

Harper withdrew the tiny blade from his patient's eye. "I thought you said they were Tajik?"

Laleh nodded, sending droplets of snowmelt off the edge of the umbrella. She adjusted so as not to get the patient wet. "The men say. Chinese soldiers on horses coming down from Tajikistan."

"How far out?"

She shrugged, sending another shower of drips. "Not far away now," she said. "On the switchbacks."

"The dogs will tell us," Harper said. Chinese military coming across the border from Tajikistan could prove problematic. Still, not only had he come out here to help people, he'd come for the adventure, too.

Both Harpers were graduates of Johns Hopkins medical school, she in obstetrics and gynecology, he in ophthalmology. They'd met in med school, found time to get to know each other in those rare moments without looming exams or clinical rotations. She'd matched with a residency program at Harvard, while he'd stayed in Baltimore. Four hundred miles may as well have been four thousand. Residency was a gut punch compared to med school, with little time for sleep, let alone study for frequent monthly tests and case presentation, but they eked and robbed and clawed a few scant moments to pen letters to each other at least once a week, often after a double or even triple shift. Naomi kept them all, numbered and cataloged in a three-ring binder.

Almost every letter (but for the ones where Monte waxed particularly poetic and lovelorn) contained at least some reference to how they wanted to someday give back, to send themselves on medical missions. He didn't have a death wish, not at all, but felt it was among the greatest of sins to cling to life so tightly while others suffered. His wife was no better, living by the mantra "What could we do if we were not afraid?" Their children called her an enabler. They weren't monks. She drove a Porsche 911 Turbo Carrera and he was building a snazzy Rotor X helicopter in the shop beside their home outside of Annapolis. But from the beginning, even before they'd had the good fortune to find each other, each had dreamed of travel to foreign lands and using their medical skills to help the less fortunate.

Now, thirty-five years, two daughters, and one grandson later, Dr. Monte Harper and Dr. Naomi Harper designated two months out of every year to rolling up their sleeves in the poorest areas of the world. Supplies and equipment were often provided through grants, but travel was always at their own expense. Both pushing sixty, they were relatively long in the tooth for the rigors of travel to places where a toilet was a spot behind a large stone and toilet paper was a smaller stone in the same spot, but both had decided early on that, like Jack London said, it was better to go out as ashes than dust.

Harper had both volunteered at the renowned Aravind Eye Hospital in southern India and worked under the direction of Dr. Sanduk Ruit at the Tilganga Eye Hospital in Kathmandu, Nepal. And everywhere he went, there were women having babies, in desperate need of post-natal care and training.

Critics at the hospital in Kabul had said the paucity of human beings in the Wakhan Corridor made it an unlikely candidate for the Harpers' time. Better to stay in the city, where they had an almost endless number of patients and, for the most part, working toilets.

As always, they smiled, listened patiently, and then did what they'd always intended to do.

The journey from Kabul to the remote grazing camps took three days, by charter plane, bongo truck, and the last twenty miles by yak train, north over the still icy mountain passes into the Big Pamir, some ten miles from the border with Tajikistan. Two weeks in, their trip was almost at an end. Naomi was ready to go see their grandchild, but Monte had fallen into the melancholy he always did when he was about to leave a place he might never return to see again.

The surgeries were fast, fifteen minutes if you knew what you were doing, faster in more sterile conditions without flyswatters and umbrellas. Harper had done thousands. He was just finishing up when his wife pulled aside the felt flap that served as a door and entered the yurt. She was dressed in mountaineering clothes, puffy down jacket over fleece, trekking pants, and a wool beanie. She'd traded her heavy boots for a pair of Keen trail shoes while they were in camp. Downright short compared to Monte's six-foot-one, Naomi was a tad on the round side. He reminded her often, and quite seriously, that he much preferred quarter horses to Thoroughbreds when it came to conformation—at which point she usually smacked him with whatever was at hand.

She tiptoed to see where he was in the procedure, and when she was sure he didn't have a knife in someone's eye, she held up a satellite phone.

Harper bandaged the patient, who was Laleh's mother, and helped her sit up. The poor woman had had nine children and Laleh was the only one who had survived. As tragic as the circumstances around him, he couldn't help but smile at the sight of the sat phone in Naomi's hand.

"Becca?" he said, the grin growing larger.

His wife nodded and then stepped outside. Harper gave postop instructions to Lelah and her mother and then followed his wife out.

Done with his final surgery, he grabbed his watch, a Breitling Emergency, from his pocket and snapped it on his wrist. Naomi had given it to him for their thirtieth anniversary. He'd grown accustomed to the hefty weight of it and he felt its absence each time he removed it during surgeries. Flabbergastingly expensive, Naomi had reasoned that they traveled to so many remote and dangerous locales that Monte needed a sixteen-thousand-dollar watch with a built-in emergency transponder. He wore it dutifully, and didn't have the heart to tell her that it might get his arm chopped off in some parts of the world.

The mounted men lined out on the switchbacks

up the valley, inching closer as Harper took the sat phone and caught up on all the news from his eldest daughter, also an ophthalmologist at Wilmer Eye Institute in Baltimore. He listened mostly, as one did to stay in the good graces of a successful twentysomething professional who was good enough to call from time to time but was not particularly interested in anything or anyone but her own goings-on.

Harper counted fourteen horses working their way down the switchbacks toward the valley floor and felt yurts and ancient stone corrals of Vagd Boi. Eleven of the animals had riders; the remaining three were pack animals. He thought it odd that the shepherds had been able to tell the approaching people were soldiers, let alone identify them as Chinese—until he saw the rifles slung over each rider's shoulder.

". . . Dad, are you still there?" his daughter said.

"Yes, yes, sweetheart," Harper said. "We start home tomorrow."

"Mom filled me in on the latest. Pretty shitty about those meds those poor people are getting out there. Mom says they have plenty of opium, though."

Harper studied the riders, working out what they might be up to, saying nothing.

"Sorry, Dad," his daughter said. "Insensitive joke."

"No, no, that's fine." He gave an emphatic

nod, though his daughter was on the phone and couldn't see it. "The meds they get here are trash. The only clinic in the valley does a yeoman's job, but . . ."

"That's what Mom was telling me," Becca said. "You're still going to speak at the ARVO conference in San Antonio? Dr. Ryan was asking me if I'd heard anything."

"I hope to," he said. "The trek out is downhill, so theoretically it should be faster. We hope to catch the first plane out of Kabul."

"Good," his daughter said. "I told Dr. Ryan about the knockoff generics. Pissed her off, too. Pretty sure her husband wants to talk to you."

Harper's attention was momentarily pulled away from the horses at that. "You're breaking up," he joked. "I thought you just said the President of the United States wants to talk to me about the bad batch of antibiotics . . ."

The soldiers were getting closer now, a half-mile away on the flat, trotting across the valley, dwarfed by the toothy peaks that rose up all around them. Afghan and Kyrgyz ponies could run at altitudes that would choke a mortal horse. It was nearing noon and the shepherds were beginning to drive their animals in for a midday milking. A flock of sheep scattered at the soldiers' approach, some of them running toward the edge of a rock precipice. A boy of twelve named Shambe raised his walking stick and shouted something. The nearest soldier must not have liked what he said. His horse humped up, spurred into action, and wheeled left, racing toward the boy as if to run him down.

"What the hell?" Harper whispered under his breath.

"Sorry, Dad," his daughter said. "I can't hear you."

"Nothing, sweetie," Harper said, distant, watching the horse bear down on the cowering boy. "Listen . . . early departure tomorrow . . . Got to run."

"Okay," she said. "Can I talk to M—"

Harper folded the antenna and stuffed the phone into his back pocket, locked on to the scene that was unfolding in front of him on the Roof of the World.

31

The soldier turned his horse at the last instant, kicking the young shepherd in the face with a boot as he rode by. The boy fell hard, his dog barking in a frenzy.

Naomi gathered herself up to bolt and go help the child, but Harper grabbed the back of her down jacket and pulled her tight beside him.

"Look," he said. "He's getting up."

"He could still be concussed," she said, shivering despite her down jacket and insulated pants. She glared at the approaching soldiers with the practiced frown of one who had raised teenage daughters.

Shambe's father and uncle ran to check on him.

Harper stifled the urge to run out himself. "Let his family handle it. We'll look him over when he gets here."

A murmur ran through the gathered crowd at the sudden violence. The yurts soon sprouted women in colorful red headscarves and dresses. Men came in from their flocks. Soon, over fifty people had crowded around the Harpers and the village headman.

"Assholes," Naomi said, eyes flashing daggers at the camouflaged men bouncing on the backs of lanky mountain horses. "This must be what it felt like when Genghis Khan and his hordes came riding in." She cocked her head slightly, squinting to get a better look. "What do you think they have on the pack horses?"

Ali, the village headman, heaved a long sigh. He was one of the few in Vagd Boi who spoke English.

"Guns," he said. "Big guns."

Naomi turned to look directly at her husband. "What on earth would they have to shoot at way the hell and gone out here? What do you think their game is?"

"I have no idea," Harper said.

They didn't have long to wait.

A stocky Chinese man wearing dark sunglasses led the way into the village. His horse, an angular gray with long legs and a dished Arabian face, stopped the moment he lifted the reins, snorting, looking grateful to get a moment's rest. Athletic and apparently accustomed to spending time on horseback, he stood easily in the stirrups, stretching, surveying the village before he settled back into his saddle. He folded his hands across the pommel and peered down at the lowly people who remained on foot. Harper judged him to be in his fifties.

The other soldiers remained mounted as well.

Two of them looked to be Tajik, including the one who had put his boot to Shambe. Harper had to pat his wife on the arm to keep her from flying at the guy's face. They were all dressed for the cold in thick camouflaged wool and heavy boots. Each was armed with a rifle, but they kept the things slung as if no one there was worth the effort.

The leader peeled off his wool hat, revealing closely cropped gunmetal hair. His cracked lips were ringed with white zinc salve, making him look like a baby yak just off the teat. Dark glacier glasses shielded his eyes from the sun, made more intense in the thin air.

"I am Colonel Tu Jian of the People's Liberation Army," he said in perfect English. "Western Theater Command, Xinjiang." He nodded toward the soldier who'd kicked Shambe. "This is my associate Captain Abdulin of the Armed Forces of the Republic of Tajikistan."

Since the colonel was speaking English, Harper addressed him directly.

"Colonel," he said. "What brings you to Afghanistan?"

"I come as Captain Abdulin's guest," he said, without a hint of irony.

Harper raised a wary eye at the other armed men. "And all the soldiers?"

Colonel Tu smiled graciously. "They are with me."

Naomi scoffed. "Guests of guests should not invite guests. How about you tell me why Captain Boot to the Head had to kick that child?"

"Captain Abdulin's business is his business. It is not mine."

"Bullshit!" Naomi said. "These are peaceful people. They deserve—"

Colonel Tu threw back his head and laughed. "It is a pity that we do not all receive what we deserve."

"No kidding," Naomi said.

The smile bled from Tu's windburned face. "You are the Americans? The Harpers?"

Monte's heart skipped a beat. Naomi squeezed his hand. Their humanitarian mission was in all the newspapers and online, so it didn't come as a surprise that this man knew their names. It was the way he said it. Formally. Like a proclamation.

"We are," Harper said. "Have you come for medical treatment?"

Colonel Tu shook his head slowly, as if addressing a small child. "Oh, no, no. I have come to protect **you**."

"Protect us from what?" Naomi asked, breathless, shivering so hard the nylon of her jacket sounded like it was whispering.

"From those who would not be happy with American spies who pretend to be physicians."

32

Japanese workers tended to stay late at the office, pushing the worst of rush hour further into the evening. The train was still unbelievably crowded, but there were not yet any white-gloved railway workers helping to smoosh people into the cars. Adara hung on to a plastic ring with her good arm, ignoring the Japanese pressed against her hip during a quick, four-minute subway ride on the Yamanote Line from Tokyo Station to Akihabara, where Yukiko Monzaki had insisted on meeting them. The team emerged at ground level into a teeming mass of people, tourists and locals alike, who had come to take part in the wonders of what many people called Electric Town.

Adara and Jack continued to walk together while Midas trailed at a distance, providing countersurveillance. They stayed connected via cell and earbuds.

Restive moans from hundreds of gamers, lined shoulder to shoulder at their "candy box" video machines, spilled onto the sidewalk each time a frosted door to this venue or that swung open to admit a new customer, mixing with the constant pinging clatter of pachinko machines that seemed to spill from everywhere but nowhere in particular. The savory smells of street food—takoyaki (balls of battered octopus), ramen, and yakitori—made Adara's mouth water as they walked. The earlier adrenaline dump had only piled on to her overall fatigue, leaving her half starved and stumbling along like a zombie.

The gash on her face was deep but straightforward, requiring nothing more than a painful scrubbing, some antiseptic, and superglue. The wounds on her arm were more problematic. She should have had someone else stitch it up for her—some of the inside stuff needed attention she didn't have time to give it. In the end, she scrubbed everything out as best she could, irrigated it with Betadine, and then superglued it shut as well. A few wraps of gauze and surgical tape would have to do for now. It was swelling some, but her fingers still worked, mostly.

She consoled herself that at least she'd have a hellaciously good scar on her cheek. Nothing wrong with her that another six or seven hours of sleep wouldn't cure—like that was ever going to happen.

Still, this place was amazing and she never got tired of it. Neon ruled, even in the early evening, giving the wide pedestrian streets a feel similar to being inside a Las Vegas casino—except the blue sky above these garish, towering buildings was real. It was a hotspot for what the Japanese called otaku culture—people with interests that consumed them, like anime, manga, and cosplay. Costumed players stood in front of opaquely windowed businesses, handing out flyers and beckoning passersby inside. About half of them were dressed like a fifteen-year-old boy's mental image of a French maid. Some added furry ears to their costumes.

"Everything around here is a transforming robot, a maid, or a transforming robot maid," Midas muttered over the phone. "Japanese men are weird as shit."

"That's hilarious," Adara said. "**Men** . . . hell, **human beings** are weird—wherever you go. People here are just willing to pull the curtain open a little wider so we all get a peek inside."

"Don't get me wrong," Midas groused. "Who among us hasn't been aroused by a sexy robot maid at least once in his life?"

Jack checked the moving map on his phone, showed it to Adara, and then gestured to a shadowed doorway beside a maid café that bathed in pink neon. The wooden placard screwed to the metal door said **Sugiyama** in Japanese script.

"This is it," Jack said. "Yuki said we should text and then come on up when we got here."

"I'll hang out on ground level," Midas said. "With all my new robot friends . . ."

"Be good," Adara said, and followed Jack through the door.

They were met immediately with a thunderous racket of crashing and stomping. Adara recognized the noise immediately as the sound of a dojo. The people upstairs were practicing the ancient martial art of kendo—charging at and striking each other about the head and chest with bamboo swords called shinai. Adara had taken a few classes from a sensei in Alexandria and found the experience exhilarating. There was a great deal of strategy to it, and points were given for aggression—which she knew from practical experience was crucial in actual battle.

As instructed, Jack sent Yuki a text letting her know they had arrived before trudging up the stairs.

They were greeted by the warm and humid air of a working gym, a place where bodies moved and sweated and sometimes bled. The dojo was relatively large, encompassing the entire level of the building that housed the maid café below. Above the dojo, accessible up a set of stairs in the café, was a pachinko parlor and several other businesses that had no signage. It was the perfect place for a member of the Public Security Intelligence Agency to practice the art of kendo without being associated with the police.

"There she is," Adara said, dipping her head toward a pretty Japanese woman in the far corner under a wall of calligraphy scrolls and a rack of wooden swords.

Like the other two dozen kendōka in the training hall, Yukiko was dressed in flowing blue hakama pantaloons, padded arm guards, and a lacquer chest protector. A blue cloth called a tenugui was wrapped around her head, holding back shoulder-length hair and protecting her scalp from the helmet she'd just removed and now carried under one arm. In her other hand, she clutched the bamboo shinai.

The benign smile she gave Adara faded when her eyes focused on Jack, and she began to stride toward them, bare feet gripping the wood floor, swishing in and out of the voluminous pantaloons. The outfit and her demeanor were eerily reminiscent of Darth Vader's.

Adara gave Jack a playful nudge. "I think she called you here to beat your ass with that stick."

"Are we sure I didn't die?" Ryan groused. "I'm pretty certain this is hell."

Yuki stopped when she reached them, smiled broadly at Adara, and then leaned forward as if bowing to an opponent during a kendo match. "It is good to see you again. Both of you." Then to Jack, "You say you need my help, after these many months."

"We do," Jack said, nodding, stammering just a little, a side of the smooth John Patrick Ryan, Jr., that Adara imagined few people ever got to see. "Yes. We . . . We think a discussion could be . . . mutually beneficial—"

"Have you ever fought with a shinai?" Yuki asked. She lifted the bamboo sword and clacked it backward against her own shoulder.

"Some," Jack said. "I suppose."

"Perhaps we should have a go, you and I, Jack-san," Yuki said. "How do you say it in America? For old times' sake . . ."

"Yuki—"

"Oh, it will be great fun." She waved away his excuses. "The path of the sword is a wonderful way to become reacquainted—footwork, that feeling of all-encompassing chaos during a violent attack . . . Do not worry about equipment. My friend, Jiro-kun, is about to go home for the evening. He is not quite as tall as you, but his armor should fit. I am sure he would not mind loaning it to you. You may use one of my swords."

Jack shot a look at Adara. "We really need to talk to you about something important."

"No doubt." Yukiko gave him a slow nod. "It has been a very long time since we spoke."

"It has," Jack said. "And I'm sorry about that."

She waved him off, grinning now, suppressing a laugh. "I am only joking, Jack! What is the saying? The phone rings both ways." She tapped him lightly on the forehead with the end of her bamboo sword. "I could have called you, but I became very busy with work. Adara-chan knows what I am talking about. We are nito-onna, she and I, women whose careers leave little time to iron our blouses—or to nurture a relationship."

Jack released a pent-up breath. "Yeah," he said, still stammering. "Yeah, I should have called, too."

"Is there someplace we could talk in private?" Adara asked. Watching Ryan twist in the wind was fun, but she was fading fast, wrinkled blouse or not.

"Of course," Yukiko said. "The sensei allows me to use his office from time to time for matters of import."

She led the way to a cramped private office not much larger than a closet, filled with wooden swords and bits of kendo gear. It was clear that this sensei preferred to be out on the dojo floor with his students over being cloistered away in an office.

Her face grew dark as Jack gave her a quick rundown about what had occurred at the hacker space. "Your CIA have already gotten themselves involved," she said, fully aware of the case. "I assume they know it was you who killed the men."

"The people who need to know know," Adara said.

Neither she nor Jack were particularly worried about Yukiko turning them in. They'd first met on an operation in Buenos Aires when the Japanese operative had shot a Paraguayan terrorist in the head under the noses of Argentine law enforcement.

"Have you seen the two dead men?" Jack asked.

Yukiko shook her head. "My agency had a representative at the scene," she said. "But Tokyo Metropolitan Police are handling it. Their Cybercrimes Division is looking at the hardware." She scanned Jack up and down with a narrow eye. "From what I am told, some appears to be missing. Am I to assume you have it?"

"We do," Adara said. "Would you mind looking at two photographs?"

Jack handed Yukiko his phone.

She scrolled through the photos, flipping back and forth. "I do not recognize the bald one," she said. "But this one . . ." She turned the phone toward Jack and Adara, displaying the photo of the Japanese man. "His name is Wada, a former member of Japan Special Forces Group 1st Company, 4th Platoon—specializing in urban warfare. He is believed to have strangled a Korean woman who was cleaning the apartment next door to his."

Adara stifled a yawn. "Seems like you know a great deal of information about a man suspected of homicide."

"True," Yukiko said. "Murder does not customarily cross into my domain. The murder was never proven, but the soldiers in Wada's platoon apparently ceased to trust him and pushed him out. It was what he did after the alleged murder that brought him to our attention. He only came to our attention some five months ago, in connection with the coordinated killing of an Australian diplomat and six of his entourage, including two Japanese guides, during a conference in Sapporo. The assassination was carried out by small hit team. At first we thought the assassins to be state actors, perhaps China or North Korea, but now we believe the murders had to do with some decisions being made regarding beef imports. We know Wada flew to Hokkaido—where Sapporo is located—a week before the murders and showed up on several security cameras in subsequent days. I will have to check and see if this other man was there as well."

"Beef . . ." Adara said. "This Aussie was killed over meat?"

"We believe so," Yukiko said. "Five billion dollars' worth of beef."

"That's reason enough to hire a hit team," Jack said.

"An extremely well-trained team," Yukiko said. "They were supplied with highly advanced weapons and the latest technology. Snipers, drones, radio jammers to disable local police communication. Witnesses at the scene all reported some version of the same thing. These assassins performed flawlessly. A local shopkeeper described it as 'like a dance.' An American Navy pilot on holiday from Atsugi said it looked as though the assassins were 'having fun.'" She peeled off the tenugui headscarf and shook out damp locks of layered, ebony hair that hung almost to her shoulders.

She might not have time to iron blouses, Adara thought, but Yukiko definitely found a minute to get herself a killer haircut. Jack noticed, too, and made that little breathy noise that men instinctively make when a woman shakes out her hair.

"I do not know if it will be of help," Yuki said, "but I placed lookouts on Wada's passport and known aliases. We know he has made at least three trips to India in the past four months. One of them as recently as three weeks ago."

"India," Ryan said. "Will you send investigators over to follow up?"

"I am not sure," Yukiko said. "I did not know Wada was involved until you showed me his photograph. I believe we would send someone eventually after the cyber unit completes their investigation. We would not send investigators such a great distance only to investigate his murders."

"Do you know where he went while he was there?" Adara asked.

"We know he flew Qatar Airways from Narita to Kempegowda International with an overnight stop in Doha."

Adara shot a glance at Jack. "Kempegowda?"

"Bangalore region," Yukiko said. "In the south."

"But nothing else?" Jack asked.

"I am sorry," she said. "No. Perhaps your CIA will have more information."

"Perhaps," Adara said. She didn't say it in front of Yukiko, but she knew what this meant and groaned inside. **Yippee. Another plane ride.**

Yukiko looked over her shoulder to make sure the door was shut. She lowered her voice though they were obviously alone. "I should not speak to foreign operatives of such matters," she said. "But I feel I must ask . . . for old times' sake. Have you ever heard of a group who calls themselves the Camarilla?"

The team made their way back to the Marriott separately. Out of habit and good OpSec, spending an hour backtracking on subways, circling, and watching one another's backs as they made several blocks and stopped at various convenience stores along the way. Jack piped up that he'd found a place that sold Takarabuneya éclairs, and offered to pick some up for everyone. The triple-cream pastries were, in Adara's estimation, the most delectable éclairs on the planet, but her stomach was still rebelling, so she declined.

Midas had already briefed Chavez by the time they reached the hotel and met in his room, inserting the room key into a slot by the door so all the lights and air-conditioning would work.

"Don't tell me," Adara said. "We're jetting off to India in ten minutes." She collapsed on one of the tiny chairs at the little two-place nook table, looking out the window at a guy selling fire-roasted sweet potatoes out of a cart on the quiet street.

"Sort of," Midas said. He scratched his beard, moving his jaw back and forth in fatigue. "You okay, my friend?"

He was completely serious and sweet. "I'm fine," she said, resting her head on the table. "Just exhausted. And probably coming down with a bug or something. You know how it is. We're always on the edge of getting something with all this travel and no sleep." She shrugged it off. "So, anyway, we're off to India?"

Jack double-checked to see if she wanted an éclair.

Tempted, she took one and tried a nibble. Just as decadent as she remembered.

"Ding wants us to start for India," Midas said. "They're working on some things on their end. We're supposed to give the computer hardware to the Agency chief of station here in Tokyo and use Foley's name to keep from getting scooped up and interrogated."

"India." Adara licked chocolate off her fingertips and took out her phone. "I'll find us some flights. Yay. Another twenty hours of jet travel . . ."

"That's the surprise," Midas said. "Helen and Country are already on their way to pick us up. Clark wanted us ready to jump whichever way we needed to jump."

Adara fanned her face like she was about to cry, only half joking. "So we're going on the G5?"

"Yep."

"When?"

"It's just us so they have room. Helen has the relief crew flying them over so they'll be good to go when they get here. Wheels up in . . ." He looked at his watch. "Fifteen hours."

"Fifteen?"

He nodded. "Fastest commercial flight is over twenty hours and it doesn't even leave until midafternoon tomorrow. Even waiting on the Gulfstream, we'll still be well ahead of that."

33

Leo Debs had read somewhere that the average person ate something like seven spiders a year while they were asleep. Almost as big as his hand, the yellow-and-black garden spider who'd set up shop between the eave and the top corner of the kitchen screen would have been a meal all by herself. It was almost three in the morning—and everyone was asleep but Debs and the bugs.

The smell of Hoppes #9 gun oil mingled pleasantly with the odor of alcohol and cigar smoke in the old ranch house. Behind Debs an old lariat hung on the rough cedar wall, blackened from slipping around a saddle horn during a dally when it had still been in the hands of a working cowboy. Above the rope was a colorized photograph of someone's prized Hereford bull. Rustic knickknacks covered most every inch of wall space—a wooden display of a dozen different kinds of barbed wire, a shotgun with a plugged barrel, and ancient metal Coca-Cola signs featuring pretty women on horseback. Craig Taylor called the motif "early-twentieth-century barbe-cue," and it was as good a place to plan a kidnap-ping as any.

The house was set up for ranching, with two baths, four regular bedrooms, and a large bunk-house area off the back of the spacious country kitchen. Everyone there was accustomed to sleep-ing on the ground in the shade of a Stryker or Humvee. Cotton sheets and actual mattresses were unimaginable luxuries.

Almost all of the men had broken their noses at some point in their lives, some multiple times, and the walls reverberated with chain saw snoring.

Statistically, at least one of them might well have been in the middle of eating a spider.

A Secret Service agent from Houston once told Debs that everything in the Texas woods either sticks, stinks, or stings—and on the isolated ranch outside Abilene, Debs had found that to be more than true. Thorny mesquite, cactus, puff adders, hornets, fire ants, skunks, all manner of venomous snakes—the place seemed a metaphor for the men of the Camarilla.

Light from the kitchen window drew an enor-mous quantity of insects to the old porch. The bug zapper hanging on the post outside worked overtime, electrocuting mosquitos and miller moths, but there were more than enough left over for **Argiope aurantia**.

Debs could almost hear Richard Attenborough's

voice narrating as a hapless cricket stumbled into the web, kicking and screaming. (How could it not be screaming with **Argiope aurantia** and her shiny black fangs bouncing long, daggerlike legs to undulate her great web like she was having so much fun?) Once she'd moved the web enough that the cricket was sufficiently snared, the huge garden spider scuttled across the silk and used her fangs to great effect before entombing her meal quickly in a wrap of sticky silk she shot from her abdomen.

Such patience. Such precision.

Leo Debs found solitude in patience. Operations like NIGHTINGALE required meticulous planning—whether it was figuring the weaponized math he needed to make an impossibly faraway shot with his .300 Winchester Magnum or the number of explosive charges, weapons loadouts, and egress plans needed to snatch the First Lady of the United States.

In truth, witnessing Vetter's ill-conceived plan with the armored car had spooked him. It was the little things that tripped you up. Everyone involved in protection knew too well the dirty little secret of the business. The main reason protection details succeeded was because very few people tested them. The Secret Service were just people, flesh and blood, easily ended. Still, Debs had trained with their agents long enough to know they could be extremely good at their jobs. To top that off, the First Lady seemed likable enough, which could make her protectors not only professional, but fierce.

He scanned the maps and models. This was not the mission to let some little detail slip by him.

Debs hunched over the long kitchen table, poring over maps and a laptop with the small portion of the San Antonio River Walk visible on Google Street View. Mainly, he relied on the hand-drawn sketches he'd made during his three recon trips.

The first trip had been necessary to formulate the plan. Trips two and three to set up the necessary hardware. Secret Service agents had done an initial study of the area but would come back later with bomb dogs and metal detectors. The river was relatively shallow around the event, less than three feet, but Debs felt sure they'd employ divers to check for IEDs. He had different plans.

Logistics for an action this precise were intense.

In the movies, nobody ever got the squirts or stress fractures from a bad taco or working out too much. A squad of mercs—always wearing some kind of ninja-looking uniforms or at the very least a black T-shirt—loaded up with a bunch of guns and did whatever deal they were getting paid for. These fictional soldiers could press the trigger on their SMGs for so long they'd set the barrel on fire in real life. The cyclic rate on the FN P90s Debs chose for NIGHTINGALE was plus or minus a thousand rounds per minute. Meaning you could dump a fifty-round magazine in under four seconds. 5.7x28 ammunition was small and relatively light as far as ammo went, but it did not rain from heaven in unlimited supplies, especially when things were turning to shit. Someone had to order that ammo, take delivery—and dispense it among the team, holding back enough for the actual mission. For NIGHTINGALE, that duty fell to Leo Debs.

The Secret Service would employ SIGs, Glocks, MP5s, MP7s, Remington shotguns, sniper rifles, helicopters, fighter aircraft, and possibly signal jammers. Camarilla operators would have only small arms—and a few explosive devices if all went as planned. Secret Service jammers, if they were used, would hinder radio communication.

Fortunately, they were talking about the First Lady and not the big guy himself. Debs had run the logistics on that scenario, too, just in case the President had decided to accompany his wife. Killing would have been possible, but a snatch was out of the question, and losses of Camarilla personnel would run north of fifty percent.

Debs ran a mechanical pencil along the route from the convention center where Cathy Ryan was supposed to give her speech and the riverside garden, where she would appear for the dedication—the spot where the dominoes would begin to fall. There was a chance he would lose someone on this trip. That was **always** a risk—by some policeman who reacted out of the norm or some soldier who had to take a piss, which put him in the right place at the wrong time . . . or a broken bootlace or a jammed weapon. They all knew that was a possibility each time they went out. Some of them—most, really—lived for the rush. Life without risk was like playing poker without stakes—boring as hell.

Even so, Debs and the others walked through every eventuality they could conceive to increase the odds of their own survival. In this case, the more Secret Service agents who died, the more of them would live. It was simple math. Sometimes that's just how it had to be. Like war. Hell, if this wasn't war, then nothing was. He'd seen plenty of war . . .

At thirty-six, Debs had lived a fair share of life in war-torn hellholes, starting with his mum's council-house flat in Grimsby. Her bedroom had a revolving door for live-in boyfriends. So far as Leo knew, none of the men was his father, or at least none of them treated him like a son. For most of his young life, his mum sported a chipped tooth or, at the very least, a black eye. He'd wanted to protect her, but she wouldn't have it. Men paid the bills, she said, and one just had to put up with a bit of rough stuff from time to time in return. By age eleven, Leo had gotten himself a baggy tracksuit and taken up with a pack of other miscreants, pinching sweets or magazines and trying not to get nicked by the cops. Then Elliott moved in. A real arsehole if there ever was one, but during the rare moments when he was sober he pretended to be the father of the house, which made Leo want to hurl.

Elliott had a bunch of tattoos, all of them hidden under his shirt, which he took off the instant he walked through the door, drunk or sober. Most were Latin phrases, like **memento mori**, or **aut neca aut necare** on his shoulders—the least painful, and thus the least badass place to get a tattoo, according to Leo's friends. But there was one, a downturned sword surrounded by flames with **Who Dares Wins** inked just above his left nipple. The crest of the Special Air Service.

Leo had been impressed for all of two minutes. What boy in his position would not have been ecstatic to find out his mum was sweatin' up the sheets with a blade from the most elite of the elite, the British SAS? But Elliott was all lies. He was careful not to actually say he was ever in the SAS, or even the military, speaking only in broad terms about when he worked with the regiment, or what happened during his time "serving the regiment." He was downright religious about keeping his ink covered when he went out. For all Leo knew, Elliott's service to the regiment had been delivering cheese.

Even so, it was Elliott who had changed the course of young Leo's life one evening. Airing out his bellicose tats and saggy man boobs over a game of cribbage, he liked to pretend they were a family. It might have been enjoyable if Leo's mum hadn't been wearing a sling on her right arm.

Leo was in the middle of planning how he could kill the man with a paring knife when he heard Elliott pontificate something about how a boy of twelve in Britain was not considered old enough to have a paper route, but he could join the Army at sixteen.

The notion of picking up a gun for Queen and country took root in young Leo's fertile mind and at the same time saved Elliott from a paring knife to the neck—for now.

Leo began the Army application pipeline when he was fifteen years and seven months. He needed permission to actually join before he was eighteen, but his mum, God love her, realized that the Army was better than ending up in prison—or worse. On his sixteenth birthday, the moment the British Army would accept him, Leo raised his right hand and became Recruit Debs.

Intelligent enough to make officers wonder why he hadn't gone to university and aggressive enough to make his sergeants happy he hadn't,

Leo thrived in the structured environment of rules, competition, and camaraderie. Three years on he gave his notice of interest to apply for the Special Air Service, the elite SAS. One of his platoon mates, a beefy Scot named McLaren, had applied as well, and accompanied Leo to Stirling Lines in Hereford for Selection.

McLaren broke an ankle during the infamous "Fan Dance," a twenty-four-kilometer ruck run in the rugged Brecon Beacons of Wales. Debs completed the whole shebang, including being stuffed into a cramped dog kennel for hours during the so-called "tactical questioning phase."

By twenty, he'd earned his sand-colored beret with downturned Excalibur, becoming an operator in D Squadron. His unflappable demeanor and superb marksmanship eventually singled him out as the top sniper in the squadron and arguably the entire corps.

Two years later, Debs ran into his mum's old boyfriend Elliott in a pub. The sleeves of his T-shirt were rolled up to reveal the Latin war ink. Debs said hello, remembered his mum's broken teeth, and casually mentioned to his mates from the regiment that there was another tattoo they might be interested in seeing.

Elliott wept-blew snot right there on the table, promising he'd get the offending ink removed.

Debs and his mates dragged the tearful piece of shite behind the pub anyway and took what didn't belong, using wet bar rags and an entire bottle of coarse salt. It was without a doubt the right thing to do, and a bonding experience to do it alongside his mates.

Debs first saw action in the Kashmir, advising India in skirmishes with Pakistan and China. Deployments to Libya followed, and then Baghdad as part of Task Force Black. Far from his old mates in Grimsby, who were likely still pinching sweets and porno mags, this was a life worth living, a brotherhood, a family.

Then a girl came into the picture at precisely the right moment to make him question his personal trajectory. Debs was twenty-eight years old and in the best shape of his life. He had twelve years of military experience under his belt, a university degree, a breast full of ribbons, and more adventures than most men in England could accumulate in five lifetimes.

But the girl wanted him home, not "off traipsing around hill and dale fighting other men's wars." Somehow, through witchery and feminine wiles, she'd convinced him to abandon his mates—the men he'd fought and bled with—and apply for a job with the Metropolitan Police. Her father was a chief superintendent with RaSP—Royalty and Specialist Protection—providing close protection to the Crown and prime minister, among other bigwigs.

A hasty marriage and two miscarriages later,

the Debs family stalled. Leo's career, on the other hand, moved ahead at lightning speed, fast-tracked by his father-in-law into a career protecting British dignitaries. Time at the Specialist Training Centre in Kent was exciting enough to hold his interest—lots of fast driving and gunplay, though not nearly so stressful as The Regiment. The actual work, however, was dull as dishwater. Debs was a man of war, bred to tactically advance toward battle. Endless monotonous hours of waiting for something to happen began to chip away at his soul. One look at his range record and senior officers had tapped him to serve as a police marksman—a more civilized term for sniper, but his job was still to shoot people.

That had salved him for a time, but again, the training was far more interesting than the job. Debs often found himself on a rooftop looking through the reticle of his Schmidt & Bender scope, idly considering what it would be like to put a round through the ear of whatever dig they were supposed to be protecting, just to shake things up a bit.

He began to think of his wife the same way a dog must feel about the vet who'd clipped his balls. In hindsight, it was nothing short of astounding that the marriage had lasted six years. The job with RaSP disintegrated shortly after the marriage, no doubt with a little nudge from his former father-in-law.

Craving the camaraderie of his old mates in D Squadron, Debs applied for readmission to the SAS. He didn't even care if they made him endure selection again. He just wanted back in.

He needed back in.

The physical requirements would be no problem. He was experienced, in peak physical shape, near, but not at, the maximum age. The Regiment should have been overjoyed to take him.

They were not.

Oceans of water had flowed under the bridge since he'd stepped away. Few remembered him, and those in charge smiled serenely as if they were witnessing a tired old man trying to relive the adventures of his youth. It turned out that his ex-father-in-law had friends in Special Forces who put a thumb on the scale. His application was denied without comment. Full stop.

Leo Debs, with easily a million pounds' worth of education in the ways of war and human conflict under his belt, found himself drifting, completely unemployable—a washout—just two months shy of his thirty-sixth birthday.

Then Simon Rook, a likable Yank and former 2nd Para in the Légion étrangère—the French Foreign Legion—had bought Debs a pint at a pub on Albany Street, not far from the Regent's Park barracks. Rook, a decade older than Debs, chatted about a life of soldiering, the good and the bad—but mostly the good. Two pints in, he invited Debs to meet a few of his mates at a private gun range.

The range turned out to be a two-hour plane ride away in the Czech Republic. At first Debs thought Rook might be MI6 or some other clandestine government organization. His time with the Regiment had pulled back the curtain on more than a few juicy tidbits the general public knew nothing about. Whatever organization Rook was fronting for, Debs saw this for what it was, a job interview.

The Czech gun range was a thing of beauty, tucked into the forested hills on the D1 motorway halfway between Prague and Brno. Rook had evidently rented the entire range, because he and his mates had the place to themselves. Debs was in heaven, once again able to wield weapons by Colt, FN, and SIG Sauer. There were Glocks, Browning Hi-Powers, and, of course, CZ pistols and rifles. They were, after all, in Czechia. Someone had done their homework and provided Debs with both an Accuracy International rifle chambered in .300 Winchester Magnum and a venerable Winchester Model 70 in .243, like his soft-kill rifle in the SAS—a joy to shoot.

The men had bonded, as soldiers often did, over gunpowder and flying brass. Everyone shot well, but Debs edged them out, both in speed and in accuracy. There were five of them. Rook, a hulking Aussie named Taylor, and an older bloke named Burt Pennington had all apparently served in the Legion together. A former operator with Poland's GROM named Nowak and a short, wiry dude from El Salvador named Fermin Pea left most of the talking to the former legionnaires. Every one of them was an excellent shot, but next to Debs, Pea appeared to be the coolest under pressure, completely unflappable. The man had spent thousands of dollars removing the many facial tattoos that had identified him as a member of Mara Salvatrucha—MS-13. Even now, when Pea turned just so to the light or ran a few dozen yards for a shooting drill, he looked like a gaunt leopard. The ghost of his ink seemed even more sinister than the tats themselves, like there was something lurking just beneath his skin.

Debs liked him straightaway.

The gun range turned out to be a chapel of sorts where like-minded men could bare their souls to the rest of the cadre, listing the deeds or errors in judgment that had gotten them booted from the careers that had once defined them.

Debs told them about rubbing off Elliott's tattoo with salt. Rook asked if he'd killed the bastard. Debs told them no with no other explanation. Lying to build his résumé wasn't in his nature.

Rook, Pennington, and Taylor had been drummed out of the Legion because of an unfortunate death and dismemberment of a Corsican prostitute. Their commanding officer, himself a frequent partaker of the dead putain's services, had considered having them deployed to some far-off place and shot, but in the end, he'd withdrawn their French passports and sent them out the front gate in disgrace. It mattered nothing to him that they were **Français par le sang versé—French by spilled blood**.

They'd circled back and cut the bastard's throat—and then searched for other outcasts who craved adventure above any cause but brotherhood.

The boss, a man they called the Spaniard, found them, then they had found Fermin Pea. He was on the run from killing the son of his patrón for sleeping with his sister. No one disrespected his sister.

Nowak had **accidentally** fragged a porucznik, or first lieutenant, in Afghanistan, a man so cowardly he was sure to get his entire platoon killed. Good riddance or not, accident or not—the Polish Army took a dim view of fragging first lieutenants.

Other men followed, slowly, carefully. You did not ask to become a member of the Camarilla—you were invited. Four members of the existing cadre took prospects to a gun range somewhere in the world and gauged their mettle, their allegiance to the brotherhood of war. If the prospective teammate passed muster, he was tentatively welcomed into the fold. Red flags meant a one-way trip to some nearby strip of greenwood and a dispassionate bullet behind the ear.

A short time after they'd taken him to Czechia, Burt confided to Debs that had he lied and told them he'd actually killed his mother's old boyfriend, he would have been taken on just such a ride. Trust, it turned out, was far more important than how many people he'd killed. Though they were impressed by that number as well. Operators with the Camarilla rarely spoke about it, but most walked through life with a sort of profound dismay that they'd made it this far alive.

34

The fan in the hall bathroom flicked on, nudging Debs from his thoughts. He heard a cough and realized it was Burt, up again to pee. The poor guy's prostate was likely the size of a tennis ball. It took him a full five minutes to finish up before he wandered out, his scared face bewildered with sleep—and something more insidious. In the old days, when Debs had first met him, Burt Pennington had been a force to be reckoned with, with a stern visage that could make grown men weep. Now his cockeyed mustache and tendency to park his lower teeth in front of his uppers made him look like a human incarnation of Sylvester the cartoon cat.

"Whatcha got there, Leo?" he asked, scratching his ass as he shuffled across the clay tile floor.

Debs leaned back and gave a long, groaning yawn, speaking softly as he might to a small child. "Going over the routes again, Burt. Timing, that sort of thing."

"Routes for what?" The older man moved closer, wide-eyed, interested to see what was going on.

Debs groaned again. "Routes for the mission . . ."

Burt touched the scar around his drooping eyelid. He did that when he needed a moment to compose himself. The angry pink flesh served as a reminder to those around him that he'd done his bit.

"Yeah." The confusion in his good eye settled as he studied the map in front of Debs. "Sure. I get it. I just meant, you know, specifically what routes. Thought I'd let you talk things through. It always helped me when we talked a plan through . . ."

"I hear you," Debs said, careful not to show pity. It was an open secret that Burt was getting worse. Burt himself knew, locked in that terrifying moment when he was hyperaware of his own failing mental state. When Leo came aboard, Burt was one of the most capable members of the Camarilla. Aggressive, the fitness level of a decathlete, and weapons skills unmatched even by Debs. Ten years older than anyone else in the group, he served as caustically blunt Dutch uncle, wise elder statesman, and even the father that many of the men never had.

The IED in Côte d'Ivoire would have killed Craig Taylor but Burt, the only one of the group wearing a Kevlar helmet, had pushed him away. The blast had scarred his face and, as evidenced with each passing day, wreaked havoc on his brain, particularly his amygdala and hypothalamus. At first some words eluded him—but they all had that problem once in a while. A year after the accident he'd wandered off on a job in Athens and they hadn't been able to find him. He'd brushed it off to getting turned around and having all comms on silent. The streets were a nightmare so the team let it slide. He seemed now to be lost most of the time, locked inside his own head. Worst of all, he'd lost all aggression, apologizing even for others' mistakes.

Some whispered for serious action, but Taylor owed the man his life.

Debs closed the notebook on the table and patted the cover. "Well, mate, we have shit-ton of work to do tomorrow."

Burt blinked his good eye. The saggy one followed, moving slower. "I . . . I know. I'm sorta hungry. Thought I might get up and fix me some eggs. You know, have an early breakfast—"

Craig Taylor wandered in from the dark hallway. "You blokes oughta get some shut-eye. It's two-thirty in the mornin'!"

"Hey, Taylor," Burt said. "Yeah, you're right. I should go back to bed." He nodded sheepishly at Debs. "Good talk, Leo."

The big Aussie got himself a Dos Equis from the kitchen fridge, popped the top, and then sauntered over to the table after Burt had gone back to the bunk room.

"Feeling confident, mate?"

Debs tossed the mechanical pencil on the table and rubbed a hand over his face. He needed to shave. The Secret Service tended to focus on scruff. "As confident as I can be pulling a job for a man who talks to dead tigers."

"Yeah, billionaires get away with a lot of shit." Taylor took a long slug of his Dos Equis and then looked up at the ceiling, rubbing tired eyes. "I hated going with Gil to that guy's office. It's funny as hell, but it's also bloody weird."

"Hard to trust a man who gets counsel from a bit of flea-bitten taxidermy."

"We don't have to trust Malhotra," Taylor said. "That asshole is scared shitless of us. Too scared to cross the Spaniard, anyway." He took a drink. "So, back to my original question. You feel good about this op? It is gonna work, right?"

"You trust me?" Debs asked.

Taylor gave him a wink and set the bottle down hard on the table, causing beer to geyser out the top and run down his hand. He licked it off, not the type to waste beer. "Like I trust a whore to give me the clap."

"Ain't it nice to have something you can count on." Debs waved a hand over his notes and sighed. "Seriously, I think we're good, mate. There's always gonna be some fly in the ointment, some variable, but we got contingencies for our contingencies."

"I'm sure," Taylor said, distant. He threw a quick look over his shoulder, making certain they were alone, then raised the beer again. "A favor, mate?"

"Of course," Debs said.

"I ever get like Burt, put a bullet in my head. It'd be a kindness."

"Righto," Debs said. "And vice versa."

Neither man said it aloud, but that day was coming for Burt. They both knew it. Everyone on the team did.

Even Burt . . . most days. You could see it in his eye.

35

Colonel Tu glanced from his watch to the sky and conferred with the Tajik Army captain about hiding the horses, split between five different yurts, no doubt to conceal them from passing satellites. Tu seemed to know exactly when they would be overhead. With no weapons but shepherd's staffs and the odd butcher knife, the Wakhi families whose houses were being turned into barns could do little but grumble their complaints. Those who grumbled too loudly earned a boot to the back.

As soon as the horses started moving the direction he wanted, the colonel barked something to his men and they began to search the Harpers. One of the soldiers, a Chinese troop named Wen, made a great show of patting down Naomi, jeering at her when he had her pull her bra away from her body so they could check beneath it. Harper moved to put a stop to the behavior and earned a swift elbow to the bridge of his nose, knocking him to the ground. Naomi shook her head.

"It's nothing," she said. But it wasn't nothing.

It was another nail in these dickheads' coffins as far as Harper was concerned.

The soldier with the elbow of iron was half Harper's age. Bull strong with the swagger of youth, he snatched the satellite phone from Harper's back pocket the moment he saw it, barking in rapid Mandarin, holding up the device, probably asking if there were any others in camp.

The soldiers meant to cut off their communication. That was a bad sign.

Harper shook his head.

Iron Elbow pointed his rifle at Harper's chest with one hand, holding the sat phone in the other, still barking. Apparently, he wasn't the trusting sort.

Harper raised his hands in surrender. "No more phones—"

The soldier's eyes settled on the Breitling Emergency Harper wore on his left wrist. He gestured at the watch with the barrel of his AK. Harper gave it to him, certain he was about to be shot for trying to hide an emergency transmitter. The soldier ogled the heavy band, nodding in approval at its heft. He let the light reflect off the broad crystal face before slipping it on his own wrist with a decisive nod. He appeared to like the watch as fancy bling rather than realizing it contained an emergency locator transmitter that would send up a signal on 406 MHz. As long as none of these assholes figured out what they had, Harper clung to the hope he'd find a way to deploy it.

Their search complete, the soldiers told the Harpers to stay put and went to check with their boss.

"He took your watch," Naomi whispered. "I was hoping—"

"Me, too," Harper said. "We'll figure out a way to get it back."

Shambe, the Wakhi shepherd boy who'd been kicked in the face, lost a canine tooth and probably had a cracked orbital bone. His father and uncle had brought him in from the pastures shortly after Colonel Tu had accused the Harpers of being spies. They'd denied it, of course, vehemently, but the colonel simply smiled and walked away.

Monte Harper had always had his hands full keeping his wife from going full mother grizzly. Now it was nearly impossible. The colonel saw she was upset and appeared to be looking for an excuse to punish her. An outside observer might have thought that Harper was more patient, because he bided his time and watched. He had in fact resolved that if this man harmed his wife, even a little, it would be both his and Colonel Tu's last day on the planet.

Naomi did what she could for the boy, pulling the remainder of the tooth—emergency dental work constituted a fair portion of their work in remote areas. He was incredibly stoic through the ordeal. She held off giving him ibuprofen, worrying he might have some internal bleeding, but gave him oxycodone for pain, a better option than the opium he would have gotten had they not been here.

The air was rare at over thirteen thousand feet and it was easy to find oneself out of breath. The poor kid lay on a pile of cushions in his father's yurt, squinting against the pain and panting like a puppy trying to escape the southern heat. His mother was busy making him halwa, a rich paste of flour, butter, and salt. A richer Afghan might have added nuts, raisins, and cardamom. Shambe's mother had none of these things, so he got something that resembled a rich and sticky roux. It was simple, easy to eat with a broken tooth, and filling for a child who got nothing but bread and milk tea day after day after day— the Wakhi version of chicken and dumplings . . . minus the chicken and stock.

Their patient tended to, the Harpers sought out Colonel Tu, who was busy overseeing the movement of his belongings from one of the packhorses to a yurt he'd commandeered. Two of his men were hauling the Harpers' belongings from their large mountaineering dome tent that had been their home for the past week and a half.

Naomi tried to wrench a bag of dirty clothing

out of a soldier's hand but he shrugged her off, shooing her away with a hostile glare. She followed him inside the yurt, puffing up like she might attack when she saw the soldiers piling her things against the wooden latticework of the yurt walls.

"We must remove the evidence you are here," the colonel said. "I have heard the Taliban has access to some satellite imagery, and possibly drone technology. It would be dangerous if they tracked you down because of a tent when we could simply take it down and have you sleep inside."

"Just where are we supposed to sleep?" Naomi sputtered, lips pursed, chin quivering.

"You may stay here if you wish," Tu said, waving his hand around the commandeered home. "Obviously. There is plenty of space. My men will divide themselves among the other dwellings."

"I can't imagine the Wakhi will be very happy about that."

"I do not care," Tu said. "Their feelings change nothing. You and your wife are spies and my men are here to protect you. To do so, they need a place to sleep."

"We are not spies!" Naomi snapped. "Why do you keep saying that?"

The colonel chuckled, shaking his head. "Of course you are."

"Seriously, sir," Harper said, trying the tactful route. "What leads you to believe we are spies?

And what exactly would we spy on here in the Wakhan?"

Tu's eyes narrowed and he smiled slyly. "Oh, you know very well, Mr. Harper. I am not going to explain it to you. That is not how these matters work."

"This is crazy!" Naomi all but shrieked. "We are physicians. Ask all these people. There!" She pointed to Laleh's mother. "Look at that woman's bandage. Could a spy replace the lens in a person's eye?"

A man beside Tu spoke up. He was younger, perhaps twenty-five, with a prominent Adam's apple and an earnest smile that made him look more like a college student than a soldier-kidnapper. His name was Shen, and he appeared to be the second-in-command. "Spies often have a subset of skills," he said, as if he were reading from a textbook and sincerely believed it.

Tu rubbed his hands together. "I must insist you remain our guests until we get to the bottom of this."

"How long do you anticipate that to be?" Harper asked.

"As long as it takes," Tu said.

"Wait just a minute," Naomi said. "We have to be on a flight out of Kabul in three days. We **are** starting down the valley tomorrow, no matter what you say."

Tu darkened, taking a step forward.

Harper braced, but the colonel stopped, tilting his head to one side as if deciding how to proceed.

"Mrs. Harper," he said. "Ultimatums are the refuge of the weak. You will leave when I say it is time for you to leave, and not a moment sooner." His countenance softened at once and he gestured to the back of the yurt, where the woman of the house cooked fresh flats of naan and a large pan of milk tea over a dung fire. "Please. Join me for dinner. I have some excellent tinned meat and plum wine to bolster this meager fare."

Harper stood his ground. "You realize that by crossing the border as an armed, uniformed army you are committing an act of war."

"Spying is an act of war," the colonel said. "This part of the world is not a safe place for spies."

"I ask again," Harper said. "Who would we spy on?"

"There are many militants in the area who, I am sure, would be keenly interested in your presence here."

"Is that a threat?" Harper asked. "You're seriously threatening to ring up some Taliban commander and hand us over to get your reward?"

"Oh," Captain Shen, the second-in-command said. "You would like that, wouldn't you?"

"What?"

"I am afraid you misunderstand me, Mr. Harper," Tu said. "I know very well that the

Taliban would not harm you. It is them for whom you spy."

"What?" Harper said again, beyond in-credulous.

"That is insane," Naomi said.

Captain Shen quoted his Intelligence 101 manual again. "A spy will deny the accusations. In the beginning."

"You must let us contact our embassy," Harper said.

"Ah," Colonel Tu said. "That will be taken care of very soon . . ."

36

Shambe's parents were relieved to have the Harpers stay in their yurt and provide the extra care for the injured boy. Colonel Tu made it clear that though there was nowhere for them to run, he'd posted a guard outside the door—for their own safety. They'd not been there long before two Chinese soldiers dragged one of the shepherds inside. He was in his late forties, old for the Wakhi, with a map of lines from weather and now fear on his deeply bronzed face. Harper recognized him as Nazir, one of his first cataract surgery patients since coming to the Pamir. His wife, Fariah, was related to the village leader. They had no living children, but she was heavily pregnant and a devoted attendee to Naomi's health classes. She came in next, face flushed with tears, eyes flitting around the smoky interior of the yurt like a terrified mouse. A third soldier followed close behind with a video camera and production light.

"This can't be good," Naomi whispered.

Nazir's hands were bound in front and his head hung down. His rolled wool pakol hat was pulled slightly to cover an abrasion over his left ear. Other than the spot over his ear, there didn't appear to be any obvious injuries. The soldiers placed his back to the felt wall, kneeling him on a cushion.

Abdulin, the Tajik Army captain, surveyed the area behind the captive, removed some colorful paper Shambe's mother had used for decoration, and tossed it on the floor, out of the frame. The soldier with the video camera looked through his viewfinder and gave a curt nod.

Colonel Tu strode in next, Harper's former assistant Laleh on his heels.

"Unfortunately," Tu said, "I don't speak Wakhi. But I do speak Russian. I understand you do as well. The girl has agreed to translate this man's statement into Russian for us."

Naomi fumed. "His statement?"

Tu put his finger to his lips. "Shhh. The movie is about to begin."

The soldiers standing on either side of Nazir each took a half-step away and then stretched black balaclavas over their heads. A red light illuminated on the video camera and Colonel Tu nodded at Laleh, who told the trembling man to begin.

His head came up slowly, his eyes, surely still tender from recent surgery, squinting at the bright production light. He cleared the phlegm from his throat and took a deep, shuddering breath.

"I am Nazir . . ." He coughed again. Licked his lips and looked at Tu, as if for guidance.

The colonel growled, low and menacing. "We talked about this," he said. Laleh translated rapidly. "Look straight into the camera. It is very simple. Repeat the words you told me before!"

Tu nodded at the cameraman again. "Begin!"

"I am Nazir Bayat. I am in good physical health and my mind is sound. I have not been tortured or harmed in any way. At this time, I wish to unburden myself with the confession of a great wrong that I have committed. For two years I have served as an agent for the East Turkestan Freedom Movement against China . . . In recent weeks, I have had numerous contacts with Taliban officials to discuss training classes"—Nazir paused, licked his lips, and then continued—"classes in the use of firearms and improvised explosives. I was . . . I was recruited to these classes . . . by Dr. Monte Harper and his wife. I am ashamed of my actions against all peaceful people in Tajikistan and our peaceful neighbors in China . . . That . . . That is all I have to say."

The red light on the video camera flicked off, leaving Nazir wallowing pitifully in the glare of the production lamp. He turned away, cringing when the soldier lowered the camera. Laleh turned to meet Harper's eye. She shook her head, apologizing without words for her part in this fiasco.

"There is a bit of weather on the horizon," Tu said. "But as soon as it passes you will be taken to China, where you will stand trial for espionage—"

Naomi, stunned from Nazir's out-of-the-blue sham confession, finally got her bearings. "You can't believe we're actually spies!"

Tu grinned and gave a little shrug. "It is not what I believe," he said, "but what the Party tribunal will believe."

Harper met the colonel's eye, glaring. He was a good six inches taller than the man and outweighed him by fifty pounds. One of the soldiers took this as a threat and struck him in the side of the head with the butt of his AK. Harper's legs went wobbly. He staggered but kept his feet.

Naomi sprang forward, but another soldier caught her by the hair and yanked her backward, throwing her to the ground.

"Enough!" the colonel roared, taking even Harper aback. "Do not be confused by my calm demeanor. My men **will** kill you if you force them."

Harper felt the sting of blood in his eye and dabbed at his brow. Naomi tried to stand again but he put out his hand, urging her to stay put.

"Even if we were spies," he said, trying to keep

from panting from overwhelming fear, "which we are not, what makes you believe that you can march into Afghanistan, where we are guests of the government, and kidnap us?"

Laleh looked up and gave a forlorn shake of her head. "Nazir is Wakhi from Tajikistan. In video, he says he from there."

"Just so," Colonel Tu harrumphed, looking pleased with himself. "For all the world knows— for all I know—you two recruited him there. Nothing in the video will give away our location. On the contrary. A Tajik man speaking of the Taliban, ISIS, and Free East Turkestan in his home country—where all of those groups pose a serious threat. It is not a great leap forward to believe you are in Tajikistan."

The colonel flicked his hand toward Nazir, beckoning him closer. The shepherd climbed shakily to his feet, without the use of his hands, and approached, head down.

"The problem is," Tu said, "our friend Nazir seems to put great trust in you. I am afraid he will recant his statement the moment he has the opportunity."

Nazir stood listening, able to grasp that there was something important being said, though he couldn't understand the words.

Tu looked directly at Harper. "That is why I need you to kill him."

"You're insane," Harper spat.

"Kill him or I'll kill both him and his pregnant wife."

"I won't," Harper whispered.

Tu gave a curt nod and two soldiers grabbed Harper's arms, while the cameraman grabbed Naomi.

Tu drew a Makarov pistol from the flap holster on his belt and made circles in the air with the barrel, as if deciding which way to point it. "Then I will kill your wife as well."

"Kill us all," Naomi whispered through clenched teeth. "He's not shooting anyone."

"Very well," Tu said, pointing the Makarov at a bewildered Nazir's temple and pulling the trigger.

The pistol crack shook the enclosed space of the yurt, causing everyone but Nazir's wife to flinch. The poor shepherd went rigid before toppling over backward. His head slammed against the carpeted floor and the stones beneath with a sickening thump. His wife sank to her knees over the body, wailing in abject sorrow. She had to list sideways to reach him because of her pregnant belly.

Colonel Tu kept the Makarov up, making circles in the air again as he studied the grieving woman.

Harper struggled against the impossible grip of the soldiers. "No! Stop! Please leave her alone!"

Tu lowered the weapon slowly and gave a sad

shake of his head. "I am not an animal, Dr. Harper," he said. "There is no need to kill his wife . . . at this time."

Naomi turned her face to the ceiling and screamed. She jerked against the single guard that held her, giving him a run for his money. "You bastard! You're insane."

Tu gave a long, exhausted groan, then looked back and forth between the Harpers. "I am not insane," he said. "On the contrary. If I were a madman, you would have a chance against me. I might make some mistake. That is not the case. I assure you."

"I swear to you," Naomi spat. "You—"

Tu raised a hand as if to strike, cutting her off. "What is the matter with you, Dr. Harper?" he snapped. "You plainly see that I will not hesitate to put a bullet in a man's skull. This is serious business, and there are plenty of people in the village with whom I can and will demonstrate that fact to you. You are sorely mistaken if you think I won't do to you what I did to poor Nazir. You believe that I need you alive." Tu sighed, calming, giving a little shrug. "And in some respects that is true." He squatted down on his haunches, leaning in closer to Naomi's face. "But you must remind yourself of this. I only need one of you."

———

The soldiers made Harper help drag Nazir's body away from camp and stuff it in a large stone enclosure where sheep were normally kept. The dead man's wife followed, weeping, but the soldiers chased her away and sent Harper back to his yurt, pantomiming that he should go to sleep, and no doubt making lewd gestures about his wife.

Shambe's father cut out the bloodstained portion of carpeting where Nazir had died and stuffed it in the fire. Overcome with exhaustion, Harper dozed in the corner while Naomi tended to Shambe, who was now running a fever.

Sometime later, he wasn't sure how long, Harper awoke to raucous laughter that drifted in from outside of the yurt when Laleh lifted the felt door and crept inside. She spoke quickly to Shambe's mother, who put a hand on her shoulder and nodded.

"Yasmin will let me sleep here tonight," Laleh said. "It is safer in here with you."

"Of course." Naomi nodded after Harper translated the girl's Russian. "I understand."

Harper motioned the girl closer so the guard outside wouldn't be able to hear. "What is the colonel doing?" he asked. "Could you see?"

"He talks on the phone a lot," Laleh said. "A satellite phone, but not yours."

"Could you tell what he was saying?"

WAKHAN CORRIDOR, AFGHANISTAN

N

TAJIKISTAN

Wakhan Corridor

AFGHANISTAN

PAKISTAN

TRIBAL VILLAGES

TAJIKISTAN

Mulung Than
Vagd Boi   • Asan Katich

PAKISTAN

© 2021 Jeffrey L. Ward

"I am sorry," the girl said. "I could hear some of it, but I could not understand it."

"That's right," Harper said, disappointed. "You don't speak Chinese."

"No," Laleh said. "He spoke in English."

Harper translated for Naomi.

"I'm not going to be able to sleep," she said. "But we should at least try and get some rest."

Shambe's mother made everyone pallets of yak felt and distributed all the blankets she had—borrowing one from her own bed to give to the Harpers.

"What are we going to do?" Naomi whispered from the darkness beside Harper. "You heard the colonel. He's holding the entire village hostage if we don't play ball. We came here to help them and now we're getting them killed, putting all of these sweet people in danger."

"That's what I don't get," Harper whispered back, his face just inches from his wife's but unable to see her. "Colonel Tu hasn't told us what he wants, except that we admit to being spies. He's using us as pawns in some bigger game. I just can't figure out what it is."

"Well," Naomi said. "Whatever it is, these poor people have no part in it. We have to do something to help them."

"I know," Harper said. It's just that I can't imagine losing y—"

The blanket rustled and she reached up to touch his cheek.

"Remember what we used to say when we decided to venture out and work in far-flung places like this?"

Harper nodded, a lump in his throat. " 'What could we get done if we were not afraid?' "

"Well, I'm so over being afraid." Naomi's words buzzed against his neck. "We've left a hell of a mark on the world, you and me. Two exceptional daughters . . . and the best grandbaby anybody's ever even heard of. I don't want to be fatalistic, but I'm not going to stand by while that bastard shoots another innocent person."

"I'm not arguing with you," Harper said.

"Good," Naomi said, snuggling in closer—as if such a thing was possible. "So we both die. Big deal. I tell you what, though. I'd really like to cut that colonel's balls off before I go."

Harper chuckled, patting her on the shoulder. "That's my girl," he said. "But let's be smart about it."

"Sure," Naomi said under her breath. "Spies . . . Can you believe that? I am so mad at that asshole who took your watch."

"He is kind of a jerk," Harper said. "How about we make a plan to get it back?"

She turned toward him. "Your watch?"

"Yeah."

"I'm intrigued," she said. "So long as I still get to, you know, do that thing to the colonel."

A loose plan began to form in Harper's head as exhaustion pulled him under. He drifted off to the smell of smoldering yak dung and a hint of soured milk.

37

"Hey, Daiwi," Sergeant First-Class Eric "Ripper" Ward said, knocking on Captain Alan Brock's containerized housing unit. "Got a second?"

The rousing beat of Corb Lund's song "Horse Soldier, Horse Soldier" spilled out from beneath the door of Brock's CHU.

Like many operators in United States Special Forces, Ward used more familiar terms when he communicated with his team commander than a traditional infantry soldier would have done. **Daiwi**, the Vietnamese term for captain, was a tradition handed down through generations of Green Berets. Ward was Operational Detachment Alpha 0312's 18Z—the operations or team sergeant. As the ODA commander, Captain Brock's job was to look up and out, calculating risk and political fallout (there could be a shitload of that), and constantly assessing each mission. The team sergeant was the team's "daddy" and ran the day-to-day show.

The members of Operational Detachment Alpha 0312 were assigned to 10th Special

Forces, 3rd Battalion, 1st Company, Team 2. Mountaineers and horse soldiers. ODA 0312, commonly called an A-team.

A military brat himself, Ward bled Army green. His Ranger father was a barrel-chested Black man from the Deep South who'd met Ward's statuesque blond German mother after a training exercise in Mittenwald. He'd grown up listening to his old man's stories, learning land nav before he was eight, doing push-ups and ruck runs for punishment for as long as he could remember. As his father said, "You could either be a smart Ranger or a strong Ranger. The more you screwed up, the more you pushed up."

Eric did enough stupid shit in his early life that his father saw to it that he became extremely fit.

Then he met Greedy, and he decided he could be both.

There was no question that Eric would join the military. His mother encouraged him to finish college and commission as an officer. Rather than offer advice, his father introduced him to an endless line of senior enlisted friends of his. Some had gone to college, some had not, but all of them had kickass careers that involved limited time driving a desk. They were leaders who stayed in the trenches sweating and bleeding with their soldiers, not rear-echelon pogues. One of them was a Special Forces sergeant the old man called "Greedy," because he had a reputation for keeping all the most difficult and unpleasant tasks for himself.

They'd sat around the campfire, Ward, his old man, and Greedy, the two men talking reverently about friends they'd lost, men they'd worked alongside. Greedy worked the tenets of Special Forces into his conversation in terms that resonated with a teenage boy. **Be a quiet professional. Be a warrior. Be an expert at the unconventional. Be a partner. Be an agile problem solver. Above all, have a noble purpose.** Greedy and his old man had toasted the United States Army "to the superlative and the shitty."

Eric could still hear the clink of their beer bottles hitting together beside the fire.

He started college to appease his mom but finished because he found he loved history and had a knack for Arabic. The recruiter had nearly pissed himself when Eric walked in with a degree in Middle Eastern Studies, a minor in Arabic, and a conversant knowledge of Farsi—and then said he wanted to enlist.

"You don't want to become an officer?"

"Not at this time, Sergeant."

"What is it you want to do in the Army?"

Ward felt like a dick all these years later that he'd been so overly dramatic, but he'd looked dead in the recruiter's eyes and said, **"De oppresso liber."**

"If I had a nickel for every kid who strutted

into this office and told me they were going to be a Green Beret . . ."

Ward couldn't help but grin at the memory, as the captain of Special Forces Operational Detachment Alpha 0312 opened the door to his CHU.

"Ripper," he said. "What's up?" Brock's brown grizzly-bear beard was mussed from leaning on his hand while he studied intel reports on his Toughbook. He wore PT gear—green T-shirt and shorts, and a pair of shower shoes.

"You see the intel about the American doctors?"

"Reading it now," Brock said. "Picked up as Taliban spies somewhere in Darshai?"

Ward nodded. "S2 has a Tajik opium dealer who believes they were transported to some shepherd camps in the north. Doesn't know where. But that still doesn't make sense. Darshai's on the road system. I can see trekking in somewhere to spy if there was worthwhile intel, but holy shit, Boss, we're talking about a bunch of sheep and rocks."

"Fair point."

"Jake got a call from that yak trader we worked with last month." **Jake** was Sergeant Thelan, the ODA 0312's 18F or intelligence sergeant. "He's hearing noise that Tajik soldiers have been coming south into the corridor. Maybe the docs were snatched and taken over the border."

Captain Brock gave a nodding shrug. "That

fits," he said. "These doctors . . . the Harpers, were supposedly doing medical work in the Big Pamir. That's less than twenty miles from Tajikistan as the crow flies."

"A crow or a Tajik chopper," Ward said. "National Missions Force is looking at possible locations in Tajikistan. Dushanbe appears to be cooperating."

Brock already knew SEAL Team 6 and Delta were, after all, the units most prepared to do hostage rescue. Still, it went against both men's grain to know something was going down without them being a part of it.

"We've worked the Corridor before," the captain said. "Higher wants to do some snooping around where the docs were doing their work. What do we know about these shepherd camps?"

"Scattered through the high country," Sergeant Ward said. "There's not enough arable land along the valley floor to grow wheat and graze their livestock, so about half the Wakhi families take the village's herds of yaks and those fat-ass sheep of theirs into the high Pamir to graze. They follow the melt up and the snow down in the fall. A summer migration of sorts. They call it a **kuch**. Like I said before, it's mostly sheep and rocks and yurts made out of yak felt. ISR from the latest Predator flyover didn't show anything out of the ordinary. The bird wasn't on station long enough to establish patterns of life or anything. I'd like to get more time on station, but every available asset is focused over Tajikistan."

"Make sure—"

"Horse Soldier, Horse Soldier" continued to play in the background and the men unconsciously stopped in reverent silence when the song reached the lines about Special Forces.

Brock took a deep breath, looking into the distance. "Something about this smells off. Have Jake check in with his favorite yak trader again— and any other local assets we have in and around the Wakhan, on the off chance that the docs are still stashed in Afghanistan. I'm going to call in a couple of favors."

Ward raised a brow. "Favors?"

"A single Predator flyover doesn't give us much to go on. I think the powers that be are putting a hell of a lot of faith in their intel that the Harpers are somewhere in Tajikistan. I mean, listen, what do they have? The Harpers' daughter reports them missing. A Tajik farmer says he saw some soldiers with people he believes to be American prisoners, and a grainy cell-phone video of a woman who bears some resemblance to Dr. Naomi Harper sneaking across a closed border. Hell, I've seen two videos this morning of the President of the United States getting a lap dance. I'm not a big believer in video evidence anymore."

"Tajik government seems to believe the video," Ward said, playing devil's advocate. "They're going apeshit about Americans spying for the Taliban in their country and from all accounts cooperating with the National Missions guys to find them."

"The only difference," Brock said, "is that the Tajiks are calling it a fugitive hunt. We're calling it a rescue."

Ward grinned. "Tomato, tomahto. Whatever we call it, it's gonna be tough to get any ISR here when they're all tasked."

ISR was Intelligence, Surveillance, and Reconnaissance, comprised of, among other platforms, satellite imagery and remotely piloted aircraft such as the Predator and Reaper. Additionally, Special Forces had several smaller RPAs like Boeing's ScanEagle, Skydio X2s, and the tiny FLIR Black Hornet.

"The military's not the only outfit out here with Predators," Brock said. "I know a guy."

A pained look flashed across Ward's face, like someone just told him he had to go to the dentist. "A CIA guy?"

"Yep." Brock smiled. "With any luck, we'll have something over Big Pamir spooled up and ready by dinner."

"That's what I like about you, sir," Ward said. "You dream big."

Brock shrugged. "Like I said, something doesn't smell right about this. The Doctors Harper might well be in Tajikistan, or China, or Pakistan . . . or dead at the bottom of some glacier crevasse."

"For sure," Ward said. "But if they're still in Afghanistan, we'll find them."

"Of that, Ripper," Brock said. "I have zero doubt."

38

It was easy to feel like a suspect after an officer involved shooting, or OIS—because you were.

Policy required both Chilly and Officer Ritchey to surrender the weapons they'd fired in the course of the incident and to provide urine samples. Detectives from Homicide and Internal Affairs waited in the wings to get statements, ready with a printed Garrity warning: **You have the right not to incriminate yourself, but it you don't talk to me, I can fire your ass.**

Mighty nice of them to look after his rights like that. Chilly knew he hadn't done anything wrong, but the process still sucked.

More leader than manager, Sergeant Johnson had replaced Scott Ritchey's handgun with his own Glock. He made certain Chilly was issued another rifle before they even cleared the scene, driving home the point that they weren't being punished for doing their jobs. Still, Johnson crossed the t's and dotted the i's, giving the powers that be what they would need to put this whole incident to bed.

Chilly knew better.

Shooting-review investigators had given both officers twenty-four hours to rest before giving any statement.

Rest . . . That was a joke.

The Abilene Police Department was housed in a recently gutted and remodeled grocery store at the western edge of the city. The municipal court and Child Advocacy Center were located in the same strip of buildings. The fresh-paint-and-carpet smell of the place always made Chilly feel like he was starting a new job. On administrative leave since the shooting, he wasn't required to be in uniform, but this was important, and he wanted the brass to know that he knew it. He came in wearing dress Wranglers and Tony Lama boots with a crisp white shirt and tie—much like the Texas Ranger and the APD detective lieutenant who met him at the employee entrance and invited him to a vacant room next to the assistant chief's office. Lieutenant Gene Moss had been on Chilly's initial interview panel. A thin man with a bristle-brush mustache, he'd always seemed fair, but hard to read. An alum of the FBI's National Academy for state and local law enforcement leaders, he was rarely without an NA lapel pin or coffee mug—or some bit of wisdom he'd gleaned while he was "at Quantico."

Ranger Will Peterson set his silverbelly Resistol hat on the table, crown down. He made it clear that he generally saw the FBI as a necessary evil, the clean end of the turd that was the federal government. A flat wooden toothpick hung in the corner of his sardonic mouth. The iconic circle-star badge was pinned to the left breast of a starched khaki shirt, custom-cut and polished from an authentic Mexican cinco peso coin by a silversmith over in Clarendon. Chilly had seen Peterson around a number of crime scenes over the years, though, as a lowly motor officer, he'd never formally been introduced. The ranger did, however, know Chilly's father, and mentioned it as they shook hands. Chilly couldn't tell if it was to let him know the Ranger was an ally, or to establish rapport with a suspect, as any good detective would do.

Probably a bit of both, judging from Peterson's reputation as a lawman.

The interview was being videotaped, with investigators from Internal Affairs and the district attorney's office taping the interview from the adjacent room, watching, ostensibly to keep Chilly from having to give two separate statements.

Chilly gave a quick rundown of everything that occurred from the time he'd attached himself to the active-shooter call until the SWAT team arrived and cleared the mall. He left nothing out, including the fact that he'd been prepared to move directly to the shooters and leave a poor pregnant woman to bleed to death in order to stop more killing.

Lieutenant Moss listened with a dispassionate half-smile, periodically taking sips from his National Academy mug. A lay minster at First Baptist Abilene during his off hours, Moss was an enigma. Chilly couldn't tell the if guy was proud of his behavior or about to recommend five days in the electric chair.

Peterson tapped a cheap ballpoint pen on his little Ranger notepad and expertly swapped corners of his mouth with the flat toothpick. "That sum it up, Officer Edwards?" he asked when Chilly was finished.

Chilly gave a curt nod. "It does, sir."

Moss raised an eyebrow, bushy to match his mustache. "So, nothing else?" He obviously thought there was something.

"No, sir," Chilly said.

Peterson raised his hand, as if a Texas Ranger needed permission to speak. "You didn't happen to run across any other shooters inside or outside of the mall?"

Chilly shook his head. "No, sir. I mean, I understand that Officer Ritchey fired his weapon, but other than Vetter and Lilly, I saw no one else."

Peterson leaned over the desk a hair, as if the next question was all-important.

"Some guy in a hood, maybe?"

"No," Chilly said. "A hood?"

"A mask." Lieutenant Moss glanced at his notes. "A balaclava."

"Definitely not," Chilly said. "I'd remember that."

Ranger Peterson leaned back in his chair again, hands folded across his chest, pondering heavily on something.

The desk phone chirped. Moss, showing a spark of emotion for the first time during the interview, snatched it up, sounding annoyed. He listened for a moment, then hung up.

"Detective Spoon wants to know if you announced yourself as a police officer prior to firing your department-issued rifle."

"I did not," Chilly said.

Moss scratched another note in his book.

Chilly decided he needed to explain. "I came under fire from the moment I entered the main concourse of the mall. At this point, I'd already activated the red and blue strobe lights on my motorcycle and I was wearing a uniform helmet and bright yellow uniform shirt."

Ranger Peterson chuckled. "Still wrapping my head around the fact that you rode your bike straight into the mall." He shook his head. "I've seen some cool shit in my day, but . . ." He glanced at Moss, who gave him a nod.

Both men relaxed noticeably.

"Most of this event was caught on mall security cameras," the lieutenant said. "Fortunately, your account matches the footage perfectly. We'd like you to take a look at something."

Moss called one of the administrative clerks and asked him to bring in a laptop. Ranger Peterson, hands still folded on his chest, eyed Chilly while Moss logged in and cued up the video footage.

"How you holding up though all this, son?"

"It's kind of surreal, sir," Chilly said honestly.

"Have you talked to your daddy about it?"

Chilly nodded. "Yes. And my brother. Weird that my older brother's been on the job six years longer than I have, half of that on FBI Hostage Rescue deployed all over the country, and I'm the one who has an OIS—as a motor officer in Abilene."

"I'm sure your dad has some good counsel for you," Peterson said. "I know he's been there himself."

"He has," Chilly said.

Moss looked up from the computer. "Our investigation isn't done," he said. "But from here, it looks like you saved a lot of lives."

Chilly shook his head. "I suppose . . . But I can't help but think that if I hadn't been bogged down with Ms. Wright and the bomb . . ." He glanced up. "I understand Vetter killed three more while I—"

"I'm going to stop you right there," Peterson said. "There's a world of difference in giving yourself an honest critique and second-guessing your every move. Lois Wright and her baby survived this ordeal because of you. That should count for something."

"I appreciate that, sir," Chilly said. "It's . . ." He stopped, changing tack. "Vetter was dragging a hostage when I got him. Did she make it?"

"She's still in ICU," Moss said. "But it sounds like she'll pull through." He tapped a finger on the notes in front of him, scanning as if to make sure he got them right. "She told paramedics that Vetter was talking about some 'spy militia' before he died. Does that mean anything to you?"

"No, nothing." Chilly shook his head. "If I'd have gotten him a few seconds earlier, maybe she wouldn't be—"

"I told you to knock that shit off," Peterson said, still calm, but leaving no room for debate. "Self-doubt has destroyed more good operators than bullets. I reckon there's no such thing as a **good** shooting, but yours looks to be honest and justified. Even so, you've got a long row to hoe ahead of you. There's surely going to be a vulture or two circling out there, ready to throw buckets of civil actions against you and the city just to see what sticks. It's best you realize from the git-go you can't do a damned thing about any of it. What you **can** do is keep your head down and remember you did your job. Leave that other shit to the nutless critics who think they know exactly how they would act under stress because they watched a couple episodes of **SEAL Team.**" Peterson took out his toothpick and flicked it into the trash can before picking a bit of wood off the tip of his tongue. "I didn't see any of them riding their motorcycle toward the sound of gunfire."

Moss gave a grinning nod and turned the laptop on the table so they could all see it.

Chilly watched the events replay from sixteen different angles on a split multiplexed computer screen. He'd lived it, but still found himself startled at how quickly things unfolded. In the bottom-right view, he watched Vetter and Blondie race out of the Sears doors, only to turn and run back inside when mall security showed up and rammed what was apparently their getaway car.

Then, inexplicably, that box on the computer screen went black.

Ranger Peterson pointed a new toothpick at the dark square. "Some wily son of a bitch shot out the camera," he said.

"The guy in the balaclava you asked me about?"

"Sounds that way," Moss said. "Good Samaritan with a gun, according to witnesses." He opened his folder and slid a stack of eight-by-ten color photographs across the table. The top one showed a white Hyundai SUV. In the next photo, a man lay on the pavement beside the vehicle's bumper, a gaping, unsurvivable wound where his throat should have been.

"Merlin Swain," Chilly said. "I've arrested him a couple of times. Petty theft, stuff like that. Goes by Zip."

"**Went** by Zip," Peterson said. "According to the driver of the white SUV, Mr. Swain threatened her and her kid with a handgun. He was in the process of jacking her car when a, in her words, 'tactical-looking dude in a mask' shot him in the neck with a rifle. She says this masked man saved her life."

Chilly took a closer look at the photo, exhaling slowly. "Rifle wounds never look the way they do in the movies . . ." He took a deep breath, shaking his head. "Interesting that whoever shot him took the time to take out the camera beforehand."

"Sure is," Peterson said. "Two quick shots, from fifteen meters. The woman from the SUV says her husband has a couple suppressors, and this guy had the same kind of thing on his rifle."

Chilly studied the photograph in thought. "Suppressed rifle, snap-shooting the camera before taking out Zip. Seems like a professional. Any Special Ops guys coming through Dyess?"

"As far as I know, Dyess is mostly an Air Mobility and bomber base," Peterson said. "But maybe so. A witness leaving the library gives the same description as the SUV driver—tall, athletic, describes the mask as 'the same kind of balaclava that Nairobi dude wore.'"

"The SAS guy," Chilly said, mulling that over.

His theory about Special Ops was sounding more and more plausible. "From the al Shabaab terrorist attack on the Westgate Mall in Kenya."

"Yep," Peterson said. "According to multiple witnesses, our guy shot Merlin Swain twice in the throat, then took his phone."

"That is some level-ten professional shit," Chilly said. "Excuse my French, L.T. I mean, in the middle of a botched robbery turned carjacking, this balaclava guy locates the only security camera, pops it, shoots Zip in the neck, leaving his face intact so he can unlock the cell phone."

Struck by a sudden thought, Chilly spread the photographs out on the table. He found what he was looking for and pushed it toward the other two men.

Ranger Peterson pulled a pair of reading glasses out of his shirt pocket and leaned in closer. "A track in the blood." He slid the photo to Moss, then looked up over the top of his glasses, waiting for Chilly to explain. "Okay?"

"It is an odd-looking print," Moss said. "You recognize it?"

Chilly took a moment to scroll through his phone and then set it on the table beside the crime scene photo. "The same boot print we found at Royce Vetter's house after his wife and son were murdered—roughly four hours before the mall shootings."

"We'll run the print through SoleMate,"

Peterson said. "Shouldn't take long to find out what kind of boot it is."

Moss pushed back from the table and got to his feet. "So we're looking for a professional shooter who executed Royce Vetter's family and then hunted down Merlin Swain, killed him, and took his phone—right here in Abilene."

"What was that Vetter was saying to his hostage?" Chilly asked, on his feet as well. "Spy militia . . . Sounds about right."

39

President Jack Ryan sat behind the Resolute desk, thinking about his recent morning with Cathy, and noting to himself that the American people benefited when their President was an emotionally whole and happy person.

Arnie van Damm shattered the pleasant mood, blustering in through the side door nearest his own office, avoiding the secretaries' suite altogether.

"And yet again," he said, "we've got a situation in Afghanistan."

As usual, van Damm wore the wrinkles on his blue pinstripe like a badge of honor—or maybe just an afterthought. A navy-blue tie angled from the loose collar of an oxford button-down like the hand of a clock pointing to four instead of six.

The chief of staff looked impatiently at his watch.

"I thought everyone would be here by now," he said.

The door from the secretaries' suite swung open mid-sentence. Mary Pat got the gist of what Arnie was saying and grimaced.

"We're ten minutes early."

Bob Burgess, Homeland Security Secretary Mark Dehart, and Beth Treviso, the secretary of health and human services, filed in behind her. Commander Robbie Forestall, deputy national security adviser, brought up the rear.

"Ten minutes," van Damm mused out loud, as if there were something morally superior about being eleven minutes early.

Ryan moved from behind the desk to take up his chair to the right of the fireplace. He waved a hand toward the twin sofas, urging everyone to make themselves comfortable. Coffee was on the way. What was to have been a strategy session on the Pharmaceutical Independence Bill was about to morph into a briefing on Afghanistan. It was out of Treviso's or Dehart's wheelhouse, but Ryan valued their input and asked them to stay.

The previous video showed a female who's believed to be Dr. Naomi Harper crossing the border into Tajikistan north of Pagol," Foley said. "This newest footage was hand delivered to an asset in Ishkashim—on the Tajikistan side—by a cutout, a traveling merchant who swears he knows nothing more than it was given to him by a Chinese man he thinks was a soldier."

"First off," Ryan said. "Have we established this is a real video?"

"Good question," Foley said. "And yes. This does not appear to be a deepfake."

"What do we know about this fellow giving the confession?" Ryan asked.

Foley tapped a pen on her notebook. "The station chief in Dushanbe says Nazir Bayat appears to have family that drifts back and forth from Tajikistan into Khushabad, Afghanistan. He's got people trying to locate some of the Bayat family now, but the Wakhi don't have cell phones or vehicles or many other means we can use to find them. It's all boots on the ground and word of mouth."

Dehart spoke next. "From what I read, the Wakhi people are virtually untouched by the wars in their country. They're not experienced in violence. Wouldn't take many armed troops to subdue them and take the Harpers captive and cart them north."

"True," the SecDef said. "There are a couple of not-so-secret PRC bases over the border in Tajikistan. One near Pak, not far from where the video was supposedly taken, and another farther east, twenty miles from the Chinese border."

Ryan took a sip of coffee, weighing that for a moment before glancing at his director of national intelligence. "How far from the Tajik border were the Harpers working?"

Foley gave a nod to the tablet computer on Forestall's lap. It faced the President and displayed a map of Afghanistan's narrow Wakhan Corridor and surrounding nations of Tajikistan, Pakistan, and China. "According to their daughter," Foley said, "the Harpers were working at any one of three sites: Mulung Than—which is the closest to the border with Tajikistan—Vagd Boi, or Asan Katich. In the Big Pamir."

Ryan laced his fingers in thought. Everyone in the room knew of his affection for **Kim**, the Rudyard Kipling novel about a small boy operating as a spy during the Great Game that brought the Wakhan Corridor into being. Where the rest of them were clearing the fog off their mental maps of the "Stans," Ryan was picturing Central Asia as it was then as compared to now.

"How many Chinese troops in this latest video?" Ryan asked.

"Four are visible in frame," Forestall said. "There's enough movement we can be sure there was a cameraman and not a tripod. So at least five."

Ryan took another sip of coffee and shook his head. "It's not unusual for the Chinese to patrol the Wakhan. Hell, what are the few Afghan forces posted out there supposed to do when a larger, better-armed group of PLA soldiers tromps over the mountains and says they want to help? That said, it's one thing to patrol and another to march across the border and kidnap Americans in the middle of a humanitarian mission." The

President peered across his cup at the DNI. "And we're one hundred percent certain the Harpers are not intelligence assets of some kind?"

"They're not ours, Mr. President," Foley said. "The area they are in is beyond remote. No Taliban presence—the Wakhi people are too poor to bleed dry and too few to chastise for lax religious practices. A handful of smugglers still use the old Silk Road route, but Chinese troop movements are so infrequent that there would be almost no useful intelligence gleaned from posting anyone out there for us or the Taliban."

"Who knew the Harpers were there?" Ryan asked. "I'm sure word spread among the Pamir that there were doctors in the house, but this sort of thing would take planning. Any idea how it got up the chain?"

"BBC did a news piece on them a couple weeks ago," Forestall said. "A journalist and her producer accompanied them in—truck, foot, yak train, the works. She stayed a couple days and then filed the story as soon as she returned to Kabul." Accustomed to briefing the President, Forestall answered the next question before it was asked. "BBC has already sent all their raw footage to Langley. The reporter says unequivocally that the only people she saw with the Harpers for the duration of her trip were Wakhi, Tajik, or Kyrgyz shepherds. No sign of any Chinese military personnel."

"One of the men in uniform behind Dr. Naomi Harper has features that suggest he might be Tajik," Burgess said. "The others appear to be People's Liberation Army. The Chinese forces commander didn't identify himself in the video, but we've confirmed him to be Colonel Tu Jian, Western Theater Command. Last we knew he was in Xinjiang."

"Accused of being spies . . ." Ryan said. "What did the video say again? Holding them 'for their own protection.' It's always some bullshit like that."

"But they're not asking for any exchange," Dehart mused.

It was a viable observation, since it wasn't exactly unknown for a country to nab a foreign visitor, accuse them of being spies, and then demand a prisoner exchange in trade.

"Nothing yet," Foley said.

"SEAL Team Six and Delta are spooling up for a possible insertion into Tajikistan," Burgess said.

"Once we have a location for them," Ryan said.

"Working on that," Burgess said. "Dushanbe has given us permission to keep a one-dot-zero orbit over the yurts near Kargush." He translated for Dehart and Treviso. "Twenty-four-hour surveillance."

"And if they're still in the Wakhan?" Ryan asked.

"Special Forces familiar with the area are

snooping into the Wakhan as well, working with their AFA commando counterparts."

Ryan shook his head. "Anybody else feel like this is exactly what Colonel Tu wants us to do? To rush in before we have enough data? The video clearly shows the Harpers are in a felt yurt. If they're in Tajikistan or the Wakhan, the people who have them will see us coming for miles. We risk putting the Harpers in harm's way if we go in without knowing exactly where they are, right down to the specific yurt—not to mention the danger to innocent Wakhi shepherds . . ." He looked around the room. "Keep me posted. What else?"

When no one else spoke up, Mary Pat said, "I wonder if we might address the recent Operation Noble Eagle incursion again."

Ryan leaned away as far as the high-back chair would let him, distancing himself from the question.

He groaned. "Okay."

Mary Pat gave a maternal this-is-for-your-own-good smile. "The fact that the pilot's family was threatened by an unknown third party suggests a probing attack. Like something bigger is at play here."

Burgess gave a slight nod, aware that Ryan didn't want to talk about this, but throwing his support behind Foley anyway.

"We're leaving the 101st at Andrews on a

heightened state of alert for a few more days," he said.

Secretary Dehart, in charge of homeland security voiced his agreement.

Ryan set his coffee mug on the side table and raised his hands. "Okay. I have enemies," he said. "I'm fully aware of that. Hell, you can't make the decisions we make and expect everyone to like you. We've got deepfake videos that show me speaking to a group of my supposed hooded Illuminati minions or addressing world-dominating bankers. The last one I saw showed me promising G20 leaders that I would nuke Russia if they don't 'return Ukraine to us'—as if Ukraine was ours to begin with. Ransomware attacks are up, what, fivefold in the past three weeks, at least one of them causing the death of U.S. citizens. And . . . yes, someone attempted to force Mr. Cantu to fly an airplane into my home. But it didn't work."

Ryan leaned forward, eyeing each person in the room in turn. "We cannot—will not be deterred. I trust in my merry band of experts to keep us all safe and allow me to move forward."

40

Burgess and Forestall excused themselves first. Foley stayed a few minutes longer, giving input where Ryan asked her, offering suggestions that he'd not considered. As Oval Office meetings went, it was a long one, lasting a whopping twenty-five minutes.

Arnie and Secretary Treviso left through the hall door, but Ryan asked Mark Dehart to remain for a moment.

"Strange times," Ryan said when the two men were alone.

"They are indeed, Mr. President," Dehart said. He opened his leather folio and removed a sheet of paper, leaning forward to pass it to Ryan, who put on a pair of readers from his desk to examine it.

"I trust this isn't a letter of resignation."

"Not at all," Dehart said. If he was flustered, he didn't show it. "You'd asked us all to prepare a list of five individuals we believe would be good candidates for the office of vice president. I apologize for being dilatory with my list, but here it is, along with my rationale for each name."

"John Nance Garner, serving as FDR's vice president, said the job of vice president was 'the spare tire on the automobile of government.'"

Dehart smiled. "Among other things, sir."

"Old Cactus Jack did have a few more colorful descriptions of the office, to be sure."

Ryan scanned the document. "You have Mary Pat Foley as your top choice. Interesting."

"You asked for an honest list, Mr. President," Dehart said. "Director Foley naturally shares your priorities ninety percent of the time. From what I've observed, she gets on board without hesitation the other ten percent."

"She does indeed." Ryan passed the paper back to Dehart. "Your list is incomplete."

"Sir?"

"I would like to have seen your name there, Mark."

Now he was flustered. "Mr. President, I . . . That's not . . ."

"You were on three other lists," Ryan said. "Including Mary Pat's. And I have to tell you, you're certainly on mine."

"Mr. President," Dehart said, sounding as if he'd just run the anchor leg of a four-by-eight-hundred-meter relay. "You are fond of quotes, so I'd channel Theodore Roosevelt here. 'I'd a great deal rather be anything, say a professor of history, than the vice president.'" A pained expression crossed his face—as Ryan knew it would.

"You are surrounded by so many who are much more capable than I—"

Ryan gave a wry chuckle. He'd used almost exactly the same lines on President Durling. Rather than dwell on the past, he leaned forward, focusing intently on Mark Dehart.

"You know what clenched my decision for me?"

The secretary closed his eyes and took a slow, deliberate breath. "I cannot imagine, Mr. President."

"At Andrews," Ryan said. "When Scott brought the vice president's body home from Japan. Of course you were respectful to Tony Hargrave's memory, but your first priority was to Special Agent Mulvaney. It's a tough thing for a Secret Service agent, losing the person they're sworn to protect, even to natural causes. You know Keenan Mulvaney by name. What kind of a cabinet secretary knows their people that well?"

"What kind of President does?" Dehart said.

"And there you go," Ryan said. "That's what I expect . . . No, that's what I require." He waited for a minute to let the conversation sink in, then said, "I am eager to hear your thoughts."

"Sir," Dehart said, swallowing hard, looking around the room as if for some way to escape. Ryan had long thought that the Oval Office seemed to have been designed to make people feel like there was no way out. "This position would set someone up who wants to run in the next election. No offense, but I've never had my eye on this office."

"I get it," Ryan said. "You don't want the job. That's what makes you the right person to do it. You've already been vetted by the Bureau and you have decent support on both sides of the aisle, so confirmation shouldn't be too painful for either of us."

Dehart exhaled again. "You know I'm here to serve, Mr. President, but I don't like it. No, sir. I do not like it at all—and frankly, neither will my wife."

"Tell Dee that the vice presidency is often described as the most boring political office in D.C."

"With all due respect," Dehart said. "It certainly didn't turn out to be boring for you."

"No," Ryan said, thinking again to the few short hours he'd held the office of vice president of the United States—before ninety percent of the government was wiped out. "It was not."

41

Downtown Washington, D.C., looked as though its inhabitants were preparing for an invading army instead of honoring the life of the late Vice President Anthony Hargrave. In truth, they were doing both.

John Clark stood beside his son-in-law. Barely able to tolerate crowds of any size, he kept his back to a large willow oak near the intersection of Pennsylvania Avenue and 4th Street. Thousands of people filled the open area between the east and west buildings of the National Gallery of Art, pouring out along Constitution Avenue from the White House all the way to the Capitol.

President Ryan had directed the secretary of defense to conduct a state funeral for Anthony Hargrave on behalf of the nation. Pursuant to his orders, the secretary of the Army designated the Military District of Washington to exercise that responsibility.

A state funeral was a massive undertaking, with myriad moving parts across all service branches and multiple government agencies overseeing security and planning logistics for dignitaries from the United States and around the world.

They'd had three days to make it happen.

Later, when the vice president's body reached the Capitol, every other face in the crowd would be military, Capitol Police, Secret Service, State Department Diplomatic Security—or someone else with a badge and gun protecting some diplomat or potentate. Security personnel were present along the procession route as well, uniformed, or, like Clark and Chavez, in civilian clothing, blending in with the crowds.

Gone were the tour buses, sidewalk T-shirt vendors, and hot dog carts that usually pocked the sidewalks along Constitution Avenue. City dump and garbage trucks blocked perpendicular streets a block away. Concrete bollards and metal fencing funneled crowds where the Secret Service and D.C. Metro wanted them—close enough to pay their respects, but not so close as to pose a threat.

Clark knew all too well that the only way to protect someone was to keep them in a concrete bunker surrounded by armed personnel. But no one stood for that for very long, no matter the threat, especially those with enough hubris to be good leaders in the first place. And even then, at some point, the enemy learned enough about your defenses to build their own bunker buster.

The speaker of the House—next in line for the presidency until Mark Dehart was sworn in—was cooling his heels at an undisclosed location away from the other members of the cabinet and congress. The designated survivor. A decapitation strike wasn't exactly unknown in the United States. A Japanese commercial airliner crashing into the Capitol building vaulted Jack Ryan into the Oval Office kicking and screaming. The powers that be took it seriously after that—for a time. The nation's level of high alert fell quickly to a state of relaxed attentiveness that grew more relaxed and less attentive with every minute that passed from the time of a disaster or security breach.

People forgot.

Not Clark.

Chavez stared west down Pennsylvania Avenue at the approaching funeral procession. Like Clark, he was gauging the mood of the crowd. Foley had asked them to roam, to act as unofficial countersurveillance during the procession.

Clark looked up Constitution at the approaching phalanx of police motorcycles. The Washington Monument rose up behind them in the distance.

A Navy chief in dress blues standing with a cadre of fellow sailors two paces away snapped a crisp, white-gloved salute as the national colors came into view. Clark, a chief in a previous life, was in civilian clothes and stifled the urge to salute as well.

The honor guard of D.C. Metropolitan Police motorcycles passed at the head of the procession, lights flashing. Behind them marched a color guard. A mounted section chief from the 3rd United States Infantry Regiment or "Old Guard" came next, followed by six matching horses drawing a four-wheeled caisson and the flag-draped coffin. Eight uniformed body bearers representing the five service branches flanked the caisson, originally built in 1918 to carry a 75mm cannon. Behind the coffin, another color guard carried the flag of the vice president. A single Old Guard troop led a riderless black horse, caparisoned with a blue blanket and saddle. Polished boots faced backward in the stirrups.

Military bands, marching personnel, flags, cannons, and a river of Class A uniforms stretched along the National Mall. The United States Secret Service, Capitol Police, and D.C. Metropolitan Police Department were heavily involved, but there could be no doubt that this was a military endeavor. All the pomp and flag-waving made Clark happy while at the same time filling him with intense sadness.

The horses drawing the caisson approached 4th Street, their clomping hoofbeats somber accompaniment to the military band playing "Hail Columbia" as the first march rounded the bend.

Chavez leaned closer to say something, but Clark raised a hand, bidding him to wait a moment. A heartbeat later, Chavez learned why.

As the coffin rolled through the intersection at a steady three miles per hour, a lone Air Force F-16 roared overhead. Four flights of five followed, one after the other, low enough that Clark felt the growl of the fighter jets' engines deep in his chest. As the last flight crossed overhead, the third plane in formation pulled skyward, leaving a noticeable gap.

"That missing man and the riderless horse always get me," Chavez said when the roar abated and before the band got too close to hear anything. "Boots backward in the stirrups so the commander can look back at his troops one last time before he leaves . . ."

Clark gave an almost imperceptible nod. "It comforts the living, I suppose."

Though he'd seen much of death, the closer Clark got to his sell-by date, he wasn't sure what he thought about it. Would he have the opportunity to look back, to check on his wife and family? His grandson? One thing he did know was that it did little good to ponder on such things for very long. Better to focus on what he **could** do while he was upright over what he might do after he was dead.

42

Today, Harjit Malhotra discussed finances and acquisitions with the tiger. He reviewed the benefits of the upcoming sale to Roth Pharmaceutical and the many obstacles and oh-so-dreadful hardships the bastard American President was putting in his way. The tiger appeared to listen intently—leastways, it did not interrupt. Kashvi, Malhotra's deliciously pretty secretary, called it "his" tiger. But that was not right at all. Though Malhotra had indeed been the one to kill it, the tiger belonged to no one. Could anyone really own a beast as fierce and beautiful as this? Kashvi was a nonsensical girl who could never have understood philosophy of any kind.

"She does have her uses, though," Malhotra said to the tiger.

He gave a little start when there was a rap at the door, thinking for a moment that the noise had somehow come from the animal. Kashvi leaned her head in, large hoop earrings dangling from succulent lobes . . . and announced the arrival of Herr Reinhardt Roth, president and majority stockholder of Roth Pharmaceutical.

Malhotra had to force himself not to rub his hands together with glee.

Almost twice Malhotra's age at sixty-one, Roth carried himself like a much younger man. He was tall and strong-jawed, with a high head and golden hair that made anyone who saw him say, "And there goes that German fellow."

Kashvi showed the man in, doting on him as a secretary was expected to dote on guests. Perhaps, Malhotra thought, a little too much, as he came around his desk to join Roth in the two side chairs of richly tanned leather from Kanpur. Kashvi took a step back once the men were seated.

"Something to drink?" Malhotra waved a hand toward the well-stocked bar along the wall adjacent to the tiger. "A Jägermeister? Or perhaps you would enjoy some exquisite Indian feni."

Herr Roth licked his lips as if tasting the air, and then looked at Kashvi, smiling politely. "Rum will do. Ice if it is good rum."

Malhotra bit his tongue, then nodded at his secretary. "Bring him a rum and ice, and a feni and lime for me."

"We have a saying in my country," Roth said, a few minutes later after Kashvi had swished away. He swirled the rum but looked directly at Malhotra as if judging his every reaction. **"A prudent pause moves business forward."**

A pause? This was exactly what he feared. Had Roth flown all the way from Munich to watch him twist in despair after he told him the deal was off? Herr Roth was much too shrewd for that. Were he to end things, he would have ended them over the phone. No, no, no. This was merely a negotiation tactic. One did not become as wealthy as Reinhardt Roth by paying the asking price for anything. And then again, one did not attain the riches Malhotra wanted by selling at a discount.

Malhotra took a drink of the cashew liquor and forced a smile. "We, too, have our sayings. One in particular has served me and my family well: **Neither a monkey who misses a branch nor a man who misses his chance can be saved."**

The German took a sip of rum and contemplated that.

"Herr Malhotra," Roth said. "This business of the Americans building facilities in Puerto Rico is worrisome, both to my board and to me personally. Perhaps we should—"

Malhotra took a chance and interrupted. "If I may, it is very premature to say the Americans **are** building facilities. This protectionist bill is yet in the early stages, likely to die on the vine in the committees of their congress." He smiled, this one genuine. "Little of worth survives those committees, and this bill has no worth at all. Not to worry . . . Not to worry."

Roth stared at the tiger for a long moment. "The eyes . . ." he said.

Malhotra nodded, happy to have a mental moment to figure out how he might salvage this deal. "Yes, the eyes are fierce, are they not? So very intense."

The German's upper lip curled into something that might have been disgust but was at the very least mild disdain. "I was going to say they were tragic." He set his empty glass on the teak side table with a resounding clunk. "More than one of my advisers believe it would be prudent to pause for a beat, suggesting that perhaps I explore the possibility of investment in Puerto Rican real estate."

Kashvi, finely attuned to noises like empty glasses hitting tables, knocked on the door before coming in to offer Roth another rum.

He handed her the glass along with a broad smile. Malhotra could not be sure, but he thought the bastard actually caressed the girl's fingers.

"Your employer is very lucky to have such a pleasant and attentive assistant." He shot her a playful wink. "No ice this time, my dear."

"Herr Roth," Malhotra said. "I assure you this bill amounts to nothing. My lobbyists and

political operatives in Washington, D.C., tell me
that it is dead on arrival. That is all there is to it.
Any speculation involving real estate in Puerto
Rico would result in Caribbean land that, though
quite picturesque, will be worth little more tomorrow than it is today. This acquisition is a very
good deal for both of us. I urge you to be stead-
fast in your resolve to follow through."

Roth finished his second rum and, to
Malhotra's momentary relief, agreed not to make
any rash decisions for one week.

Kashvi showed him out, blushing and tittering
at his many compliments. He was an old letch,
but she was only doing what she'd been asked
to do.

Malhotra returned to his desk and snatched
up the phone the moment the door swung shut.
He had no time for this. The closing on the
sale was scheduled for just over a week away—
and Malhotra stood to lose billions if it did not
proceed.

The other end of the line picked up. It was
the Spaniard's personal line. Malhotra was in no
mood to deal with an assistant.

"Yes."

"It has to happen soon," Malhotra said. Gil
knew exactly what "it" was. "The very point of
all this is to hit the American President where it
hurts him most. A handful of Internet scams and

obviously fictitious movies are not doing the job! I want her taken and I want her taken now!"

"We have it well in hand, sir," the Spaniard said. "These things cannot be rushed—"

"That is ridiculous!" Malhotra all but screamed. "You have had this assignment for months. Two weeks ago would not have been rushed. I am not sure you comprehend the importance of timing."

"Our plan is sound," Gil said. "And we will follow through as the timeline dictates. But you have my word, it will happen soon enough to keep your German buyer in tow."

"It had better," Malhotra said, feeling only slightly foolish for threatening a man who surely had a half-dozen aliases and an army of killers at his beck and call.

"Was there anything else?" the Spaniard asked. "If not, I will get you a situation report."

"Yes," Malhotra said. "Yes, yes, a situation report." And then he ended the call.

Exhausted from both encounters, he slumped forward, elbows on his desk, chin on his hands. He shook his head sadly at the tiger. "Do not fret, my good friend. You are not tragic. You are fierce—"

There was a gentle knock at the door and Kashvi stuck her head in. "Did you need me, sir?"

He sat up and flicked his hand for her to come in.

"What did you think of Herr Roth?"

She shrugged. "I don't know. He seemed to me to be nice enough."

"We need the man," Malhotra mused, mostly to himself. "But I find something quite sinister about him." He looked up quickly. "Don't you?"

"To be honest," Kashvi said, "I did not pay much attention to him. My job is to take care of you, H.M."

Malhotra could not help but smile. It was not uncommon for Indian employees to address superiors by their initials. When Kashvi did it, it was a sign that she wanted to be playful, to calm him down and coax him off the proverbial ledge. She showed remarkable intelligence for someone in her status, much more than his designer girlfriend.

"What would I do without you, my sweet Kashvi?"

She shrugged again, deftly opening the top button on her blouse, as if by accident.

He leaned back in his chair and flicked his hand toward the tiger.

"Now go stand over there. I want to look at you both."

43

Historically, it was not unheard of for the office of vice president to go unfilled for some time, years even. Ryan pushed and cajoled and called in virtually every marker he ever held, as well as some future favors, in order to convince the Senate to hold a confirmation hearing. The American people needed some continuity and Ryan aimed to give it to them. The full threat board probably didn't hurt to speed things along.

Just less than a week after Tony Hargrave's untimely death, Mark Dehart, son of a dairyman from Pennsylvania, former senator, and most recently secretary of homeland security, was sworn in on the floor of the Senate chamber as the vice president of the United States by Associate Supreme Court Justice Irene Palmer, a Ryan appointee, also from Pennsylvania. Dehart's college sweetheart stood at his side holding the family Bible. Their four adult children and nine grandchildren, half of them redheads like their grandmother, stood with him in support.

Keenan Mulvaney, special agent in charge of

VPPD, walked with him to the armored limousine and motorcade that took him to a small reception in the White House. His staff had already prepared his office in the Old Executive Office Building across the White House Campus as well as his smaller office in the West Wing, down the hall from the Oval.

There would be a larger reception later, after a little more time had passed from Tony Hargrave's death. This one was small, in the Roosevelt Room, with Ryan's cabinet and a handful of others Dehart would be working with. As homeland security secretary, he already knew his way around the White House.

"Cathy wanted me to apologize," Ryan said. "She wishes that she could be here." He couldn't help but notice the stunned looks in the vice president's eyes. His wife, busy talking to her new chief of staff, wasn't much better. Ryan couldn't blame them.

"Completely understandable," Dehart said. "To be honest, I wish I was in San Antonio listening to her speech instead of here now, Mr. President."

Ryan leaned in closer. "In the Oval, with everyone present, it's fine to address me as Mr. President, to give dignity to the office and all. Everywhere else, I'd just as soon you call me Jack." He chuckled. "Hell, I wish everyone would just call me Jack."

"I'll try, Mr. President."

"Don't try, Mr. Vice President." Ryan grinned. "See to it. That's a direct order."

Scott Adler worked his way through the crowd and extended his hand. "Congratulations, Mr. Vice President."

"I appreciate it, Mr. Secretary," Dehart said.

"Scott," Adler said. "You outrank me."

"I wish things had turned out differently," Dehart said. "That there had been no need for me in this office."

Adler smiled. "As my dear mother used to say, 'vus vet zayn, vet zayn.' What will happen . . . will happen. You will do fine, sir. The country is lucky to have you."

Ryan saw Foley and Burgess approaching and glanced at his watch.

The DNI and the SecDef gave their regards to the new vice president and then looked at Ryan.

"A few developments on the Wakhan Corridor issue, sir," Foley said.

"Very well," Ryan said. "Is Robbie Forestall up to speed on everything?"

"He is," Burgess said.

"Then have him brief the vice president," Ryan said. "If you don't mind, you can bring me up to speed on Air Force One."

"Of course," Foley said. Like everyone in Jack Ryan's orbit, she was accustomed to frequent impromptu flights.

"I'm sorry to run, Mark," Ryan said. "But welcome aboard."

"Thank you, Mr. President . . . Jack," Dehart said. "Here's looking forward to a supremely uneventful term."

"Uneventful?" Ryan raised a brow and then chuckled. "Have you met me?"

44

Leo Debs realized something was off by the time he parked. He'd expected all the surface streets within four blocks of the Alamo to be blocked off. He expected there to be a helicopter or two overhead, even now, this early before the event. Barricades, bollards, and plastic fencing were naturally the order of the day when someone like the First Lady of the United States came to visit. He'd not expected there to be such an army.

Not for the NIGHTINGALE.

Law-enforcement officers from San Antonio PD, Park Police, and Bexar County, not to mention the Secret Service, crawled the brick streets and walkways around the Alamo like an invasive species of ants.

He checked his watch, a Citizen Eco-Drive. Considering the money he made with the Camarilla, he could have easily afforded a Rolex or an IWC, but watches like that got you noticed, and that was the last thing he needed at the moment.

NIGHTINGALE would be wheels-down at

Lackland Air Force Base in half an hour. There were easily double the number of personnel he'd counted on this early in the game. Debs locked the door to his truck with the key fob and cursed under his breath as a khaki-clad pair of park officers patrolled by him on the sidewalk, chatting about a girl one of them was trying to woo. A man in a light windbreaker and a flesh-colored earpiece walked past from the south, eyeing the rooftops across the street as if looking for snipers. It was as if the bloody Queen herself was about to arrive.

Debs ignored them and took a folded map from his hip pocket, checking it as any tourist might, though every sidewalk, street, and alley were burned into his memory.

Walking routes hadn't been closed yet. That wouldn't happen for another hour, and Debs was able to trot down the steps off Market Street to reach the River Walk without drawing undue attention. He kept his eyes wide, in awe of all the hubbub, as anyone would when surrounded by so many guns and badges. Too much swagger was dangerous.

The first rule of thumb in most any ambush was to arrive early, but in this case, time on station meant the possibility of arousing suspicion. It was difficult to appear benign for long, especially for battle-hardened men like those with the Camarilla.

They'd all driven down from Abilene, twelve of them in four separate vehicles. Ramos, who'd been Colombian Search Bloc in his past life, and a former German GSG 9 operator named Himmel were in the counterfeit Bexar County ambulance, sitting in front of a barbecue joint in Schertz, twenty miles away. Pea and Rook were already in place, in their respective rooftop nests. The Secret Service would be focused primarily on shooters who threatened the First Lady. Pea and Rook took up positions to take out the snipers themselves. Any partial view of the venue below was added value. Taylor and the others would arrive at the river soon after Debs gave them the all-clear. Moving separately toward their assigned location.

Debs ambled his way along the river toward the target site where NIGHTINGALE would dedicate the memorial.

It was refreshing to work with professionals who knew what they needed to do and when they needed to do it. The money didn't hurt, but none of them were in it for that. Who else got to run an op like this one, right here under the noses of the most sophisticated protective organization in the world?

And still, something was wrong here.

He sorted out the problem as he approached the convention center, the location of the ARVO conference where NIGHTINGALE was slated to give the keynote later that afternoon. Two Secret Service agents—junior, from the lack of disillusioned stain on their earnest faces—stood by as a man with an acetylene torch spot-welded a manhole cover in place next to the river. This was not something that was done at the last minute. NIGHTINGALE's itinerary must have changed . . .

Debs froze when he saw scuba divers in the water. The San Antonio River was shallow, but the Secret Service left nothing to chance and checked the submerged area adjacent to the conference venue. That was going to be a problem if they did it up and down the river. A brisk walk toward the target venue eased his mind. The area directly between the convention center and the river was cordoned off with increased security protocols around the perimeter. It made perfect sense. POTUS had made a change in his schedule.

He was coming to watch his wife's speech.

Debs's mind went into overdrive as he wove his way through tourists, maintenance personnel, and myriad law enforcement along the River Walk. If the President had decided to attend the dedication ceremony with NIGHTINGALE, then everything he'd put in place was for nothing. Security for the First Lady was excellent, but the protective net around POTUS was exponentially more complex both in hardware and the sheer number of boots on the ground.

Two uniformed Park Police officers and a woman in a khaki vest Debs took for Secret Service stood post beside the draped memorial on the riverbank. There were no divers in the water there, or, more important, upriver two hundred feet adjacent to a lone palmetto bush. The area had no doubt been swept earlier and the three post-standers were there to make sure it stayed clean. The fact that they were present at all actually calmed Debs a notch. If they'd found even one item that he'd left underwater farther along the bank, the White House would have canceled NIGHTINGALE's participation in the event altogether.

Twenty feet from the post-standers, Debs took out his phone as if to make a call, and breathed easier when he saw he was still receiving a good GPS signal. The President evidently wouldn't make it for the memorial dedication, otherwise this place would be overrun with steely-eyed agents like the convention center.

Debs stood for a moment and watched a lone mallard drake, cocky and brightly plumed, swimming in circles, frantically attempting to attract the attention of a mottled brown hen who squatted fluffed and ambivalent on the riverbank.

This turn of events could well be a stroke of

luck. Agents looking after POTUS and FLOTUS were all part of the same protective detail—PPD. They melded into one when the President and his wife were together and those on the ground would be looking outbound in anticipation, unable to stop themselves from subconsciously getting ready for the big cheese to arrive. After all, who would bother with the drab little hen when her fancy mate was on his way.

Debs checked his watch again. Wheels-down in twenty minutes.

Debs opened up the encrypted Signal app on his phone and thumb-typed a message.

NIGHTINGALE IS GO

He pressed send and watched the string of eleven thumbs-up signs appear on his screen.

Slipping the phone into his pocket, he stood on the bank for another full minute, savoring the serenity of the place, thinking of the bedlam that was to come—and savoring that as well. A dozen yards away in the San Antonio River, the green-headed mallard drake swam his ass off looking regal and self-important while the hen sulked on the bank, close enough for Debs to kick if he'd been so inclined.

"Spoiler alert, mate," he whispered. "We're not after you. We're here for the missus . . ."

45

It was horses, or, more specifically, the lack of horses that drew Sergeant First Class Jake Thelan, ODA 0312's 18F (intelligence sergeant) to look more closely at the collection of felt yurts and stone animal enclosures comprising the Wakhi summer grazing village of Vagd Boi.

Captain Brock was still working on the persistent ISR. He'd requested a one-dot-zero, or twenty-four/seven surveillance, using several platforms, but his Agency contact got them the periodic use of a CIA Predator. Everything else was committed north, on locations where the Harpers were supposed to be now. Thelan worried that it was groupthink or, more bluntly, group blindness to any alternative other than the scenario posited by the Battalion S2's shop that kept everyone moving in the same direction once they started down any given path. The institutional inertia created by a unit as large as the National Missions Force made of hard-charging Tier One SEAL Team 6 and Delta type A personalities required a significant amount of effort to move even a few degrees. Oh, the teams were some of the most capable men Thelan had ever worked with. Personally, in smaller units, they were nimble and responsive to change—but they also went where they were pointed, and right now, their bosses were aiming them at two particular villages across the Pamir River in Tajikistan. No one had actually put eyes on the Harpers or their Chinese captors, but Reaper footage showed two Yongshi military jeeps partially hidden under camouflage netting twenty miles northeast of Ishkashim. No one was keen to throw finite surveillance resources at a spot where the Harpers had been, when a significant amount of signal and imagery intelligence lent credence to the notion that the Harpers were being held in Tajikistan.

Even periodic use of the CIA Pred was better than nothing. Far better.

The General Atomics MQ-1 Predator carried only a single Hellfire missile, but they were easier to come by than the faster and more heavily armed Reapers.

While the National Missions Force was getting up and ready to move once they had a target fixed in Tajikistan, ODA 0312's 18F sat down in the team room with Captain Brock, Warrant Officer Guzman, and Ripper Ward, the ops sergeant.

Thelan slid identical copies of the eight-by-ten photos across the table to each of the other men.

"What are we looking at, Jake?" Guzman asked.

"Three sheep pens, Chief," Thelan said, stating the obvious and earning a narrow look from the warrant officer. "Full of animals. The Wakhi move their yurts as they follow the grass up and down the valley," the 18F continued. "But there are several of these stone corrals where they return each year for their summer encampments. They bring their livestock into the enclosures at night to protect them from wolves—which my local agents tell me are a big problem. Other than the odd rusted-out Soviet rifle, rock pens and dogs are about their only defense."

"And these enclosures are in Vagd Boi?" Captain Brock tapped the photograph in front of him.

"Correct." Thelan turned his topo map toward the men and traced a line with a grease pencil and then pointed to a spot on the Wakhan highway just south of the border with Tajikistan. "So we know the Harpers got a permit to go into the Wakhan. They got it stamped when they came through Goz Khun two weeks ago with a driver and then hired a yak train to pack all their medical gear and camp supplies in from Wazud, where their permit was also logged, and they made the twenty miles or so push in the Big Pamir summer villages of Kund-a-Thur, Mulung Than, Vagd Boi, and Asan Katich."

Sergeant Ward spun his photo in a slow 360, looking at it from all angles.

Thelan gave them a beat, and then distributed another set of photos around the table.

Guzman studied the second photo side by side with the first and then shook his head. "I still don't see what I'm looking—wait a minute. There are horses in the first photo but none in the second."

"I count six," Brock said. "They're stuffed in with the sheep. Maybe seven, but that one could be a yak's ass."

"Right," Thelan said, sliding a third set of images across the table, and then a fourth.

"Okay, no horses here," the captain said. "Did we ever see anyone ride away?"

"No, sir," Thelan said. "The first image was taken nine hours ago, shortly after the Pred went on station. We aren't sure which village the Harpers were in when they were taken, so we've got it patrolling over all four. The camps are strung out all along the valley, just far enough apart that the ARGUS can't keep all of them in view at the same time."

Guzman pushed the photos away, like he was folding a poker hand. "So where'd they go, these horses?"

That's what's interesting," Thelan said. "They just disappeared. My money is on the yurts."

"They're large enough to hide a few horses," Sergeant Ward said. "I'm sure you're watching for women bringing in more than the normal number of water pails, etc., to see what deviates from what we'd consider normal patterns of life."

"We are," Thelan said. "And we stand ready to box the horses in Vagd Boi when the Pred picks them up again."

The ARGUS-IS, or Autonomous Real-Time Ground Ubiquitous Surveillance Imaging System, within the MQ-1's Gorgon Stare pod, had the capability of drawing a colored box around up to sixty-five different targets of interest within a fifteen-square-mile field of view and then tracking the individual movements within those boxes for as long as it remained on station.

Ward perused the map. "None of these other villages have horses?"

"It's mostly sheep and some yaks," Thelan said. "But they do have a few. The thing is, their horses are doing what horses are supposed to do in the Big Pamir, hanging out by the water, hauling stuff. There's the off chance they could be having some kind of festival and a big buzkashi tournament."

Guzman drummed thick fingers on the table. "Those buzkashi horses are beasts. I rode one once early on my first deployment and that son of a bitch bit pretty much everybody we got close to."

"Guess you'd get pissy, too," Ward said, "if your rider was quirting the hell out of other dudes for control of a headless goat carcass."

"I loved that horse," Guzman said. "At any

rate, are we sure the horses hanging out by the water in Mulung Than or Asan Katich aren't the same horses from the rock corral in Vagd Boi?"

"Image analysts say they are not," Thelan said.

Brock leaned back in his chair and ran a callused hand over his curly mop, then stretched his chin out to scratch his whiskered neck.

Sergeant Thelan and the others perked up. Every soldier on ODA 0312 knew the boss was pondering on some serious shit when he did the head-rub-chin-scratch maneuver.

"Jake," Brock said. "We're not going to change anybody's mind showing them photos of horses that aren't there. But those horses have to be somewhere, and the fact that the Predator isn't picking them up is curious."

"They could be concealed in the shadow of a rock," Guzman said, playing devil's advocate. "You said it yourself, Boss. It can be hard to tell the difference between a horse and a yak's ass when the lighting is wrong."

Brock raised a wary brow. "You really think that?"

"No, Captain, I do not," Guzman said. "I'm with Jake on this. I think those sons of bitches are hiding their horses in one of those yurts."

"Okay, then," Brock said. "The boys and girls up north are still probing a launch into Tajikistan, and rightly so. The evidence that the Harpers are there does point that way. But Sergeant Thelan's mission analysis has nudged the needle at least a hair toward the village of Vagd Boi." He shot a glance at Thelan. "What's the population of Vagd Boi supposed to be?"

"Around fifty, according to my local contact, a yak trader in Goz Khun."

"Fifty," Brock said, looking perplexed. "That's a lot of innocents running around in the crossfire if we attempt a rescue without fixing the target to a specific dwelling."

"The chief and I have been looking at all the angles for infiltration since this thing started," Sergeant Ward said, open hand over the map. "I'm leaning toward splitting. Split Team Alpha does a HAHO infil south of Mulung Than, working down to set up a three-man sniper observation post overlooking Vagd Boi. They will find and fix the target from the ground. Has to stand off a good distance, though. Every shepherd in this valley has at least one dog. Those dogs are loud and they are ferocious."

"Volkodav." Thelan gave a solemn nod. "Wolf crusher."

Most everyone on the team had at least one story to tell about a run-in with a massive Central Asian Ovcharka, protective and distrustful of strangers. The locals cut off their ears when they were puppies, giving the wolves less to grab on to during a fight and adding to their angry appearance.

Ward continued. "Once the target is fixed, Split Team Bravo infils with a helicopter assault force of ANA kandak commandos with three UH-60s—ten and ten and ten—thirty guys or even two Black Hawks and a Chinook, then we can take seventy. They finish the bad guys and rescue the hostages."

The team worked off the F3EAD mission model: Find, Fix, Finish, and then Exploit, Analyze, Disseminate any pertinent intelligence.

Brock glanced at Guzman, who gave a nod of approval.

"I like it," Brock said. "Get with Colonel Habib and see if he's amenable to you and Split Team Bravo accompanying a company of his kandak commandos in the HAF once we fix the target. Fifty would be nice. Sixty would be better. I'd like an overwhelming show of force on this."

Special Forces soldiers had a close working relationship with their Indigenous partners in the commando units, training and often deploying alongside them.

Guzman gave a sardonic nod. "The new 18 Echo is still feeling sketchy about trusting the Indigs. Afraid one of them is gonna drop him in the grease if things go sideways."

"Sergeant Megnas is new," Ward said. "He'll learn pretty quickly just like we all did. If they're wearing ball caps with the crunch brims, dipping

Copenhagen, and listening to Mas-todon, they're on our side."

"Yup," Thelan said. "That's what I told him, 'If their kit looks like our kit, we're good.'"

"Ripper," Brock said to Sergeant Ward. "You and the chief get the HAF jocked up for an early-morning assault. I'll take Jake and the new guy with me on the HAHO jump tonight."

Thelan wanted to smack his hand on the table and cheer, but instead he nodded and said, "Yes, Captain. Pakol hat and shalwar kameez," he asked. "Dress like a local?"

"Bring them," Brock said. "But we'll be in uniform. And I want everyone with M-4s and Glock 19s for interoperability. Sorry, Ripper. I know you're a SIG guy, but with virtually everyone else busy up north, we need to be as self-sufficient as possible. Jake, last time I saw you on the range you were hot shit with your new MRAD."

"Well, thank you, Boss," the intel sergeant said. "I'll bring her along."

The weapons sergeants on the team got the first two newly issued Barrett Multi-Role Adaptive Design (MRAD) Mark 22 rifles, but Thelan's skills as a long-range marksman were widely known with him regularly smacking sixteen-ounce Rip It cans at a thousand yards with his Remington M24. Sergeant Ward saw to it that he got the third gun, complete with a Nightforce optic. While Thelan loved his old Remington, the Barrett Mark 22 was like getting eight guns in one and had the advantage of allowing troops to switch between eight different calibers from .338 Lapua down to 6.5 Creedmoor. Pretty sweet deal. He'd worked up some good data on the Lapua and decided to bring the rifle set up with that reach-out-and-touch-someone caliber. A stinging Jake.

"Megnas still working with his little drone projects?" Brock asked.

"He is," Ward said. "Bryant Megnas is kind of a cyber nerd. I thought Raspberry Pi was something you ate until he got here. Real gamer. Easily the best personal reconnaissance drone operator we have."

"Good. Have him pack a couple of the little recon Hornets."

Guzman began to chuckle. "So much for the new kid working with people whose kit looks like his kit. You guys are gonna be out among 'em."

Brock smiled. "He'll do fine." He tapped the map with his index finger and looked up at his 18F. "We're talking about a distance of around twelve miles from the end of the road to Vagd Boi."

"Correct," Thelan said.

Brock checked his watch, a Rolex Submariner with black face and no date. It was the quintessential timepiece of a Green Beret, but so far

Thelan's wife hadn't warmed to the idea of him spending over eight grand on a new watch when his G-SHOCK was working just fine.

This deployment. For sure.

"I'd like my Alpha Team ready by dusk," Brock said. He rubbed a hand over the top of his head and then gave his neck a good long scratch, but if he was coming up with some cool plan, he kept it to himself.

46

Dr. Cathy Ryan felt the familiar pop-whine in her ears as the C-32 began its descent into San Antonio. It was a rare occurrence for Ryan to second-guess her lot in life, but the two women sitting across the table made her feel, if only for a fleeting moment, that maybe she was missing out. Dr. Marci Troxell, commander, United States Navy, and Acting Special Agent in Charge Karen Sato seemed to have dozens of inside jokes. They'd spent the first few minutes after boarding at Andrews catching up and comparing notes on their hectic lives. A raised brow from Troxell when Sato mentioned a cute lawyer from Justice she was dating. A knowing nod from the Secret Service agent when the White House physician spoke of her struggle to shave a few seconds off the swimming segment of her triathlon times.

Friends, Dr. Ryan thought. What a novel notion. Someday she would have the freedom for luxuries like that—when she could travel without dragging along an entourage of staff and security in a hundred-million-dollar airplane.

Friends or not, ten minutes into the three-and-a-half-hour flight, Sato and Troxell were all business. The interior of the airplane almost demanded it.

The C-32 carrying the First Lady used the call sign Executive One Foxtrot, the **F** designation for family of the President. One of four 45-seat military VIP versions of a Boeing 757, it was operated under the Presidential Airlift Group, Air Mobility Command's 89th Airlift Wing at Andrews. The same plane became Air Force Two if the vice president was on board. Officials like the secretary of state or defense utilized one of several VIP aircraft in the Wing, at which point the planes were designated Special Air Mission, or SAM, along with the tail number.

Not nearly as sophisticated as the Boeing VC-25 that customarily served as Air Force One, the C-32s were nonetheless well appointed. This particular one had been recently upgraded, swapping the stodgy navy-blue government seating for plush whiskey-colored leather and upgraded wood conference tables. Flat-screen televisions were situated on most every bulkhead, including the more tightly packed aft section, where media and Secret Service personnel whiled away the flights.

There was a private office up front, normally used by the vice president. Ryan had written her keynote and practiced it ad nauseam. (Poor

Jack.) She preferred to be around other people and planted herself at the small conference table on the port side. It was set up in a vis-à-vis configuration with a single seat (customarily occupied by the ranking person on the aircraft) and two aft-facing and slightly smaller seats on the opposite side of a polished teak table.

Maureen "Mo" Richardson, the agent in charge of the FLOTUS protection detail, was away at her sister's wedding, leaving Sato to run the San Antonio trip. A triathlete like Troxell, Karen Sato was beyond fit, with the flint-hard eyes that seemed to Cathy to be a requirement for Secret Service agents, at least those assigned "inside the bubble" or next to the First Family. Sato's hair was long but she kept it up in a tight bun when she was working. Today she wore khaki slacks and a light wool blazer over a ballistic vest, SIG Sauer pistol, extra ammunition, handcuffs, and radio. There was probably some kind of folding knife in there, too. It wasn't lost on the First Lady that Sato lugged all this around specifically to protect her. A pair of neat Asolo trail shoes rounded out the ensemble—"fighting over fashion," Sato said, joking with Troxell about some television cop show where the female lead wore "no shit, three-inch heels to hunt the bad guys."

Regina Shepherd, Dr. Ryan's longtime chief of staff, sat across the aisle, yielding her customary seat across from Ryan to Sato, who'd spent the last hour going over security plans and protocols with Troxell one final time before wheels-down. Vice President Hargrave's unfortunate death weighed heavily on everyone's mind. As White House physician on this trip, Troxell would be nearby.

If Cathy Ryan had a friend in the West Wing, it was Marci Troxell. They shared a love of medicine, of course, but it was more than that. Troxell's children were older. Her husband was a career Naval officer, a rear admiral stationed at the Pentagon. She knew what it was like to have a powerhouse husband, teenagers, and a career. White House medical staff served on a rotation, but more often than not, Dr. Troxell accompanied the First Lady when she traveled out of town.

With the briefings out of the way and landing imminent, the women stowed folders and settled into their seats. Troxell asked Sato if she planned to run the Manassas Mini sprint triathlon later that summer. Cathy listened to them chat, wondered which was more difficult, protecting someone or being the someone who was protected. A no-brainer, really. Having someone hover over you could be tedious, but doing the protecting was fraught with danger and boredom and being away from home . . . and more danger. Ryan had visited the U.S. Secret Service training center in Beltsville several times over the years, especially when Jack Junior was younger. The agents had taken him under their wing, palling around, mentoring, and even teaching him to shoot. Damn it. Her stomach ached when she thought too hard about where all that had gotten her oldest son.

Oh, Jack, she thought. **A mother always knows.**

Just because she spent much of her time becoming an expert on a piece of real estate the size of a nickel at the back of the human eye didn't mean she couldn't see what was going on in front of her face.

Even Jack Senior thought she was unaware of the "situation." No doubt they both believed they were sparing her hours of fear and grief, so she let them go on thinking they had her fooled. It was nothing short of astounding that such a bonehead in that regard could be so successful at running the country. Her Jacks, Senior and Junior, would continue to do unthinkably dangerous things for the good of the nation. They were good at it. She shouldn't blame them just because they happened to enjoy it, too.

The First Lady gave a slow shake of her head to clear her mind and looked out the window. The runway rose up to meet them. Executive One Foxtrot's wheels greased onto the tarmac.

———

Leo Debs shrouded his laser focus with a bumbling walk and, he hoped, a far-off look of incompetence.

Fermin Pea reported that NIGHTINGALE had arrived at the convention center. She and her detail of Secret Service agents were on their way to the dedication site with three local luminaries in tow. These dignitaries, all women with the San Antonio Youth Literacy Society, walked beside the First Lady. Debs made the mental adjustments needed to account for the slightly wider space between armed Secret Service agents as the detail was forced to spread slightly, and the ammunition required to drop the three new women in the party.

A dozen yards away, outside the cordoned zone flanked by Secret Service and a seemingly insurmountable wall of uniformed law enforcement standing shoulder to shoulder, Debs and the others watched NIGHTINGALE's approach, surrounded by nine Secret Service agents in a tight diamond formation, made somewhat more narrow than customary because of the confines of the River Walk. Her advance agent, a muscular kid with Hollywood blond hair who was probably thinking about his wife and kids, reached the bend by the dedication site.

And it begins, Debs thought.

Phones up and down the river began to chirp

and buzz. The Asian agent directly behind the First Lady moved forward three seconds after Ramos activated the Emergency Broadcast System text. Debs knew this would be Karen Sato, the substitute special agent in charge. She'd kept her eyes up, not consulted her phone, but was responding only to the buzzing, longer and more urgent than a normal text notification. Still walking, she tapped the First Lady on the shoulder, then cocked her head slightly, listening to a voice in her earpiece, another agent informing her of the emergency alert warning of the natural gas leak a mile away.

Debs smiled inside, imagining how he would react to the news if he were in her shoes.

A gas leak, you say? Do I really want to submarine the First Lady's event because of some minor problem that's over a mile away?

Special Agent Sato paused for a moment, causing the entire detail to stop. She cast a quick glance over her shoulder, clearly considering calling an exfil.

Debs held his breath. If this sneaky bitch listened to her gut and turned around right then and returned to the convention center, she and her team would live through the day—and it was the Camarilla who would be submarined.

She whispered something to the First Lady, who nodded and pulled her sweater tighter across her chest, as if she'd gotten a sudden chill—or sensed that something bad was about to happen. NIGHTINGALE then consulted with the jowly woman from San Antonio in the entourage beside her, who smiled and shook her wide face and waved a hand across the eastern horizon. Debs could almost hear her. **Oh, hon, don't you worry about a little gas leak. That kind of thing happens all the time . . .**

Special Agent Sato gave a noncommittal shrug and the agents began to move again—with the notion of possible explosions planted subliminally in their heads.

On an apartment rooftop four blocks to the east, Ramos activated the six DJI Inspire 2 drones. The M67 grenade on board each device weighed slightly less than four hundred grams, a hundred grams less than the drone's payload capacity. The UAVs rose from the rooftop, well outside the secure perimeter. Accelerating to fifty miles an hour in seconds, they sped toward the venue, homing on the GPS coordinates Debs had set, independent of any pilot input.

Twenty seconds later, the first grenade tumbled into the crowd. Five seconds after that the second rolled off the tiny balsawood tray suspended from the drone. And then the third, each sending jagged shards of shrapnel into everyone within fifty feet, and each progressively closer to the First Lady.

Though absent balls of fire and not nearly so

dramatic as depicted by Hollywood, the grenade explosions were still extremely loud and palpable, thumping chests and adding to the confusion.

Pea and Rook had taken out all four Secret Service snipers by the time the fourth grenade tumbled into the crowd. It struck an elderly man in the shoulder, slowing its descent, and then detonated at knee level.

Special Agent Karen Sato threw her arm around Cathy Ryan and, shielded by the collapsed diamond formation of her protective detail, began to run—directly toward Debs and his team.

Behind Debs and his men, the Counter Assault Team would be coming down the steps in less than ten seconds, armed to the teeth and ready to pluck the First Lady out of danger, but Debs didn't worry. He was, in fact, counting on the timing of their arrival.

47

John Clark, Chavez, and Caruso stood over the conference table at Hendley Associates, poring over a spread of personnel folders—dossiers of prospective recruits to The Campus.

This wasn't a job you applied for. It was invitation only—by referral, from trusted sources. Everyone in the room would die for the others—and had proven it time and time again. Nine times out of ten they each knew what the others would be thinking. An air of mutual respect and comradery permeated the team. They genuinely liked one another. New blood was sorely needed, but with it came the real chance of upending the balance. No one in the room took this exercise lightly.

They'd begun with ten names, and so far narrowed it down to six. Every file on the table represented a stellar individual, but in Clark's mind, two front-runners had begun to emerge, equally interesting. A Marine captain with Fleet Anti-Terrorism Security Team, single, fluent in German and Russian, a collegiate boxer, drove race cars in his spare time—and a female CIA officer whose mother was Saudi American and father Japanese. In Japan she was called "hafu" and looked down upon, but her fluency in four languages and her self-described ambiguous ethnicity made her a high-value recruit for the CIA. She came highly recommended by DNI Foley—just short of an order to at the very least give her a look.

Ding finished reading her file for the second time and held it aloft. "She's been involved in some high-level ops," he said.

The door to the conference room flew open and Gavin Biery barged in.

Everyone looked up at the same time.

"Hey, Gav," Clark said. "What's going on?"

Instead of speaking, the portly IT director cast his eyes frantically around the room. He snatched up the remote and switched on the flat-screen TV.

"Gavin?" Dom said. "You okay, bud?"

Biery shook his head, jabbing the remote toward the television. "Just look."

At first, Clark thought he was witnessing the bedlam of a mass shooting, then he read the chyron across the bottom of the screen.

"Someone get Jack Junior on the phone."

48

TEN MINUTES EARLIER

Cathy Ryan felt Karen Sato's hand on her shoulder, the first indication that anything was wrong. The Secret Service never just reached out and touched you unless it was something serious—a threat or even someone in the crowd with a water balloon. When you felt the hand you were supposed to go with it, follow their lead. Move where they directed you—away from danger . . . to safety. **Trust them. They had it worked out.**

Karen leaned forward, explaining the emergency broadcast message about a gas leak. Everyone was getting the alert now, phones buzzing like cicadas. Sonya Rodriquez, Cathy's host, explained that it was a mile away. "No problem," the smiling woman said, giddy to be there. "We will be fine here on our beautiful river."

They'd not gone ten steps before a muffled crack shook the ground like a distant clap of thunder. Special Agent Sato's hand gripped Cathy's shoulder more firmly at the sound. Another explosion sent up a chorus of screams. Still behind them, toward the convention center, but getting closer. Bits of debris skittered into the river, plopping like a child tossing in small stones.

"This way," Sato barked. Her fist twisted the fabric of Cathy's jacket, directing her firmly toward a three-story stucco hotel to the right.

A third explosion ripped through the awning in the building next to the hotel, close enough to be deafening. The crowd began to stampede, the mass of panicked bodies pushing the Secret Service detail toward the river no matter how many guns they had. Cathy had worked the emergency department enough early in her career to recognize the screams of wounded and dying. Marci Troxell was back there, keeping her distance so she wouldn't be injured in the same attack. Now Cathy worried that her distance might have gotten her hurt—or worse.

"Shit!" Sato muttered. "This is no gas leak!"

Pushed along with the river of panic, half deaf from the last explosion, Cathy was vaguely aware of Sato directing resources over the radio, calling in the heavily armed Secret Service Counter Assault Team down from street level via an alternate route. A fourth explosion, this one muffled, threw up a geyser from the river behind them, close enough to spray the entire Secret Service detail with water.

Twenty feet ahead, directly in their path, two

uniformed officers inexplicably fell face-first into the concrete walk. The threat—which had been to the rear, was at least partially in front of them. Rather than duck or try to protect themselves, the two Secret Service agents in the lead stood straighter, making themselves larger targets, shielding Cathy. They fell simultaneously, as if wilting under an unseen force.

Cathy's first instinct was to rush forward and help. The Secret Service had tried in vain to drill that out of her in Beltsville. AOP drills, they called them—attack on the principal. The agents had always yelled the direction of the threat. Gun left! Gun right! But the threats were everywhere now. Explosions, screams, trampling feet—and gunfire.

A hail of bullets mowed law enforcement and terrified bystanders alike. A spatter of blood splashed Cathy's cheek when the agent to her left was hit. A boy . . . he was just a boy, not even as old as Jack—

Karen Sato grabbed her by her shoulder, pulling her away from danger. Then her hand fell away, and she, too, stumbled, pitching forward face-first onto the River Walk, leaving Cathy standing alone.

She looked up to see men with machine guns advancing quickly toward her. **The Secret Service CAT? No, they weren't dressed right for that—**

The man leading the way let his gun fall and ran straight into Cathy, driving her sideways with the full weight of his body. At the same time, something sharp impacted her thigh. This bastard had stuck her with something! They toppled over the low curb and hit the water hard, Cathy's arms pinned hopelessly to her sides. She held her breath, resisting the urge to scream as the man drove her to the silty bottom. Still face-to-face and rolling like a croc spinning its prey, he wedged her under a concrete overhang, a sort of lip that kept them from floating to the surface. Mere seconds after they'd hit the water, a massive **whoomf** from above sent a pressure wave through the water, slamming into her chest and sending a jolt of pain through her ears. Another explosion—larger than any of the others, this one right on top of them.

Cathy's mind reeled, fighting panic. Her lungs screamed for air. Whatever drug he'd injected made it impossible to move her legs, to fight back at all. It was too dark to see, but she felt the man shove something roughly against her mouth, bashing again and again at her lips until she opened them. He pinched her cheeks together, holding whatever it was in place. A cloud of bubbles burbled around her face and she realized she was supposed to breathe. A respirator.

Mind racing, she gulped for air. Had this person saved her from the blast above or was he an enemy? The drugs were taking effect now. The logical part of her brain realized the man had given her ketamine. She felt as if she were floating outside her own body, watching this bastard hold her under—and spiders, myriad spiders, fanged, covered with thick black fur, able to swim like fish. The ketamine. She willed herself to stay focused, but it was no use. Bombs, gunfire, death, and now swimming spiders. The logical part of Cathy Ryan's brain took a backseat to overwhelming panic. A cloud of bubbles erupted around her regulator, filled with her shattered screams.

49

Leo Debs stretched a brunette wig over NIGHTINGALE's blond hair and smeared half her face with mud before he brought her sputtering out of the water ninety seconds after the bomb detonated. The ketamine dart had rendered her dazed and compliant for the time being, but that could wear off at any moment. He thought he'd delivered the full syringe, but he'd hit her on the move and there was always a chance the needle had slipped out and spilled a portion onto the ground. Not to mention that this bitch was probably metabolizing the stuff like a racehorse. She'd kneed him in the groin twice in the milliseconds before he'd taken her into the river, and nearly bitten his ear off. He kept one arm around her shoulder, as if to console her, as he led her up the nearby concrete steps. He'd left a canvas fireman's jacket with the respirators and he wore it now—slimy from two weeks in the water, but amid all the chaos, no one would notice.

The rest of the team came out of the water at the same time—all but a man named Dufort. Debs had seen him fall, the victim of a Secret Service bullet. But he was nowhere to be found now. The explosion had swept a twenty-meter circle and mowed down everyone and everything else for another twenty, killing or maiming everyone on the approaching Secret Service CAT.

No explosive-detection dogs had ever cleared this area for devices. The First Lady was never supposed to come this far.

The air smelled scorched, like steam and burned flesh. Walking wounded—law enforcement and civilian—milled at the edges of the blast radius, some wailing, some blinking in stupefied silence, holding severed appendages or clutching ragged wounds where those appendages should have been. Secret Service and local law enforcement who'd been posted around the periphery began to pour in, pistols drawn, leaping over bodies, desperately trying to get eyes on the First Lady. It was as if she'd been blown off the map. The sheer number of dead and dying overwhelmed initial attempts and an organized response.

Those who could walk helped those who could not, terrified that another bomb might go off at any moment. Debs, clothes sodden, feigned a limp, and led his injured patient past frantic agents and mortally wounded civilians, up the steps to the waiting ambulance. The rest of the team moved to street level with the fleeing crowd, joining Debs and NIGHTINGALE.

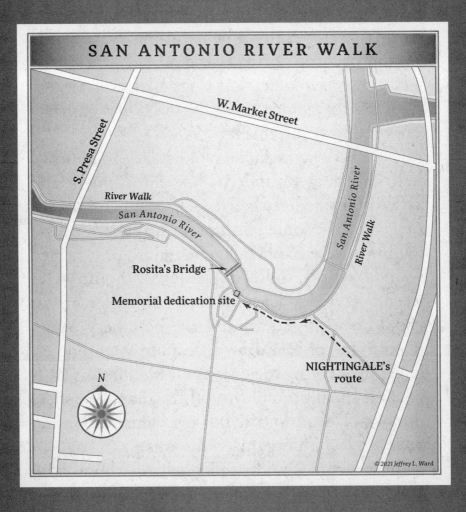

SAN ANTONIO RIVER WALK

Debs banged his fist on the interior wall as soon as everyone was on board and the back doors were shut.

"Go! Go! Go!"

Sirens wailed, arriving from every direction. They passed five oncoming ambulances before they'd gone as many blocks. Ramos drove northwest, away from the city, lights and siren because that's what everyone would expect. They'd lost Luc Dufort. But losses happened. Other than that, things could not have gone more smoothly. He nodded somberly to himself. Some of the poor sods were still operating under the impression that the explosions had been caused by a gas leak. With any luck, they'd be halfway to Abilene before the Secret Service picked through the bodies of all the mangled agents and realized the First Lady was gone.

Debs banged his head softly against the back of his seat and closed his eyes, congratulating himself on a nearly perfect operation.

And then NIGHTINGALE woke up and kicked him in the ribs.

50

The President's office on board Air Force One was located in the nose of the Boeing VC-25 aircraft, below the flight deck and in between his private suite (with a surprisingly comfortable bed) and a medical compartment staffed with a nurse and, today, Dr. Jason Bailey, chief of the White House Medical Unit. Sometimes called the Flying Oval Office, sophisticated satellite communications systems and comfortable surroundings allowed the President to work with virtually no interruption posed by travel.

Hands flat on a sizable working desk, Ryan leaned back in his swiveling leather chair. Mary Pat Foley sat in a nearly identical chair across the desk. Secretary of Defense Burgess and the chairman of the Joint Chiefs, General Tom Vogel, occupied a wraparound couch along the bulkhead.

Absent dangerous weather or a bona fide emergency, Air Force One was never vectored or held. When air traffic control heard the call sign, they waved the plane to the head of the line, wherever she was. The flight from Andrews Air Force Base to San Antonio took a commercial airliner three and a half hours, give or take. Ryan had been in the air a little over two and half, and his ears were already beginning to pop as the pilots began their initial descent into Lackland.

His advisers had spent the first hour briefing him on the situation with the Harpers in Afghanistan. They'd left him alone with his thoughts for most of the flight, but returned ten minutes ago. Arnie was aft, in the Secret Service cabin, going over a couple logistical issues that would impact Gary Montgomery's team.

Foley slid a folder containing a series of satellite images across the desk. Relatively clear, despite pockets of fog and shadows from cloud cover, at first glance, the photos showed herds of sheep and little else. A concentration of nine yurts set among what appeared to be cairns of stone did have half a dozen horses picketed with a few shaggy yaks. General Vogel pointed out a mound of debris, probably garbage, he thought, in the shadow of a large rock outcropping east of one of the yurts.

Ryan pushed the folder back across the desk to Foley. "We're thinking these horses could belong to the . . ." He paused, cocking his head at the sudden heaviness in his stomach as the aircraft began to climb. The water in a tumbler on Ryan's desk vibrated slightly as the pilot added power to the Boeing's GE turbofan engines.

General Vogel, also a pilot, noticed it, too. Air Force One did not miss approaches.

"Someone want to find out why we're not land—"

Arnie van Damm burst through the office door with Gary Montgomery tight on his heels. He glanced quickly around the desk until he found the remote, clicking on the flat-screen television behind Ryan's head. Montgomery folded his arms across his chest, uncharacteristically unsure of what to do with his hands. The chief of staff's bald head was flushed red as if he'd sprinted the length of the airplane to get here.

Ryan's eyes narrowed, feeling a sudden pressure in his stomach along with the weight of the men's dark mood. Neither of these two was the sort to panic, but this was as near to it as he'd ever seen.

Van Damm's voice came in a reverent whisper. "Mr. President," he said. "There's been an incident in San Antonio."

"An incident?" Ryan tensed, looking back and forth. "What the hell does that mean? What kind of event?"

Montgomery stepped forward, rescuing the chief of staff. "The First Lady's detail was ambushed, Mr. President—"

Ryan shot to his feet. "Ambushed? What about Cathy?"

"Unaccounted for, sir," Montgomery said.

"Everyone on the scene is scouring the area as we speak."

"Unaccounted for?" Ryan repeated, feeling gutted, then furious. "She's surrounded by, what, fifty of your people who are supposed to be protecting her, Gary, and you've got the balls to tell me that she's unaccounted for?"

"We only have initial reports," van Damm said. "A series of explosions. Some early reports of gunfire, but those are as of yet unconfirmed."

"Bombs?" Ryan fumed, teeth clenched so tight he thought they might shatter. He focused his rage on Montgomery. "Are you shitting me? Don't you people check for little things like explosives?" He slammed his palm against the table. "I want us on the ground. Now!"

Van Damm looked sideways at Foley.

"That's not advisable, Mr. President," she said.

"Security protocols won't allow us to land during an ongoing threat," Montgomery said.

"Protocols my ass," Ryan snapped. "Get me on the ground. Your security protocols obviously didn't do shit to protect the First Lady."

"Sir," Burgess offered. "You'll be of much more use to all involved, including the First Lady, if you are somewhere safe. No one knows yet what's happening down there."

"All the more reason for me to be on the scene." He snatched up the phone and called the pilots directly. "Colonel Caine. Turn this airplane around and put us on the ground in Lackland without delay."

The pilot's response was immediate and the plane began to bank to the right.

"Mr. President," Montgomery said. "We can't protect you—"

"I'd say that's obvious," Ryan snapped.

"Sir," Foley said. "I'm begging you to think this through. Whatever happened down there, it could well be part of a larger scheme to draw you in. Please take a breath before you charge in."

Van Damm spoke again. "The assistant special agent in charge of the FBI San Antonio is en route to coordinate as we speak."

"What?" Ryan wheeled. "Why not the SAIC? I suppose he has more important issues than finding the First Lady of the United States—"

Van Damm locked eyes with Ryan, the way friends do when they have something difficult to say. "Jack. Barb Crawford, the special agent in charge in San Antonio, was on the River Walk about a hundred feet from Cathy. According to a Bexar County Sheriff's investigator at the scene, Crawford was killed in one of the initial blasts."

Exasperated, Ryan turned to the television. He collapsed into his chair when he saw the aerial footage of all the carnage.

Inky smoke rose from a smoldering building. A wide circle along the water's edge looked as if it had been swept clear around a dark smudge in the broken concrete walk. Ryan held his breath, taking in the scene as it unfolded in front of him, struggling—and failing—to look at it analytically. This was the epicenter of the blast. Dead and wounded still lay scattered up and down the river, with uniformed EMS personnel only now working their way through, triaging those who deemed savable. One woman sat at the base of a metal pole, clutching a charred stump where her left knee used to be. Dozens of scenes of trauma and shock filled the screen. A Park Police patrol boat motored slowly through the green water, two officers wielding long wooden poles, the boat pausing only at bodies that were likely female, then left them bobbing in place after a quick check, and moved on to the next. The reality hit Ryan like a slap. The men in the boat were searching for his wife among the dead.

His white-hot rage cooled before a cold chill of shame and despair. He turned away, distancing himself from the images on the screen, terrified that he would see Cathy's face when the river patrol rolled a floating corpse. He caught Gary Montgomery's eye.

"Mr. President," the agent said. "If I might be excused to handle coordination with my counterpart in San Antonio."

Ryan gave a slow nod. "Of course."

Montgomery turned to leave, but Ryan stopped him, asking a question to which he already knew the answer.

"Gary," he whispered. "What about Karen?"

"Special Agent Sato is dead, Mr. President," Montgomery said, stone-faced, all business. "Five of the others confirmed dead, the rest of the First Lady's detail are still missing."

"I'm so sorry," Ryan said.

Montgomery gave a curt nod, grim. "Understood, sir. May I be excused?"

"Of course," Ryan said. He started to say more, to apologize again, but Foley's cell rang, cutting him off. The Secret Service agent shut the door behind him.

Ordinarily Foley wouldn't have taken a call during a meeting with the President, but she snatched the phone from her jacket pocket immediately.

"We're sure?" she asked after a few seconds. "Good work. Send it to my e-mail. I'll access it from here . . . All right . . . Contact me direct when you have anything else."

She slipped the phone in her pocket and nodded at Ryan. "We have security camera footage of someone pushing Cathy into the river seconds before the last explosion."

Ryan rubbed a hand over his scalp. "After she went in?"

"The blast knocked out the camera," Foley

said. "We're only able to see the portion uploaded to the Web prior to that time. But we now know that Cathy was alive when she went into the water—and that she was below the surface during detonation."

Ryan looked back at the television, numb, taking in little.

"Jack," Foley said. "I really need you to do the right thing here and turn us around."

"You need?" Ryan said.

"Yes." Foley was adamant now. "I have seventeen intelligence agencies and all the technology that goes with them at my disposal. Let me get back to D.C. and do my job."

Ryan sat in silence, staring at the awful images on the screen.

Foley prodded again. "Jack, there is a very large list of people both abroad and at home who will see your relationship with Cathy as a weakness. If you barge into this unknown chaos in San Antonio and throw your weight around like you just did with Gary you will play right into their hands. You are the President of the United States, but as your adviser and your friend, I am telling you that if you do not turn this plane around right now, that might not be the case by the end of the day."

51

John Clark and the others crowded around the conference table in horror and watched the footage from San Antonio unfold on two flat-screen televisions. Adara, Midas, and Jack Junior were on the phone, watching the news from the Business Aviation terminal at Narita, where the G5 was now refueling.

Gavin was recording the feed from every outlet for later scrutiny. If they couldn't be on the scene, Clark wanted to look at every possible angle. He'd noted three blast signatures so far, two considerably smaller than the one reported to be the last.

Clark's phone buzzed, alerting him to the video file he'd been expecting from Mary Pat. He left the news playing on the left screen and cast the video from his phone to the television on the right.

"Heads up," he said. "Jack, I'm sending you a video. You'll want to watch it."

Ryan didn't respond, so Adara answered for him. "He's opening it now."

The security camera video had no sound, but

it clearly showed a squad of men in white shirts meeting the First Lady's detail as they fled the explosions to the rear. All the men were wearing hats, shielding their faces from the camera, and all of them fired submachine guns as they advanced. Secret Service agents fell as if they'd been gassed, leaving Cathy Ryan the only one on her feet. All agents down, the apparent leader of the attack parked his gun expertly on a sling behind a holstered pistol and ran straight for Cathy, driving her sideways and into the river. One of the attackers fell, caught by gunfire from somewhere off-screen.

"There!" Jack's voice came over the line, loud and electric like he was about to jump out of his skin. "Right there. We can ID that son of a bitch and see who his pals are."

Clark used his thumb to advance the video frame by frame, slow enough to see the attacker hit her in the thigh with something.

"Run it in slow-mo," he said.

"A syringe," Adara said. "That's a good sign."

All of Jack's emotions erupted at once, spewing over the line. "Why don't you go ahead and enlighten us with your clever observations, Sherman. How? How could someone drugging my mother and then shoving her into the river possibly be viewed as a good sign?"

Adara's patient sigh was audible. "Because they didn't shoot her, Jack. They drugged her, then took her underwater to protect her from the blast of that last street-sweeper explosion that mowed down everyone within a hundred-foot circle."

Both hands on the conference table, Dom leaned closer to the Polycom speaker. "Adara's right, Jack," he said. "They want her alive."

"Yeah, well," Ryan said, "I want them dead. Change of plans. We're taking the G5 to Texas."

"Negative," Clark said. "You need to be with your father."

"Who is at this moment in San Antonio," Jack said.

"No," Clark said. "He is not. There's no way in hell they're going to land Air Force One and put the President in the middle of all that. He's inbound to D.C. as we speak. I imagine he could use a call from his son about now."

"I can be more useful working with you."

No," Clark said, his voice growing a hard edge. "You really wouldn't be. Midas and Adara are going to put you on a commercial flight to D.C. and then they're going to continue on with this mission in the Gulfstream."

"You're still sending them to India?"

"I am," Clark said. "But you're coming home. You hear me?"

Jack's breath came hard over the line, like a fighting bull working up the steam to charge.

"Listen to me, son," Clark said. "Your old man

has been my friend for a long time. And if I know my friend, he needs his family. So go now. That's an order."

Gerry Hendley arrived seconds after Clark ended the call. As the founder of The Campus, the former U.S. senator generally left tactical and strategic decisions to Clark or Chavez, but frequently added his two cents during operational planning sessions or after-action reviews. It was common for him to pop in at any time.

"Ryan coming home?" he said, taking a seat along the wall and out of the way.

"Yes, sir," Chavez said.

"Wise."

"Listen up," Clark said, accustomed to plowing ahead. Hendley would stop him if he had something important. "I want everyone thinking of possible next moves. As Jack pointed out, we have the dead attacker to ID. The Bureau is looking at exactly the same footage that we are, so they'll be all over that. Gavin, download any SigInt coming into Liberty Crossing from the FBI or any source pertinent to the First Lady." He gathered the recruiting files as he spoke. "Everything else we've been working on takes a backseat."

"We'll find her," Chavez said.

Clark heaved a long and exhausted sigh. "I don't

need to tell any of you all how volatile this situation is. Every law-enforcement agency in the U.S. is looking for Cathy Ryan while a sizable number of assholes in the world are looking for some way to exploit this situation." He gave Chavez a nod. "Cathy Ryan is my friend. Her husband is closer than any brother I could have, so, yes, if she is alive, we **will** find her. And if she's dead, we will hunt down those who killed her . . ."

Caruso took a half-step forward. Amid all the chaos it was easy to forget that the First Lady was his aunt.

"You okay to continue with this?" Clark asked.

"I'd be pissed if I couldn't, John," Caruso said. "I mean, I'm as okay as any of us are. You were one hundred percent right to send Jack to meet his dad, but we're all family. I don't see a situation where this isn't personal for any of us."

"Good to hear," Clark said.

Chavez stepped closer to the flat-screen television and pointed out two charred circular patterns on the concrete, not far from the convention center. "It's like they were driving the detail into a trap," he said. "Whoever did this went to a hell of a lot of trouble to keep the First Lady alive. They'll attempt to use her as leverage—a ransom, prisoner exchange, something. That buys us some time."

"It does," Caruso said, cocking his head, brow raised as if struck with a sudden notion. He turned to speak directly to Clark. "Listen, the Bureau is swarming all over this by now. I'm still on the books. As far as anyone in the field offices know I'm just some Headquarters puke. If you can get Director Foley to grease the skids for me at the Hoover Building, I'll head to Texas. I know Gavin has feeds from Fort Meade and Langley locked in, and Foley will keep us apprised, but that takes time. It's a sure bet I'll be able to get us better real-time intel if I'm boots on the ground."

Clark rubbed his face, tamping back the emotions of the moment. Seeing the red mist of revenge did nothing for Cathy Ryan. "Very well," he said. "Ding. You go with him. He can introduce you as his protégé from DOJ. There will be so many 'other government agency' types, you get a hall pass from the director of national intelligence and no one will bat an eyelash."

"Roger that," Chavez said. They were all accustomed to bouncing at a moment's notice and kept go-bags with gear and clothing for a variety of situations and locations at the office.

Clark gave Caruso's assessment a nod of approval. "The FBI is extremely good at what they do—and so is the Agency if this goes international. Neither, however, are known to be particularly nimble. Find out what you can as soon as you can and we'll jump on the info right away, deconflicting through Foley's office."

"I've got everything I need here," Caruso said, glancing at Ding, who gave him a thumbs-up. "Okay, then. We'll be on the next plane south." Then to Clark, "I do have one request, though. When you speak to Director Foley . . ."

52

Chilly Edwards recognized Rene Tatum the moment she walked in Rockin Rollerz Craft Burger Co. and started to scan the dining room. He wasn't certain she was looking for him, but it made sense. He **was** the guy who shot and killed her stepfather.

He sat alone in the rear of the dining room, his back to the wall—a habit instilled in him by his old man from the time he and his brother were small. His go-to place and his go-to meal when he was feeling off: a chicken-fried steak sandwich, tots, and Nasty Sauce. Greasy, soul-lifting deliciousness, it was the perfect late lunch—until Margaret Vetter's daughter locked eyes with him and marched across the room.

Her Wranglers were starched with a razor crease up the front of each impossibly long leg, naturally faded from time, not by some machine to make them stylishly distressed. Snug at the rear end but loose in the thighs, working jeans. She'd rolled the sleeves of a white pearl-snap Western shirt above strong forearms and tan elbows, bronzed for the same reason her Wranglers were faded. A gold barrel-racing buckle and scuffed Tony Lama boots said she was the real deal. Every barrel racer Chilly had ever known who was any good—and he'd known a fair number—was a tough cookie, as apt to crack a beer bottle over some cowboy's head in a bar fight as any man. Her blond hair was cut pixie short with a freshly buzzed side shave, giving her a punk-cowgirl look if there was such a thing.

It certainly made her look like she meant business.

Chilly glanced at her hands and her waist-band—no weapon that he could see. Still, he pushed away from the table and stood before she got to him, wiping the Nasty Sauce off his hands and dropping the napkin on the table.

"Officer Edwards?" she said, tight, like she might break down in tears at any moment.

He nodded. "Yes, ma'am."

"Can I please talk to you for a minute?" Her eyes were red and swollen. She sniffed back a sob.

"I don't know if that would be a good idea," Chilly said.

"Please," she said. "I know this is weird comin' from me, considering—"

"How'd you find me?"

"Pretended to be an old girlfriend and asked your neighbor where you'd be when you were feeling low. Told him I wanted to console you, after the shooting and all."

"Well, shit," Chilly said. His name hadn't been officially released to the media yet, but there were enough witnesses who saw him ride into the mall on his Harley that the fact he was the officer who took out Vetter wasn't exactly breaking news. He was going to have a heart-to-heart with his neighbors about giving up his favorite lunch spot to strange women. "How about I call the on-duty detective for you? She'll be able to answer your questions."

"I heard you were at the trailer," Rene said, charging forward. "With my mama and little brother."

"Listen to me. I . . . really shouldn't be talking to you at all."

"Look." Rene met his eyes and did not blink. "You think I'm upset because you're the one who killed Royce."

"I have to admit that thought did cross my mind."

"Well, I'm not," Rene went on. "You just saved me the trouble of capping that asshole myself."

"I'm not so sure he killed your mother," Chilly said, regretting the words the moment they left his mouth.

"I don't think so, either. At least not directly." She looked around the dining room. "Now, can we please sit down? People are starting to stare at us."

Chilly groaned, waving a hand at the chair

across from him. This would probably get him fired, which would completely torpedo his chances of getting hired with the FBI. Still, his father had taught him to listen to people in trouble—and if anyone was in trouble, it was this poor woman who'd just lost most of her family to bloody murder.

"What can I do for you?"

"Honestly," she said. "I don't really know what I'm trying to accomplish here. I agree that Royce Vetter didn't pull the trigger, but I'd bet everything I own that it was his crazy end-of-days conspiracy theories that got my mama and little brother murdered." She leaned in, elbows on the table. "I talked to my mama on the phone the morning she got killed. She said Royce was losing his shit over some militia guys who he thought were following him. But Royce Vetter was always losing his shit about some imagined threat, so I didn't think much of it at the time."

"Militia?" Vetter's hostage in the mall had heard him say something about a "spy militia." Chilly made a mental note to talk to the homicide detectives about it but kept that to himself.

"Yeah," Rene said. "I'm saying there's something else going on, something connected to Royce but bigger than him. Something my mother found out about and they shut her up."

"Who's 'they'?"

"I wish I knew," Rene said. "But it needs to be checked—"

A murmur ran through the dining room and all the waitstaff came around the counter to watch the TV. One of them turned up the volume.

"Holy crap!" Rene whispered.

A knot formed in Chilly's gut as he watched footage of an attack on the First Lady of the United States in San Antonio. He gasped, unable to think of anything to say.

His SWAT phone began to chime as text after text came in from his team members.

ARE YOU SEEING THIS?

WHAT THE HELL, DUDE . . .

YOU THINK THEY'LL CALL US DOWN TO HELP?

BET YOU WISH YOU WERE HRT NOW, CHILL!

SADDLE UP, BOYS . . .

THIS IS CRAZY!!

Then, from the SWAT sergeant:

CHECK YOUR KIT AND STAY BY YOUR PHONES.

Rene Tatum lay her forehead on the table and began to cry.

"Hey," Chilly said softly, tentatively touching her on the shoulder. "You okay?"

She raised up slightly, arms still flat on the table. Tears streaming from bloodshot eyes. "No," she said. "I'm not okay at all." She nodded sideways at the television. "Don't you get it? Y'all's bosses are likely to send half of you down to help hunt down the assholes who took the President's wife. My mama's murder was on the back burner to begin with. It ain't even on the stove anymore."

53

It was well after midnight, but Malhotra had kept Herr Roth out for dinner and drinks, giddy with the prospect of how the German would react to the stupendous news of the American First Lady's kidnapping. Kashvi had come, too, wearing a little black dress that she kept at work for emergencies like this. She was, in fact, the only reason Roth had agreed to stay out so late. The old goat seemed quite interested in her, so Malhotra took advantage of it.

They'd heard the news in the limo, and Malhotra insisted they return to his office to watch it unfold on the television in his office.

It was not going as he had planned.

Malhotra pretended to be concerned, as one would be when something so tragic occurred anywhere in the world. But Roth was distant, looking at Kashvi more than he watched the events on the television.

"This is most horrible," Malhotra said, forcing a knitted brow. He nursed a glass of feni Kashvi had poured for him. It was late and he had a headache, but this was a moment to celebrate.

Roth, too, held a drink, an apricot brandy this time. He took his eyes off Malhotra's secretary long enough to gaze into his glass. "I wonder," he said, "if these tragic circumstances might not make President Ryan solidify his resolve."

"What?" Malhotra sat up straighter. "How do you mean?"

"With his agenda," Roth said. "You know how Americans are. Stubborn, vengeful. If he believes someone is forcing his hand, he may well . . . How do they say it? Double down."

"No, no, no." Malhotra had to summon all his self-control not to shout. "My people in Washington have assured me that Ryan was already losing political will. Surely this will serve to make him reflect on what is truly important. I would, in fact, be extremely surprised if he is still in office tomorrow."

"Perhaps," Roth said. "This is so upsetting. That someone would stoop to killing the poor man's wife."

"We do not know if she is dead," Kashvi offered. She'd grown accustomed to the evening banter and let the familiarity bleed over once they returned to the office. A serious mistake.

"That is true." Roth turned suddenly to look straight at Malhotra. "May I be completely frank with you?"

"Always," Malhotra said.

"It is the waiting that bothers me. Once

I have made a decision to proceed, I want to proceed. All of my poor decisions in life have come when I had time to overthink them." He threw back the remainder of his brandy, half the glass. "I only wish this were over and the deal was done."

Kashvi gave an almost imperceptible nod.

Malhotra tried to keep his face from twitching. With all the alcohol in his system, Roth did not appear to notice.

"My attorneys have completed their review," Malhotra said. "The timing is completely up to you."

Kashvi hustled over, little black dress swishing, and poured the German another brandy. **Good girl.**

"This is very interesting," Roth said. "We could move forward almost at once."

"At your earliest convenience."

Roth stood, unsteady, holding out his hand for Kashvi to help him. "Very well."

"Tomorrow, then?"

"Ha," Roth said. "I suppose that is a possibility. But my attorneys will be in touch with your attorneys."

Roth called his driver, who came in to retrieve him from the outer office. Kashvi touched him on the hand as he left.

"You did well," Malhotra said after the door shut, leaving him and his secretary alone.

"Thank you, H.M.," she said. "That was too much fun."

Malhotra smiled, tamping back the jealous rage in his belly. She was only doing what he asked her to do. He just wished she did not seem to enjoy it so much.

"One more thing," he said. "A small change to the contract. Buried deep, so even his lawyers will not notice."

54

Cathy Ryan tasted blood. So incredibly thirsty. Her hands had gone numb for some reason. And she needed to get up and pee.

Consciousness came slowly, like a black curtain that let in only a sliver of light, parting by slow degrees to reveal the world outside the darkness.

She was on her side, hands tied or cuffed behind her back—she couldn't feel them, so it was impossible to tell. The hem of her skirt was bunched at mid-thigh. There was little she could do about modesty but pull her legs into a fetal position.

In some kind of vehicle, older, with a bad suspension and on a rough road, judging from the bounce and squeaking springs. A van, considering the row of boots she could see in front of her. The black cotton hood that was supposed to cover her eyes had ridden up, perhaps in a struggle. Had she fought when they'd given her the ketamine dart? She couldn't remember much of anything, but she brightened at the idea that she might have kicked the hell out of these pricks . . . whoever they were. Her muscles sure felt as if she'd been in a fight. Her neck, unsupported by any pillow, felt like it was about to pop off every time they hit a bump. It made sense. They had to be taking back roads to keep off the radar.

Cathy wasn't sure how long she'd been unconscious, but every cop in the country would be looking for her soon if they weren't already. A sob caught hard in her throat when she thought about Karen Sato and the rest of her Secret Service detail.

". . . long is he supposed to be gone?" someone asked.

"Not long," another man said. "You know him. He'll kill her quick." The man chuckled. "He might stick around for a few minutes after. You know him—"

A deep baritone voice interrupted the chatter of the group. Australian and brash, this one sounded like he was in charge, or wanted to be.

"Keep it slow," the Aussie said. "I doubt they've had time to set up roadblocks this far out, but I'm not keen to meet up with any highway patrol trooper eager to make a name for himself. The eyes of Texas wouldn't look too kindly on what we're doing at the moment."

"Texas is the least of our worries," an American voice said, deadpan. "I'd be much more concerned about this little thing called the federal death penalty."

A Hispanic voice spoke next, soft, breathy. Cathy could see his boots if she turned her head.

"We capped a shitload of secret squirrels. I wonder if they'd have more than one trial."

"They'd shoot us on sight," the Aussie said. "I got six, for sure, and probably twice that many who happened to be in the way—"

"Stop it!" Cathy banged her head sideways against the vehicle floor, pushing the hood up even higher. A man with dirty-blond hair jumped, startled by her sudden movement. Everyone around her looked like soldiers. Lean, fit, eyes that had seen conflict. "I said stop it!" Her voice grew louder and more ragged with every word. "What is the matter with you? Talking about killing my friends like a bunch of glib teenage boys playing some video game. Those were good people with families! You murdered them without a thought." Her chest shuddered with runaway sobs as she broke down. "They were just doing their jobs—"

"No shit," the American said, unmoved. "Unfortunately for them, that job was to protect you, which put them in the way."

"Better to keep your gob hole shut, Your Highness," the Australian said. "Be silent and cooperative and you'll make it out of here alive."

"No, I won't," Cathy spat. "I've seen your faces. There's no way you're letting me walk away from this. You know it and I know it."

The Aussie put a hand on her thigh, under her skirt. "Maybe," he said. "I hate to be a stereotype here, but we're just a bunch of blokes who haven't see a woman in weeks. You're a little long in the tooth, but . . ." His voice trailed off for a moment, then he said, "I mean really, we have a mission to think about, but . . . you know, boys are gonna be boys—"

Cathy used her hips and core to rise up like a snake, spitting and cursing, red with rage. She twisted, hands behind her back, and sank her teeth into the Aussie's exposed forearm.

He slammed a fist into her temple, knocking her to the floor amid a shower of lights and color.

She writhed there, whimpering, groaning. "You might as well kill me now."

Someone Cathy couldn't see spoke next. He sounded British, his voice muffled as if he'd been napping. "What exactly did you expect her to do, nimrod? Feeling her up like that."

"I expected her to be more civilized," the Australian snapped.

"Hilarious!" the Brit said. The van rocked a little as he stood up and hovered over Cathy, still looking at the Aussie. "Let's you and me gun down a few dozen people, toss this one in a dark lorry where you can take the opportunity to give her knickers a little grope. Yeah, mate, that'll bring out the most civilized behavior in anyone."

Cathy cringed as the Brit knelt beside her. The

next moment she felt a sharp pinch in her thigh. The bastard had hit her with another tranquilizer. Her racing heart put it into her system almost at once. The Brit's voice clawed its way into her brain as she drifted off.

"Civilized," the Brit said again. "That's rich. We might well need to produce a little proof-of-life video. Leave her alone."

"For now," the Aussie said.

"Yeah," the Brit said. "For now."

55

For the first time in a very long while Mary Pat Foley thought she might actually cry full-on blubbering tears.

The White House Situation Room was often called the Meatgrinder for the rough-and-tumble discussions that led to decisions that impacted the world. At the moment, the Cabinet Room was doing some meat grinding of its own. Located off the President's secretaries' suite opposite the Oval Office, the room was now packed to the gunnels. The fifteen leather chairs around the polished table were occupied by the principal officers of the executive departments who would decide pursuant to Section 4 of the Twenty-Fifth Amendment if the President was unable to discharge the powers and duties of his office. The President's chair—the back of which was slightly taller than the rest—looked forlorn as it sat empty in front of the Rose Garden windows.

The vice president was also absent, odd, because the outcome of this proceeding would surely affect him in momentous ways.

It took a majority of the cabinet to invoke

Section 4, but the fifteen principal executives made it clear they wanted to hear from a litany of experts—on the Constitution and on Jack Ryan.

D/FBI Wilson and D/CIA Canfield sat in chairs against the wall with over a dozen members of congress—including the speaker of the House, the Senate president pro tempore, and, maddeningly, Senator Michelle Chadwick.

Though the crowd was shoulder to shoulder, the room was uncharacteristically quiet with most content to let everyone else do the talking, then watch the mood of the room and follow the majority. So far, that majority sat or stood and stared at their own feet, nodding in tacit agreement while Chadwick piped on. She'd been making her case for the past five minutes, her helmetlike bowl of mouse-brown hair bobbing every time she nodded at the obvious rightness of her argument.

Jack Ryan simply had to be forced aside.

Mary Pat Foley felt like she might vomit. Even the busts of George Washington and Benjamin Franklin that perched in alcoves on either side of the fireplace looked disgusted at the smarmy senator's pitch. Never what anyone with a brain would call an ally, in recent days Chadwick had worked with Ryan. He'd offered to let her take the lion's share of the credit for the pharma bill, he'd strategized, planned, broken bread with this bitch, and now she had the balls to stand in his

Cabinet Room and advocate tossing him to the curb like a piece of trash mere hours after his wife had been kidnapped.

"... all know the President and I have had a somewhat rocky relationship," Chadwick said, as if reading Foley's mind. "But I must admit that I've come to respect if not agree with Jack Ryan on most issues of consequence. I have also been around him enough to see firsthand the strength of the relationship he has with his wife. I've observed him to be a highly intelligent individual, but circumstances such as we face at this moment cloud the judgment of even the most intelligent people—"

Foley stood from her seat—the chair that would have been directly across from Ryan, had he been present to defend himself. She cleared her throat with gusto, making apparent her contempt for this nonsense that was happening before her eyes.

"Senator Chadwick has worked with President Ryan for . . . a handful of days, so she considers herself an expert on his character and behavior. Many of you around this table have worked with him for years. I have known him for more than half of his life—half of my life. I have known Jack Ryan since there was an Iron Curtain—and he and I worked behind it. I have personally observed him face situations more stressful than I could have ever imagined, and he did so with grace and aplomb. I can assure you that he was clearheaded then and he is clearheaded now."

Rhonda Sanders, the Senate president pro tempore, spoke up. "But is he really? I deeply respect the President, but how could anyone be clearheaded in this situation? In many ways, the fact that Ryan is so close with his wife is all the more reason to question his ability to make rational decisions at the moment."

"Jack Ryan can," Foley said. "And he will."

"Were you there?" Chadwick asked.

Foley took a deep breath, not bothering to hide her glare. "Was I where, Senator?"

"When President Ryan got the news about San Antonio," Chadwick said, much too smugly for Foley's taste—like an attorney about to discredit someone on the witness stand. "I mean, did he get angry or keep his cool? He was on Air Force One at the time, the boss, the most powerful man on plane . . . on the planet. Was his initial reaction to show concern for all the dead, or did he blame others in the room for what happened to his wife?"

Foley's gaze shifted from Bob Burgess to General Vogel. The chairman of the Joint Chiefs was one of the six people in the President's office on Air Force One when Ryan first learned of the San Antonio attack. Someone had leaked the details to Chadwick. Foley hadn't done it, and she was sure it wasn't Burgess or van Damm. Gary

Montgomery had taken the brunt of Ryan's outburst, but he didn't seem the type to spill tea. That left Vogel. The general caught her looking at him and met her gaze with the stony resolve of someone who knew they were in the right.

Bastard.

"I'm not going to discuss the specifics of a meeting with the President of the United States," Foley said, her eyes lingering on the general as she spoke to Chadwick. "That would be most unprofessional, and possibly even against the law."

Dan Murray, the attorney general, considered that for a moment and gave a little shrug as if to concede that the last might or might not be true. Still, his side-eye at General Vogel made it clear he was with Foley on this.

Chadwick raised both hands, palms out. "Don't misunderstand me, Madam Director," she said. "Am I wrong that President Ryan acted as any of us would have when he learned his wife was in danger? I would assume he would respond like a human being—a sudden burst of anger before calming down and looking at things rationally. The problem is, when someone very literally has their finger on the button that could start a war, bursts of human emotion have grave consequences." She sighed, chest heaving, shoulders falling—drama queen that she was. "Listen, no one in this room wants to get rid of him—"

"Oh, is that right?" Foley shot back. "Are you serious? You can stand there and ask us to honestly believe that you don't want Jack Ryan out of office? That's been your war cry for as long as I've even known who you are."

"Of course I want him out of office," Chadwick said. "But not this way. That should happen at the ballot box. Look, we don't negotiate with terrorists. Right?"

Both the speaker of the House and Senate president pro tempore nodded in agreement. Regina Barnes, secretary of commerce, nodded, then caught herself and began to toy with her crystal water glass.

"We certainly do not," Foley said, thinking that Chadwick was a terrorist herself.

"Let's be honest, then." Chadwick plowed ahead. "How does one even consider not capitulating to some pirate's demands when the love of your life has a gun to her head?"

"Pirates?" Foley scoffed. "I'm not going to entertain hypotheticals—"

Brian Watts, the speaker of the House, chimed in. "I'm afraid that's exactly what we have to do."

Foley waved that off. "There have been no demands—"

The door suddenly opened and Jack Ryan strode through, looking smaller, more fragile than Foley had ever seen him—and still, he filled up the room.

Everyone scrambled to their feet.

"Yet," he said. "There have been no demands yet."

A murmur rumbled around the table. The speaker of the House shifted back and forth on his feet, squirming.

Ryan shot Mary Pat a friendly, if exhausted smile. Hair disheveled, eyes bloodshot, he stood inside the door, drawn, like he'd aged ten years in the last few hours. "No one has contacted us yet. But the demands will come. We have enough experience with bad men to be certain of that."

The Secret Service had grown more than twitchy after the attack in Texas and Gary Montgomery stood extra-close to the President, as if trying to shield him from all the sorrow raining down on him. Vice President Dehart came in next, with Keenan Mulvaney, the special agent in charge of his protective detail.

Foley's hand shot to her mouth when she realized what was happening.

"Jack—"

Ryan shook his head, tears welling in his eyes now. "It's okay, Mary Pat." He held up a single sheet of paper. "Madame President Pro Tempore, Mr. Speaker, I have . . . I have here a letter, drafted . . ." He stopped, took a ragged breath. "A letter that . . ." He swallowed hard, attempting to regain his composure. "Tell you what, I'll just read it."

**To the Honorable Brian Watts, Speaker
United States House of Representatives:
Honorable Rhonda Sanders
President Pro Tempore
United States Senate**

In consultation with my personal counsel and the attorney general of the United States, I have deemed it in the best interest of the country for me to temporarily step aside pursuant to Section 3 of the Twenty-Fifth Amendment and cede the authority of my office to Vice President Mark Dehart, who will assume these powers and duties as Acting President of the United States.

I am fully capable of discharging the duties of the office, but hold fast to a belief that it is vital to the nation and the world that the decisions made by the office of the President are not colored by fear or threat of reprisal to members of my family. It is to that end that I temporarily cede these powers of the President.

I shall advise you when I feel it appropriate to resume the discharge of the constitutional duties of the office. God Bless us all and God Bless the United States of America.

**Sincerely,
John Patrick Ryan**

Foley shot Dan Murray a wounded you-could-have-told-me look. The attorney general merely shrugged and nodded at Ryan. He was following orders. Foley knew what it meant to keep a confidence. She would have done the same thing. She glared at General Vogel again. Unlike some people.

"The Constitution states that the powers and duties of the presidency will immediately cede to the vice president in this instance," Ryan said.

"Jack—" Foley said, hopelessness pressing against her heart.

Ryan gave her a wan smile. "It's the right thing to do, Mary Pat. Everyone in this room knows it, even . . . especially me." He turned to Dehart. "Now, Mr. President, I know you have a country to run, but I'd be forever in your debt if you would do everything in your power to find my wife. I will be in the Residence."

56

Harper woke to the sound of rustling felt and a bitter gust of wind through the open door of the yurt. Murmuring voices and the sound of clanging pans carried through the darkness. He panicked when he realized Naomi wasn't beside him, but relaxed a notch when he saw her familiar silhouette by the glow of the firepit. It was early and cold—he could see his breath curling through the shadows.

Wakhi shepherds rose before dawn, the women tending their fires while men saw to their flocks, checking them to make certain no wolves had taken any during the night. Laleh must have been out doing her share of the early milking, and she'd brought Farhad, the village headman, in with her.

Shambe's mother bustled around the fire, working with Naomi to prepare the breakfast of bread and salted milk tea—that they ate every day. She welcomed her visitor and invited him to share the simple meal.

Laleh spoke rapidly in her native tongue, urging the headman forward.

"He heard news," she said to Harper in Russian.

Harper groaned to his feet and put a hand over his heart.

"Salaam alaykum," he said.

Farhad returned the greeting, then added "Good morning" in English.

Harper rubbed a hand over his face, pushing the cobwebs out of his brain. Blessedly, Naomi brought each of them a bowl of shirchoy.

Harper rolled his sleeping mats out of the way and motioned for Farhad to take a seat. "Laleh says you have news."

"The Chinese colonel," the village headman whispered, looking over his shoulder and then leaning in. "I hear him talk on phone."

Harper shot a glance at Laleh, who stood by watching. Orange light from the dung fire danced on her face. Smoke hung around her, suspended on the chilly air.

Farhad gave an excited nod. "Yes. English. Colonel very angry. Say he cannot . . . return China. He wait for chopper to pick him up from Pakistan. Not happy about it. Very angry to wait. He say he want to be gone by now. He stop talking when his captain come in. I think captain not know about Pakistan."

"Pakistan?" Harper took a deep breath, willing his heart to slow down. It made no sense, but then none of this did. Getting a message out was suddenly all-important if the colonel never had any intention of taking them back to China.

As near as Harper could tell, the soldier who had his watch was named Wen, but Harper thought of him as Iron Elbow. There seemed little to distinguish him from his fellow soldiers.

Harper lowered his voice. "I need to retrieve my watch," he said in Russian for Laleh's benefit, and then in English for Farhad. All the back-and-forth gave him a killer headache.

Laleh surprised him when she knew exactly who he was talking about. "Soldier Wen, he is bad man," she said. "Most of them are only boys. Young. Doing their jobs. Wen and his friend Fang are nasty. They talk nasty to girls. Spy on us when we wash this morning."

Harper shot a glance at Naomi, an idea forming in his mind. It was dangerous, but no more dangerous than sitting around waiting for bad things to unfold.

"Have you gone behind the rock yet?" he asked Naomi. It was their euphemism for taking a pee break. The men of the village knew to steer clear of that particular boulder, leaving it for the women only.

"I did," she said. "Before you woke up."

"What if I asked you to make another trip?"

She squinted at him through the hazy firelight.

"What are you talking about?"

Instead of explaining in detail, he had Laleh ask Shambe's mother if she had a large knife. She retrieved a stout boning knife from a leather roll beneath her cooking pots and demonstrated its keen edge by shaving the back of her arm. Wicked sharp, it had a thick spine and an eight-inch curved blade.

Harper tested its heft, and then put a hand on Naomi's shoulder. "Wait five minutes and then go to the rock. Be obvious enough that he sees you, but don't do anything out of the ordinary."

"What . . . What is your plan here?"

Harper touched her on the cheek. "What could we do if we were not afraid?"

Young Shambe perked up at the chatter going on around him, then crawled out of his quilts to a spot along the back wall. He removed a wooden pin from the scissorlike frame, allowing him to lift two of the pieces free. On hands and knees, he poked his head out through a seam in the heavy felt matting that formed the skin of the dwelling. Satisfied the coast was clear, he ducked back inside and motioned toward the makeshift exit.

Laleh gave an excited nod. "He say you go this way. Out of sight."

Harper kissed his wife, keeping the blade up and down beside his leg.

"Give me five minutes."

"Monte—"

He kissed her again, once on the forehead,

once on the lips. "What could we do . . ." he said again, and then ducked out Shambe's secret exit into the morning chill.

Harper was met with the sound of phlegmy coughing, rebelling lungs of the soldiers not accustomed to living on the Roof of the World— and the people who lived here breathing the soot of dung fires day in and day out. Sheep bleated to his right and his left. Hundreds of hooves clicked and snapped against clattering stone. Two women chatted while they milked their animals, the vibrant hiss of liquid hitting the sides of metal containers carrying through the frosty dawn. It was still incredibly dark.

The nine yurts of Vagd Boi were spaced with fifteen to twenty yards between each one, close enough that any of the soldiers could have easily seen Harper had they stepped around back to check. But all of the dwellings faced the animal pens and, from the look of them, had only one way in and out.

Harper held his breath. Every move he made seemed to produce a deafening noise. His own heartbeat was surely audible at the other end of the camp. He squatted outside the yurt, curved blade in hand, and slowed his breathing. The women's rock was visible through the gathering dawn, a black shadow roughly the size of a minivan. The mountains loomed larger around the valley, an impenetrable fortress of rock and ice.

Harper padded quickly across the open ground, instinctively crouching as he moved, though it would have done little good. There was nothing but barren rock between the yurts and his destination.

There was only one vantage point from which to spy on the women, the remnants of a stone sheep pen, little more than a pile of stones now, a corral that had fallen in on itself to become a cairn. Harper knelt there, taking care not to cut off the circulation in his legs. He had to be able to move instantly when the time came. Funny the things one thought about when waiting to murder a man.

He'd only just gotten relatively settled when he heard Naomi's distinctive cough. Clattering rocks. Sniffing. A shuddering sigh as she walked between Harper's hiding place and the latrine rock.

Then the sound of more rocks near the yurts. Someone was following her—as expected.

Harper's pulse whooshed in his ears, making it almost impossible to hear. It had to be Wen. If it was not, this was pointless. His grip tightened on the knife and he had to make a conscious effort not to squeeze so hard he cramped his arm.

He was far too old for this. Hell, anyone would

be too old for what he had in mind—no matter their age.

Too late to turn back, he watched Wen's silhouette saunter into view, a scant thirty feet behind Naomi. When you had a gun—and a bunch of friends with guns—there was little need to hide just to leer at an unarmed woman while she took her morning pee.

Naomi shrugged off her jacket, making a show of pulling the tail of her shirt out of her waistband, completely entrancing the soldier.

Harper crept forward slowly at first, knife pointed forward, expecting Wen to turn at any moment, intent on charging forward if he did.

The human body was a marvelous but fragile thing, a hairless ape with thin skin, no claws, and blunt canines. The eyes and smallish ears faced forward, focused on hunting rather than protecting oneself from another hunter.

Monte Harper was a physician with decades of study in anatomy and physiology. He'd gone elbow-deep in cadavers and living patients during med school and internship, working long hours in trauma wards, surgery, and intensive care. He was intimately familiar with every system of the body—and what it took to disrupt them. If his extensive medical training had taught him anything, it was that killing a human being was a relatively straightforward if not easy process.

Simply speaking, you had to deprive the brain of oxygen. When boiled all down to the bones, as it were, that was really the only thing that caused death. Choking—no oxygen to the brain. Bleeding to death—no blood to carry oxygen to the brain. Heart attack, cancer shut down the organs. Decapitation—same, same, same.

Harper needed it to happen quicky and quietly.

Kidneys made the perfect target. No ribs to contend with, two to choose from, and each was entangled in a vast network of veins and nerves. A wound to a kidney would not only start the bleeding processes, but would inflict immediate, overwhelming pain, in theory at least, robbing Wen of his powerful iron elbow. It wouldn't be quick, but it was a start.

Naomi coughed again, fumbling with the snap on her pants.

Wen leaned sideways, shuffling his feet as he watched, tensing suddenly as if he'd heard something.

Harper hit him before he turned, driving the eight-inch blade into the soft flesh of the man's loins, while at the same time snaking an arm around to cover his mouth and keep him from crying out.

Unaccustomed to such gruesome work, Harper let his finger stray into the soldier's mouth. Wen clamped down hard, Harper's wedding ring blocking the worst of the bite. It didn't matter.

He was too involved in the task at hand to feel anything but rage.

Seething, Harper withdrew the blade from Wen's back and, hand still clasping the thrashing man's face, plunged it into the side of his neck. He'd watched the village headman dispatch a sheep for a feast when they'd arrived, using a similar blade to cut off its head. He copied the maneuver.

An arc of blood sprayed the air in front of the two men. Eyes flying wide in the darkness, Wen relaxed his grip on Harper's finger and slid to the ground.

Naomi rushed to help, her boots clattering as she tiptoed quickly across the rocky ground. There was some agonal breathing, twitching legs, gruesome things Harper had blocked from his mind about violent deaths he'd witnessed in the emergency room. He attempted to shield his wife from the obscene sight of the dying man, but she shrugged him aside.

"We're past that," she whispered. "We have to get him behind those stones before someone sees us."

Harper stooped to remove his watch, wiping it free of blood before returning it to his own wrist, hidden under the sleeve of his down jacket.

Footfalls to their right caused them both to freeze.

It was Farhad, leading a horse.

"One of the soldier horses," he said. "They keep him hobbled because he always try run away."

The horse stomped a foot, blowing hard, nickering nervously at the smell of blood. But for the howl of wolves, animal sounds hardly raised an eyebrow in camp.

Naomi held the trembling animal while Harper and Farhad hefted Wen's body onto the horse. The Wakhi headman was accustomed to tying loads on pack animals and made short work of lashing the dead soldier across the horse's back with a thick yak-hair rope.

"What about his rifle?" Naomi said.

Harper shook his head. "It has to go, too. If they find it here, they'll know he didn't run away."

"If they are searching us for guns, it'll be too late to worry about that," she said.

"Touché," he admitted, shaking badly now from the killing. "We'll stash it in the yurt with us."

Farhad started to lead the horse to the south. "It will run downhill once we are out of the village. The soldiers might hear and try to chase, so I will take it far. I should go before it gets light enough for them to see."

Harper put a trembling hand on Farhad's shoulder. "Thank you," he said.

"Thank you, Breaker of Rocks."

"The watch," Naomi said.

"Right," Harper said, feeling foolish for waiting

this long. He unscrewed the small cap at the base of the face, like a second crown. Then, making sure he had a clear view of the sky, he pulled the cap away, extending a thin antenna wire that, until now, had been coiled inside the watch.

57

FBI Special Agent Kelsey Callahan spied Dominic Caruso when he badged his way through the door across the cavernous convention center ballroom and cursed a happy curse under her breath. It would be good to see the bastard, but the fact that he was even here meant things were about to get weirder than they already were. Her previous work with the ruggedly mysterious quoter of Italian proverbs and keeper of secrets had been pleasant, in a torturous sort of way that made her want to at once pull her hair out and hug the guy. It shouldn't have come as a surprise that he'd parachuted in to save the day. Considering the circumstances, Texas was about to get an enema of counterintelligence squad weenies from FBI HQ.

She'd not been on the ground long, just a couple hours, long enough to get her stuff stowed, get an initial briefing, and catch a short glimpse of the carnage along the River Walk just over a football field away. Caruso had sure gotten here fast if he came from D.C., only adding to his mystique. So far he'd not seen her, and Callahan moved behind a pocket of milling agents. It was fairly simple to blend in with all the other blue windbreakers, and she hoped to keep it that way until she got a better handle on the situation. She couldn't do anything about her red hair.

The leader of the multiagency Dallas area Crimes Against Children Task Force found herself on a Southwest jet out of Love Field less than two hours after the first hint of trouble along the River Walk. She'd been on the treadmill when the special agent in charge called her personally. A call from the Old Man was like a lightning bolt from Zeus, rarely a good thing, but as soon as he told her about the First Lady, she'd forgotten any trepidation, grabbed the go-bag under her desk, and jumped on the first flight to San Antonio. She'd pulled a pair of jeans over her running shorts but settled for the merino wool hooded T-shirt she'd been running in, giving her the look like she'd just left the boxing gym. Her red hair was still pulled back in a thick ponytail.

She arrived in San Antonio with the first wave of agents, greeted by ashen-faced rental car personnel who welcomed them like a liberating army.

If the FBI was good at anything—and they were very good at a lot of things—they excelled at springing up ad hoc emergency operations centers before the dust settled after a violent incident. Quarterly case-file inspections ensured that the entire Bureau was organized and scrutinized down to the cellular (individual agent) level. Every office had at least one crisis response agent and volume upon volume of crisis response plans, digitized, but also in print in the event of an electromagnetic pulse attack or any number of scenarios that might render computers useless lumps of plastic and glass. Though there was no specific scenario titled "First Lady Kidnapping," there were enough similar scenarios to set up the scaffolding for an investigation. Drills, joint training scenarios complete with role players and active multiagency emergency operations centers.

Multiheaded demon-dog bureaucracy that they were, when the FBI needed to jump, they could jump. Fast.

Surviving Secret Service personnel had notified their command post of the attack on FLOTUS in real time. There had, of course, been FBI special agents on the ground with state and local LEOs, working the crowd, gleaning intelligence on protesters, possible terrorist actors, but generally staying out of the Secret Service's way. The death toll of state and local officers was at sixteen at the moment and ticking upward at an alarming rate. Conflicting reports put Secret Service casualties at twenty-three or twenty-six. Along with the SAIC, two FBI counterintel agents were confirmed dead, another suffering from a concussion when the stampeding crowd knocked her into a concrete planter. She'd been the first to alert the command center to the attack. Calls poured in after that, from other agents, Bexar County 911, and concerned citizens.

San Antonio command center ran the information up the flagpole to FBI Headquarters in D.C., where it landed in the hands of a call-taker on SIOC Watch. The Strategic Information and Operations Center, or SIOC, made it possible for the FBI to take global command after an attack against U.S. interests. With forty thousand square feet of work space and over sixty miles of fiberoptic cable, the SIOC allowed the Bureau to keep a common operating picture (COP) on deployed FBI national assets, and disperse intelligence information enterprise-wide, including to regional Joint Terrorism Task Forces.

The SIOC Watch commander pushed the information to the Critical Incident and Operations Unit, which coordinated the activation of operational and support personnel from headquarters and the FBI field offices nearest to San Antonio. Within three hours, an army of special agents, analysts, IT, and administrative staff descended on the Henry B. González Convention Center, setting up shop in the Stars at Night Ballroom. At fifty-four thousand square feet, the ballroom was larger than the sixty-three people on-site needed at the moment, but the First Lady was missing, so their ranks would grow exponentially as the minutes ticked by.

The natural inclination was to throw everything and everyone at an incident like this, but
there were still plenty of bad actors out there,
champing at the bit to capitalize on the misery
of the moment. If every squad leader and uniformed officer in Texas followed their instincts
and rushed to the River Walk, the voids in their
own jurisdictions would be vulnerable to all
manner of criminal activity.

Callahan counted herself fortunate she was
one of the initial wave.

Personnel from Dallas, Houston, El Paso,
and Oklahoma City were first to arrive. IT and
TSCM (technical surveillance countermeasures)
specialists went to work immediately identifying weaknesses in the ad hoc command center
itself like speakers that could be turned into listening devices on the other end of the line by
a simple reverse in wiring, sweeping for listening devices, and setting up a false wall of plastic
sheeting to create a room within the room. With
the President's wife missing, there were certain to
be discussions at the highest levels, necessitating
a sensitive compartmented information facility,
or SCIF, in the middle of a hotel ballroom.

The Bureau had roughly thirty-five thousand
employees, so it was easy to get lost, but major
assignments tended to be like old home week,
despite the horrendous circumstances. Callahan
had run into half a dozen agents she'd not seen

in years shortly after arriving. To her chagrin, the Texas Rangers also had a presence. Ranger Lyle Anderson, her rawboned ex-husband, was there, up front with the bosses who were about to give a briefing to the buzzing crowd, which in the last few minutes had jumped from fewer than seventy to almost two hundred state, local, and federal LEOs. The San Antonio fire chief stood alongside SAIC Crowley, but all his employees were already hard at work at the river. Uniformed officers, mostly from neighboring counties since Bexar County had their hands full, staffed the doors, facing outbound. No one knew who'd mounted the attack, and force protection was on everyone's mind. Tough to focus on investigating a crime if you were constantly worried about getting shot or blown to pieces.

Initial jump teams of ATF and FBI explosive and crime scene experts were already boots on the ground by the river along with an army of fire and medical personnel, but to find the First Lady, they needed to cast the widest net possible. Walt Crowley, the special agent in charge of the Houston Field Office, tapped on his mic to get the briefing under way.

Crowley welcomed everyone with a grave voice befitting the occasion and promised to keep it brief so they could all get moving. He began with what they knew, which was little except for the initial casualty count: sixty-one confirmed dead, seventy-four seriously wounded, and an unconfirmed number of missing—including the First Lady.

Listening, Callahan leaned against a long table, glancing around the crowd and wondering who would be assigned to her team. When she turned back, Dominic Caruso stood beside her.

Time was of the essence, so SAIC Crowley finished the briefing in record time, slightly out of breath when he was finished—as one would expect him to be with Cathy Ryan's life in the balance. He directed all the state and local officers to Bill Jordan, the United States marshal for the Western District of Texas, who would swear them all in as special deputies for the duration of the ad hoc task force, allowing them to follow federal guidelines and legal precedent along with their federal counterparts.

There was surely a large murder board somewhere (though no one called it that) back at the SIOC, but coordinating the endeavors of hundreds of investigators required something more sophisticated. Everyone present had provided a cell number when they'd signed in. Texts were going out to designated squad leaders in the next five minutes, followed by team assignments shortly after. Squad leaders would be given links to their specific assignments.

Waiting, like everyone else, Caruso extended a hand. Callahan took it, pulling him in for a back-slapping brotherhood hug. He was surprised that she was this glad to see him.

He stepped back, keeping her hand long enough to show genuine affection but not long enough to be weird, and then hooked a thumb toward the stocky Hispanic man beside him.

"Special Agent Kelsey Callahan," he said. "I'd like you to meet my colleague from Main Justice. He's—"

She stepped forward and shook the man's hand, cutting off Caruso mid-sentence. "Let me guess, John Doe or Smith or Jones."

The man smiled, clasping her hand firmly, looking her directly in the eye as he shook it. "Domingo Chavez," he said. "My friends call me Ding."

"Ah," Callahan said. "You work with Caruso's last spooky friend, John . . . what was his name?"

"I know him well," Chavez said, but didn't clarify.

"Puts you in good company," Callahan said. "I'm reasonably certain your buddy, John, was responsible for some extralegal interrogations and a couple of murders."

"Wouldn't know about that," Chavez said.

"See," Caruso said. "I told you she wasn't the type to hold things back."

Callahan folded her arms across her chest. "Look, Caruso, it's great to see you again, but I'm not sure it's a good idea for you to get yourself assigned to my squad."

Dom's cell phone began to buzz in his hand. He scrolled through the message before turning it toward Callahan so she could read it.

"Now hang on just one damn minute," she said. "I'm assigned to **you**, not the other way around?"

Caruso gave a shrugging nod. "Looks that way."

"Now it makes sense why my assignment came from the Old Man himself instead of a supervisor or the ASAC," she said. "You asked for me personally, didn't you?"

"I did," Caruso said. "Look at it this way, Kelsey, the other squads are going to be doing God's work, that's certain, but our team is comprised of just the three of us. We'll be nimble and more democratic in our process."

"Democratic?" Callahan mused, unconvinced. "So no one is really in charge?"

"So to speak," Caruso said. "Unless you count the director of national intelligence. Because she tells me to jump, I jump."

58

If Callahan was butt-hurt, she got over it quickly and ran Caruso and Ding Chavez through what she'd learned so far. With two hours longer at the scene of the attack, she was the resident expert of their team. Caruso found himself doubly glad to have her on the team. She was honest and capable and had just enough ego to march into gunfire but not so much that she always had to do it alone—or even in the lead.

". . . initial review of the scant security footage we've gathered corroborates witness statements that the first explosives were dropped from small drones—three of which have been recovered in various stages of being trampled by fleeing bystanders and victims. They're on the way to the lab now but a preliminary examination indicates the aircraft were set to home on specific GPS coordinates—"

"Making antidrone guns that scramble radio communication ineffective," Chavez noted.

"Correct," Callahan said. "Disrupt the RF signal controlling the drone and it simply returns home—or to a programmed location it thinks is home. The tech exists to disrupt GPS systems, but it could unintentionally affect other devices. Sophisticated drones, like our military UAVs, are shielded."

"And these?" Caruso asked.

Callahan shook her head. "Nope. The ones we found were off-the-shelf DJIs with a small balsa-wood platform added for the grenade. They simply flew to the programmed spot, dropped their payload, and stayed until they ran out of juice."

Chavez pursed his lips, thinking, then said, "I'm extremely surprised the Service didn't see these things earlier. They had countersnipers, didn't they?"

"They did indeed," Callahan said, giving a mournful shake of her head. "Uniformed Division had two sets." She pointed to the map, indicating the rooftops of two adjacent hotels overlooking the area where the First Lady had been supposed to attend the dedication. "The initial text warning of a possible gas leak was followed by a display of Roman candles, drawing their attention away long enough for shooters to get into position and take them all out. Much of the River Walk might as well be in the bottom of a Dixie Cup, as far as visibility from air assets goes. Angles from buildings along the route block the view unless the aircraft hovers directly overhead. One of the drones flew straight down the river to its home coordinates, deploying a screen of smoke about a hundred feet above the crowd."

"But the last explosion," Chavez said. "That one appears to have been much bigger."

"It was," Callahan said. "A hell of a lot bigger."

"A larger drone?" Caruso asked.

"We don't think so." Callahan referred them to the map again. "Secret Service explosive-detection dogs cleared the area around the event site from the convention center to about a hundred yards west of Rosita's Bridge all the way to the South Presa Street overpass. The area here, between the Presa and Navarro Street bridges where the larger blast occurred, was outside the sweep zone. It looks like a conventional bomb was placed there earlier. ATF is still collecting evidence to discern type of explosive, but it was big enough to kill or maim everyone on the south walk and cause some substantial injuries on the north side of the river."

Caruso ran the tip of his index finger along the map. "So they dropped grenade after grenade on the crowd, driving the First Lady and her protective detail west—"

"Like lambs to the slaughter," Callahan said. "The attackers didn't have to bother with getting past a secure perimeter. They just waited for their targets to come to them. Search teams are finding a shitload of 5.7x28 brass."

"FNs," Chavez mused, shaking his head.

"Yep," Callahan said. "And with no regard for who they hit, the attackers appeared to have just shot everyone who wasn't Cathy Ryan." She pulled up new video of men and white shirts emerging from the water after the blast. One of them led an injured female with dark hair toward the steps leading up to Navarro Street. They passed a responding Sheriff's deputy, who pointed the way to street level before rushing off to look for survivors.

"That's her," Caruso whispered. "They took her into the water to protect her from the blast, covered her blond hair with a wig, and just led her right past everyone responding to the explosions."

"It's mathematical in its brilliance," Chavez said.

"No kidding," Callahan said. "It appears they walked her up to a waiting ambulance on Navarro, which transported her and the attack team out with lights and sirens. Bexar County deputies found the ambulance abandoned off the 410 loop south of Lackland Air Force Base."

Caruso sighed. "Wiped clean of prints and DNA, I'm sure."

"On fire," Callahan said.

"Any IDs from facial recognition yet?" Chavez asked, watching the footage of the men emerging from the water again.

"Not these from the river," Callahan said. "But one of the bad guys appears to be among the dead. He took a round to the jaw from Secret Service, judging from the video. No ID or documents on the body, but we used what was left of his face to get a preliminary ID." She paused a beat, as if for effect. "Fits the scenario. Luc Dufort, former French National Police, Recherche, Assistance, Intervention, Dissuasion Unit."

"A RAID operator," Caruso said. "You're right. That does fit. Those guys burn through practice ammo like the rest of us breathe air."

"And he'd have plenty of expertise in VIP protection," Chavez said. His phone buzzed and he stepped away to take the call.

"Our friends at Langley tell us he turned merc a couple of years ago," Callahan said. "After RAID cut him loose for conduct unbecoming. Something about an underage girl." She peered at Caruso. "Surprising how quickly I get answers to questions like that when the First Lady goes missing."

"Glad to hear it," Caruso said. "Since she's my aunt."

Callahan took a half-step backward. "No shit?"

"No shit," Caruso said.

"I'm really sorry to hear that," she said.

"Thank you," Caruso said. "I'll be fine, but it does give me extra incentive to find her."

"Surprising that they're letting you work this."

"You think?"

She groaned. "Not really, since you're with that mysterious Headquarters component."

Caruso gave her a tired smile. "You know how it is."

Chavez slipped the phone back into his pocket and rejoined the conversation. He nodded to Caruso. "We've got the go-ahead from Director Foley."

"The go-ahead?" Callahan said, incredulous. "What the hell? You are high enough up the food chain that you get calls from the director of national intelligence?"

Chavez looked around to make certain there was plenty of distance between them and the nearest knot of agents. "That was our friend John," he said. "He's got the director of national intelligence on speed dial. So let me ask you, what's the first thing that comes to mind when you hear 'Camarilla'?"

"Human trafficking," Callahan said. "Not trafficking, but whacking traffickers. A group of former-military-turned-mercenaries run from somewhere in Europe. Contractors who don't pay much attention to the black-and-white niceties of the law." She narrowed a wary eye at Caruso. "I had your spooky friend, John, pegged as a Camarilla—and you, too, to be honest."

"Well," Chavez said. "We're not. Anything besides extrajudicial killing of human traffickers?"

"Even that's not concrete," she said. "Nothing more than rumors. No actual names to attach to any file. More like a series of events that all bear the same sophisticated signature for which no one claims responsibility. Military coups in East Africa, a couple assassinations in Eastern Europe, the Caribbean, things that have the look of state actors, but not the fingerprint. It's the same way scientists know there's a black hole, by the effects of something they can't see on the things around it. Camarilla—the little room, the unofficial cabinet—they fit the bill for this in spades. Whoever took the First Lady definitely had some serious training. It virtually had to be a group of former military who drilled this until their execution was flawless." Her nose scrunched up in thought. "Even if we're right and it is them, no one knows any more than what I've told you—a faceless group run out of a shadowy place somewhere in Europe."

"But now we have the dead former RAID operative," Caruso said. "We can get someone running down his past, contacts, next of kin, basically crawl up the collective asses of anyone and everyone who's ever known him until we find some connection. In the meantime, there's a Bosnian Serb cooling his jets in a Buenos Aires hospital who may know something about the Camarilla."

"And what makes you think that?" Callahan asked.

Caruso shot her what he hoped was a we're-all-on-the-same-team grin. "Because he got us confused with them when we chased him down on the river and he got shot—and therein lies the problem. I'm not sure he's in good enough health to talk to us. I'll give you everything we have and maybe you can get the legat to drop in and check his pulse. See what he knows."

FBI legats, or legal attachés, were special agents stationed in key cities around the world, working closely with local law enforcement, security services, and government officials.

"Or," Caruso said. "You could go see him yourself."

"Where are you going?"

"That remains to be seen. I'm with you for now. But the guy who handled Begić's security is still in the wind," Chavez said. "He wasn't on our radar until our recent encounter, but I have photos. I'll get them for you and we can both work on trying to ID him."

"Wait," Callahan said. "You have a different facial-recognition database than the Bureau—Never mind. Of course you do."

"I said we'd give you copies," Dom said. "Whoever he is, it's a pretty good bet that this guy is the one who told his boss the Camarilla might be coming for him. For all we know, they really were and we merely beat them to it. Begić is responsible for the rape of dozens of women when he was a young man during the war. It stands to reason that one of those women might come from a family wealthy and connected enough to hire the Camarilla to go after him."

He turned and looked around the hive of activity in the conference hall–turned–command post. "I need to find a secure terminal."

Callahan smirked. "FBI cybersecurity and Technical Surveillance Countermeasures people set this whole place up. This is about as secure as it gets."

Ding gave a contemplative nod. "He means secure from you guys."

"Come on," Dom said. "We'll fill you in on everything on the way."

"Everything?"

He shrugged. "Most things."

Callahan stopped in her tracks. "Hang on a second. We're operating under the assumption that the Camarilla, a group of former soldiers who hunt down human traffickers and war criminals, is at the same time responsible for murdering at least seventy-five people and abducting the First Lady? All for the money?"

Chavez looked at her and shook his head. "I don't think they're doing it for the money."

"Why, then?"

Chavez and Caruso spoke in unison.

"For fun."

59

The moment Dr. Monte Harper extended the wire antenna on the Breitling Emergency, the watch began to broadcast a distress signal at 406 MHz to the nearest COSPAS-SARSAT satellite in five-second bursts every two minutes.

A joint venture among Russia, the United States, and Europe, the Cosmicheskaya Sistyema Poiska Avariynich Sudov–Search and Rescue Satellite-Aided Tracking system piggybacked equipment on a variety of satellites at various altitudes, including seventy-two medium Earth orbit search-and-rescue (MEOSAR) satellites. Among these MEOSAR was a group of four earth observation satellites collectively known as the A-train.

The twenty-three-foot-long caboose of the A-train, Aura's primary mission was to monitor the earth's climate and air quality, but piggybacked on board was additional SARSAT equipment needed to receive the distress signal and pinpoint its location. Once received, Aura broadcast the information back to ground control, which simultaneously notified the Search and

Rescue Point of Contact (SPOC) associated with the country code of the device and the SPOC associated with the distress beacon's point of origin—in this case the Mission Control Centers in Suitland, Maryland, and Ankara, Turkey, respectively. Both SPOCs notified the Consolidated Personnel Recovery Center with the remaining military in Afghanistan that someone in the Wakhan had sent up a virtual flare.

Under normal circumstances, the coordination center would dispatch search-and-rescue assets immediately. In this case, the information was intercepted by an other government agency case officer (read "CIA") who'd asked to be notified if a signal of any kind was picked up from the eastern end of the Wakhan Corridor. The case officer sent this information directly to his boss at Langley, who pushed it up to D/CIA, who forwarded it to the ODNI. Mary Pat Foley informed Acting President Mark Dehart forty-one minutes after the emergency locator beacon antenna on the Breitling was deployed and A-train satellites had traveled almost halfway around the planet.

Scott Adler, Bob Burgess, and General Vogel entered the Oval Office shortly after Foley arrived. Vogel shot her a half-smile—a lot for a guy with his stony expression. Chadwick had been projecting, grasping at straws about President Ryan's behavior on Air Force One. No one had leaked. Chadwick had just realized Ryan was a human being and subject to human emotions.

They'd all seen the shepherd's video confession implicating the Harpers as spies. The experts at Fort Meade judged it authentic, at least insofar that it wasn't a deepfake—but even a layman could see the confession was under duress. The file had been scrubbed of metadata, but what little remained was consistent with location tags on other video, leading analysts to conclude that it was shot in Tajikistan.

"This signal came from a watch?" Dehart asked.

"That's correct, sir," Foley said. "According to the ID number that communicated with SARSAT. A Breitling Emergency Mission."

"On the spendy side, I'd imagine," Dehart said.

"On the order of ten grand or better new," the SecDef said.

Dehart drummed his fingers on the desktop. "I'm no operator, but it would seem to me that a watch like that would be taken from a prisoner the moment he was arrested."

"Maybe they didn't know what it was," Adler offered.

"They'd know it was expensive," Foley said. "So you're right. It's odd that the Harpers would still be in possession of it. Could be a trap, or whoever has it is just monkeying around without knowing what it does."

"I've spoken at length to Foreign Minister Wang," Scott Adler said. "He assured me he is not personally aware of any issues in Tajikistan or the Wakhan, but will make it a priority to discuss it in the Zhongnanhai."

"Like a car salesman going to talk to the manager," the SecDef said.

"I get that a lot," Adler said. "And frankly, I give it a lot, too. Nature of the beast. Wang is relatively new. Considering what happened to the last foreign minister when he crossed Zhou, he's treading lightly. I'll get him back on the line and up the ante on our end."

Dehart leaned back in his chair . . . Jack's chair. Foley pushed the thought out of her mind.

"Are we one hundred percent sure the Harpers are not somehow connected to U.S. intelligence?"

"We are, sir," Foley said. The question demonstrated that the man wasn't going to go off half-cocked. She gave him that. Still, it made her crazy to think about going into a situation like this without Jack Ryan.

"Anything that might make Beijing believe they're spies?"

"Nothing that would send up a red flag for me if I was looking at them," Foley said. "Certainly not spies for the Taliban. They are a husband-and-wife team of physicians who volunteer their time fixing eyes and helping new mothers in some of the poorest places on earth. Nothing more."

"Is there anything of strategic value in this part of the world?"

"Other than the Chinese base across the border in Tajikistan?" Burgess said. "No. The Wakhan is so remote that the war has never reached it. Shepherds and yak herders. Any useful military intelligence would be extremely sporadic, on the order of patrols one or two times a year, and we can get that from satellites or a UAV."

"The Harpers' daughter completed a retina surgery fellowship under Cathy Ryan's supervision," Foley said. "It's not common knowledge, but it's out there, and it could give the Chinese a lever to pull if they knew about it."

Dehart sighed. "You know what they say about privacy on the Internet these days. 'There isn't any. Get over it.' If we know, then they know or will soon—if they're looking." He drummed long fingers on the desk, pondering the way Jack would over a slow sip from his favorite USMC coffee mug. "Something isn't right here," he continued. "We need to look at the subtext of what's happening. Has Beijing ever admitted to their bases in Tajikistan?"

Burgess shook his head. "They have not, sir."

"Then why put themselves in a position where they might be forced to do that now?"

"Any inkling that the Harpers might have traveled into Tajikistan on their own?"

"Not according to their daughter," Foley said.

"Last word she got was that they were about to begin the trek down the valley by yak train. There's a road in Tajikistan that parallels the border. They could have gotten out by truck."

"So they were taken in the Wakhan," Dehart mused. "He pushed a ballpoint pen across an imaginary line on the Resolute desk. "Chinese forces, who are not supposed to be in Tajikistan in the first place, cross the border into Afghanistan . . . That's a hell of a lot of borders to cross in order to grab someone you know isn't a spy. What's their endgame? Maybe they do already know about that connection with Dr. Ryan."

"Maybe," Adler offered. "But that's a card I believe they would have played earlier in order to get the President's attention."

"You're right," Foley said. "And even if they did know, it still doesn't make sense. Not that Beijing has anything to fear from Kabul, but an incursion like that is an act of war. Besides, they're courting the Taliban of late, not trying to antagonize them by arresting their supposed operatives."

Dehart turned to the secretary of defense. "No more specifics coming out of Tajikistan, patterns of life, that sort of thing?"

"Nothing out of the ordinary, sir," Burgess said. "And there's an ODA out of Mazar-i-Sharif gathering intel in the Wakhan." He paused. "And ODA is Operational Detachment—"

Dehart raised an open hand, smiling, but clearly not wanting to be spoon-fed. "Thank you, Mr. Secretary. I know what an A-team is." He sighed. "Okay. It's time I played the role of unpredictable acting President."

Adler spoke next. "I'll get with the foreign minister on the SVTC."

"Hold off on that," Dehart said. "Let's get Communications to set up a call with Zhou as soon as possible. This is something that should be handled president to president." He caught Foley's eye. "Acting though I may be. I'm an unknown quantity. Maybe we can catch Zhou on his back foot. Get a glimpse of what he's up to."

Burgess gave a nod of approval. "Zhou won't know if you're bluffing."

"Exactly," Dehart said.

Dehart got to his feet, prompting the others to stand as well.

"I'll see to setting up your call with President Zhou," Adler said.

"Very well," Dehart said. "Director Foley, would you stay back for a moment."

"How'd I do?" he asked after the others had gone.

"Sir?"

"I can see you're grading me," he said. "It's to be expected, I suppose. I'd do the same thing if I were in your shoes. What would President Ryan have done differently?"

Foley gave him a motherly wink. "Not a thing, sir," she said. "Not a thing."

"I don't, you know," Dehart said.

"You don't what, sir?"

"Bluff."

"Due respect," Foley said. "But you could be bluffing right now."

"I could," Dehart said. "But I'm not."

"Just continue to do what you're doing, Mr. President," Foley said. "You'll be fine."

60

Jack found his father sitting in the dark in the Residence dining room, elbows on the table, face buried in his hands. The Old Man glanced up when Jack came in, a tragically sad smile spreading across his face, the kind of smile that is a precursor to tears, resignation—an all-is-lost smile. Jack had seen it on others, but never his dad.

Jack grabbed his father and drew him close in an all-encompassing bear hug. He felt so small and fragile, absent the vibrance and vigor that set him apart from mere mortals.

Jack stepped back, holding him at arms' length. "What can I do?"

"What can any of us do, son," Ryan said.

"Sally?"

"I've come to find out she's the rock among us," he said. "Like . . . Like your mother."

"She's here?"

He sighed. "In the kitchen with the kids, trying to keep them from falling apart. I think she expects you to take care of that with me."

"Or vice versa." Jack chuckled, his lips set in a grim line. "Any update at all?"

"Nothing," Ryan said. "It is killing me, but I have to stay back and let them handle it. It's too confusing otherwise. The last thing your mother needs is for those trying to find her to be confused about who is in charge of the mission. No, this requires a clear head and a dispassionate investigation—as much as I don't want to admit it. Now, if I knew who was behind this, clear heads and cool demeanors would be out the window."

"Tell me about it."

His father took a deep breath. "The others?"

"Clark?"

"Yes."

"He's running things on our end, deconflicting with Mary Pat. We have some leads, but nothing concrete. Dom's embedded with the FBI in San Antonio."

"Good to hear," the Old Man said. "It sounds trite, but we have to trust our friends to do the right thing."

Jack rubbed a hand across his face. "Dad . . . I'm not sure I can stand by while she's out there."

"I know the feeling," the Old Man said. "And I share it, but there's a reason they don't recommend people with access to nuclear weapons go after those who have kidnapped their best friend."

"Or their mother," Jack said.

"Ah," the Old Man said. "But you don't have access to nukes."

"Shows what you know, Dad," Jack said. "I'd sure as hell be able to find some if I needed them." He groaned and pulled his father in for a tight embrace. "I just feel like I should be doing something."

"You are, son," Ryan said. "You really are."

61

Watches move, Captain," Sergeant Megnas said. ODA 0312's new 18E communications sergeant hunkered behind a jagged slab of stone the size of a dump truck two miles from the village of Vagd Boi.

Megnas was heavily freckled, with shockingly red hair. So far, the rest of the team had resisted the urge to call him "Red" or "Howdy" or "Doody" or anything quite that obvious. Besides, nicknames had to be earned.

"What's your point, Sergeant Megnas?" Brock asked, slipping the satellite phone back in the pouch on his chest rig. Moments before, they'd received word that someone had activated the emergency locator beacon on Monte Harper's Breitling watch—putting it within four hundred meters of the village of Vagd Boi. They'd stopped for a moment to touch bases via sat phone with Split Team Bravo and make any necessary adjustments to their plan.

Sunrise was still a couple hours away. Absent a scintilla of light pollution, the Roof of the World was draped with a blanket of stars. Stopped here on the side of this barren mountain looking up at the brilliant night sky, he wished he could share the moment with his little boy—minus the sixty pounds of weapons, ammo, and supplies . . . and that whole going-to-battle thing.

"I'm just sayin' that it seems like a ten-thousand-dollar watch would be the first thing captors would take off a prisoner," Megnas said, breaking the spell.

"And you'd be right," Thelan said. "But taken with the disappearing horses, it makes for a pretty damn compelling argument that the Harpers are still in Vagd Boi."

"True," Megnas said. "It's just weird that the ELT is going off now, so long after they were captured."

"You are absolutely correct," Brock said. "A local might be playing with the crown and accidently deployed the ELT. It could be a trap. Or the Harpers might have been under surveillance until now and this is the first time they've been able to deploy the antenna."

"Yep," Thelan said. "And the only way to find out is to go find out."

"Roger that," Megnas said. "I don't want you to think I'm not on board."

"Not at all," Brock said.

A horse nickered softly in the darkness behind them, pawing at the rocky ground with its hoof.

Megnas soothed the animal with a low voice

born of experience. "Whoooa, boy. It's all good . . ."

Special Forces soldiers were expected to think outside the box, to improvise. Sergeant Thelan had come up with the first mission adjustment before they'd even jumped. They'd arrive at Mulung Than in the early-morning hours, meeting one of Thelan's contacts and buying his horses for the ride into Vagd Boi. The Wakhi man knew the soldiers would have no need for the horses after this trip, and as long as they did not get shot or fall into a ravine, he would have them back after it was over, essentially renting his horses for the same price as selling them. A good deal for all parties.

Years of war had all but decimated Afghan horse breeds like the lanky Qatghani ridden by Special Forces soldiers and Northern Alliance early in the war, but Tajik and Kyrgyz mountain breeds now trickled back and forth across the border. For all but a very few people of the Wakhan, a horse was a tool that provided four legs and a strong back and, in the case of mares, milk. Thelan's contact, a man named Kalakov (the nickname Afghans often gave to the Russian AK-47 rifle) was one of the few who knew his horses and cared about the breed, or at least purported to. According to him, these three mounts were all pure Qatghani Afghan horses with good feet and sound lungs. Brock's, an angular dun with a large head that reminded him of the bucket on a backhoe, was supposed to have been a champion of buzkashi—the violent headless-goat-grabbing free-for-all scrum that was, according to locals, eighty percent horse and twenty percent rider.

Central Asian saddles were hard, wooden affairs with a deep seat between the upswept horn and high cantle—not the most comfortable things in the world, but secure, which was more important for a horse soldier. Kalakov threw in three saddles for five thousand afghanis each—about sixty bucks, knowing he'd get them back as well.

Contrary to his computer nerd reputation, Megnas had grown up on a ranch in southern Idaho, and though he'd groused about the skinny Afghan horses, he was the best rider of the three of them, almost giddy to be atop his lanky bay.

The soldiers still wore their uniform and kit, but switched boonies for pakol hats, and draped the long Afghan robe over top to break up the outline once it started getting light.

Thelan held up a hand, motioning for everyone to stop. His horse, a dappled gray, wheeled, picking up some distant noise before their human ears caught it.

"You hear that?" Thelan said.

Brock reined in the dun, using leg pressure to keep it from prancing—or at least trying to.

Then he caught the sound of clattering rocks and labored breathing.

"Captain!" Thelan said, spurring his horse toward a rock outcrop. "I think somebody's charging at us."

The three men reached the cover of the outcrop and spun their horses as a single horse cantered by, blowing and wheezing from terror and exhaustion. The outline of a body tied over its back was barely visible in blue darkness.

Brock, M-4 in one hand, reins in the other, pointed the rifle toward the fleeing animal.

"Grab it!"

Megnas brought up the rear of the column, putting him closest to the horse. Wheeling his bay, he leaned forward, giving the animal its head, urging it forward. The bay, not winded and encumbered by a lifeless flopping corpse, caught the runner in a dozen long strides. Megnas leaned over at the run and grabbed the terrified animal by the bridle, reining in his own horse to bring them both to a jogging stop.

Megnas led the horse back to the rock outcrop while Brock and Thelan kept watch to make certain there weren't more horses with live riders on their way down the trail.

"This is some weird shit," Thelan said, checking the dead man's uniform. "PLA soldier. Looks like his throat's been cut."

"I'd say that makes for pretty damned good

odds that we found them," Brock said. "Disappearing horses from the ISR, the Breitling ELT, and now this dead Chinese guy." He took the satellite phone from its pouch and extended the antenna. "Let's scoot up there and pin it down to an exact location for the HAF."

Some five hundred kilometers away, the helicopter assault force comprised of Chief Guzman, Sergeant Ward, along with the remaining seven team members of ODA 0321 and sixty Afghan National Army commandos, lifted off in two Sikorsky UH-60 Black Hawks and a single Boeing CH-47 Chinook.

They were ninety minutes out.

62

olonel Tu paced back and forth like a caged tiger. He'd changed into a pakol hat and shalwar kameez. All his soldiers had opted for the traditional loose pants and thigh-length shirt to one degree or another, presumably to foil any satellite surveillance.

The colonel seemed about to break at every turn. He growled at the Harpers and lashed out at his own soldiers if they crossed him in the most insignificant matter. Harper assumed his mood had to do with the fact that his ride wasn't coming as quickly as he wanted it to, but whatever the reason, everyone went out of their way to avoid the man, even his aide-de-camp, Captain Shen.

Harper was busy putting clove oil on Shambe's broken tooth when the colonel shoved aside the yurt flap and barged inside, stooping to clear the header. The soldier with the video camera came in next, followed by two soldiers with un-slung rifles. Captain Shen brought up the rear.

Tu smoothed the front of his tunic with both hands and stood up straight, beckoning Harper closer with a braided leather quirt.

"The time has come for you to give your confession," Tu said.

Harper bowed his head. "I'm happy to—"

"Not you!" Tu barked. "Your wife."

Naomi stood from where she was helping Shambe's mother with the bread, neck arched, seething. "I swear to you—"

Tu waved her off. "Please spare me your threats. I do not have the time for such silly ways. You will read what I have prepared or I will shoot your husband in the head. Refuse again, and it will happen instantly."

Naomi's knees started to buckle. She wobbled, and would have fallen, but Shambe's mother caught her. Blinking, she caught Harper's eye and shook her head. "I'm so, so sorry, sweetheart." A sob caught hard in her throat. "I know what we decided, but . . . I can't let him kill you."

"It's okay," Harper said. "It's . . . all okay—"

"Shut up!" The colonel grabbed her by the hair and jerked her off her feet, dragging her across the carpeted floor.

Harper lunged to stop him, but the colonel simply drew his pistol and pressed it against Naomi's temple.

"Her blood and brains will make a fine confession."

Harper stopped in his tracks and raised both hands. "Okay, okay."

Tu shoved Naomi against the lattice frame

and gray-brown felt of the yurt. Outside, toothy shadows marched in from the west across the valley floor as the sun rose behind the jagged peaks to the east, bathing the sheep and dogs and gathered shepherds in morning blue. One of Tu's soldiers stood facing the yurt with his video cameraman, boots planted wide to keep him steady. He pointed to the yurt door and a soldier tied it open to allow in more light. Another knelt below the camera with a clipboard holding the script for Naomi's sham confession. The videographer switched on a small bank of LEDs, then looked up from his viewfinder and gave a curt nod. He was ready.

One of the Tajik soldiers grabbed Harper and held him to the side, out of frame. Tu pointed the pistol at Naomi. For a horrible fleeting instant Harper thought Tu meant to execute her— but he swung the pistol toward Harper.

"If she attempts to communicate any hidden messages by, say, blinking a code with her eyes or substituting words from the script provided, I will shoot you in the head. Argue with me in any way or deviate from my instructions and I will shoot you in the head. Immediately." He glared over his shoulder at Naomi, the muzzle of the black Makarov still rock steady at Harper's face. "Do I make myself clear?"

"I understand," Naomi said, gathering her composure.

"Good," Tu said, giving a little sigh, as if he'd just dodged a bullet. "Now you will confess your lies and deceit to the world—"

A baby-faced soldier ducked through the open door, face flushed, rifle clutched across his chest. He cleared his throat.

The colonel spun on him, growling something Harper couldn't understand.

Captain Shen strode over to see what the soldier wanted, and then stepped back to relay the information. The colonel twisted the leather quirt in his fist and flushed a deep shade of crimson as he listened.

He bellowed a string of orders at the young troop, spittle flying from his lips. At length he turned and smoothed the front of his uniform tunic once again. Outwardly he looked calm, but his voice betrayed him. He flicked the quirt toward Naomi.

"Get on with it!"

Harper couldn't understand the words, but he got the tone. Tu had just learned that one of his men had deserted and fled the camp with one of the horses. Had the colonel doubted this story, Harper would have been shot then and there. Judging from the unhinged look in the man's eye, it wasn't exactly off the table. Colonel Tu was scared, and fear pushed men to violence. Harper knew this all too well.

The colonel smacked his own thigh with the leather quirt and then growled at the cameraman.

Naomi began to read, but Harper wasn't looking at her. Instead, he focused on a small bird that hovered like a hummingbird at the door. The bird pivoted, scanning the room, its lens pointed directly at Harper.

63

Acting President Dehart asked Foley to remain in the Oval Office during the call with President Zhou. Secretary of State Adler was also present, along with Bob Burgess, General Vogel of the Joint Chiefs, a secretary, and two Mandarin interpreters, one of whom also worked for WHMO—the White House Military Office.

Foley wasn't surprised he'd want a deep outfield of advisers around him for this call. As a former senator from Pennsylvania, Dehart wasn't exactly steeped in foreign policy experience. He was, however, patient and shrewd, qualities he would desperately need to deal with Beijing.

Dehart remained behind the Resolute desk, eyes closed in thought while Betty Martin stood by with the handset, waiting for the communications office to connect the call. Foley took one of the side chairs, across from him, pen and yellow legal pad at the ready, in case she needed to write him a note mid-call. From personal experience, she knew that if anyone ever took the time to listen to recordings of important calls, the tell-tale scratch of scribbled notes on paper would be fairly constant in the background.

Betty Martin stood a hair straighter. "Please hold for the President of the United States . . ." She spoke into the handset, then turned to Dehart. "Mr. President, I have President Zhou."

At his nod, Martin put the call on speaker and returned the handset to its cradle, retreating to the windows overlooking the Rose Garden until she was needed again.

Here we go, Foley thought. **Hell of a way to begin a new job.** She smiled, and gave Dehart a hearty thumbs-up.

"Zhou Zhuxi," Dehart said. "Thank you for agreeing to speak with me." Dehart's use of **Zhuxi** drew raised brows from the interpreters. The honorific title could be translated as **president** in English, but was generally understood to mean **chairman** in Mandarin. Speaking in both Mandarin and English could have been considered a rube move, but Dehart pulled it off with aplomb.

"Of course," Zhou said in English. "Please convey our most sincere condolences to President Ryan for this despicable hardship. Whatever else comes from our discussions now and in the future, you must believe we wish for Mrs. Ryan's safe and speedy return."

"Thank you," Dehart said. "I will pass along your kind sentiments." He skipped further niceties and, to Foley's relief, any apologies for his inexperience, going straight for the meat of the matter—the yolk of the egg, as Ryan liked to call it.

". . . As you can see," Dehart said, after a thumbnail review of the current situation in the Wakhan Corridor, "something is very wrong. I feel certain that your military would in no case invade a foreign power under these circumstances. I would take the liberty to guess that you have a rogue officer who has surely overstepped his authority."

"Mr. President," Zhou said. "I can assure you that I will get to the bottom of this matter."

"And I appreciate that," Dehart said. "I really do. But I must be frank with you, sir. We are under a great deal of stress in this country, searching for the criminals who have abducted our First Lady. Some in the administration might believe that this incident coming on the heels of that abduction is evidence of involvement on the part of Beijing—"

The response came back in rapid-fire Mandarin, which was translated by a female aide on President Zhou's end. "We deeply resent any implication of involvement in Mrs. Ryan's abduction. Such accusations are an inauspicious beginning, to be sure—"

"I understand," Dehart said, calm but direct. "I am only being candid about how some feel. You can imagine who." Dehart looked up long enough to give the secretary of defense a playful wink. "I personally do not believe China to have a hand in this. I am, as we say here, putting all my cards on the table. Our evidence has clearly shown that Chinese forces are on the ground in the Wakhan. I feel certain that you, sir, knew nothing of their presence—"

Zhou started to speak, again in Mandarin, but Dehart kept talking, his previously controlled voice rising in pitch and volume with each word.

"I am merely making you aware that I will not allow U.S. citizens to be bullied by aggressors who have invaded a sovereign country in which those citizens are guests on a humanitarian mission."

"I will look into the matter," Zhou said, this time in curt English. "You have my assurance."

"You do that, Mr. President," Dehart said. "But in the meantime, I would advise you to keep anyone you care for out of Afghanistan—because with God as my witness, anyone standing between me and my people will be wiped from the face of this earth."

I don't see him wanting to fight us in Afghanistan," Burgess said. "Not a hundred miles in from the Chinese border."

Dehart rubbed his eyes with a thumb and fore-finger. Betty Martin came in with two Tylenol and three ibuprofen and a glass of water. "Maybe so," he said, tossing back the meds and half the glass of water. "But if he does, my first act in office will be to start World War III."

The director of national intelligence stood by the fireplace, listening, watching Dehart work. She was impressed, not only with the demeanor of the man and how he'd so quickly risen to the occasion, but with the wisdom of the man who'd chosen him for the job. For the third time that day, Mary Pat Foley, whose eyes had seen so much human meanness and brutality over the years as to become numb to most everything, welled with tears.

64

Tally-ho," Megnas said, comparing the image on the Black Hornet's video feed to a printed copy of the Harpers' passport photos. "Those're our hostages."

He and Brock remained in the saddle, having approached to within two hundred meters of the village under cover of darkness. For the time being, the wind was in their faces, so the massive dogs hadn't smelled them yet. Sergeant Thelan peered through the Nightforce scope on his Barrett, gathering intel the old-fashioned way.

Brock watched the feed as well while Megnas worked the nano-drone's controller. Small enough to carry in a chest rig, the FLIR Black Hornet was essentially an unmanned helicopter system that carried sophisticated cameras. It had a range of just over a mile and could stay airborne for almost half an hour.

"Some of the dogs are noticing it," Thelan said, staying on his gun. "Barking some, but that's working to our advantage. It's got everyone looking at the mountains for wolves so they can't see what's right in front of them.

"Get out of there."

"Roger that," Megnas said. Then, "Hang on, sir. Hostage is raising his fingers . . . I think he's giving us a troop count."

"Good to know," Brock said. "Let's get—"

"Shit!" Megnas said.

"What now?"

Megnas worked the controls on his console. "It's gone dark."

Thelan's calm voice buzzed against his rifle. "Damned dog jumped up and snatched it, Captain. The bad guys are looking it over now— going apeshit."

Brock was already on the horn to the HAF. They'd found and fixed the target—now it was time to finish it.

"They're four minutes out," Brock said.

Still on horseback, Megnas opened his fingers to let a second Black Hornet escape into the air and speed toward the encampment. "I'll have eyes on again in three."

"Flying Crossbow," Thelan whispered. "Second dwelling to the left of the target. They're onto us."

The PLA Feinu-6 Flying Crossbow was a third-generation man portable surface-to-air missile, perfectly suited to shooting down helicopters.

"How many?" Brock asked.

"One so far," Thelan said. "He hasn't put it to his shoulder yet . . ."

The rules of engagement were clear. Enemy combatants held Americans against their will. Rescue was imminent, and if one of those combatants picked up a weapon and pointed it— Thelan would put the proverbial warhead on his forehead. No command from Brock would be necessary.

The **wap wap wap** of rotors hitting the thin high-altitude air echoed up the valley.

"Shouldn't have done that," Thelan said, taking a deep breath and settling behind the Barrett.

Harper rushed to Naomi at the sound of the approaching helicopters. Colonel Tu and his men rushed out of the yurt, scanning the mountains while Captain Shen crushed the tiny drone in his fist and threw it on the ground in contempt.

Unwilling to step into the rapidly devolving madness outside, the Harpers lay flat on their bellies at the door, shoulder to shoulder, and watched it unfold.

Less than twenty feet away, a soldier carrying a missile stumbled forward, the top half his head suddenly just gone. Harper pulled his wife closer, urging her to look away. She shrugged him off. Soldiers ran this way and that, leading horses outside from where they'd had them stashed inside various yurts. Most of the sheep and yaks were down valley grazing, but the few that remained in camp began to bleat and mill excitedly at all the commotion.

Colonel Tu stood in the shadow of one of the stone pens, screaming into his satellite phone—like a spoiled child who couldn't get anybody to listen to him.

Two Black Hawk helicopters hove into view, their rotor beats bouncing off the surrounding mountains in a throaty drumbeat that was surely the most beautiful noise Monte Harper had ever heard. A big twin-rotor Chinook followed, all three of the birds bearing down hot and fast in a spectacular show of force.

Tu shoved the satellite phone at his aide, pointing at it and screaming. Harper imagined him saying "You try!" but couldn't be sure. Whatever he'd said, he abandoned the phone to Captain Shen and ran toward his horse as the Black Hawks beat in. He slowed when he saw the missile, and stooped to pick it up, immediately meeting the same fate as the soldier before.

"He's out of the picture," Harper said over the drumbeat of approaching choppers.

"I see that," Naomi said, shuddering beside him.

"We need to be still," Harper said to everyone in the yurt. "Hands on our heads, and make ourselves as nonthreatening as possible."

The helicopters disgorged man after man, all of

whom began to move toward the village as soon as their boots hit the ground.

Two Chinese soldiers and one Tajik leapt on their horses and tore down the valley, whipping their animals to gain every ounce of speed. Harper felt Naomi catch her breath beside him.

"What?"

"Would you look at that," she gasped. "Coming straight at these bastards."

Harper followed her gaze to see two new animals galloping up the valley directly toward them. The men on them were large, somewhat dwarfing their mounts, and dressed in a distinctive desert camouflage and boonie hats.

Horse soldiers.

Guzman, Ward, the rest of ODA 0312, and the ANA commandos descended on the village in such a show of force that the only two fatalities were the soldier who'd foolishly tried to use the FN-6 Crossbow, and the idiot colonel when he attempted to pick the thing up.

Sergeant Thelan had remained in his hide covering the HAF's arrival while Brock and Megnas cut off the mounted soldiers' attempted escape.

The Afghan major tasked his commandos with lining up the PLA and Tajik soldiers, restraining them and securing their weapons.

Leaving the prisoners to the ANA forces,

Sergeant Ward saw to it the team collected exploitable evidence to be sent up the chain for analysis—including the late Chinese colonel's satellite phone, which his aide-de-camp had gotten rid of like it was radioactive.

Weinrick, the senior 18D—medical sergeant—stood beside the Harpers in front of one of the yurts checking their condition when Brock trotted up and dismounted.

"Captain," the 18D said. "These folks have had a bit of a rough time. Think we can give 'em a ride?"

Ward came up just then with a middle-aged Wakhi woman whose husband the colonel had apparently murdered. Through an ANA commando kandak interpreter named Hashem, the woman told them that she had crept to where the colonel was staying, intent on killing him to avenge her husband's death. The captain had come and scared her away, but before she left, she'd overheard the colonel talking on his phone—in English.

65

Senator Michelle Chadwick shut the door to her condo and pitched the keys on the side table in the tiled foyer. Her grandfather had always told her, the house is great, but the foyer is what sells the place. It's the first thing and the last thing a buyer sees and, more important, they imagine it will be the first things their friends see when they come to visit. Her grandfather was a foyer fanatic. He was also a millionaire many times over, so she tended to listen to the man growing up. He would have been proud of her had he seen this place—nice Arlington neighborhood. Low crime. Just far enough from D.C. Granddad would not have approved of her house dog. Dogs were for the ranch. Period. They drove down the value of your property and ruined the yard—

Speaking of that. Chadwick gave a little smooch. Where was her dog. Weird that he hadn't met her at the door. Border collie and Scottsdale night wanderer, he was always at the door to meet her.

"Hondo!" Chadwick gave another smooch. "Mama's home—"

She heard a yelp from the bathroom and scratching. The little turd had gotten himself trapped.

"How about a walk before Nick—"

Chadwick froze as she rounded the corner and spotted the man sitting on her sofa wearing nothing but a pair of jogging shorts and paper shoe covers like surgeons used. He glanced up when she came in—like he was bored. He sipped a glass of tea while he read some papers spread out on the coffee table. A black pistol lay on the table beside a stack of file folders. She knew enough about guns to recognize the suppressor on the end of the barrel.

Chadwick's knees very nearly buckled. She grabbed the wall for support.

Shoe covers, a silencer . . . this was bad . . .

"How did you get in here?" She tried to mask her terror with aggression.

He wasn't a large man, not much taller than Chadwick's five-seven if at all. He had maybe twenty pounds on her, but all of that looked like ropy muscle. And she was only fifteen feet away. All he had to do was flick his hand and pull the trigger—which he obviously planned to do, soon, from the look on his face. If she could just get him talking. She glanced at the clock on the mantel. Five minutes should do it. She would filibuster her own murder.

"I have money," she said. "It's in the safe if you want me to open it."

He shook his head, sneering.

Something about him was off. Was he wearing makeup? No. It was like he had spots all over his torso and up his neck and face. Like one of those ghost leopards . . .

She changed tack and nodded at the papers on the table.

"What's all this?" She was genuinely curious. Assassins took files, they didn't leave them.

"Michelle, Michelle, Michelle," the man said. He took a sip of tea, watching her the entire time. His hand was steady, his eyes dead, like a doll's. "What's the deal with this shit?" He stuck his tongue out. "You don't believe in sweet tea?"

She couldn't think of a thing to say. He lifted the pistol.

"Wha . . . What about the papers?" She asked again.

"Your stocks." He set the glass on the coffee table and pulled the top envelope toward him. "Let's see here, this one is for Galindo Pharmaceutical Corporation out of San Juan. And here's some options for Trax Medical, based in Caguas. I gotta tell you, Michelle. This looks suspicious. You did mention these on that . . . what do you call it, your financial disclosure form you gotta do every year? You did do that, right?"

"I . . . I've never seen those before and you know it."

The man slouched back in her couch cushions, gesturing at her with the pistol. "You know why nobody likes you, Michelle?"

"Why's that?"

"I watched you on television and I figured it out," the man said. "You don't just act like you're right. You act like everyone else is a dumbass."

"What makes you think you can come in here and threaten me?"

He laughed and got to his feet, groaning at the effort.

Surprisingly, he left the gun where it was and walked over to face her, hands behind his back.

A steely resolve flooded her veins. "I'm not going to let you touch me."

He laughed and swatted the end of her nose.

"You mean like that?"

"You bastard!"

"Oh, Michelle . . ." He struck quickly, hitting her hard in the floating rib, knocking the wind out of her.

She breathed out hard, clutching the wall to stay standing, speaking through gritted teeth. "You . . . You hit like a pussy."

He nodded to her belly. "I didn't hit you," he said, and then held up a blade. "I stabbed you."

She swayed in place, teetering there for a moment before collapsing to land on her butt.

The man walked back to the couch and wiped his knife blade on the fabric.

"Shouldn't be long now," he said. "Pretty sure I nicked your liver."

Hondo heard her cries and launched into a barking fit in the bathroom.

She clutched her stomach, looking down to see blood oozing between her fingers. "Please," she whispered. "Please don't hurt my dog."

The door rattled behind her. She'd almost stalled long enough. Her boyfriend was here. An ATF agent. He'd be armed . . .

Almost.

She screamed. "Niiiiiick!" Her head spun and she wasn't sure any words even came out of her mouth.

She tried again, but with the same result.

The man shot her twice. Once in the chest. The second shot struck her below her left eye.

Well, this turned into a real shitfest, Fermin Pea thought as he capped the senator and fled out the balcony door, putting at least one round into the big dude who'd come through the front door with his guns blazing. Pea knew for sure he'd hit the guy. He heard the familiar slap of the bullet finding a home. He just couldn't tell if it was lethal. It didn't matter. He'd hit the bitch in the eye. She was finished. The documents were in place and the big dude hadn't gotten more than a fleeting look at him. Sure, the cops would still have his clothes, folded on the couch. He'd thought he'd take them off to keep from getting blood on them when he did the close work on the senator. If the big guy hadn't showed up he could have had a good time. Slow. Methodical, like the old days, not these boring political killings where you had to get in and out and couldn't take your time. Then the big guy rushed his hand and he had to haul ass. Bad deal all around.

Pea knew they could get his DNA off the clothes. He watched **CSI**. But they'd have to catch him to have anything to compare it to, and he didn't intend to let that happen. He dumped the gun in the shrubs and took off at a jog down the block. For all anyone knew, he was just out for an evening run. He made it to the first intersection before a couple of chicks in a blue Dodge Dart rolled down their windows and asked if he'd escaped from the asylum. They pointed at the puffy paper covers on his shoes and laughed their asses off. If he'd still had the pistol he would have shot them.

66

Operational Detachment Alpha 0312 turned Colonel Tu's satellite phone over to the in-country cyber specialist. The device was not password protected and call logs for the past three weeks were easily obtained. The list of numbers went up the chain and then laterally to CIA, who passed it directly to Liberty Crossing.

One of Mary Pat Foley's analysts had been waiting for word since the Breitling Emergency locator beacon went online—and hand carried the information to Foley's office, sliding an annotated spreadsheet across the director's desk.

The intel analyst, a twenty-six-year-old mother of two with a master's in economics from Baylor, stepped back and folded her arms across her chest. She reminded Foley of herself back in the day, a young mother on the job. She'd not only found subscriber data from all the numbers—two of which were apparent burner phones pinging off towers in Afghanistan—but done a deep dive into the background of the number Colonel Tu had called thirteen times in the past four days,

MalhotraMed Pharmaceuticals in Hyderabad, India.

"This is really good work, Katie," Foley said, picking up the desk phone. For a fleeting moment, she thought about calling Jack directly, but talked herself out of it. It was what he would want, but not what he would do. He was smart enough to know that he had to stay out of this completely. If he showed his face, simply to see what was going on, people would bend to his wishes by sheer force of his personality whether he asked them to or not.

"Jodie," Foley said as soon as her assistant picked up. "Please let my security detail know I need to go the White House as soon as possible."

Please," Dehart said, waving a hand toward the couch after she'd given him a thumbnail rundown of the information from the A-team. One of the numbers on the satellite phone was to a bank in the Cayman Islands. They hadn't been able to access his accounts yet, but it didn't take much of a leap to understand Malhotra had paid him to grab the Harpers.

"And the Harpers' daughter works with the First Lady," Dehart said, connecting the dots.

"Becca Harper did her fellowship under Dr. Ryan," Foley said. "If the President mistakenly sent Delta and or SEAL Team Six into Tajikistan to save his family friends relying on bad intel . . ."

"I get the picture," Dehart said. "Could it be this baldly simple? A billionaire with a pending buyout on shaky ground pays a Chinese colonel to kidnap two doctors in order to embarrass the President, to take his mind off a pharmaceutical bill?"

Foley groaned. "He's trying to sell his company to a German buyer, I'd imagine for a considerable fortune. This bill stands to put the kibosh on the sale. What would someone not do to save a multibillion-dollar deal? You said we should look at subtext of the actions. And the intelligence from the colonel's satellite phone is pretty damning. We have to look at the sudden abundance of deepfake videos purporting to show President Ryan in compromising positions. The ransomware attacks. The Harpers. When taken in total, it's been an effective active measures campaign to push many of our initiatives to the sidelines, expending the time and energy of the President and the nation."

"Begs the obvious question," Dehart said. "So we think this Harjit Malhotra is behind the First Lady's abduction?"

"No smoking gun," she said. "Yet. But you and I both know he is. We know the Japanese operative at the hacker space in Tokyo had made several trips to India in recent weeks."

"How exactly did we come up with that information again?"

Foley took a deep breath and held it before exhaling slowly.

Dehart gave her a wary side-eye. "What is it? I feel like you're about to tell me my dog has died and gone to a better place."

"Mr. President," she said. "We've discussed the possibility of a rogue group of former military operators—"

"The Camarilla," Dehart said. "Mercenaries. Highly trained guns for hire. I understand one of the men at the hacker space was formerly attached to Japanese Special Forces."

"Yes, sir," Foley said. "There's something else at play here that you should be made aware of, considering."

More side-eye.

Foley took another breath, feeling like she was about to confess some grievous but explainable sin. "There is . . . a group of sorts that President Ryan stood up several years ago. Once I divulge what I am about to tell you, you will be one of a very small circle of people who even know of the group's existence."

Dehart was on his feet by the time she finished. She'd not given him any names yet, but would have had he asked. Though acting, he **was** the commander in chief, which meant he was her boss. The boss. Ryan was smart, and if he trusted Dehart enough to hand him the reins of this runaway horse, then who was Foley to think otherwise. If she waited and he learned of The Campus some other way, any semblance of trust would vanish.

Dehart turned away, hands clasped behind his back, then suddenly wheeled. "So what you're telling me is that we are using our own off-the-books good Camarilla to hunt down this bad Camarilla."

"The Campus," Foley said. "But yes. Essentially, you are correct."

"And they're in India as we speak, following up on the Japanese soldier?"

"Correct," Foley said. "It was a Campus contact with Japanese intelligence that pointed us that way."

"So intelligence agencies from other nations know of The Campus?"

"Intelligence is a world of smoke and mirrors, sir," Foley reminded him. "In almost every case where they have to make contact, it is assumed they are from CIA or one of our other intelligence agencies."

"I see," Dehart said. He was asking good questions, the kind Foley would have asked were this sprung on her out of the blue.

"Who's in charge of this Campus, their

day-to-day?" He raised a hand and shook his head before she could answer. "I don't want to know details at the moment. Our priority now is to get Cathy Ryan home and safe. I assume you'll have them see what they can find on Malhotra and then turn it over to the FBI legat. It just occurs to me, every CIA chief of station I've ever met goes completely berserk if anyone comes into their bailiwick without checking in. Do your Campus folks do that?"

"They do not," Foley said. "But I make informal checks to deconflict, make sure they're not stepping into an ongoing operation."

"Very well," Dehart said. "With any luck, I'll only be in this office for a few more hours." He stopped pacing and looked hard at Foley. "But if through some tragic turn of events I end up here for a longer stint of time, then we are going to have a very long talk about the status of this off-the-books Campus."

"They do incredible work, Mr. President," Foley said.

"I have no doubt," Dehart said. "But we'll still need to talk about it." He closed his eyes. "Yes. A very lonely place indeed."

67

Cathy Ryan woke on her side with something hard biting into the flesh above her ankle. She couldn't feel her hands, but the muscles in her neck were on fire. She shook her head, trying to remember anything beyond the persistent tinnitus that squealed unceasingly in her ears.

A wave of nausea washed over her, from the aftermath of the drugs. There'd been spiders, big, hairy, jumping spiders, which likely meant a ketamine dart. And maybe midazolam, there were so many holes in her memory.

She was blindfolded—hooded really, something soft, not hard like she imagined hoods would be when she watched spy movies with Jack . . . **Jack! What have I gotten myself into?**

She'd learned long ago not to take sight for granted, going so far as to blindfold herself for a full twenty-four hours during her ophthalmology residency so she could experience what her patients did when she performed a tarsorrhaphy—sewing the eyelids together to protect the cornea after a burn or during Bell's palsy, when the patient could not close and lubricate their own eyes.

She'd always tried to put herself in her patients' shoes—and this would certainly help with that when she got out . . . if she got out.

The hood material was porous enough she could tell it was light in the room, but she had no idea if it came from a bulb or a window. She held her breath, straining to hear anything over the pounding of her heart that might help her get a sense of the situation.

She tried to sit up, heard the rattle of a chain, and realized her right wrist was secured to something.

She didn't know how long she'd been a prisoner. There had been a van ride. But before that . . . She remembered Karen Sato trying to lead her to safety. The rest of the detail falling under a volley of gunfire, in slow motion like one those violent Sergio Leone movies that were Jack Senior and Jack Junior's guilty pleasure. The whole thing was surreal. Unthinkable.

She found herself beginning to hyperventilate, panic overriding any shred of coherent thought she had left in her fevered brain. She willed her breath to slow. She was alive . . . But why? Surely not for any ransom. There were richer people with far less security than she had. Were they terrorists trying to make some statement? If all they wanted was headlines, she'd have already had a bullet in the brain. The only reason to keep her alive was as leverage—over her husband.

The one in the van had said something after they'd taken her . . . What was it?

They needed her "intact . . ."

What the hell did that even mean? Alive? Not cut into pieces? Not yet raped?

"Oh, Jack," she whispered. "I don't know what they want you to do, but—"

A deep voice sent her recoiling backward as if slapped.

"You hungry, Miss?" the voice said, rough and gravelly, but polite.

She held her breath, waiting for someone to hit her or inject her with some drug again. When that didn't happen, she gave an involuntary sob, fighting the fear that threatened to completely overwhelm her.

"You can take the hood off," the voice said, absent even a hint of malice. "If you want to."

Cathy realized her left hand was free and yanked the hood off immediately, blinking at the sudden brightness from the naked bulb above her.

She found herself dressed in blue hospital scrubs, in a ten-by-ten bedroom, chained to a wrought-iron bedframe. A leg iron connected her left ankle to an eyebolt set in a five-gallon bucket of concrete, presumably allowing her to move around, albeit slowly, if they ever uncuffed her wrist. There were no sheets or blankets on the stained mattress—not that she needed any. The room was sweltering and dank, smelling of mildew and old socks. The trunk of a twisted tree stood outside the dusty pane of a single window. It was covered with steel burglar bars, but oddly enough had no curtains or shades. The light from outside and the bright bulb did little to cheer the faded yellow wallpaper.

The bed squeaked and her muscles protested as she swung her legs slowly to the ground, getting her bearings. A wave of nausea washed over her as she realized someone had changed her out of clothing and into the scrubs.

"My name's Burt," the man said. "You don't look so good." He didn't exactly sound handicapped, but something was definitely going on here. Kidnappers didn't speak this way.

"Hi, Burt," Cathy said, disarmed by the innocence in his voice. "Where am I?"

He chuckled. "To tell you the truth, I don't know for sure. They don't tell me much."

Dressed in jeans and a pearl-snap Western shirt, he looked to be in his late forties, tall, muscular, with a thick mop of silver hair and a large pink scar on the right side of his face from the middle of his forehead to his ear and halfway down his cheek—like he'd fallen asleep in the sun. He held out a paper plate in both hands, like her kids used to do when they made her breakfast in bed on Mother's Day.

"I made you some eggs."

She nodded, still squinting, smacking her lips. "I could use some water."

"Ah," he said, holding the plate in his left hand while he reached into his back pocket with his right and pulled out a bottle of water. "I almost forgot this."

She took the bottle and drank it greedily, careful not to waste a drop. She didn't know what was going on with Burt, but not everyone here was as easygoing as he.

He stood and watched her eat. "My name's Burt," he said, grimacing as soon as the words left his mouth. "Well, shit, I already told you that. I'd forget my head if it wasn't tied on."

Cathy finished the eggs and a piece of dry toast, wondering if it would be her last meal. Perversely, her thoughts jumped to attending autopsies in med school, and watching the pathologist catalog the contents of the victims' stomachs. Would this be what they found if they discovered her body? She shook off the thought and looked up at her jailer.

"You doing okay, Burt?" she asked.

He nodded. "Why wouldn't I be?"

"I don't know if they told you or not, but I'm a doctor." She pointed to her own eye, rattling the chain. "You've got a little ptosis going on there."

He frowned. "What's that mean?"

"Droopy eye," she said, pulling her eye open

with a thumb and forefinger. "I need you to lift your lid open for me. Can you do that?"

He did. "I knew my eye was screwed up."

"Let me ask you," Cathy said. "Are you having headaches?"

He gave an exhausted laugh at that. "Oh, hell, yeah," he said. "You got no idea."

"I can't diagnose you for sure," she said. "But the ptosis, the way your pupil is dilated and sort of lazy, looking down and out like it is, I'm guessing you've got something called third nerve palsy. I'm not joking here. That's a sign of a possible aneurysm."

He took a step backward. "An aneurysm? You mean like a stroke?"

"Like a weakness in your vessel," she said, "pressing on the nerves. You should definitely get it checked out."

"I'll do that," he said. "Thanks, Doc." He took the empty plate. "Need anything else?"

"A restroom?" Not only did she need to go, but Burt seemed like the right one to ask.

"In there." He took a cuff key from his belt and released her wrist, nodding to a door she'd thought was a closet. "I'm not allowed to unhook you from the bucket. Not sure why. You seem nice to me, but you must have done something pretty bad."

"That's okay, Burt," Cathy said. She dragged

the bucket to the bathroom. "Don't forget to check out that eye."

"Are you kidding me?" Burt said. "I don't have room in my brain to think about anything else right now. I don't think the guys are going to like it much, though."

68

Burt locked her wrist to the bed again and left her alone. A dead bolt slid home with a resounding **clunk** as soon as he shut the door.

She looked around the room, trying to settle her mind enough to come up with some sort of plan. She'd read so many stories of miraculous escapes. Kidnapped women who were their own rescue, who saved themselves by prizing open a window, unscrewing a door hinge, or even overcoming their captors with a rock or stick or . . . She scanned the bedroom. There was nothing there. No weapon. Nothing but a bucket full of concrete that she could barely even drag.

She drifted off, sleeping fitfully, but better now that she'd lost the hood and her body had metabolized the last of the drugs they'd given her. She dreamed of Jack, calling in the military to drop bombs on these assholes that had taken her. Of sweet little Jack Junior, tall and strong now, with his scratchy beard and secret job—kicking in the door with guns blazing to save his mother's life—

A rattle at the door shook her awake and the

silly fantasy evaporated. Shuddering through a painful stretch, she swung her legs off the bed at the same time the door flew open. Cathy opened her eyes wide to see a stocky man bearing down directly for her, cursing wildly, shaking his fists. The room was small and he reached her in two steps, rearing back and planting a heavy boot directly in the center of her chest.

Driven backward, she slammed hard against the wall, wrenching her captive wrist against the chain. A searing white light exploded in her head. She tried to cry out, but the brutal kick had paralyzed her diaphragm. The man was on her in an instant, pushing her face-first into the filthy mattress, his knee grinding into her kidney.

Somehow, she found enough breath to whimper, which seemed to enrage him even more.

Spittle flew from his lips, wetting her cheek as he leaned into her, screaming. His words flew out on a torrent of hot, stinking breath. ". . . ignorant bitch! You have no idea what you've done! You think you're so smart, takin' advantage of my mate!" He grabbed her hair, arching her neck, exposing her throat. "You think Burt's a decent bloke, do you?" He laughed maniacally. "Well, let me tell you something, Doctor. He's just like all the rest of us, maybe worse. Before . . . Before the accident, he'd have been first in line to bend you over the bed!"

She whimpered. "I . . . I didn't—"

"No, I guess you didn't!" He shoved her forward, deep into the mattress, making it impossible to breathe. Leaning in close against the side of her face. She tried to struggle but could barely move, chained hand and foot as she was and trapped under the press of his impossible weight. "You had to go and scare the shit outta him . . ." The man was crying now, screaming, cursing into her ear, wracked with sobs. "I gotta kill my mate . . . because of—"

Cathy was fading quickly from lack of air. She was vaguely aware of others flooding into the room. The weight on her back lessened as someone dragged her attacker off of her, still cursing. He got in one last kick to her thigh before they pulled him away.

Croaking in a lungful of air, she recoiled from the blow, curling into a ball as best she could around the chains.

"She killed him!" the man sobbed. "It's her fault. You all know it—"

"Get him out of here," another man said. The Brit. Cathy remembered him from the van—the one who'd killed Karen, and then pushed Cathy into the river.

The Aussie jerked free and rushed her again, grabbing her by the hair again and wrenching her head back as if to break her neck.

She let loose a terrified scream, feral, from

somewhere she'd never had to go before, then broke down in pitiful infantile whimpers.

The Brit hit the Aussie hard in the side of the neck, causing him to release her hair, not knocking him out—or even down.

"Taylor!" he barked. "Not yet!"

Two other men tried to grab the big Aussie's arms but he cursed and shrugged them off. "Okay, okay!" He glared at the Brit under a heavy brow. "But I get to be the one! You got me, mate?"

The Brit nodded. "That's fine." He dipped his head toward the door and the other men. "Leave us for a minute. I need to explain some things to our guest."

The Brit produced a bottle of water and offered it to Cathy. "Apologies for all that," he said. "He got you pretty good. Should have never let it happen."

Cathy shuddered, trying to regain her composure. She moved her jaw back and forth. "I think I chipped one of my teeth . . . and broke a rib."

"I'm not surprised," the Brit sighed, as if he was talking about the weather. "A size eleven like that gives you a punt, you're bound to break a rib or two."

"Who are you?"

"Well," the Brit said. "It's not who **we** are that matters. Who **you** are is why you're here."

She pressed a hand on her knee to keep her

leg from bouncing like a sewing machine. "You mean because of who my husband is . . ."

"Just so," the Brit said.

"Why not just kill me?"

"Oh, don't fret too much over what I said to Taylor—"

"You said 'not yet'!" Cathy blurted. "That means it's—"

The Brit raised his hand. "Don't get your knickers all knotted up, Ms. Cathy. I had to talk him down or he **would** have killed you right then and there. That bloke's capable of some pretty brutal shit."

"Apparently so was Burt," Cathy said.

The Brit smiled softly, some memory flashing in his eyes. "Oh, ma'am, you have no idea."

"Did that man . . ." Cathy shuddered again. "Taylor . . . He said he had to kill Burt."

"Burt's still alive and kicking," the Brit said. "Taylor's beside himself because he and Burt were best mates for years now. Came up together in the Legion. I wasn't there, but the two of them were in Africa after they'd already joined up with us . . . on a job when poor old Burt took the brunt of an IED that by all rights should have hit Taylor. Saved his life, for sure."

"So . . . So I messed up by trying to help his friend?"

"You messed up by putting it into his mind

that he's sick. Now all he talks about is going to hospital . . . We caught the stupid bastard walking toward the gate ten minutes ago . . ." The Brit looked her in the eye and gave a slow shake of his head. "Can't have that. Not now."

Cathy fell against the wall, summoning every ounce of control she had left to keep from breaking down in front of this man.

"I've seen your faces," she said. "You call each other by name in front of me . . . You don't plan to trade me for any ransom."

He flopped down on the mattress beside her, close, like they were old friends. "Don't overthink this, Cathy." He patted her on the thigh. "I have a master plan."

"You do?" She laughed. "Because all I've seen is a bunch of men who are so out of control that you're about to murder one of your own for trying to go to the doctor."

The Brit was silent for a long time, just sitting there, looking at her, hardly blinking. Then he put his hand on her thigh again and gave it a harsh squeeze. "You're right, you know. You're not going to make it out of this—though I suspect some part of you believes deep down that your husband will use his power to call his FBI Hostage Rescue and his Navy SEALs, pull every weapon he can think of out of his presidential ass to save the little woman. Well, sweetheart—"

"He's not even President by now," Cathy spat. "I know my husband. He would step aside rather than compromise the integrity of the office."

The Brit cocked his head to one side, gave her thigh another pat, and then left without another word.

So, Cathy thought, Jack had really done it. She'd been right, and saw the truth of it in the Brit's eyes.

Stepping down from the presidency under the circumstances would have been impossibly difficult, but she had no doubt that's what he would do—even if it meant letting her die.

"Good for you, Jack Ryan," she whispered, banging her head softly against the wall. "Good for you . . ."

69

I cannot believe that creepy little asshole left her alive," Craig Taylor muttered, turning his iPad so Leo Debs and the others could see the article. The entire news cycle was story after story about the near fatal attack on Senator Michelle Chadwick's life. The Aussie smacked himself in the forehead. "I reckon this makes what? Three times. Gil wanted this Chadwick bitch pegged as a sellout and I reckon our little Salvadoran buddy has single-handedly turned her into a martyr."

Rook sat on the couch in a pair of cutoffs and a T-shirt, a dip of snuff in his lower lip. He spat into an empty plastic Dr Pepper bottle while he played poker on his phone.

Soulis had a camera torn apart on the table opposite Debs, soldering the guts of the thing.

Everyone but Burt wore a pistol and most had their rifles within reach—M-4s; all the FNs were either at the bottom of the San Antonio River or in an FBI evidence locker by now. It didn't matter. They were all clean, untraceable to anyone that mattered.

Burt stood at the kitchen sink doing the dishes,

stared down at the water in an empty pot, looking at his reflection. "I looked up ptosis and that third-nerve shit online," he said. "Dr. Cathy's right. I think there might be something serious wrong with me."

Taylor looked up at Debs, fuming. "Something's got to be done."

"I know."

Everyone in the room froze when Debs's cell chimed on the table. He glanced at the CCTV screen on the counter and watched a white Impala pull through the gate.

"Pea's back," he said. "Coming up the road now."

Rook spat into his Dr Pepper bottle. "He's got some 'splaining to do."

Pea was bouncing when he came through the door, in time to the Salvadoran cumbia he was always humming or whistling. He fell silent when he noticed everyone was looking at him.

He dropped his duffel on the floor. "What?"

"What, my ass," Taylor said. "The bitch ain't quite dead."

"Are you serious?" Pea strode across the room to study the news story, but Taylor yanked the iPad away. "You got a phone. Google that shit yourself."

"This could be a real problem, Fermin," Debs said. "Did you tell her anything?"

Pea looked up from thumb-typing on his

phone. "Did I what? Hell, no! Dude! I'm telling you, I shot her in the face."

"Oh, yeah, you did," Rook said, holding up his phone. "There's a lovely photo of her in the hospital with a Band-Aid under her eye."

"What happened, Fermin?" Debs said. "You told me just the other day you always make sure now after those last two failures."

"And I do," Pea said. "But then that big dude crashed in and surprised me and was all 'ATF!' and trying to cap my ass, so I had to get out of there fast."

Soulis looked up from his camera. "The article says they have evidence."

"They got nothing," Pea said. "The papers I was supposed to leave. But they speak for themselves. Her name's on the documents. They're legal."

"Nothing else?"

Pea groaned, admitting, "My clothes."

"You took your clothes off?" Taylor smacked himself in the forehead again. Rook spit.

"I reckon you could have burned us down, dickhead," Taylor said.

"But I didn't," Pea said.

"Hey, Fermin," Burt said. "Did you hear? I might have an aneurysm in my third nerve . . ."

"What's he talking about?"

"You think you could run me to the doctor later?"

Pea looked at Debs, who gave a sad shake of his head.

"Has he really got an aneurysm?"

"Hell if I know," Taylor said. "But somebody has to take care of this."

"I know," Debs said, pushing away from the table to stand. He press-checked the Browning Hi-Power to make sure there was a round in the chamber and then returned it to the holster on his hip. "Burt," he said, forcing a smile. "Come on, I'll help you take the trash down to the burn pit."

Eager to please, Burt dried his hands on a dish towel and then grabbed two bags out of the kitchen trash cans. "This many soldiers makes a shitload of garbage, don't we, Leo?"

"Yes, we do, sir," Debs said. "Pea, grab your rifle and come with us."

"Why me?"

Taylor glared at him. "I ain't doing it. And it wouldn't hurt for you to atone."

"Whatever," Pea said. "I told you it wasn't may fault."

"Your rifle," Debs said.

"I can get my rifle if you want, Leo," Burt said. "I don't mind."

"Nah, mate," Debs said. "It's all good. Pea's just coming along for security. Heaps of people trying to get to us now, since we have Dr. Cathy here."

"Yeah," Burt said. "You're right. Can't be too careful."

Everyone else in the room bowed their heads.

"Hell of a thing to come home to," Pea said.

They didn't ever burn in the burn pit. That would have put out too much smoke, and too much smoke would draw attention. The neighbors knew they were here, of course; most thought there was some oil or gas speculation going on and the Camarilla men did nothing to suggest otherwise.

The walk was a short one, less than fifty yards from the ranch house to a long trench, dug with a backhoe some thirty feet long and fifteen feet deep in the red earth and crumbling layers of gray limestone. Two shovels stood upright, stuck into the clay next to two fifty-five-gallon barrels full of quicklime—to help the garbage dissolve without the aid of a fire. They'd burn everything before they pulled out for good—which, if things went well, would be any day now. If they did not go well, it could be any minute.

Burt threw the trash bags in one by one, and then stood at the lip of the trench. There was a fine view of a stock tank in the little swale below, where water ran down the hill to form a little circle of marshy green against the gnarly mesquite and cedar breaks. A cool wind was blowing down and away, so they didn't have to contend with the smell of garbage.

Burt stared off into the distance. The breeze picked up and tousled his long silver hair.

"I'm sick," he said, surprising both of the other men with his candor. "But I'm not stupid."

Debs took two steps back. Pea unslung his rifle and looked over his shoulder at Debs. "Are you sure, cabrón?"

Burt nodded and gazed across the valley.

Fermin Pea shrugged. "This is some awful shit," he said, and raised his rifle, an instant before Leo Debs shot him in the back of the head.

Pea dropped to his knees and then pitched forward, tumbling headlong into the trench.

Burt stood frozen in place, looking down but not moving his head. When nothing else happened, he turned slowly and stared wide-eyed at Debs.

"I thought you were gonna end me," he whispered.

"Not today, brother," Debs said. "Not today."

Debs pried the lid off a drum of quicklime with a screwdriver he'd brought along for that purpose.

Burt grabbed the other shovel to help.

"How come, Leo?" the older man asked. "Why Fermin and not me?"

Debs leaned on his shovel handle. "You said it yourself, mate. You're sick. You can't be held accountable for the mistakes you make. Pea didn't have an excuse. He screwed up three times. That was going to get us all killed. We took a vote."

They both stood there for a time, Burt thinking whatever thoughts he was capable of and Debs coming to the realization that Cathy Ryan was right. This whole thing was falling apart.

Burt suddenly looked up, then began to nod, apparently having stumbled onto a great truth. "Leo," he said. "When there's a vote on me, would you . . . you know, will you take care of things? It'd be awful hard on Taylor if he had to be the one."

"Sure thing," Debs said, and began to toss shovels of quicklime into the trash pit on his dead friend's body . . .

70

An hour east of Bengaluru, India, Helen Reid, the pilot in command of the Hendley Associates Gulfstream 550, turned her airplane north toward Hyderabad, a bustling and blossoming city of some seven million people ringed with lakes and set among rolling green hills. Reid informed Midas and Adara that they were adjusting course and that Director Foley was expecting their call.

The director of national intelligence sounded exhausted as she briefed the two operatives on what she knew.

"Malhotra stands to lose a great sum of money if our Pharma Independence Bill frightens off his buyer," Foley said. "We have evidence that links him to the rogue PLA colonel in Afghanistan. And with your former Japan Special Forces soldier making recent trips to central India, it's no stretch to believe Malhotra is tied up with the ransomware attacks."

"And if he's hired his little band of mercs to do all that," Adara said, "then he's involved with the First Lady's abduction."

"Exactly," Foley said. "The FBI legal attaché and the Agency station chief in New Delhi have been put on alert but don't have the details. The legat has contacts in Hyderabad City and Telangana State Police."

"Due respect, ma'am," Midas said. "But we're talking about a billionaire."

"Indeed," Foley said. "He could have tendrils everywhere. That's why you two will go in first, get a feel for what we're looking at before we pull the trigger on anything."

"I say we black-bag the guy," Adara said. "Take him somewhere and start shooting pieces of him off until he tells us where they're holding the First Lady."

"Nothing's off the table," Foley said. "I don't have to tell you that time is of the essence here. See what you can find out and get back with him as soon as practical."

71

Cathy Ryan rolled over in bed, silently cursing Jack for not getting up and killing that annoying cricket. She would do it, but something was wrong with her arm. That was going to be a problem. She needed that arm to do a retinopexy this morning. The damned cricket would not shut up . . . She opened one eye, and there was Jack, sitting across the room, talking to Mary Pat, confiding some secret . . .

Cathy turned over, getting madder by the second that he would do this to her—then her wrist jerked short from the chain. Groggy, she rolled back toward her restraints, taking the pressure off her shoulder and elbow.

On her back, she stared up at the ceiling. That was messed up. She'd never dreamed about Mary Pat like that before. They were friends. Good friends. Jack wouldn't . . . Would he? She'd been through the wringer with this man of hers, IRA terrorists, spies, assassins, former Soviet military officers who called to speak with him privately in his study. His tragically meteoric ascendance to the White House. They'd raised four children together.

You couldn't be married for as long as they had without getting to know a guy. Could you? Cathy understood what made the man tick better than anyone in the world. But there were just so many secrets that he had to keep . . .

It was different with Mary Pat. She saw Jack every day, sat down with him over tea and toast or whatever they happened to be serving in the Navy mess across from the Situation Room. They routinely discussed little things like the fate of the free world. Hell, the fate of the whole world. Mary Pat Foley was a spy, a keeper of secrets, and had been most of her life. She understood parts of John Patrick Ryan that Cathy would never see, the fight against cabals and conspiracies that the press never got wind of unless something went terribly wrong. Cathy knew more than the average citizen. She was, after all, sleeping with the guy. But he held things back. She didn't have the requisite clearance, sure, but mostly he wanted to protect her from the ugliness—the part of him that ordered Air Force bombers to rain death on some country where a lot of bad guys, and certainly a few not-so-bad guys, were bound to die. The part of him that called dead service members' families and listened to them weep, thanking him for his kindness or cursing his name because he had sent them there in the first place. It didn't matter. Jack sat through them all. Mary Pat was often there, sitting in a chair that should have her name engraved on it beside the Resolute desk. She provided moral support during those horrific moments, the moments from which he shielded Cathy.

"He's lucky to have you, Mary Pat," she whispered. "He'll need you all the more when I'm gone . . ."

She scooted and flopped onto her side, rattling the restrictive chains as she pulled her legs and arms into a fetal position.

These men were going to kill her—sooner rather than later. She hadn't eaten since the salami sandwich a sullen Greek man had brought her for lunch hours ago. A single lightbulb on the ceiling burned all day long, but it was getting dark outside, which put it a little after eight. The Greek guy had left a plastic bucket near her bed, close enough she could reach it without anyone having to unchain her wrist.

A gifted conversationalist, he'd tossed her the sandwich and a bottle of water, pointed to the bucket, and said "Piss there" before stalking out of the room.

She buried her face in the filthy mattress, wracked with sobs, past caring about whatever had caused the stains. At any moment, the door would open again. Killing her was on their list, but she was certain from the looks in their eyes they had other things in mind for her before they pulled the trigger.

A quiet whisper caused her to freeze, still face-down on the bed.

"Hey . . ."

She drew herself into a ball, eyes shut tight.

"Ms. Cathy," the voice said. It was Burt. A white undershirt accentuated well-developed shoulders and displayed numerous scars. The body said old soldier but the look on his face said innocent little boy.

She rolled over, blinking at the bright light above.

Burt stood at the edge of the bed, towering over her. "Were you telling me the truth about my third nerve? Or were you only trying to escape?"

Cathy scooted into a sitting position, dragging the weighted bucket as she pulled her knees up. She was careful not to squeak the bed and bring anyone else in to check. Burt hadn't been in to see her since the big Aussie's violent outburst, and she felt certain he wasn't supposed to be here now.

"I told you the truth," she said. "You do have a problem and it might be very serious. But I have to admit I hoped you might be glad I warned you and it would stop you from hurting me."

"I don't hurt people," he said. "I used to. Killed a lot of folks. Hurt women, too. But not now. They didn't deserve it . . ."

"It's good you stopped," Cathy said, shuddering.

"They killed Pea," he blurted. "He deserved it."

"Pea?"

"Yeah." He sighed. "They're going to kill us, too. You and me." He gazed down at her, moving his jaw back and forth, clearly wrestling with something.

"We don't deserve that," Cathy said.

"**You** don't," Burt said. She started to say more, but he put his finger to his lips. "I wish you wouldn't talk so much while I'm trying to think."

Then he turned and walked out of the room, pulling the door shut quietly behind him.

Cathy choked back a sob. She'd already resigned herself to death. But now poor Burt and his traumatic brain injury had stepped in and added a glimmer of light on a dark horizon. Hope was hell, but it was better than the alternative.

Rene Tatum didn't want to make the hour drive between Eastland and Abilene every day, but she couldn't just go home. She had to stick around and figure out who killed her mother. At first, she thought she'd just stay at the trailer. The cops said they were done with it. She was a big girl and felt certain she could deal with any fears that went along with spending the night in a house where her mother and brother were brutally shot to death. What she hadn't counted on was the mess.

As it turned out, there was no crime scene fairy who came and ripped out the carpet, scrubbed the spatter off the walls, or mopped blood and gore off the tile after a killing. The cops just locked the doors and left. They weren't responsible. So Rene did what she'd always done when it came to the messes left behind by her mama's bad decisions. She put on a pair of kitchen gloves, hitched up her big-girl panties, and cleaned up as best she could.

She'd never been much of a crier, preferring to let only the pillow see her tears. So she scrubbed and thought and scrubbed some more, mulling over everything she could remember about the last few conversations with her mom. They'd talked every other day, at least.

By the time she finished and carried the buckets and rags out to the trash can, she'd come up with a list of people to talk to and places to check out. In the meantime, Rene had just enough money on her credit card to get a motel for a couple nights. There was no staying in a place where she'd cleaned bits of her family off the wall, not now, not ever.

She'd checked three different leads from some of Royce's old paperwork she found in her mom's kitchen drawers. The guy at the gun shop bent over backward to help, but it was clear he didn't know anything—except that Royce Vetter was an asshole and treated his wife like crap. The mechanic at the body shop wasn't much better, swearing he would have taken Vetter's head off with a spanner wrench if someone else hadn't gotten to him first. It turned out that the armored car driver was his brother-in-law and he was sure Royce had gotten the intel for his botched robbery while he was hanging out at the shop mooching free coffee.

Finally, late in the day, an elderly man who sold ham radios out of his garage told her he'd heard Royce talking to his friends about going shooting out near the old Spivey place. She remembered her mother saying Royce and his moron friends liked to practice their little war games off Buffalo Gap Road. She went to school with one of the Spivey girls—long gone to Dallas or Houston by now—and had a general idea of where the place was.

It was getting dark and probably wouldn't pan out anyway, but she decided to take a ride and get a feel for the place where Royce Vetter had spent his time preparing for the end of days.

She was almost to the gate when she saw the old guy, climbing through the five-strand barbed-wire fence. He was older, with longish gray hair that tousled in the evening breeze and a tight wife-beater shirt that said he wasn't a stranger to hard work. He shielded his eyes from her headlights.

If he was a killer, he sure as hell didn't look like it. Some kind of injury on his face . . . and the look of sheer bewilderment, like he didn't quite know where he was. She'd seen that look before, on bull riders when they first stood up after a getting slammed to the dirt by fifteen hundred pounds of angry bovine. This guy kept looking over his shoulder like he was running for something. Or hiding.

Against her better judgment, Rene pulled over to see if he needed help. Cell in hand, she dialed Chilly Edwards at the same time.

He picked up on the first ring.

"Where are you?" she asked.

"Meeting my dad at the Olive Garden," he said. "Late dinner. Why?"

The dazed man walked to her passenger side and got in, flopping into the seat like he'd been expecting her. "I'm Burt," he said. "I might have an aneurysm in my third nerve."

She gave the man a nodding smile, filling Edwards in quickly, telling him she'd just picked up a guy named Burt. He stopped her when she mentioned where Royce had gone to shoot.

"Hang on. Did you say Spivey?"

"I did," Rene said. "Listen. I think my new friend Burt might have wandered away from home. I've decided I shouldn't check this place out by myself. Any chance you could meet me somewhere? This is getting weird."

"Drive on back toward town," Edwards said. "I'll come to you."

Burt patted the dash. "We should go. They have cameras at the gate."

"What did he say?" Edwards asked. "Cameras?"

"Hold on." Rene lowered the phone to her lap as a white Impala rolled down the dirt road from the direction of the main houses. A stern-looking man got out and opened the gate. The driver remained behind the wheel. She shot a glance at Burt. "Do you know those guys?"

He nodded. "That's my friend Taylor."

She'd turned off the motor to save gas, and there was no guarantee that it would start up again until the third or fourth try. The Impala rolled through the gate and turned toward her, headlights glaring on the windscreen. Burt's buddy, Taylor, hadn't gotten back in the car, but walked toward her now, pistol in his hand, silhouetted by the headlights. He gave a single shake of his head, sneering like he wouldn't hesitate to shoot her if she attempted to leave.

Rene kept the phone down and out of sight so the approaching men wouldn't notice it. "Chilly," she said. "You better get out here quick!"

She left the line open and nudged the phone between the seats before Taylor reached her window. He motioned her out of the truck with the pistol before reaching in and grabbing the phone.

He held it up so she could see the screen. Locked. She cursed herself. She must have accidentally ended the call.

"Nice try," Taylor said. His Australian accent would have been much more interesting if he hadn't had a gun in her face.

Twelve miles away, Chilly Edwards threw his Ford Expedition in gear and drove out of the Olive Garden parking lot, heading down Clack until he could jump on 84. He called his SWAT sergeant while he drove and filled him in about Rene Tatum's phone call and her trip out to the old Spivey ranch.

"Yeah. Sounded like she had some older guy who'd walked away from his family. Weird, though. She was telling me about him and then all of a sudden told me I'd better get out there . . . Then it went dead."

"And she's not calling you back?"

"Not so far," Chilly said. "I'm going to swing out that way and see what's going on. Thought I should let someone know." He waited a beat, thinking, then said, "Hey, remember how Vetter said something to his hostage right before he died?"

"Something like 'spy militia.'"

"Right," Chilly said. "Rene told me Royce

Vetter thought he was being followed by some militia group. What if he was saying 'Spivey militia'?"

"Yeah," Sergeant Johnson said. "I don't like the sound of that at all. I'll get a Taylor County unit heading that way, too, for backup. Call me back as soon as you make contact with Tatum."

"Will do, Sarge," Chilly said. "I know I'm probably turning this whole deal into something that it's not. She probably just lost service. The hills out there can make it iffy."

"Probably so," Johnson said, though neither man believed this was the case.

"I'll call you," Chilly said, preparing to end the call.

Johnson stopped him. "Hang on," he said. "You have your kit?"

Chilly glanced over his shoulder at the mountain of SWAT gear. The rest of the team carried issued tactical gear and weapons in their work rigs, but since his assigned rig was a Harley-Davidson, he carried his in the back of his personal vehicle.

"Always," he said.

72

Midas and Adara left everything but their backpacks in the Gulfstream and cleared Indian Customs and Immigration under their cover passports.

It was early, not quite seven in the morning. Rush hour was in full swing, though Adara had never been in Indian traffic when it did not seem like rush hour. An Uber would have been more convenient and probably quicker, but Harjit Malhotra had already shown he kept hackers on the payroll. Using a mobile app to summon a ride that would leave a digital trail of their journey seemed counterintuitive to their mission. Instead, they paid five hundred rupees in cash—about seven dollars—for the forty-five-minute cab ride to Banjara Hills.

Adara settled into her seat. She was unsure what time zone her body was actually on, but felt much better after the long nap on the Gulfstream. Being able to stretch out in the back without worrying about some dude in 4C ogling you made for a restful sleep. By the time the taxi driver turned north on P.V. Narasimha Rao

Expressway Adara felt almost back to her old self—physically, anyway.

Apparently, she didn't look it.

Midas let his head loll to the left, staring at her, one eyebrow raised. Though he didn't always act it, Bartosz "Midas" Jankowski was the oldest of the operatives besides Chavez and Clark— a decade older than Adara. He'd already spent one career in the Army—Ranger, Special Forces ODA, and the Unit—what he called 1st SFOD-Delta, where he retired as a lieutenant colonel. He'd been around the block, seen some pretty sketchy things, which, in Adara's estimation, gave him the right to joke a bit about the vagaries of life that could flat reduce a lesser person to tears. She reckoned that was how he stayed relatively sane. Sometimes, he seemed even younger than Jack—which was saying something. Midas was direct and goofy and often profane and Adara loved him like an older brother.

Now he was doing the CAT scan thing with his eyes. "Do I need to worry about you?"

Adara scoffed, looking away to escape his gaze and focus on the sea of motorcycles and luxury cars on the expressway. "What's that supposed to mean?"

"It means we're about to go snooping around the offices of a billionaire who might very well have the wherewithal—and the stones to . . ." He glanced at the driver and left the rest unsaid.

"I'm just tired," she said. "Why? Do I look like shit after traveling some thirty thousand miles in the past five days?"

"Not at all," Midas said, completely serious. "It's just that, by now, you'd usually be regaling me with tidbits of knowledge about local color and history. 'Hyderabad was home to the richest man in the world until a few decades ago. It's known as the city of pearls and flowers. Both the Hope Diamond and the Koh-i-Noor diamond in the British Crown are from mines outside Hyderabad . . . Google and Microsoft are building huge campuses here as are many pharmaceutical companies . . .'"

She sat up a little straighter. "Is that all true?"

"Yep," Midas said. "And you usually tell us where the ice-cream shops with the best ratings are located. I'm not sure we can run the op without that intel." He smiled as the cab slowed. They opened their doors to the honk and clatter of morning traffic, a block from their target. The smells of strong tobacco and garbage and vehicle exhaust swirled in the humid city air, not quite covering the odor of spiced meats and fried dough. Adara swallowed back her nausea and tried to ignore the press of people on the sidewalk, men and women talking, drinking tea, chattering on their phones—like any other big city in the world.

"Look, my friend," Midas said after he paid

the driver and stood next to Adara on the sidewalk. "There is a reason I'm single. I'm no good at this. I don't know whether to try and help you, thereby incurring your great and terrible wrath or keep my mouth shut and just let you puke all over my shoes."

"I'm fine," she said, waiting for the cabbie to disappear into traffic before pushing into the flow of the crowd toward their target address. "I am just fine. A baby, a gallstone . . . how am I supposed to know? I've never had either."

Herr Roth stood quickly once he'd signed the papers, snapping to attention with a little bow that Malhotra had come to think of as uniquely German. Flanked by four attorneys, he wheeled quickly toward the door, hardly glancing out the floor-to-ceiling windows that ran the entire wall of the conference room. Up until a few seconds before, the fifteenth-floor view overlooking the verdant woods of KBR Park had belonged to Malhotra and it stung a little to see it wasted on the new owner.

Roth took the time to shake Malhotra's hand, thanking him for "doing business" and then vanishing out the polished teak door—as if he had purchased a soft drink and not a multibillion-dollar company. Billionaires could be odd ducks, Malhotra thought, reveling in the notion.

Kashvi was still seated, one chair to Malhotra's right, whispering something to one of the three attorneys on MalhotraMed's payroll. They were all young men, years younger than Roth's lawyers, who either had gray hair or no hair at all. But they were smart and devoted and had drawn up an airtight contract. Best of all, Kashvi had worked with them that very morning to remove the provision for a cooling-off period. Once the contract was signed and notarized, the deal was done. Finé.

Roth, the fickle man that he was, would not be able to back out now.

The air was suddenly sweeter than it had been only moments before.

In a gesture of great magnitude, he thanked those present for their service. Kashvi gathered the contract paperwork in a large leather folio and held it to her chest.

"Shall I file this, H.M., or did you want to take it and show it to your best friend?"

The youngest of the attorneys, a graduate of the prestigious National Law School in Bengaluru, ducked his head and coughed, sounding suspiciously as if he hid a snicker.

Kashvi looked innocently, blinking wide brown eyes, then said, "I will put them on your desk."

"Yes," Malhotra said. "Yes . . . My desk."

He followed her to his office like a puppy, still attempting to suss out what was going on here.

The floor suddenly seemed a bit uneven under his feet. Something was off. He shook his head, chalking it up to the enormous emotional release of becoming over ten billion dollars richer with the stroke of a pen.

73

Chilly tried Rene Tatum's phone twice and got nothing but voicemail.

Abilene PD Detective Ian Lewis had done the interview on Royce Vetter's hostage. He was one Academy class ahead of Chilly so they'd essentially come up through Patrol together.

Chilly called him on the way out to Buffalo Gap to find out if the woman had ever given a better statement.

"She did," Lewis said, hedging his words. "But I can't give you anything. She's a witness to your officer-involved. And anyway, aren't you on admin leave?"

"Moss told me I'm good to go," Chilly said. "Mall cameras got the entire event."

"They did," Lewis said.

"Look," Chilly said. "I'm not asking anything about the shooting. I just need to know what Vetter was ranting beforehand."

"You know," Lewis said. "His normal end of days apocalypse shit. And something about a spy mission or militia. Witness couldn't tell which."

"Spivey militia," Chilly said, half to himself.

"Yeah," Lewis said. "It could have been that."

"I need to call dispatch and see if they can do an emergency locate on a phone."

"I'm at the PD now," Lewis said. "Better if I ask since this sounds like it's part of a homicide investigation. I'll call you right back."

Chilly was just passing the Walgreens on Buffalo Gap Road when his phone buzzed.

"No luck with the phone," Lewis said. "Not pinging off any tower."

Chilly slowed a quarter-mile from the old Spivey place. It was dark, but he expected to see Rene's truck on the side of the road. The man she'd picked up—Burt wasn't it—had said something about cameras by the gate so Chilly decided to do a recon drive and check it out. Sure enough, he saw two in his peripheral vision as he went. He caught a glimpse of tire tracks in his headlights, though he was going much too fast to get any sense of detail.

It took him ten minutes to make the long block, continuing half a mile down to take a series of lefts that eventually brought him back on his original approach to the Spivey place without backtracking in front of the camera gates.

This time he killed his lights a quarter-mile out. He pulled to the side of the road well short of the gate, out of view of the cameras, and got out to look around on foot. It was well into dusk, the time when as a kid, his parents called him in. It seemed light enough, but the moment he went in the house and looked out the window it was dark.

Headlights appeared to the south and a quick phone call confirmed it was the Taylor County Sheriff's deputy responding. Chilly gave him a quick brief of the situation, informed him of the cameras, and asked him to hang back a quarter-mile until he'd taken a look around.

He shrugged on a chest rig, with a set of ceramic rifle plates and grabbed the M-4 carbine from the locking collar in his backseat. This situation was getting weirder by the minute. Pistols were for fighting your way back to a long gun, and he wanted to avoid that scenario altogether.

Slinging the rifle, he shielded the glow from his small Streamlight with his hand, hoping to avoid casting any glare toward the cameras, and played it along the crushed limestone surface of the road. He'd noticed Rene Tatum drove a dually pickup in the parking lot of Rockin Rollerz when he'd first met her. As he suspected, tracks from a set of dual wheels pulled off the road and then continued up the gravel before turning into the Spivey gate—which was secured with a padlock.

He was about to take a step when his light played across a set of footprints in the dust, where he imagined Rene's driver's-side door would have been in relation to the tires. And there it was, the unmistakable boot print he'd seen in blood both at the scene of the Vetters' murders and the mall parking lot beside Zip's body. Chilly took the time to snap a quick photo of the print—keeping a weather eye on the gate, and then trotted back to his SUV.

He opened the tailgate and punched the code into the secure drawer where he kept his rifle and optics. The Accuracy International .308 rifle, Suppressed Armament Systems Arbiter suppressor, and Nightforce scope together were worth nearly eight grand, not something you just left lying in the backseat. Accustomed to rolling out in a hurry, Chilly kept all his sniper gear in one bag, two during winter months. He'd been about to meet his dad for a late dinner when Rene had called and was dressed in Wranglers and a Western shirt. That wasn't a problem, but the Tony Lama boots weren't optimum for hoofing in through the brush with a rifle and pack. He kicked them off quickly and, not wanting to be caught barefoot if someone came barreling down the road, slipped into a pair of Salomon GTX trail shoes with cable laces. Easier to put on than boots.

Situating the earpiece, he called Sergeant Johnson while he did a quick double check of his gear.

Radio, personal wound kit, rifle and optic

(in a drag bag), armor, three ten-round mags for the .308 (one of them barrier penetrating), four seventeen-round mags for his Glock, Broco "Jimmy" mini prybar, plastic zip-ties, two flash-lights, night-vision monocular, Leatherman, water, and a couple candy bars. It sounded like a lot, but most of the kit was on his belt or chest rig—low profile so he'd be able to set up in a prone position. A folding Zero Tolerance knife was in his pocket. He resisted the urge to carry flash-bangs and other nice-to-have items. He didn't want to be weighed down, but neither did he want to be caught in the brush without the necessary equipment. Rather than opting for a full ghillie suit, he grabbed a camo mesh sniper veil and a smaller ghillie hood—essentially a BDU top covered in uneven jute rags he'd sewn on himself. Before closing the tailgate, he grabbed one last item from his pack and stuffed it in the only spare pouch on his vest.

Sergeant Johnson answered on the fourth ring. "Talk to me."

Chilly filled him in quickly, location, tire tracks, cameras on the gate—and the boot print. "Lieutenant Moss was going to run the other two through SoleMate," Chilly said. "Things got away from me and I never heard if they came up with anything."

"They got a hit," Johnson said. "Print was made by an Altberg Aqua. A UK brand."

"England?"

"Yep," Johnson said. "I've got the team spooled up. We'll be en route to your location in twenty minutes. Barth and Fujimoto are driving the BearCat out."

"Copy that," Chilly said, reminding the sergeant of the cameras at the gate. "I'd have them hang back a hundred meters or so. Can't see the ranch house from the road, but they may be able to see lights."

"Sheriff's deputy ever show?"

"He's standing by a quarter-mile to the south," Chilly said. "If you're good with it, I'm going to go ahead and work my way closer to get a good eyeball on the house." Before the sergeant could answer, Chilly made his case. "Rene Tatum is up there, Boss. Her phone has gone dark—and the guy who moved her truck was present at a double murder, not to mention the mall shootings. If this isn't a hostage situation . . ."

"I read you," Johnson said. "But be careful. We usually go in loud and proud during a hostage rescue. We're going to treat this like a high-risk warrant. In other words, easy does it. They don't know we're there yet. So get close, but not too close. Don't tip our hand until the rest of us arrive."

"Copy," Chilly said. "I'll check in as soon as I'm in a good position."

"Okay," Johnson said. "But don't forget where

you found those Altberg boot prints. That guy sounds like a pro."

Chilly climbed through the barbed-wire fence before shouldering his rifle and drag bag and then started to trot toward the old Spivey place. He moved quickly at first, using the night-vision monocular to chart a path around prickly pear cactus and under thorny mesquite. He could move fast now, covering the semi-open hills, but if these were the kind of people he believed they were, they wouldn't just have cameras on the gate.

74

Kashvi set the folio on Malhotra's desk and took a step back, batting her eyes. "We have not talked about what you will do now."

"I had not given it much thought." Malhotra flipped through the paperwork, gloating at Herr Roth's signature—the signature that had made him an extremely wealthy man. "Whatever I wish, I suppose."

"Ah," she said. "That will be fulfilling."

He couldn't tell if she was impressed at his new wealth or if she was making fun of him.

"Tell me, sir," she said, finally showing him a little deference. "With the cooling-off period removed from the contract—"

Malhotra shot to his feet, then abruptly sat again, pulling his chair closer to get the best view possible at the contract before him. "Am I reading this wrong? This says one-point-one billion . . ." He thumbed through the documents. "The payments should not be broken into increments . . ."

She stepped closer, one hand on the desk, the other on his shoulder, pressing her thigh against him.

She perused the contract, perfectly manicured nail tapping the line that indicated the purchase price of MalhotraMed. "The numbers are correct."

"But this is a fraction . . . A mere tenth of the agreed-upon sum!" Panic fluttered in Malhotra's belly, growing, bloating until he could hardly breathe. He shuffled quickly through the pages, searching for some explanation to this travesty. His voice twanged like an overtight guitar string. "This cannot be! This paperwork has gone through dozens of hands. It has been thoroughly vetted. I checked the paperwork myself . . ."

"As did I," Kashvi said.

He glanced up to see her smiling down on him. Gloating.

He gasped. "You! You made the changes. But this is impossible." He pounded the table. "It will not stand! You . . . You are working for Roth! That is disgusting. He is old enough to be your father . . . your grandfather. My attorneys will see to this. I am not worried . . ."

"Oh, H.M.," she said and sighed. "You poor, blind, stupid man. I am sure your friend the tiger saw this coming. Frankly, I am surprised the beast did not warn you over this betrayal and backstabbery. You see, your attorneys are, in point of fact, Herr Roth's attorneys. They and I will remain with the company long after you and your stuffed beast have gone."

He pounded on the contract. "No court will—"

Something hard hit his ribs and he glanced down to see the howdah pistol in Kashvi's hand. The hammer was cocked, her manicured finger curled around the trigger. Her body, which had been so supple and tender such a short time ago, had turned cold and hard as stone.

"No court will ever hear of it," she said. She leaned in close, her breath hot against his skin as she whispered in his ear. The howdah pistol seemed ready to snap his ribs as she pushed it against him with such cruel force. "And your private soldiers . . . They are Herr Roth's private soldiers. He wishes to thank you for footing the cost of their services—"

His eyes locked with Kashvi, Malhotra's fingers searched for the katar dagger on his desk, found it, and curled around the crosspiece.

The elevator chimed as the doors slid open on the fifteenth floor. Midas and Adara stepped into a deserted lobby. The sign behind the receptionist's desk said **MalhotraMed Pharmaceuticals**. They were in the right place.

All business now, Adara focused on the mission at hand and not her other woes. To his credit, Midas hadn't mentioned it again.

"You think they're closed?" Midas whispered.

"I smell perfume," Adara said. "And cologne. Someone's been here this morning."

"One of your many superpowers," Midas said. "Let's go check—"

A deafening boom came from down the hall, followed by angry shouting and a short scream.

Both Adara and Midas froze, looking down the hallway and then at each other.

Another scream. This one from a man. Maybe. Screams were hard to pin down by gender.

Unarmed, the operators moved quickly but carefully, following the sound of thrashing and more frustrated shouting until they reached the wooden door. It was tall and ornate and led to a corner office, leaving little doubt it belonged to the owner of the company. The secretary's desk out front was empty, but for a small gym bag in the seat of the swivel chair. Midas found a metal statue of a dancing woman and grabbed it for a makeshift weapon.

Adara put a hand on the door, ready to pull it open.

Inside, a woman cursed, obviously in distress.

Midas gave a grim nod and they rolled inside.

Adara had learned long ago not to have preconceived notions when entering an unknown room. But she was genuinely surprised by what she saw.

An Indian woman struggled with a wounded Harjit Malhotra against a full-size mount of a

Bengal tiger just inside the door. It took a split second to realize they were fighting over what Adara first thought was a sawed-off shotgun but realized was a large-caliber pistol. Startled by the new arrivals, the Indian woman jerked away, allowing Malhotra to gain control of the weapon as she rushed for the open door.

"I got him," Midas said, lunging for the pistol.

Adara grabbed a handful of hair as the woman ran past, yanking her sideways. The woman stumbled, cursing, swinging wildly as she worked to regain her balance. A wide blade whooshed past Adara's face.

Shit! A gun and a knife . . .

The woman lashed out again, brandishing the dagger. Adara stepped offline, pivoting, narrowly avoiding a slash to her forearm—which was already bandaged from her encounter in Japan.

The woman rushed at her again, slashing, cursing. Adara snatched up the first thing she could find, an open book on a stand inside the door. About the size of an old encyclopedia, it had a stiff leather binding. She slammed the book shut and, grabbing it in both hands, deflected the blade, bashing the woman in the side of the head as she rushed by.

It was a glancing blow. Adara knew it would do little to finish the fight, but took advantage of the split second it bought her and sprang forward. Trapping the point of the blade with the face of the heavy book, she drove the woman backward—straight into Midas, who cuffed her in the back of the head with the heavy-barreled pistol.

The knife fell to the floor. The woman staggered, clinging to the stuffed tiger in a vain attempt to keep her feet, before sliding into a sullen heap on the carpet.

Adara kicked the knife away, and then pushed the woman facedown on the carpet. She didn't want any more guns or blades showing up out of nowhere. The woman moaned, clutching the back of her head.

Adara shot a glance at Midas, who still held the pistol, which was now aimed in at the woman.

"I'll have a talk with her if you want to take a look at this guy," he said. "Large-caliber gunshot wound to the ribs."

There was no mistaking Harjit Malhotra. She recognized him easily from the Internet pics she'd studied as soon as Foley had brought them up to speed on the Chinese colonel's phone calls. As usual, she'd expected someone bigger, more imposing, larger than life. The man before her was small, insignificant—and bleeding to death. His head lolled. Blood curtained his teeth. His words escaped on a breathy croak. "Hospital . . . Need doctor . . ."

Adara lifted the tail of his shirt, assessing the damage. The entry wound was almost an inch across, the skin around it tattooed with unburned powder from a contact shot. Black blood and gore oozed from a tattered hole large enough that she could clearly see the horrific damage inside. The large-caliber ball had clipped the bottom of one lung, angling downward to turn his guts to hamburger. Pressurized gases, injected from the blast with the muzzle pressed firmly against his skin, separated and ruptured organs well out of the path of the ball.

There was little she could do for him, little anyone could do, but she kept that to herself. Instead, she tore open a pack of clotting agent from her bag and began to stuff it gently but firmly into the wound.

He looked up at her, grimacing with pain. "Are you . . . doctor?"

"A medic," she said. "We're calling you an ambulance, but you need to help us."

"I need a doctor—"

She gambled, cutting to the chase.

"The First Lady. Where is she?"

"I . . . who are you?"

Adara spoke slowly but firmly, her face inches from the man's. "Where is Cathy Ryan?"

Malhotra's eyes fluttered. He licked his lips, smearing them with blood. "They took . . . everything . . ."

"I'm going to help you," Adara said. "But I need you to tell me where the First Lady is."

"I do not know," he said. "It is the truth." He struggled to sit up straighter and reached a trembling hand at the girl. "Her . . . She will know."

Midas put a hand on Adara's shoulder, leaning in to whisper in her ear that the ambulance was on the way. The last thing they wanted was for these two to die with some bit of evidence in their heads.

"Who took her?" Adara asked, making use of the time until medics arrived.

"Gil . . ." he said. "Señor Gil . . . The Camarilla . . ." He laughed, wincing from the effort. "Reinhardt Roth . . . behind this . . . took your President's wife . . ."

Adara stuffed more gauze into the wound, pressing sharply on a shattered rib to keep Malhotra's attention.

"Where is she?"

"I . . . I do not know," he said through clenched teeth. "That's the truth . . . not far."

"Not far from where?"

"Please!" he whispered. "I need a doctor . . ."

"I can't do anything for you until you tell me the truth."

His body shuddered and he fell still. She put a hand on his neck. No pulse.

"Let's go!" Midas snapped. Adara turned in time to see him stand from where he'd been kneeling beside the girl, whose wrists were now bound behind her back with a length of electrical cord.

"We can't leave until—"

"I've got something," Midas said, motioning toward the door. He leaned closer to Adara and whispered, "She doesn't know much, but I think she told me what she does. FBI legat will have a chat with her, but you and I need to get out of here before we get tied up with the police. Grab his laptop and phone. I'll get hers."

"Well?" Adara asked as they sprinted toward the stairs. The paramedics would be on the elevator. The first thing they'd done when they'd arrived at the building was scope out where the stairs exited off the lobby.

"**The gap,**" Midas said, hitting the steps at a run. They were halfway down the first flight before the door above slammed shut. "Apparently, the Camarilla men have visited Malhotra with their boss."

"Gil," Adara said. The sound of their boots slapping concrete echoed in the stairwell.

"Yep," Midas said. "She overheard one of the men she believes eventually took Dr. Ryan say something about a place he called 'the gap' or something like it."

"And she just told you that?"

"I threatened to let you shoot her."

"Really."

Midas looked sideways, rounding the landing to start down another flight of stairs. "Yep. Apparently, you have a look."

"The gap . . ." Adara repeated. "That's not much."

"It's not nothing," Midas said.

"We'll see," Adara said.

"Wish we coulda talked to that stuffed tiger," Midas said. "I'll bet that scabby old son of a bitch has some stories . . ."

75

Your password!" Debs barked, leaning in close so he was nose to nose with the blond girl they'd found snooping around outside the front gate. She had an older phone without facial recognition. It did have a fingerprint biometric password, but the girl's hands were so chapped from working outside that it wasn't functional. He needed an actual number to get in.

They'd duct-taped her wrists and tied her to one of the high-back kitchen chairs, setting her in the middle of the living room. Rook had stripped her down to bra and panties, ostensibly to search her for weapons. Debs knew the guy was just a letch, but taking away clothing was Interrogation 101. It left her feeling vulnerable and set her nerves on edge, which was exactly what they needed at the moment. Now, surrounded by scarred and hard-bitten men who'd not had a moment alone with a woman in months, her chin quivered like Jell-O in an earthquake. Her knee bounced like the foot on a sewing machine. She was terrified, but she was also tough, which was going to be a problem—for her.

"The password," he asked again.

"I can't remember," she said, rolling her lips to keep her teeth from chattering. It didn't help.

Craig Taylor stepped in and hit her hard in the side of the head, knocking over the chair. On her side, unable to right herself, she spit blood and looked at him, blinking. If anything, the blow had only hardened her resolve.

Debs and Soulis lifted the chair back up. The Greek openly sniffed her hair during the process and threw his head back and howled at the ceiling. It sent a chill down Debs's spine, and he wasn't the one tied half-naked to a chair.

He groaned. "I can't help you if you don't help me."

Burt slumped at the table, head down like a boy in time-out. He looked up, arms still folded. "I don't think you should hit her, Craig. It wasn't her fault."

Taylor's face flushed a deep crimson, tendons in his neck knotting, veins pulsing like he might spontaneously combust at any moment.

"You need to get out of my sight, mate!" he said. "Go. Get to your room. Now. I'll come talk to you when we're done here."

Burt shot a glance at Debs, who gave him a nod. The older man rose and shuffled off toward his bedroom, waving off the other men as he walked by, as if they disgusted hem. Something was going to have to be done with him. Soon. The thought of it sent a pulse of white-hot anger through Debs's body. He reached for the blond woman's hand and tried to pry her little finger off the arm of the chair.

"Noooo!" she said through gritted teeth. It was more growl than scream. Taylor grabbed a handful of hair, jerking her head back and momentarily taking her mind off her hand, allowing Debs to bend her pinkie finger backward until it snapped, or, in reality, dislocated at the base. Now came the scream.

"Yooooouuu . . . b . . . b . . . astaaard!" she said, wheezing, hyperventilating, blowing bubbles of saliva in an effort to deal with the pain. She gazed down wide-eyed at her finger, which now stuck straight up at a right angle to the back of her hand.

"The password to your phone," Debs said again.

Her voice was one of a wounded animal, cornered, dangerous. Blue eyes blazed at him like icy daggers. "I . . . I . . . told you . . . I can't remember."

Debs sighed. This was going to take longer than he thought, and time was not something in great supply. "Burt said you called someone. Who was it?"

"My boyfriend!" she leaned slightly toward

her dislocated finger, a bird favoring her injured wing, and craned her neck to look up at him. "Why are you doing this to me? I've never done anything to you."

Debs squatted lower so he could study her face. "I've seen you somewhere before, haven't I?"

She gave an adamant shake of her head. "I'd remember your ugly face."

"No," he said. "I've definitely seen you . . ." A foggy memory began to squeeze its way to the fore. "Wait a minute . . . What's your name?"

"Rene," she said. "Rene Tatum."

A smile crept over Leo Debs's face as he realized where he'd seen her, and then vanished just as quickly when the ramifications of what that meant sank in. "Was your mother named Margaret Vetter?"

The girl broke into uncontrollable sobs, jerking at her taped wrists, lurching against her bindings so hard she tipped over her own chair. Debs took a deep breath, working through what he needed to do next. This girl knew who he was. Somehow, she'd figured out that he'd murdered her mother, which meant the call she'd made was surely to the police.

"Gentlemen," he said, straining to retain his composure. "This is a wrap."

He needed to explain no further. Everyone in the room knew. They needed to kill both women and get out of there. Immediately.

76

FBI and U.S. Secret Service Protective Intelligence analysts provided teams on the multiagency task force with thousands of leads in the hours immediately following Cathy Ryan's abduction. Social media, news agencies, and telephone banks gleaned well over nine thousand. Some of them from well-meaning citizens who'd seen **something** and felt compelled to say **something**. The vast majority, though, were from crackpots. Some, the FBI believed, were from foreign actors, adding to the smokescreen and mirrors that law enforcement was already dealing with. Sophisticated computer programs scoured years of Secret Service threat investigations, searching names, faces, location, grievances for any link to any recently reported tip, or ties to the San Antonio area. Hundreds of manifestos mailed to politicians or filed with district court clerks around the country were scanned for key phrases. Some were typed, but an overwhelming number were handwritten in meticulous block letters so tiny as to require a magnifying glass to read them. They had all been investigated before, but that was before anyone had actually followed through.

One agent compared the review to reading the social media comments about a news piece on politics or religion. The crazies poured out like an overflowing sewer.

Due to the sophisticated technical nature of the kidnapping, any person of interest with a military or law-enforcement background was flagged. Intelligence agencies combed old files and interviewed assets, searching for any link to foreign actors, state or otherwise. Every experienced agent knew, though, that it was the ones who never spoke up who were the most worrisome.

Mary Pat Foley had directed Dr. Marci Troxell, Cathy Ryan's primary White House physician, to find Dom, Chavez, and Callahan sitting at a bank of secure computers on the edge of the San Antonio convention center command post.

Mouse-brown hair disheveled, her eyes wild, she looked as though she might fall down if she did not sit soon. They all stood and offered her a chair. She'd been one of the last of the First Lady's entourage to see her. Her face looked sunburned, probably burned from the blast, and she still wore the same gray suit. The knees were ripped, stained with blood, and one shoulder of her jacket had been ripped away. Most telling of all were the cuffs of her long-sleeve white blouse, both of which had been soaked to the wrist in the blood of the many people she'd tended to when she could not locate the First Lady.

Troxell had little to offer in the way of new information, but she did confirm that Cathy Ryan was upright and walking of her own accord when the unknown man had grabbed her and pushed her into the water. She'd been a scant hundred feet away when the largest blast detonated and swept the River Walk clean of anyone within a twenty-meter circle. Troxell had been bowled over by the blast but had clamored to her feet in time to see the same man who'd pushed the First Lady into the water escorting her up the steps to street level.

"She was wearing a wig," Troxell said. "But I know Dr. Ryan. I can recognize her walk . . ." She shook her head, eyes unfocused, staring at nothing.

Ding's phone buzzed. It was Midas and Adara. He put them on speaker.

". . . We're turning their computers and phones over to the Agency contact here," he said. "Hopefully they can get some actionable intel. Listen, does the word 'gap' mean anything to you? Malhotra's secretary heard one of the Camarilla guys use the word in relation to where they were supposed to be setting up shop."

"**Gap . . .**" Caruso shot a look at Callahan. "You're the resident Texan," he said. "That sound like any place here?"

"The Gap," she said. "Like the store?"

"I don't think so," Midas said. "Could be, I guess, but that would suck. There's probably hundreds of those."

"You know," Callahan said, eyes narrowed, thinking. "There are lots of 'gap' names in Texas. Basically any valley between the hills that early settlers could get a wagon through, they called it a gap. Indian Gap, Buffalo Gap, Cranfills Gap—"

Dr. Troxell's head snapped up. "I read something about Buffalo Gap on the flight here . . ." She rubbed her face with the heels of both hands, and then patted her jacket pockets. "I can't remember what it was and I don't have my phone anymore."

Caruso was already busy typing "Buffalo Gap" into the Panasonic Toughbook on the folding table in front of him. He scanned the article, reading aloud. "'A rural community south of Abilene settled in—"

"That's it!" Dr, Troxell said. "Abilene. They just had a big mall shooting there. A half-dozen or more dead and the shooters. It was in the Secret Service area brief. Happened a couple hundred miles away, but close enough the advance agents let us know."

"That's right," Callahan said. "A botched

armored car robbery. The Bureau sent a squad over."

"There you go!" Caruso pounded his fist on the table. "Kidnappings don't happen in a vacuum. We need to get HRT moving toward Abilene ASAP."

Kelsey Callahan got to her feet. "I'll let them know what we've got."

"Do that," Chavez said, his cell phone already in his hand. "I'll brief the DNI. She'll make sure Director Wilson lets the HRT commander know the intel is trustworthy."

"Good deal," Caruso said. "And I'll get with Abilene PD, drill down and see what else they have going on. They're bound to have an idea with this many bad actors operating in their bailiwick."

He took out his phone and then had a sudden thought, calling out to Callahan, who was already walking across the expansive conference hall toward the command desks. She stopped in her tracks and turned, miffed at being called off mission.

"We need to get to Abilene, too," he said. "And it's what, a three-hour drive?"

"More like four," she said. "If we want to arrive alive."

"Think you can score us a DPS helicopter?"

"I can try," she said.

"I seem to remember your ex-husband is a Texas Ranger. I'll bet he could set us up."

"Yep," she said and groaned. "That he is. I'll get it done."

Operators with the FBI's Hostage Rescue Team, already kitted up and ready, lifted off from Lackland Air Force Base in two Bureau UH-60 Black Hawks en route to Abilene fifteen minutes after the go order came down the pike. Though they had no specific address, Director Wilson assured them that the information would be forthcoming.

77

Wearing the shaggy jute ghillie hood, with the dark mesh veil draped over his rifle and the upper portion of his body, Chilly Edwards lay on his belly in the grass, hidden behind the ears of a prickly pear. The smell of earth and sun-dried grass flowed along the rocky ground in invisible rivulets and streams of air as temperatures dropped now that the sun was down. Chilly caught another odor, too, the smell of decaying garbage, maybe a dead cow—or something more sinister.

He had a decent view of the back of the house. A small tool shed stood some fifty feet off the southeast corner. Between house and the shed was a brick barbecue pit, surrounded by several lawn chairs, tattered and frayed, like they had not seen use in years. Four windows ran along the back of the house, two of which were large enough to offer some semblance of a view. One, over what looked to be the dining room or kitchen, was directly behind a hanging bug zapper. There were people inside, but the roof of a covered patio obstructed the top third of Chilly's view. He noted three different sets of legs—males, he thought—though it was difficult to tell looking through the tiny circle of glass.

He'd hoped to get closer but reasoned that a murderer with cameras on the gate might also have cameras on their perimeter. Considering the old Spivey ranch covered the greater part of a "section," or one square mile, it also stood to reason that any cameras would be wireless. One of the guys on the SWAT team had been playing around with TSCM—technical surveillance and countermeasures, suggesting that since virtually every meth head and heroin dealer had some kind of camera or surveillance system, a simple Wi-Fi/cellular signal detector should be added to everyone's kit. Official purchase hadn't been approved by the brass, but they were relatively inexpensive so a lot of guys bought their own.

Though his scanner wasn't sophisticated enough to find individual cameras, Chilly was able to avoid the strongest signals, crawling to just over a hundred and sixty yards from the old ranch house before he hit a wall of static that made him think he should go no farther until the rest of the team arrived.

His job was to observe, pass intel up the chain, and, when initiated by the bad guy, end a life to save one. The last thing he wanted to do was stumble in and alert the target, setting into motion a set of violent events because he'd shown himself.

Unlike military snipers he'd read and studied who engaged targets at extremely long ranges, Chilly had no reason to adjust his scope to take into account the Coriolis effect from the spinning earth. But even at a relatively close one hundred and sixty yards, precision shooting involved weaponized math.

His rifle was sighted in to point of aim at one hundred yards. Hunters often joked about their rifles being capable of shooting good enough or "minute of deer." Snipers who took aim at human targets, particularly where innocent hostages might take up half the scope picture, spoke in more precise terms. Minute of angle, or MOA, essentially meant one inch at one hundred yards. A rifle capable of shooting one MOA could put rounds inside a one-inch box at one hundred yards, a two-inch box at two hundred yards, and so on, with ten inches of room to spare at a thousand yards, still no small feat at almost two-thirds of a mile, where the crosshairs of the scope obscured the target.

In order to maintain this level of accuracy, shooters kept meticulous notes, called DOPE, or data on previous engagements, documenting where their rounds impacted at specific distances, allowing them to either make adjustments via the turning turrets on their scope or use the hashmarks in the reticle to account for bullet arc and drop.

Chilly's Nightforce scope allowed for .25 MOA adjustments. His DOPE had him correcting up .75 MOA at a hundred and fifty yards and 1.5 MOA at two hundred yards. On flat ground, he would have split the difference, adjusting one MOA, but since his nest was looking down at an approximate thirty degrees, he had to do a little math. He'd hated trigonometry in high school and vowed he would never, ever, ever utilize such inane stuff in whatever field he chose. Then he found himself on the range, doing things like multiplying the actual distance to target by the cosine of the angle to come up with the adjusted range. In this case, one hundred and thirty-eight yards.

All in all, it was a minor adjustment, the difference between a forehead shot and bullet between the eyes—well within the headbox. Though the .308 projectile would cover the distance in less than a quarter of a second, it was not instantaneous. People moved, wind gusted, hostages stumbled. A great deal could happen in the span of a breath.

Unwilling to take his eye off the scope, Chilly scanned the back of the house, adjusting his body just enough to gain a slightly wider field of view. One of them moved, and he caught a glimpse of

Rene, or half of her anyway, tied to a chair, alive but beaten.

Chilly took a deep breath, about to jump on the phone and report when a door at the far corner of the house yawned open and a head peeked out. It was a male, gray hair, older. The scar on half his face was illuminated by the light spilling out of the windows. The man looked back and forth, checking for threats, and then waved to someone behind him.

Moments later, a blond woman crept out behind him, crouching, holding on to the man's belt.

Chilly checked the focus on his scope and then took a deep settling breath before pressing the PTT button on his radio, hoping like hell the encryption was working.

"Johnson, Johnson, Chilly."

"Go for Johnson."

"Sarge," Chilly said, willing himself to stay calm. "I've got eyes on the First Lady."

Thanks to Kelsey Callahan's ex-husband, Caruso and the others were able to hitch a ride to Abilene on the DPS AS350 helicopter. Caruso was on the phone with the Abilene PD assistant chief when the word came in from their SWAT team. He briefed Chavez, who called Mary Pat to update her at the same time APD SWAT was apprising HRT operators of the situation on the ground.

Everyone from the Acting President of the United States down agreed, local SWAT was all well and good, but HRT was less than twenty minutes out. APD should hold what they had and let the operators do what they did best.

C opy that," Chilly Edwards said, his voice buzzing against his hand on the rifle. "I'm sitting tight."

The SWAT team was in place, with operators on both sides of the perimeter while Chilly kept eyes on the back. The armored BearCat was parked just out of camera view on the road beyond the front gate. The responding HRT commander made it clear. APD was to keep things buttoned up until they got there. Initiate nothing.

The First Lady and her old companion had stalled behind the brick barbecue, seemingly trying to make a plan. Chilly kept watch through his scope, willing them to just stay there. HRT would land and take care of the people inside, hopefully saving Rene, but at least Mrs. Ryan would be safe. If she moved, they would likely see her on the cameras . . .

The porch lights suddenly flicked on and a stocky man stepped out of the kitchen door, shouting something Chilly couldn't make out.

He kept his hand hidden, behind his leg, but Chilly caught a glimpse of a pistol. The door at the other end of the house—the one the First Lady had come out of—opened and a second man stuck his head out. He was taller, younger. Chilly designated the two men "Thick" and "Thin" respectively. Thin had a rifle, making him the more dangerous of the two.

Chilly operated on a principle called HIPA— Hostile Intent and Present Ability. These guys both had weapons and both were shouting, erratic, actively looking for the First Lady. As soon as Chilly pulled the trigger, he would start a chain reaction that might lead to the death of a hostage. He had no idea how many shooters were inside the house, ready to kill Rene or come out blasting with heavy weapons and overwhelm the First Lady's position.

Law enforcement snipers shied away from initiating action themselves. Their primary mission was to save lives, more often than not outlasting their target.

Active life-taking changed the dynamic— initiating an immediate response.

Thin's head snapped up, hearing something at the brick barbecue. He lifted the rifle—

Chilly shot him in the ear before he took a step.

Machinelike, he worked the bolt, ejecting the spent round and chambering another, adjusting to bring Thick into his reticle. Anticipating a slight duck in posture if the man reacted to his previous shot, Chilly took a scant moment to settle, held at the man's chin and then sent it. The round caught him in the lower jaw, clipping his brain stem.

Another man, this one with dark, slicked-back hair, stuck his head out the kitchen door, pistol in hand—and came face-to-face with a third round from Chilly's rifle. This one fell backward, landing inside the house.

The house went black, leaving nothing but the eerie glow of the bug zapper.

"We are compromised," Chilly said, speaking for the first time since pulling the trigger.

The comforting heartbeat **whomp** of the HRT Black Hawks thrummed as they approached, blacked out. Chilly gave a quick rundown on the dead targets, the First Lady and her companion's location, and reminded everyone's of Rene's location inside. Last, he reminded them of his own location, so some HRT door-gunner wearing NVGs wouldn't take him for a hostile.

A voice Chilly didn't recognize spilled over the radio and into his ear, gruff, and not especially happy. "We have you, APD Sierra Unit. Stay put. You've done enough already."

Rebuked or not, Chilly continued to watch the doors, providing overwatch for the First Lady in the event more shooters ventured outside.

They did not.

78

HRT operators fast-roped from the two Black Hawks, overwhelming the remaining Camarilla soldiers with speed and violence of action. Chilly's earlier shots had robbed them of surprise. They'd killed six and taken three prisoners, all of whom were wounded, trying to go down fighting. Rene Tatum had the presence of mind to tip her chair over, getting her out of the crossfire. She survived with a nine-millimeter wound to the hip and fractures in her wrist and jaw.

A six-person team of operators went directly from the chopper to the First Lady, knocking Burt Pennington to the ground and cuffing him while they enveloped her in a blanket and whisked her back to the helicopter, which by this point had landed in a field some fifty yards from the house.

By the time this helicopter had lifted off, Jack Ryan had conveyed a pre-written letter to the speaker of the House and the Senate president pro tempore, advising that he was once again assuming the duties of his office. Gary Montgomery and Maureen Richardson flew with him and all his children via Marine One to Andrews, where they boarded Air Force One for the three-hour trip to San Antonio.

Kashvi Chada, Malhotra's secretary, had kept meticulous notes on her laptop computer, apparently to protect herself should events unwind as they had. Confronted with the evidence of her own documents, she rolled over quickly on Herr Reinhardt Roth.

Malhotra, it seemed, had been a puppet, footing the bills while Roth pulled the strings. The idea to kidnap the First Lady had indeed been Malhotra's, but it was Roth who put him in touch with Señor Gil and the Camarilla.

Three days after Cathy Ryan's rescue, Reinhardt Roth was arrested by the Bundespolizei. But he was a very rich man, and his army of lawyers saw to it that he was granted bail while he mounted a "vigorous defense to these spurious charges." Unfortunately for him, an army of actual killers stood to lose a great deal if he ever decided to cooperate. Two days after his release, he suffered a tragic fall from the balcony of his upscale Bogenhausen penthouse apartment.

———

Among the dead at the Buffalo Gap property were nine former soldiers from several world militaries, including an Australian national identified as Craig Taylor, formerly of the French Foreign Legion, and a British citizen named Leo Darby Debs of the London Metropolitan Police.

Contrary to notes taken by Malhotra's secretary, the Spanish military had no record of a special operator named Gil. No one at Liberty Crossing or the seventeen intelligence agencies under Mary Pat Foley's purview could find any trace of the man. A thorough search of security footage from MalhotraMed Pharma Corp revealed images of Craig Taylor, Leo Debs, and the Japanese soldier named Wada, but the man who was with them was always just out of frame.

For the time being, Foley's team still referred to him as Señor Gil and represented him with a black silhouette.

Mary Pat Foley made it her general rule to steer clear of meetings with Campus personnel. She made an exception at a small get-together at Hendley Associates' upstairs office, where, as far as anyone on her protective detail knew, she was paying a visit to the President's son to celebrate the safe return of the First Lady. She made sure to get a moment alone with Adara Sherman, the talented young operative Clark could not stop talking about.

"Are you good?" she asked, standing in the corner of the conference room, glass of sparkling water in a manicured hand.

"I am, Madam Director," Sherman said. "Thank you for asking."

Foley nodded, considering the response and where to go next. "I hear this was a hell of a trip," she said.

Sherman looked at her with a raised brow. "You may have heard that I was . . ." She paused.

Foley glanced at Caruso, who stood at the other end of the table, out of earshot but clearly interested in what they were talking about. "You were what?"

"You're the . . . frigging director of national intelligence, ma'am," Sherman said. "Considering the job I do, it's easy for me to believe you've heard I might be pregnant."

Foley gave a knowing nod. "None of my business."

"Well, I'm not," Sherman said. "I mean, I was, I think, but now I'm not."

Foley could have said that she'd been there, but it seemed self-serving. Better to let the young woman talk . . . or not.

"The thing is," Adara said. "I was terrified at first, scared to tell Dom, horrified to tell Clark, but then when . . . I wasn't anymore . . ." She sighed. "I was devastated." She looked directly into Foley's eyes. "You've read the reports. You think it could have been the fight in Japan? Or India?"

"Maybe," Foley said. "But probably not. Women have been having babies for . . . well, you know. Ed and I raised two sons while we were working behind the Iron Curtain." She started to say more, but put her hand on Adara's arm instead. "Listen, you're doing well here, absolutely stellar, the way your bosses tell it. But you're awash in a sea of testosterone. You and I should compare notes, have dinner, woman to woman . . . spy to spy."

I suppose you found out the secret of the office," Jack Ryan said from behind the Resolute desk.

Dehart gazed out the windows that overlooked the Rose Garden, before turning to meet Ryan's eye.

"How is that, Mr. President?"

"That the office of the most powerful individual on the planet still has as much authority over some things as old King Canute had over the tide. Sometimes, in fact, the office itself is a weakness."

"That's the truth," Dehart said. "I need you to do me a favor and don't die."

Ryan gave him a wry smile. "That's the plan." He gestured toward the fireplace and went to join Dehart there.

"I can tell something is weighing on you, Mark."

"Mr. President," Dehart said. "If details about this . . . this Campus ever come to light . . . and they will, congress will naturally draw bright parallels between them and this Camarilla outfit."

"Of course they will," Ryan said. "That's what congress does. And on the surface they'd be right. A small group of highly trained and experienced individuals running complex intelligence and tactical operations. But you don't have to dig too deep to see that the Campus operatives have a key quality that the Camarilla lacks."

Dehart looked out the window again, still coming to grips with all this. "A noble purpose," he said.

"Exactly," Ryan said. "That Center of Gravity that Clausewitz spoke of. These men and women are nothing short of exceptional. If they go down, then so will I. It's a gamble I am willing to take."

Dehart started to speak, stopped, took a deep breath, meeting Ryan's eye. "If I've learned anything over the past few weeks and months, it is to trust you, sir. And I do, so I will remain quiet on this, and, as you say, if you go down, I go down." He raised his finger to make a point. "But it still makes me uncomfortable. So if you'd prefer to have someone else as your vice president, I understand and would happily step aside to 'spend more time with my family' when enough time has passed to make it politically expedient."

Ryan leaned back in his chair, hands folded, content and calm for the first time in days.

"Mr. Vice President, you are my choice." He chuckled. "And anyway, when have you ever known me to be politically expedient?" He got to his feet. "Now, if you'll excuse me, I have the unpleasant task of visiting Senator Chadwick in the hospital."

"Now, that's politically expedient," Dehart said. And then added. "It is also the right thing to do."

Six days after the First Lady's rescue, Chilly Edwards sat on his Harley-Davidson Electra Glide, running radar on Interstate 20. A good word from someone in D.C. had seen to it that the shooting investigation went quickly and he was cleared to go back on full duty as soon as he got the nod from the department psychologist.

The HRT commander the night of the incident looked over the evidence of what went down, said he understood, but was clearly pissed. He assured Chilly the events of the rescue would have no bearing on his pending application with the FBI, but then offhandedly did mention there was a lot going on and some applications took time. Chilly's brother told him to "chill," that things would calm down soon enough, but he'd resigned himself to many more happy years with his buds at the Abilene Police Department. It wasn't like it was a bad gig.

Then a black GMC Denali blew by doing ninety.

It pulled over immediately, apparently not having seen the marked APD motor until it was too late.

Chilly lit up the truck even though it was already stopped, called it in, and rode the quarter-mile forward to park on the shoulder of the highway behind it. He approached on the passenger side, hands free, blading a little before he reached the doorpost. There were two men in the car, a shorter, stocky Hispanic guy behind the wheel and an older guy with thinning gray hair who looked like he ate a roll of barbed wire for lunch.

Both were cool as cucumbers, polite, cooperative, almost to the point of deferential. Chilly pegged them as military right off the bat. He issued the driver, whose name was Chavez, a citation for speeding, and then said, "Y'all visiting Dyess?"

The older guy shook his head. "No, sir," he said. "Actually, we're here to offer you a job."

"I got a job," Chilly said. **Weirdos** . . .

"I get it," the older man said. Both men kept their hands visible at all times, remaining calm, easygoing. "It's out of the blue. You are going to get a phone call in about sixty seconds that will establish our bona fides. We're going to head up here to Lytle Land & Cattle and grab us a steak around six this evening. Change out of that bright yellow shirt and meet us there if you're interested."

"Okay . . ."

The driver, Mr. Chavez, leaned forward, grinning. "Are we good to go?"

"We're all done here," Chilly said, shaking his head.

Chavez put the truck in gear and then leaned forward one more time. "Word of advice. You don't want to be on your bike when you get that phone call. It can be overwhelming."

Chilly gave a thumbs-up. "All righty, then. Thanks for your courtesy."

Yep. The crazies were out today.

He stepped back to his bike, watching the black GMC merge with passing traffic. His phone buzzed in his pocket.

"Officer Edwards," he said.

"Officer Steven Edwards," the voice said. "This is the White House operator. Please hold for the President of the United States."

TOM CLANCY was the author of more than eighteen #1 **New York Times** bestselling novels. His first effort, **The Hunt for Red October**, sold briskly as a result of rave reviews, then catapulted onto the bestseller list after President Reagan pronounced it "the perfect yarn." Clancy was the undisputed master at blending exceptional realism and authenticity, intricate plotting, and razor-sharp suspense. He passed away in October 2013.

TOMCLANCY.COM

MARC CAMERON is a retired Chief Deputy U.S. Marshal and twenty-nine-year law enforcement veteran. He is the author of the **New York Times** bestselling Jericho Quinn thrillers and the Arliss Cutter mystery series; his short stories have appeared in **The Saturday Evening Post** and **Boys' Life** magazine. Cameron is a certified law enforcement scuba diver and a mantracking instructor, and holds a second-degree black belt in jujitsu. An avid sailor and adventure motorcyclist, he lives in Alaska with his beautiful bride and BMW motorcycle.

LIKE WHAT YOU'VE READ?

Try these titles,
also available in large print:

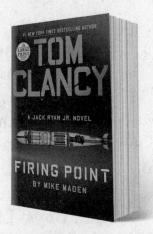

**Tom Clancy
Shadow of the Dragon**
ISBN 978-0-593-34053-0

**Tom Clancy
Target Acquired**
ISBN 978-0-593-41432-3

**Tom Clancy
Firing Point**
ISBN 978-0-593-28595-4

For more information on large print titles, visit
www.penguinrandomhouse.com/large-print-format-books